Romantic Suspense

Danger. Passion. Drama.

Texas Kidnapping Target
Laura Scott

Alaskan Wilderness Peril
Beth Carpenter

MILLS & BOON

TEXAS KIDNAPPING TARGET
© 2024 by Laura Iding
Philippine Copyright 2024
Australian Copyright 2024
New Zealand Copyright 2024

First Published 2024
First Australian Paperback Edition 2024
ISBN 978 1 038 93905 0

ALASKAN WILDERNESS PERIL
© 2024 by Lisa Deckert
Philippine Copyright 2024
Australian Copyright 2024
New Zealand Copyright 2024

First Published 2024
First Australian Paperback Edition 2024
ISBN 978 1 038 93905 0

MIX
Paper | Supporting
responsible forestry
FSC® C001695

Published by
Harlequin Mills & Boon
An imprint of Harlequin Enterprises (Australia) Pty Limited
(ABN 47 001 180 918), a subsidiary of HarperCollins
Publishers Australia Pty Limited
(ABN 36 009 913 517)
Level 19, 201 Elizabeth Street
SYDNEY NSW 2000 AUSTRALIA

Cover art used by arrangement with Harlequin Books S.A.. All rights reserved.

Printed and bound in Australia by McPherson's Printing Group

Texas Kidnapping Target
Laura Scott

MILLS & BOON

Laura Scott has always loved romance and read faith-based books by Grace Livingston Hill in her teenage years. She's thrilled to have been given the opportunity to retire from thirty-eight years of nursing to become a full-time author. Laura has published over thirty books for Love Inspired Suspense. She has two adult children and lives in Milwaukee, Wisconsin, with her husband of thirty-five years. Please visit Laura at laurascottbooks.com, as she loves to hear from her readers.

Books by Laura Scott

Hiding in Plain Sight
Amish Holiday Vendetta
Deadly Amish Abduction
Tracked Through the Woods
Kidnapping Cold Case
Guarding His Secret Son

Justice Seekers

Soldier's Christmas Secrets
Guarded by the Soldier
Wyoming Mountain Escape
Hiding His Holiday Witness
Rocky Mountain Standoff
Fugitive Hunt

Mountain Country K-9 Unit

Baby Protection Mission

Texas Justice

Texas Kidnapping Target

Visit the Author Profile page at millsandboon.com.au
for more titles.

In whom we have redemption through his blood,
even the forgiveness of sins.
—*Colossians* 1:14

This book is dedicated to my wonderful
critique group. Thanks for all the brainstorming help!

Chapter One

A soft cry brought Mari Lynch instantly awake. Heart thudding, she strained to listen. Silence. Was Theo having a nightmare?

She slid out of bed, the hardwood floor icy cold beneath her bare feet. She grabbed the 12-gauge shotgun leaning next to her bed. Wearing nothing but her flannel pajamas, she hurried down the hall to her four-year-old son's room.

"Mommy!"

Theo's cry had her wrenching the door open. A blast of cold air hit her face. She gasped at the sight of a masked man looming over her son's bed, reaching for Theo.

"Stop or I'll shoot!"

Instantly, the intruder spun away from the boy, ducked back out the window and took off at a sprint. She wanted to fire the gun but couldn't make herself pull the trigger. Darting toward the open window, she aimed the barrel of the shotgun at his disappearing shadow. Seconds later, he vanished behind the barn.

"Theo!" She turned toward her son. He jumped off his bed and launched himself at her still holding his favorite stuffed dog, Charlie to his chest. She caught him close, her heart hammering against her ribs.

What was going on? Who had tried to kidnap her son?

She belatedly noticed the window was completely gone. It took her a moment to understand the intruder had used a glass cutter to access the house.

Her house! To get her son!

Whirling away from the open window, she took Theo from the room, slamming the door shut behind her. Then hurried to the kitchen to call 911. Her Whistling Creek Ranch was twenty miles outside of Fredericksburg, so she didn't anticipate a quick response.

But she needed to report this to the police.

Mari wished she'd reported the stranger she'd glimpsed walking the tree line of her property last night, too. Likely the same man who'd just tried to grab her son, although he hadn't been wearing a ski mask. She'd reached for her shotgun then too, but by the time she'd returned to the window, he was gone.

He must have been casing her house. Figuring out which window was Theo's. But why attempt to kidnap her son?

After the dispatcher promised to send Deputy Strawn to the ranch, she carried Theo into her room. She quickly changed into jeans and a warm forest green sweater. She stuffed her feet into work boots in case she needed to head outside.

"Who was that scary man?" Theo had calmed down a bit, still gripping his stuffed dog Charlie tightly.

"I don't know, sweetheart." She wasn't sure what to say. How to explain to her son what was really going on here. She didn't want to frighten him. "Maybe he was lost. Or was homeless and wanted a place to stay."

"He told me to come wif him." Theo gazed at her from wide, blue eyes. "I didn't wanna go."

Her mouth went dry with fear and she silently prayed her ex-husband hadn't sent someone after their son. But who else would do such a thing? Her last, extremely tense meeting with Roy flashed in her mind.

She scooped Theo up and carried him into the living room.

She needed to get that window boarded up, as soon as possible. Maybe Deputy Strawn would keep watch outside while she managed that task.

Christmas tree lights brightened the room. The New Year holiday was only five days away, and Theo had asked if they could keep the tree up longer. All the way to his birthday, on January 2.

Setting Theo down on the sofa, she took a moment to feed split logs into the wood-burning stove to combat the cold air seeping from Theo's room. When she turned back to her son, the sight of a black SUV pulling up to the house caught her eye.

The intruder?

She dashed into her room, grabbed the shotgun and returned to the living room. She hovered along the wall close to the large picture window overlooking her front yard.

A man wearing a Stetson slid out from behind the wheel to stand next to the SUV. It was too soon for Deputy Strawn to show up—she'd barely made the call five minutes ago. Was this a trick? A way to force her to drop her guard? The guy blatantly stared at her house, without any attempt to be subtle.

Anger spurred her forward. "Stay on the sofa, Theo."

"Okay, Mommy."

She flung the front door open and stepped out onto the covered porch, the top eves decorated with Christmas lights. She lifted the shotgun to her shoulder and aimed the barrel squarely at the intruder's chest. "Do not come any closer. Turn around, get back in your car and drive away."

He froze, lifting his hands in a gesture of surrender. A glint of silver caught her eye. He wore a silver star on his chest. He was a lawman, a Texas Ranger, not someone associated with Roy. Yet she didn't relax. He'd gotten here too quickly for her piece of mind.

"Ma'am, I'm Ranger Sam Hayward. Will you please put the gun down?"

"Why are you here?" She did not lower the weapon one iota.

He wasn't too far away that she couldn't see the way his eyebrow arched upward at her less than welcoming tone. "I want to ask you a few questions, that's all."

"At this hour? It's eleven o'clock at night." She paused, then asked, "Did the sheriff's department send you?"

"What? No." He looked startled by her question. "I just need to talk to you."

"Come back tomorrow."

Again he looked surprised. "Ma'am, please. I'm not here to hurt you. Quite the opposite." He paused. "I would really appreciate if y'all would lower that shotgun."

They stared at each other for a long second. With a sigh, she lowered the weapon. She couldn't continue standing here, leaving Theo unprotected in case the assailant decided to return. "Fine. Come inside."

"Thank you, ma'am." He gave her a nod, mounted the steps to the porch then entered her house. He looked around curiously, his gaze landing on Theo, who was thankfully still curled up in the corner of the couch.

She didn't offer him a seat or anything to drink. Setting the shotgun aside, she crossed her arms over her chest. "What is this about?"

"Have you seen your ex-husband?"

Her stomach clenched as her worst fears were realized. "No. He's in prison. There would be visitor logs that would prove I have not been to see him since our divorce two years ago." A divorce that had become final shortly after Roy was found guilty of murder by a jury of his peers and subsequently incarcerated for life, without the possibility of parole.

Ranger Hayward held her gaze for a long moment. "Roy Carlton isn't in jail. He escaped."

What? Her heart lodged in her throat, making it impossible to speak. To breathe. Theo! Had Roy tried to kidnap their son? *No! Please, Lord Jesus, no!*

"When?" Her voice was little more than a croak. This couldn't be happening.

"He was declared missing over ninety minutes ago." The ranger's mouth thinned. "He managed to escape from the hospital while apparently faking an illness."

Her mouth opened, but no words came out.

"You have every right to be angry," he said with a slight nod. "This shouldn't have happened. That's why I'm here. I wanted to check in on you and your son. Also to ask if you have any idea where your ex-husband might be hiding."

The words hammered into her brain like nails into a barn door. She managed to pull herself together. "I think he was here a few minutes ago. A man wearing a ski mask cut through the glass in Theo's room and tried to grab him."

"Here?" The ranger's eyes widened. "Show me."

She scooped Theo and Charlie into her arms and led the way down the hall to her son's room. She pushed the door open and gestured for him to go in. "He cut the glass on the window."

"I need to search the property." The ranger glanced at her with concern. "Will you be okay here for a few minutes?"

"Yes, but you should know I saw a man outside the ranch house yesterday evening, too. Not close, near the tree line."

His expression was grim. "Stay inside and keep that shotgun handy."

She forced a nod, her thoughts spinning like a tornado.

Roy had escaped. She and Theo were in danger.

Her nightmare was far from over. The real terror had just begun.

Sam turned and headed outside. He couldn't believe Roy had gotten to the Whistling Creek so fast! The escaped convict must have had a ride waiting for him. He wished he and his fellow rangers, Jackson Woodlow, Marshall Branson and Tucker Powell, hadn't spent so much time searching around the hospital campus for Roy Carlton. After thirty minutes of finding nothing, he'd left them to it, taking the responsibility to head out to the ranch.

Having Carlton's ex-wife step outside with a shotgun leveled at his chest had been unexpected. Granted most Texans owned guns, but she'd surprised him. Oddly, he respected her for it.

And better understood her hostility after learning about the attempted abduction of her son.

He left the house via the front door, then headed toward the back of the ranch house to scour the area around her son's window. Using his flashlight, he peered at the ground. There were overlapping footprints in the snow and mud. Nothing useful.

He turned to sweep the area. To his surprise, Ms. Lynch leaned out the window. "He disappeared behind the barn."

"Understood." He crossed toward the outbuilding. The barn was long but apparently empty as he could see the herd of cattle gathered near a lean-to shelter.

He took his time, making sure no one was hiding inside the barn, or anywhere nearby. It was likely Carlton had fled the area, but he needed to be sure.

As he worked on clearing the immediate area around the house, he wondered if the would-be kidnapper was really Roy Carlton, or someone else. Carlton had help getting away from the hospital, that much was for sure. But ninety minutes wasn't a lot of time for Roy to have escaped, gotten a change of clothes and a ride to reach the Whistling Creek ranch in time to snatch the kid.

Carlton could have arranged for his accomplice to do the deed. The prosecutor on the case didn't believe Roy had acted alone in the murder of Austin City Manager Hank George.

Unfortunately, Carlton hadn't named anyone else as being involved. Not even in exchange for a lighter sentence.

And truthfully, Roy Carlton struck him as the kind of guy who wouldn't hesitate to do just that.

Then again, Carlton had left his DNA at the scene of the crime. His attempt to ditch the gun hadn't worked either. The weapon had been found in a dumpster a few blocks from the location of George's body and Carlton's fingerprints had been found on the handle. The combination of the two critical pieces of evidence had ensured a swift and just guilty verdict from the jury.

Sam focused on the immediate threat. Once he'd cleared the area around the house, and poked his head inside the barn and chicken coop, he widened his search radius. Unfortunately, the Whistling Creek property was large and spacious. Frustrating to admit Carlton could be hiding anywhere in the woods, despite the frigid temps.

He spied a long row of hay spread out along the short side of the barn for the cattle to eat during the winter. He crossed over, kicking at several clumps to make sure nobody was hiding beneath it.

He didn't find anything. Bypassing the rest of the open pasture area, he headed for the line of trees. He slowed his pace, inspecting the area closely for signs someone had been there.

And there it was. A broken twig. Another one a few feet away. He continued following the faint trail, the ground softer here, somewhat protected by the trees. Was this the path Carlton had taken? Or the intruder Ms. Lynch had seen the previous night?

Could they be one and the same? If so, the kidnapper wasn't Carlton as he escaped two hours ago.

For a few yards he didn't see anything. Just as he was about to stop and backtrack, he found what he was looking for.

Another partial heel print, the rounded area indicating the assailant had moved farther away from the ranch house.

For a moment he hesitated. Was he following the right trail? This area of the ranch was rather remote, and he couldn't say for sure the tracks he'd found belonged to the assailant who'd tried to kidnap Ms. Lynch's son.

He scowled and turned to look behind him. He'd gone so

far that he could no longer see the ranch house. Just the side of the barn where the hay was kept.

Sam stood for a long moment, listening as the wind rustled the trees. The sound of water trickling along a rocky bed reached his ears. From Whistling Creek?

He moved closer, scanning the woods for anyone lurking nearby. Mari Lynch hadn't mentioned the intruder carrying a gun, but almost everyone in Texas had one, which meant he could easily have the business end of a rifle pointed directly at him as he moved through the woods.

Finding the creek, he paused and listened again. Despite the freezing temperatures, there was a still a bit of water trickling along the rocky bed. If this cold snap continued, he figured the creek would freeze over before long.

Around here, the temperatures warmed during the day especially when the sun was out. He was about to turn away, when a dark shape caught his eye.

It almost looked as if a garbage bag was stuck between the ground and some bushes along the creek. Too small to be a person. Dismissing it as a non-threat, he kept going. He needed to keep searching Mari's property, to make sure Carlton wasn't hiding somewhere.

He took his time scouring the ground. Either he was losing his touch or the intruder hadn't come up this way.

He preferred to believe it was the latter.

Sam lengthened his stride to cover the ground more quickly. If the intruder had been here, there was no sign of him now. Either because he was hiding deeper on the ranch property, or because he'd angled off in another direction, joining an accomplice.

Throwing one leg, then the other over the plank fencing around the pasture, he approached the barn. Several of the cows turned wide, placid faces in his direction, apparently curious. Playing his light along the ground, he noted it was muddy here in the pasture. Well, mud mixed with cow pies. The scent was pungent. Cattle hooves had churned up the ground, especially near a large water trough.

No human footprints from what he could see, although they would have been easy to hide in this mess.

It was years since he'd been on a ranch. He came from a family of lawmen, starting with his granddad, his father and now him. But his high school friend Cameron had worked a ranch, and Sam had spent more than enough time there to learn the ropes.

He didn't miss it, not really. But he hadn't minded those summers working outside with the livestock either.

As much as he wanted to head back up to the ranch house, he hesitated. The garbage bag at the creek nagged at him.

He should have checked it out. It didn't seem possible Roy Carlton or anyone else had used it as a hiding spot. The bag had likely been left behind by kids using the creek as a place to hang out. Thoughtful of them to gather their garbage together. Even as that thought entered his head, he realized that wasn't likely. Since when did teenagers clean up after themselves?

Since never.

Moving quickly, he turned and jogged down to the patch of trees. He spotted the large black garbage bag again, on the opposite side of the creek. Stepping carefully on the slippery rocks, he crossed the water.

Footprints, several of them, immediately caught his attention. He still thought it was likely kids, but as he grew closer, it was obvious that there were only two sets of footprints.

One larger, and one smaller.

Moving cautiously now, he approached the garbage bag. As before, he stared at it for a long time. It never moved. Easing closer, he poked it with the toe of his boot. Whatever was inside was firm and unyielding, rather than soft like garbage.

He sniffed the air, catching the faint scent of decay. Dead animals? Or something worse? Dread cloaked him as he bent to untie the ends of the garbage bag.

The minute the ends fell away, a horrific odor engulfed him. It was all Sam could do not to lose his fried chicken dinner.

He stumbled backward, breathing through his mouth to avoid the awful stench. This was far worse than cow patties, that was for sure.

When he was certain he wouldn't puke, he stepped forward. Donning gloves from his pocket, he gripped the edge of the bag and peered inside.

A man's pale, lifeless face stared up at him.

Not Roy Carlton—it was someone he didn't recognize. The same guy Mari had seen walking the tree line? Maybe. He rummaged for his cell phone and snapped a picture of the dead man's face in case he didn't have an ID on him.

Without disturbing the body, he tried to ascertain how the guy had died. Using a gloved hand, he pushed the corpse to see better. There it was. A bloody mess covered the guy's chest and abdomen, even some pock marks in his face now that he was looking more closely. This damage had not been done by a rifle or handgun.

This was the work of a shotgun.

Unwilling to destroy evidence, he dropped the edge of the bag and stepped away. Stripping off the gloves, he used his phone to call Jackson.

"We haven't found him," Jackson said in lieu of a greeting. "Hate to admit it, but Carlton is in the wind."

"I found a dead guy stuffed in a large garbage bag on Mari Lynch's property." He paused, then continued, "A masked intruder cut the window of her son's bedroom out and attempted to grab the child. Possibly Carlton, himself. She chased him away, so I've been searching her property. I don't know for sure the dead man is related to Carlton's vanishing act, but we need the state crime lab here, pronto."

"You're positive it's not Carlton?" Jackson's voice held a note of hope. "Sure would help us if it was."

He couldn't help smiling. "I'm sure. It's not him. Like I

said, Carlton may have tried to grab his son. Mari Lynch saw a man walking down along her the tree line yesterday evening. I'm no expert, but this guy could have been sitting here since then. We'll need the medical examiner to tell us the approximate time of death."

"Do you think she killed him?" Jackson asked.

"No." Although the image of Mari standing on her front porch holding a shotgun, just like that of the murder weapon, flashed in his mind. Was he wrong about her? It wouldn't be the first time he'd trusted the wrong woman.

If he hadn't been with the Texas Rangers, and had intended her or her son harm, he had no doubt she'd have fired first and asked questions later.

"I can't say for sure," he amended. "She has a 12-gauge shotgun. And I believe this guy died of a close encounter with a similar weapon. Forensics will tell us more once they get him out of the garbage bag and on the slab."

Jackson whistled. "Sounds to me like she had the means and potential motive to have done the deed."

Difficult to imagine Mari stuffing a man's body into a garbage bag, unless it was her ex. Besides, someone had tried to abduct her son. "I need to talk to her."

"I'll get the medical examiner and crime scene techs there," Jackson said. "Stick around. Tuck, Marsh and I will be there soon. We'll need you to pinpoint the location of the body."

"Will do. After I speak with Ms. Lynch, I'll come back to stand guard over him."

Jackson was silent for a moment, as if trying to understand why he would even consider breaking protocol. Sam knew his priority was to protect the woman and her son from Roy Carlton.

"Fine," Jackson finally said. "See y'all, soon."

"Thanks." He disconnected the call. He made one last sweep of the area, making sure no one was lurking nearby. If this was the man Mari had seen, then the body hadn't been here more than twenty-four hours. Remaining untouched except, of course, by whoever had killed him and stuck him in there.

And where was Carlton? He turned and hustled up to the ranch house, hoping he wasn't making a grave mistake.

That Mari Lynch was a victim, not a cold-blooded killer like her ex-husband.

Chapter Two

What was taking him so long? Keeping Theo tucked into a warm blanket on the sofa, Mari had moved from one window to the next, searching for the ranger. He'd spent a fair amount of time in the rear of the house, where the intruder had escaped. Then he'd headed into the woods.

Her father had built the ranch house on the property in a way that the barn out back obstructed her view to a certain extent. It wouldn't have mattered, except for the very real threat of danger.

She silently prayed Roy wasn't lingering nearby. Or maybe it would be better if he was; that way the ranger would find him, arrest him and toss him back in jail.

Where he belonged.

Why had he tried to grab Theo? Questions spun through her mind as she tried to make sense of it all. As far as she could tell, Roy had nothing to gain by coming here. It was, after all, the first place the Rangers had searched for him.

Keeping the shotgun close, she busied herself by making coffee. Normally she didn't drink caffeine this late, but the attempted abduction and Roy's escape from prison convinced her she wouldn't sleep much, anyway.

Not until her ex was no longer a threat.

She wished, not for the first time, that she hadn't married Roy Carlton. Yet she could not regret having Theo. Her son was everything to her. Her main reason for living. She'd named him after her father, Theodore Lynch. And the moment her divorce was final, she'd legally changed their last name back to Lynch.

Glancing at her watch, she wondered again what was taking the deputy so long. A glimpse of movement through the window had her sucking in a harsh breath. Then she relaxed, recognizing Ranger Sam Hayward. His grim facial expression appeared to be carved in stone. He was alone, so she assumed he hadn't found Roy. Yet there was a somber aura about him that indicated something was wrong. Her stomach knotted as she let him in.

"Ma'am." He nodded and removed his hat, running his fingers through his thick dark hair.

"Did you find Roy?" She couldn't help but ask.

"Afraid not."

She bit her lip and turned away. "Help yourself to some coffee. I need you to watch over Theo while I board up the window in his room."

"Wait." His sharp tone had her turning to face him. "Please sit."

Eyeing him warily, she did so. "What's wrong?" She couldn't take the heavy silence. "You look upset or angry."

He met her gaze. "I found a dead man stuffed in a plastic garbage bag down at Whistling Creek."

What? She blinked, swayed and had to grab the edge of the table to keep from tumbling off the seat. "Roy?"

"Not your ex-husband." He continued holding her gaze, as if he might be able to read her mind. "Possibly the man you'd glimpsed walking along the trees. I'd like you to identify him."

Not Roy. She told herself it was wrong to have hoped Roy would be dead, where he could no longer hurt her or Theo. Then again, it wouldn't make sense that Roy was dead when he'd just tried to grab her son. "I don't understand. Why would someone kill him and leave him on my property?"

"Good question." Sam's gaze slid to her shotgun propped against the wall, then back to her. "Did you shoot him?"

The question was a punch to her chest. For a moment she couldn't speak, could barely think. Why would he assume she'd killed him?

The shotgun.

"Dear Lord Jesus help me," she whispered in a heartfelt prayer. This couldn't be happening. The man he'd discovered must have been killed with a shotgun.

She found the strength to look at the ranger. "I did not shoot him. Or anyone. I—I couldn't even bring myself to shoot the intruder in the back as he ran away from the house after trying to grab Theo."

His gaze didn't waver from hers. "Maybe this guy threatened you and your son. So you followed him down to the creek and shot him. Your guilt over that act prevented you from being able to shoot the masked intruder."

"I didn't!" There was no way to hide the desperation in her tone. "I wouldn't shoot someone for being on my property."

"Not even Roy Carlton?"

"No." She lowered he gaze. If Roy had come toward her in a threatening manner or had a gun, she may have been able to shoot him. In truth, she'd rather not find out what she was capable of.

Ranger Sam pulled out his phone and thumbed the screen. Then he turned it toward her. "Does he look familiar?"

She inwardly recoiled from the gruesome sight but forced herself to look at him. Was he a friend of Roy's? Maybe. She searched her memory. "No."

"He's not the guy you saw yesterday?"

She shook her head helplessly. "He was too far away to get a good look at his face. And he walked away from the house, so no. I cannot say that this is the same man."

Wordlessly, he tucked the phone back into his pocket. "I have the medical examiner, crime scene techs and a couple of rangers on the way. I need to head back down to the creek. Please stay inside. We may have more questions for you."

The reality of the situation sank deep into her bones. This was just the beginning. "I called the sheriff's department about the attempt on Theo." She glanced toward the window overlooking her driveway. "I expect Deputy Strawn any minute."

"Good. Hold off on repairing the window until he gets here."

Swallowing hard, she nodded. "Okay. I—do you need to take the shotgun?"

He arched a brow. "Not yet. Shotguns shells are full of pellets as I'm sure you know. It's not like we can match the pellets in this guy's body to the ones in your shotgun shells, the way we can match a slug to the corresponding weapon that fired it."

The fact that he'd already considered it was almost as awful as the way he'd asked her if she'd killed a man.

Then again, she had stepped out to greet him with the barrel of her shotgun. Her nerves were on edge from the recent attempt to grab Theo, but in hindsight, she should have handled his arrival differently.

She inwardly winced at her foolishness.

Without saying anything more, Sam Hayward turned and left. She didn't move as he closed the door behind him.

Who had killed that man and why? Was it connected to Roy's escape? If the dead man was the same guy she'd seen walking past her home, the timing of his death had to be prior to Roy's escape. Yet she felt certain Roy had been here, cutting through the glass of Theo's window and crawling inside to grab him. There's no one else who would want to take her son.

The two incidents had to be connected. But she couldn't begin to comprehend how. Or why.

"Mommy?" She glanced up to see Theo sitting up on the sofa, rubbing his eyes. He wore superhero footie pajamas that were already getting small for him. Her son was growing like a weed. "Is it morning?"

"No, sweetheart. It's late." She stood on shaky legs and crossed to her son. She sat on the sofa, lifted him into her arms and hugged him close. "You should try to get some sleep."

"Did the ranger find the scary man?" Theo asked.

Her heart squeezed at his words. "The ranger, Mr. Sam, has made sure the scary man is long gone. You don't have to worry about him anymore." That wasn't entirely true, but she didn't want her son to be afraid. She was worried sick enough for the both of them.

"I'm thirsty." Theo rested his head on her shoulder. "Can I have chocolate milk?"

She usually saved that treat for special occasions. Tonight she'd make an exception. She forced a smile. "Sure. But then you need to stretch out on the sofa again, okay? We'll pretend we're camping and sleep in the living room tonight."

"Okay."

After setting Theo on his booster seat, she turned to the fridge. She poured a small amount of chocolate milk in a plastic cup and handed it to Theo.

With a grin he took a large gulp. Then he glanced up at the curtain rod over the sink, where she'd recently set the stuffed elf that had been handed down by her father. "Billy the elf is watching me," Theo whispered.

Many of the kids at Theo's preschool shared antics of their Elf on the Shelf. Harmless fun that helped to keep Theo in line during the Christmas holiday. Since his birthday wasn't too far off, she'd kept the elf theme going even though Christmas had passed.

"He's always watching to see if you're good or bad," she reminded him. "Don't forget, your birthday is coming up. That means you need to listen to me, without complaining."

Theo nodded, his eyes wide. Then he downed the rest of his

chocolate milk. Over his shoulder she could see headlights approaching in the distance. Finally Deputy Strawn had arrived.

She lifted her son up and out of his booster seat and carried him to the sofa. He was getting big now that he was almost five. Soon she wouldn't be able to carry him around.

After tucking him in next to Charlie, his stuffed dog, she bent to kiss his cheek. "More policemen are here. Be good and stay here, okay?"

"'Kay." Theo yawned and hugged Charlie close.

She stared down at him for a long moment before heading to the door to let the deputy in.

First Roy or some other masked stranger had tried to abduct Theo and now there was a dead man down by the creek.

What next? She was afraid to find out.

She closed her eyes and lifted her heart in prayer.

Lord Jesus, keep my son safe in Your loving arms. Amen.

Sam was glad to find the dead man's body in the exact same position as when he'd left it. He stayed back, partially because of the smell and to avoid trampling the crime scene any more than he had.

As he gazed around the area, he didn't see any obvious signs of blood. Granted, there could be some farther away, he hadn't checked every inch of the terrain, but the more he considered the location of the garbage bag, the more he believed the guy had been dumped here after being killed elsewhere.

Now that he was here, he knew it wasn't likely Mari Lynch had anything to do with this dead guy. She couldn't have killed him, stuffed him in the bag and dragged him all the way down here. There had been no sign of something heavy being dragged across the hard ground, and he couldn't believe she would do something like this so close to her young son.

But it was entirely possible someone had killed the guy and plopped him here, hoping to implicate her.

And how did this fit into the abduction attempt on her son?

Did Mari know something she shouldn't? Was she more involved in Roy's criminal past than she was letting on?

His mind didn't want to go there, but he also knew better than to his trust her. Once burned, twice shy and all that. Besides, she'd handled the shotgun like a pro. Despite her claim that she hadn't been able to shoot at the man running away, he doubted she'd hesitate to protect herself and her son.

His phone vibrated. Pulling it from his pocket, he saw Jackson's name. He didn't even get a chance to say hello.

"Sam? Where are you?"

"Are you in the driveway?" He turned to glance up toward the house. It was far away, but he thought he could see the faint glow of headlights.

"Yeah, we just pulled in behind a Deputy Strawn. He's interviewing Carlton's ex about the attempted kidnapping. Where is this creek you mentioned?"

Sam gave him directions on how to find the wooded area near Whistling Creek. It didn't take long for Jackson, Marshall and Tucker to hoof it down the property line to join him.

Tuck shook his head when he saw the plastic bag. "Dude must be pretty small to be shoved in there."

"That was my thought, too." Sam stared at the garbage bag. "He's crammed in tight, so I couldn't get a good look."

"You reckon he's missing body parts?" Jackson asked.

Nothing would surprise him at this point. He shrugged. "Anything is possible. I didn't want to disturb the body, so all I did was make sure he was dead."

"I'll take your word for it," Marshall muttered. He tugged the brim of his hat down. "Wonder how long this guy would have been sitting out here if you hadn't come out to check on the ex-wife."

Jackson arched a brow. "Did Carlton's ex-wife send you down here?"

"No, I volunteered to search the area for Roy." He tried not to sound defensive. "A man wearing a ski mask cut through the window of her son's room and tried to grab him."

"So she says," Marshall drawled.

He sighed. "I highly doubt she cut the window herself in the dead of winter. And I'm sure if we talk to the boy, he'll confirm the incident."

There was a moment of silence as the rest of the rangers digested this information.

"Don't like this." Tuck frowned, glancing around the remote area. "Smells like a trap."

"Maybe it was, and our dead guy walked right into it. Ms. Lynch saw a man headed this way yesterday evening, but she couldn't recognize the picture I took of our guy. Could be she saw him going to meet someone else. Two people came here to discuss something important. One left, the other's dead."

"And they used her property for the meeting place, because—why?" Jackson asked.

"That's a good question. Along with how this dude factors into the abduction attempt on her son." Sam waved a hand. "No blood in the immediate area. First step would be to find the spot where the shooting took place."

"You'd think the ex-wife would have heard a gunshot, even one originating down here," Tucker mused.

Tuck made a good point. "True." He mentally kicked himself for not asking her about that.

Jackson's phone buzzed. "This is the medical examiner." He stepped away to take the call. Sam listened as Jackson provided directions for the rest of the team. The local cops would want in on this, too. But if the dead guy was connected to Roy Carlton, the rangers could pull rank. The Texas Rangers operated under the department of public safety. They handled major crimes, assisted in capturing escaped convicts, investigated public corruption, reviewed cold cases, and just about anything else the governor assigned to them. They only had jurisdiction in Texas, unlike the Federal Marshals who could go across state lines.

Texas was big enough to keep them plenty busy.

Within twenty minutes, the scene around the dead body was lit up brighter than Mari's Christmas tree. The medical examiner stood beside Sam as the crime scene techs photographed the bag, the ground and anything else that seemed remotely interesting.

When the techs and local deputies had spread out to search the surrounding area for the actual crime scene, the medical examiner, an older man with white hair by the name of Earl Bond, stepped up to the body bag. Covered from head to toe in gloves and protective gear, he peeled away the plastic bag, revealing their victim.

The man was bigger than he'd assumed as Earl unfolded him from the confines of the bag. Thankfully, he wasn't missing any body parts. Sam realized the guy had been stuffed in there like a rag doll, easier to do before rigor set in.

When Earl had their victim stretched out on the ground, though, Sam figured his original conjecture about the man's size had been correct. By his estimation, the guy was roughly about five feet eight or nine inches tall. On the shorter side and skinny, too, which had allowed the perp to stuff him in the garbage bag.

"Shotgun blast to the chest," Earl said in a voice muffled by his mask. The smell was worse now that the body was out of the garbage bag and stretched out on the ground. "Based on the amount of decomp, which is slower than normal in cold weather, I'd say he's been here about twenty-four hours give or take a few. I don't see any other wounds, but this light isn't great. I'll know more when I get him on the table."

"No spent shells inside the bag?" Tucker asked.

"Nothing but the victim and body fluids." Earl glanced up at them. "That suggests he was stuffed inside shortly after his death. Maybe even standing in the bag prior to getting shot."

That was an unusual way to kill someone, but the attempt may have been to minimize the mess. Of course, if that was the killer's goal, using a shotgun was counterintuitive. A bullet to the brain would have done the trick.

"Anything else strike you as unusual?" Sam asked.

Earl shrugged. "No ID or wallet, but that's typical. I need to examine him closer. You'll want fingerprints, I assume."

"Yep." Sam gestured for a tech to come over. "Please get his prints so we can run them through AFIS. The sooner we know who he is, the better."

"Okay." The tech went to work. Sam stared at the dead man's face, wishing he looked even remotely familiar.

"We need to interview Ms. Lynch," Jackson said. "This is her property, she owns a gun similar to the murder weapon, and if this guy is related to Carlton's escape, we could be looking at motive."

"I can take the lead." The offer popped out of Sam's mouth before he could think twice.

Tuck arched a brow. "Oh yeah?"

"I have a rapport with her." Sam needed to prove to himself, and to his buddies, that he could be objective. "I think she'll open up to me. Besides, let's not forget someone tried to grab her son. There's far more to this situation than meets the eye."

"I'll go with you," Jackson said quickly. "Tuck and Marshall can stay here."

"Sure, stick us with the dead guy," Tucker muttered sourly.

Sam smiled and clapped him on the shoulder. "Look on the bright side, he can't talk back."

Turning away, he led the way up to the ranch house. The light was still on in the kitchen. He had no doubt Mari Lynch was still awake.

As they stepped up onto the porch the door opened. To his surprise, she held a hammer in her hand. He eyed it warily as she stepped back. "Come in."

"Thanks." He cleared his throat and stepped over the threshold. "This is Ranger Jackson Woodlow. Jackson, this is Ms. Maribelle Lynch."

"Nice to meet you," Mari said. She set the hammer on the table. "Please call me Mari. I—uh, just finished boarding up the window in Theo's room. Would you like coffee?"

"Yes, please," Jackson said.

"Thanks, we'd appreciate that," Sam added.

She filled two mugs and brought them to the table. After a quick glance toward the sofa, where her son was resting, she took a seat. "Did you find Roy? Or get an ID for the dead man?"

"Not yet." He shrugged out of his jacket, then dropped into the chair across from hers. Jackson did the same. "Trust me, finding Roy is important. But we also need to know where you were yesterday."

"All day?" She frowned, tucking a strand of her dark, wavy hair behind her ear. "I start my day gathering eggs from the chicken coop."

"And that's what you did yesterday?" he pressed.

She flushed. "Yes. I fed the chickens then gathered eggs. Then I headed out to check the cattle, making sure they have enough hay to eat and water to drink, and that there weren't any other issues. I make them move around to get their blood circulating when it's cold. When those chores were finished, I took Theo to run errands with me. He's usually in preschool but they're closed between the Christmas and New Year holiday. He's in a 4-K program even though he'll be five on January second. He won't start kindergarten until next year."

"Then what?" Jackson asked. "You had Theo with you the entire time?"

"Yes. I had gathered enough eggs to sell them at the local feedstore. I dropped off four dozen from the past week then picked up a few items at the store for dinner." She folded her hands around her coffee cup. "I came home, checked on the cattle again, gathered more eggs then made lunch. Theo and I played games in the afternoon until dinnertime." She abruptly sighed. "My life is boring. Routine. I take care of the ranch, and my son."

"Please go on," Sam encouraged. "What happened after dinner?"

"I gave Theo an hour of television time while I made another run through the chicken coop for eggs then washed dishes. I was just finishing that when I saw the stranger in the cowboy hat walking near the tree line. I didn't see his face, though. Mostly his back."

"Did you hear gunfire?" Sam asked.

She frowned. "I sometimes hear gunfire in the distance. Mr. Fleming, the rancher next door, shoots at coyotes who get too close to his livestock. I—honestly may not have paid much attention. But what does any of this have to do with Roy? He must be the one who tried to abduct Theo."

Before he could answer, a text came in on his phone. The local police had arrived, and they knew the dead guy. He lifted his gaze to Mari's. "Do you know a man by the name of Jeff Abbott?"

The color drained from her face. She stared at him for a long moment. "I—uh, haven't seen him in a long time."

"You do know him." He made it a statement, not a question.

"I—yes. He was the best man at our wedding."

"But you didn't recognize his face when I showed it to you."

She bit her lip, looking pale. "I—didn't. Maybe I should have, but I didn't."

It was the connection they needed to Roy Carlton's escape. And maybe even to the recent attempt to snatch Theo.

Unfortunately, it would have been impossible for Carlton to escape the hospital and to get here in time to kill his former best man. But he may have gotten here in time to break into his son's room.

"Did you get along with Mr. Abbott?" Jackson asked.

Mari spread her hands wide. "I barely knew him. He was at our wedding, but I didn't talk to him much. We didn't hang out together, if that's what you're asking. I doubt I said ten words to him. And that was almost six years ago."

"You don't have any reason to want him dead," Sam said.

A wounded expression darkened her gaze, before she lifted her chin. "No. I haven't seen Jeff since our wedding. And since I was separated for more than a year before I got divorced two years ago, I would have no reason to interact with him." She glared at him. "You still haven't said anything about the attempt to kidnap my son. I'm sorry about Jeff, truly. But you must understand that Theo's safety is my only concern."

"I do, yes," Sam said with a nod. "But I didn't find Roy Carlton nearby."

"Then go out there and keep looking!" She jumped to her feet, pointing to the door, anger darkening her green eyes. "Find him before he tries again."

Sam glanced at Jackson, who gave a slight shrug.

She was right. A dead man shouldn't take priority over a near kidnapping. And the two incidents were obviously related. "We will."

"Ma'am," Jackson said with a nod.

As they left, he glanced over his shoulder to see her standing there, her arms crossed over her chest, looking as if she were on the brink of falling apart.

And it made him angry with himself that he wanted to go back inside to comfort her.

Chapter Three

Mari held it together long enough to shut the door behind the two men. After clicking the dead bolt into place, she sank into a chair and buried her face in her hands.

What in the world was going on? Where was Roy? Why had he come to take Theo? And who had killed Jeff Abbott with a shotgun, leaving him on her property?

To frame her? Possibly, but she hadn't been arrested.

At least, not yet.

Even that didn't make a lot of sense. What was the point of sending her to jail? She was hardly rich, barely managing to keep the ranch turning a profit. Sure, the two hundred and fifty acres of land, the modest home and outbuildings, including the original ranch house, were worth roughly six million on paper. But in truth there were lots of ranches for sale in the state of Texas, and precious few buyers willing to sign on the dotted line for long hours of work with little profit to show for it. "Land rich, cash poor" was how ranchers saw themselves.

Taking several deep breaths, she pulled herself together. She had not murdered anyone. Had she heard a gunshot sometime last night? She searched her memory but couldn't say for certain. And she would have been concerned about a gunshot after seeing a stranger. Maybe she'd been asleep. Yet living alone with Theo made her more likely to awaken easily.

She swallowed hard. Not hearing or reporting the gunfire wouldn't help prove her innocence. It wasn't easy, but she would place her trust in the process. Put her faith in the Texas Rangers' ability to find Roy and the truth about who had killed Jeff Abbott.

The more she thought about it, the more she struggled to understand what her ex hoped to accomplish by grabbing Theo. A ransom? Forcing her hand to what, sign over the ranch? He was an escaped convict on the run, it wasn't as if he could stay here and live his life.

But he could force her to sign the ranch over to someone else.

A chill snaked down her spine. That must be it. How that motive factored into the murder of Jeff Abbott, she had no idea.

She stood and carried the empty coffee mugs to the sink. Then she headed to the master bedroom to grab another quilt.

Through the window, she could see the glow of lights in the distance. For all she knew, they would be down at the crime scene for hours yet. Would the presence of the lawmen keep Roy at bay?

She prayed it would.

Turning, she headed back to the living room sofa. Theo had fallen asleep, Charlie tucked under his chin. She stretched out beside him, hiking the quilt to her chest.

She tried to relax, but her mind kept jumping from Roy's escape from prison, his attempt to grab Theo and then to Jeff's murder.

It was hard to admit how naive she'd been to marry Roy Carlton. He'd seemed so nice, and attentive. But if she were honest, she could remember a few instances when his temper had flared, his eyes turning ice-cold.

Why she'd ignored the red flags, she couldn't say. She'd just chosen to believe the words he said, rather than his actions. Once they were married, things had changed. First he'd used his tongue to lash out, but his anger had escalated to him slapping her. Then one night, he'd smacked her hard enough that she'd fallen to the floor.

Never again.

She opened her eyes and stared up at the ceiling. Then she turned to gaze at the Christmas tree. The twinkling lights didn't bring her joy the way they usually did.

How had Roy escaped? Ranger Sam Hayward had claimed it shouldn't have happened, but she didn't know how Roy had pulled it off.

Unless he'd had help.

Jeff Abbott was dead, so he couldn't have been Roy's accomplice. But someone else must have set the escape plan in motion. Maybe Roy had threatened to expose others if they didn't help him get out of jail.

She wouldn't put anything past him. He was cruel enough to threaten to take her son from her, knowing Theo was the most important person in her life.

Her son was the *only* person in her life.

She must have dozed because she awoke with a start. Shifting the quilt out of the way, she rose and looked outside. Sam Hayward's SUV was gone. As were the police cars. She rushed into her bedroom, and discovered the area down by the creek was dark. A shiver slid down her spine as she realized the police and rangers were gone.

She was alone with Theo.

A wave of apprehension washed over her. Had they given up searching for Roy? There was a part of her that was glad Jeff's dead body had been taken away. But the acres of ranchland stretched endlessly around her. The Whistling Creek Ranch was closer to Austin than San Antonio. Her property was relatively remote, with plenty of trees and scrub brush that might provide places for Roy—or anyone else for that matter—to hide.

Jeff's dead body was proof of that.

She turned away from the window and returned to the living room. The police and rangers had searched the area, making sure Roy wasn't nearby. After all, finding her escaped ex was the only reason Sam Hayward had come.

To find Roy. And to let her know about his escape.

Yet she couldn't sit still. She'd nailed plywood over Theo's missing window, but that didn't mean Roy wouldn't try again. Moving from window to window, she was slightly reassured when there was no sign of anyone lurking nearby.

Her father's shotgun was tucked in the corner between the kitchen cabinet and the wall. She took it now and held it beneath her arm, the muzzle pointing to the floor.

She didn't like having a gun around the house, especially with her almost-five-year-old living there. She'd taught Theo to stay away from the weapon, and he'd been good about that so far. But she would feel much better once Roy was tossed back in jail and the man who'd murdered Jeff was caught.

Soon, Lord, please? I ask You to provide guidance for the police to find those responsible. And please, keep Theo safe in Your care!

The prayer brought a bit of comfort to her ragged nerves. Since the hour was approaching four in the morning, she decided to give up on sleep. This was going to be one of those days where she drank an inordinate amount of coffee.

The Christmas lights along the front of the house, combined with the Christmas tree in the corner of the living room, provided enough illumination that she didn't need to turn on additional lighting. Once the coffee was ready, she carried the mug into the living room, propped the shotgun within reach, then sank into the cushy rocker recliner that had once been her dad's favorite.

Oh, how she missed him, especially at times like this. Her father had dedicated his life to ranching, taking over the land from his father, her grandfather. Her mother had passed away when she was twenty years old and away at college. Maybe that loss had played a role in her falling for Roy.

Or maybe he'd exploited her feelings and manipulated her, by being the kind and supportive boyfriend she'd needed.

Only to let his real personality leak through once they were married. She'd been on the brink of leaving him when she'd discovered she was pregnant.

She sincerely tried to make things work. But it was only a year after Theo was born that Roy first slapped her. The second blow was harder. She'd finally confided in her father and had returned home to the ranch. Two weeks later, Roy was arrested for murder. She'd filed for divorce that same day, regardless of the outcome of his trial. Yet it had still taken a full year for her divorce to become final.

Secretly, she'd been relieved to use it as an excuse to cut him from her and Theo's life. Thankfully, the judge had agreed to grant her sole custody of their son.

It had been no surprise that Roy had been found guilty. And that should have been the end of the terror.

Clearly, it wasn't.

Losing her father fourteen months ago had felt as if God had pulled the rug out from underneath her. She'd leaned on her faith, but it wasn't easy. Obviously, she knew what ranching entailed, having grown up doing chores. It made her smile that her dad had chosen to use four-wheelers rather than horses to ride the property. But being the sole owner and operator of the ranch was a huge responsibility.

She desperately needed to keep the ranch profitable, not just for herself, but for Theo.

Would her son even want the legacy of the ranch? She told herself this wasn't the time to worry about that. Her only goal was to provide a safe and happy childhood for him.

It didn't seem like too much to ask.

"Mommy?"

She turned to see Theo sitting up on the sofa again. She quickly moved over to join him. He burrowed against her, his face turned so he could see the Christmas tree lights.

"Is it time to get up?"

"Not yet, it's still the middle of the night." Normally, he slept until seven.

There was nothing normal about this night.

"Did the police catch the scary man?"

She closed her eyes and wished desperately the answer was yes. "Not yet, but soon. We're safe here. No one will hurt us."

He nodded, relaxing against her, seemingly mesmerized by the lights on the tree. Holding him close, she pressed a kiss to the top of his head, enjoying the scent of his baby shampoo.

This was a keen reminder of how God had blessed her. This was worth facing adversity.

And she silently promised once again to do whatever was necessary to protect her son.

Hiding in a thatch of brush that provided him a direct visual of Mari's ranch house, Sam stamped his feet to increase circulation to his lower extremities. Man, it was cold. He breathed on his gloved hands, attempting to infuse them with warmth.

Allowing his fingers and toes to go numb would not help if he had to act quickly to apprehend Roy Carlton.

Or the perp who had murdered Jeff Abbott.

Tucker, Marshall and Jackson had eyed him suspiciously when he'd offered to stand guard near the Whistling Creek Ranch in case either Roy or the killer showed up. But they hadn't argued, simply letting him know to call if he needed anything.

Yeah, the only thing he needed was a bonfire or a space heater. The way things were going, he'd turn into an ice sculpture before morning.

He couldn't stand the idea of Roy returning to make a second attempt to grab the boy. And no matter how comfortable Mari was with a shotgun, he didn't consider her a suspect either.

The abduction attempt on her son was enough to convince him she was an innocent victim in this. Jackson thought it was suspicious that she hadn't recognized the dead man. Sam figured the guy had been nothing more than a blip on her radar.

He was touched by the loving and caring way she treated her son. His own mother had abandoned him when he was eight. His father had moved in with his parents so they could help raise him. He'd never seen or heard from his mother again.

After joining the Texas Rangers, he'd searched for her. It wasn't hard. He'd discovered she'd died of a drug overdose four years after she'd left him. In hindsight, her leaving him with his father to be raised with his grandparents was probably the best thing she could have done. Yet he still hated knowing she hadn't cared enough to enter rehab and get clean.

Old news, he thought. Not important tonight. Yeah, the longer he stood there, the more he realized it had been foolish to stand guard like this. The likelihood of Roy returning here so soon was slim.

But he couldn't turn his back on a single mother and her son, knowing they were in potential danger.

He decided to take another walk around the property to keep his blood moving. He'd made the loop around the ranch house, barn and main pasture twice now, without seeing anything suspicious. The last time he'd gone past, the cattle hadn't even bothered to look at him.

His breath came out in puffs as he crossed the yard, dead grass, leaves and sticks crunching beneath his feet. He would have given just about anything for a cup of hot coffee, but that would have to wait.

Safety first. Creature comforts came second.

A spike of adrenaline helped warm him from the inside out. Every sense on alert, he moved slowly and carefully, making his way down the property line. It was the same path he'd taken earlier that night. The one leading to Whistling Creek.

And Jeff Abbott's dead body.

While the crime scene techs had worked on collecting evidence, including discovering the location of a bloody area roughly fifty yards farther back from the location of the body near the creek, where they believed the actual crime had taken place—he and the others had learned that Jeff Abbott was the stepson of Grayson Beaumont, the mayor of Austin, Texas.

Which was very interesting, since Roy had been convicted of murdering the mayor's city manager, Hank George. Word on the street was that Mayor Grayson Beaumont and City Manager Hank George had been close. So why kill Jeff Abbott, the mayor's stepson? Was this related to Hank George's murder? Was someone sending a message to the mayor by killing those close to him? Or was this related to something else?

Something illegal? In his mind, that was the working theory.

That political link had sealed the deal of the case remaining with the Texas Rangers. The governor had called their chief personally, who had then called Sam to request he take the lead in the investigation into Hank George's murder and Carlton's subsequent escape.

He would not, could not, mess this up by allowing a pretty face to distract him. One colossal mistake in trusting the wrong woman was enough. He'd been taken in by a pretty face and a sob story about abuse, only to be drawn into a trap that had nearly killed him and his fellow rangers.

Given that, he wasn't about to trust Mari so easily.

Despite being chilled to the bone, he didn't hurry as he encircled the property, carefully scanning his surroundings. He wondered just how much of the acreage Mari owned beyond the pastures and grazing areas that stretched before him.

Using his phone, he'd done a bit of research on her but hadn't learned much. He'd found the obituary related to her father's death, but that was about all.

There had been no sign of her on social media, which had been surprising. Then again, maybe not, considering her ex-husband was a murderer.

He wasn't active on social media, either, but that was due

to his being in law enforcement and making more than a few enemies along the course of his career.

He paused at the corner of the barn, accustomed now to the pungent scent and sounds of the animals around him. Seeing nothing alarming, he moved on to the chicken coop, then headed back up around the corner of the house until he was out front.

He abruptly stopped when he caught a glimpse of Mari holding her son on the sofa. The two of them seemed to gaze at the brightly lit Christmas tree tucked in the corner of the room, although from this angle it was hard to say for certain.

His heart squeezed in his chest at the poignant sight.

Mari was beautiful with her long, dark hair and green eyes. Incredibly amazing in how she so obviously cared for her son.

Tuck was right. His emotions were getting the better of him, and not in a good way.

He eased back, staying out of sight. For one thing, he didn't want to frighten her. For another, he wasn't there to spy on her like some peeping Tom.

His intent had been honorable. He'd stayed behind to make sure Roy Carlton or some other perp didn't show up to make another grab at Theo. Or worse.

A fear that was apparently unjustified.

He moved back even farther, far enough that he couldn't see inside the house without using a scope.

Still, it wasn't easy to push the image of Mari and Theo from his mind as he continued walking the perimeter. It was tempting to head for the road and walk the half mile until he reached the wooded spot where he'd left his SUV.

Staying here was a mistake. All he'd accomplished was adding to the confusion in his mind over Mari and freezing his backside off.

Bad news all around.

The snap of a twig caught his attention. He froze, then lowered into a crouch while sweeping his gaze around the area.

Wildlife? Or something more threatening?

He was almost seventy yards from the ranch house. He silently moved into a better position so that he could see the front porch, the string of Christmas lights and the large picture window in the living room.

Mari and Theo were still on the sofa. Long seconds passed, without any other sound disturbing the silence of the night. Sam figured the sound had been from either a white-tailed deer or maybe a coyote.

Yet something kept him hiding there. Waiting.

Watching.

His gaze narrowed on a small patch of brush located directly across from the ranch house. Had the branches moved?

He frowned. There was a gentle breeze coming in from the north, but not enough to have made the tree limbs sway.

Tucking his chin, he breathed into the front of his leather jacket. If someone was out there, he didn't want to give away his location with his breath making puffs of steam in the air.

For long minutes all was still. He couldn't see anyone hiding over there, and mentally kicked himself for not bringing a pair of binoculars.

He'd just convinced himself that his mind was playing tricks on him, when he saw movement again. Narrowing his gaze, he held his breath and watched.

His blood coalesced into ice.

There was a man out there. The perp was stretched out on the cold hard ground, which was why he hadn't noticed him.

But there was no mistaking him now. And worse, Sam was pretty sure the guy had a rifle.

Roy Carlton? Or someone else?

With excruciating slowness, he pulled his Sig Sauer P320 from his belt holster. The guy was a good seventy-five yards away and close to the ground, making accuracy with a handgun a challenge.

The distance didn't concern him. Firing a warning shot

would be just as effective. He preferred to take the perp alive, especially if the man out there was Carlton.

Too bad there was no decent cover between his current position and the guy. Impossible to sneak up behind him.

So be it. Sam lifted and sighted his weapon, preparing to fire at a spot above the gunman's head.

The sharp crack from the rifle came first, followed by the sound of glass breaking. Less than a nanosecond later, Sam fired in return, even as his heart thudded painfully in his chest.

The shooter had targeted the large picture window, the same location where Mari had been sitting with her son!

Had they been hit? He thumbed 911 on his phone without taking his eyes off the location of the shooter. Just as the dispatcher answered, he saw movement within the brush. A dark shadow rose to his feet.

No! He was going to get away!

Abandoning the call, Sam sprinted after the perp, desperately wishing his fellow rangers were there to back him up.

Chapter Four

When the window behind her shattered seconds after she heard gunfire, Mari instinctively ducked, then rolled off the sofa and onto the floor with Theo, covering his small body with hers.

Roy was out there!

Theo began to cry; the loud crack of gunfire and the broken window had frightened him. It had scared her, too. She was afraid to stand, worried Roy would take a second shot at them. But they needed to get out of there.

Far away from the ranch house.

"It's okay, Theo. We're fine. We'll get to safety." Striving to remain calm, she waited for one agonizing minute then the next, before lifting herself up on her hands and knees. She raised her head and tried to see over the back of the sofa but couldn't.

She still had the quilt and took a moment to toss it over the broken shards of glass covering the floor. It was the best she could do under the circumstances. "We're going to crawl down the hall, okay? Can you do that?"

Theo sniffled loudly and nodded. "Is the scary man out there?"

A helpless wave of fury hit hard. Why was Roy doing this?

Traumatizing his own son? He'd escaped from prison—why hadn't he headed south to cross the Mexican border? Did he honestly hate her this much? She swallowed hard. "I'm not sure what happened. Could be Mr. Fleming is shooting at coyotes again and missed."

"He hit our house?" Theo's eyes were wide.

She didn't want to lie to him, but she didn't want to scare him more than he already was. "I really don't know. We're going to keep our heads down, just in case. We need to crawl down the hall to my room."

Theo nodded and held his stuffed dog in one hand as he crawled with her across the living room and toward the hallway leading to the bedrooms. There was no more gunfire, but she couldn't help but think that Roy was still out there.

Waiting for a second chance to kill them.

Please, Lord Jesus, keep us safe in Your care!

The silent prayer helped soothe her nerves. The most important thing now was that she and Theo were unharmed. Yet they couldn't stay here at the ranch house.

Her car was in the garage and that faced the same direction from where the gunfire had originated. The car would have been better, but thankfully, she had the four-wheelers out back in the barn.

Using one of them should help her get Theo to the Fleming property. She didn't like the idea of placing the older man in harm's way, but what choice did she have?

She would do whatever was necessary to save her son.

Mari paused in the hallway, remembering her phone was still on the kitchen counter. Unfortunately, the shotgun was in the living room. Should she go back to grab it? Maybe not. But the phone was a necessity.

She hesitated, then rose to a crouch just high enough to snatch it off the charger. Then she and Theo continued crawling to the master bedroom as she used her thumb to dial 911.

As earlier, she doubted the response would be quick, but she made the call anyway.

"911, what is your emergency," the calm female voice on the other end of the line asked.

"This is Mari Lynch at the Whistling Creek Ranch. Someone shot through the front window of my house. My son and I are in danger. Send the police!"

"Okay, I'm dispatching two deputies to your home right now. Are you or your son hurt?"

Did being scared to death count? Probably not. "We're not hurt. But the shooter could still be outside! I need you to hurry."

"I'm here for you, ma'am. Please stay on the line."

"I can't." She couldn't take care of Theo while holding her phone. "Just get the deputies here as quickly as possible." Without saying anything more, she disconnected and shoved the phone in her pocket. Then she rose to her feet and scooped Theo into her arms.

"This way." She entered her room, staying away from the bedroom windows. It was possible Roy would have already run around to the back of the house. "In the closet."

It was the only place she could think of to use as a safe hideout for Theo.

Her son crawled inside the space, clutching Charlie to his chest. She quickly changed into warm clothing, suitable for heading outside. Her hands were shaking, but she did her best to stay focused.

The goal was to avoid being hit by gunfire while getting Theo out of there safely. No easy task. She was about to head into Theo's room for his clothes when she heard a voice calling her name.

"Mari? It's Sam. Are you and Theo okay?"

Sam? She hesitated. Why would Sam be here? The male voice didn't sound like Roy's, but she hadn't seen him in so long she couldn't be sure it wasn't her ex-husband out there trying to play a trick on her. She pressed her hand to her mouth to keep from screaming.

"Mari? Please tell me you're both okay." The low male voice held a note of urgency. "I saw the guy who shot your window, but he got away."

She bit down hard on her lip, trying to understand what happened. How could Sam have seen the guy who shot at her house?

"Mari?" His voice was louder now, and she finally opened her bedroom door to peer out. Sam hovered in the hallway, concern etched on his features. "I had to crawl through the broken window to get in, as you had the dead bolt on. Where's Theo? Is he okay, too?"

"You were watching my house outside in the cold?" She hadn't meant for her tone to sound accusing.

"Yes. I was worried Roy might come back." He held her gaze. "I'm sorry I wasn't fast enough to prevent him from taking that shot. I fired back, but he took off running. I gave chase but lost him on the road. He had a car stashed there and managed to escape before I could grab him."

"Mommy?" Theo's voice came from the closet.

"Right here, sweetie." She turned toward the open closet door. "You can come out, now. Mr. Sam is here to help us."

Theo came over to stand beside her. He gazed up at Sam. "Did you find the scary man?"

"I chased him away," Sam said. "And I promise to protect you and your mom so you don't have to be afraid of the scary man, okay?"

"Okay." Her son nodded, then turned his face into her side as if suddenly shy. She put her arm around his slim body, hugging him close.

She found herself relaxing just a bit. She eyed Sam critically, noticing how red his face was from the cold. "You must be freezing if you were really outside all this time. I can make coffee."

"Stay here for a few minutes. I want to board up that front window." Sam hesitated, then added, "I called 911. Deputies should be on the way."

"I called them as well. Thanks for taking care of the window."

Sam nodded and moved away.

Having Sam there helped tremendously. It made sense that the Rangers would have someone watching her house in case Roy decided to return.

And he had. Or someone had, she silently amended. To be fair, she didn't know for sure the shooter was Roy. It could be someone Roy had hired.

But why? Getting access to the ranch was the only thing that made sense, but killing her wouldn't help Roy get his hands on it.

However, kidnapping Theo could possibly lead to that. Even so, it didn't quite make sense. Unless Roy's accomplices didn't know the true financial status of the ranch.

"Mommy? I'm hungry." Theo gazed up at her with light blue eyes that he'd inherited from his father.

"Soon. First we need to get you out of your pajamas." She knew there would be no going back to sleep after this. "When Mr. Sam has the window fixed, I'll make breakfast."

Theo nodded and turned to grab his stuffed dog from the closet floor. Without putting up a fuss, he allowed her to take him into his room for clothes. The bedroom was chilly, so they didn't linger.

"Mari? You and Theo can come out now," Sam called.

He'd gotten the window fixed faster than she'd anticipated. She took Theo's hand and led him back to the kitchen. The living area was much darker with the large sheets of plywood covering the window. Sam had picked up the shards of glass, too, and placed the quilt on the sofa. Shivering, she crossed over to feed more wood into the cast-iron, wood-burning stove.

"I'll do that," Sam quickly offered.

"Oh, uh, thanks. I'll start the coffee and then make breakfast." She wasn't used to having someone to pitch in with chores. Taking a moment to snag the shotgun, more to keep it out of Theo's reach, she hurried into the kitchen.

She set the shotgun in the alcove near the pantry, then went to work. Making coffee didn't take long. She had plenty of eggs and some leftover bacon, too.

"Scrambled or over easy?" she asked.

"Whatever you're having is fine." Sam flashed a smile. "I like them either way."

"Theo prefers scrambled, if that's okay."

"Works for me." Sam scowled and crossed to the kitchen window. "I'm surprised the deputies aren't here yet."

"One of the downsides of living out here." She poured coffee into a mug and handed it to him. "Hopefully, they'll arrive soon."

"We may need to relocate you and Theo to a safe house," he said in a low voice. "Just long enough for us to find and arrest Roy Carlton."

She frowned, then turned back to the stove. She turned the bacon, before glancing at him. "I want to be safe and to have Roy arrested as soon as possible. But I can't just leave the livestock to perish. I depend on both the eggs from my chickens and meat from the cattle to provide for us."

"I understand your concern," he agreed. "But if you're staying, then so am I."

She glanced at him over her shoulder. On one hand, he had some nerve announcing he was moving into her home. Then again, Roy had tried to kidnap Theo, and had fired at them through the window.

"Okay. Then we'll stay here together," she said. Sam was far too attractive for her peace of mind, but she trusted him to keep her safe. Theo, too.

She hoped and prayed the rest of the rangers worked twice as hard to find Roy so her life could return to normal.

* * *

Sam knew Tuck, Marsh and Jackson would have a fit when they learned he'd offered to stay indefinitely, providing Mari and Theo his protection. It wasn't smart to get emotionally involved, yet he had made the right decision to stay on the property overnight. A gunman had shown up and nearly killed the young mother and her son.

Roy or one of his accomplices? He couldn't say for sure but had called Tucker to let him know about the incident. Unfortunately, the rear plate of the truck was covered in mud, so he hadn't been able to get a plate number. He did give Tuck a general description of the vehicle, though, and had a feeling his fellow rangers would all be here soon enough.

And where in the world were those deputies? A single mother living alone and reporting gunfire should have garnered a quicker response.

Seconds later, he heard the rumble of car engines. He moved toward the closest window and nodded with satisfaction when he noticed two squads had responded.

It was about time. He set his coffee on the table, then moved to the door. "The deputies are here."

"Okay. I'll hold off on making the eggs until we're finished." She handed her son a strip of bacon and a sippy cup she'd filled with chocolate milk. "Behave, Theo. We need to talk to the policemen."

Theo nodded, gulping his milk. The little boy was a trouper, handing all the commotion better than Sam had expected.

It made him angry to know that the little boy and his mother were living in fear. First the attempted kidnapping, then finding Abbott's dead body and now this.

It all had to be related to Roy Carlton. Or his accomplices. He really wished he'd been able to grab the shooter.

The two deputies identified themselves as Adam Grendel and Trey Drake.

Grendel took the lead. "We received two 911 calls about this shooting. From each of you?" He pointed to him and Mari.

"Yes. I'm Texas Ranger Sam Hayward. I'm working with several rangers to find escaped convict Roy Carlton. Ms. Mari Lynch is Roy's ex-wife."

"I heard on the way over that there was also an attempted abduction, earlier?" Grendel asked. "Strawn took that call."

"Yes, a masked man broke into my son Theo's room and tried to take him." Mari put her hands on Theo's shoulders. "I threatened him with my shotgun and he took off."

"A scary man," Theo added.

"I see." Grendel turned to Sam. "And you just happened to be sitting on the property when a gunman fired through the main window?"

"Yes. I stayed because I was afraid Roy Carlton would return to finish what he'd started. And it seems as if he did." Grendel's statement about the window had him abruptly turning and crossing the living room. He ran his fingers over the wall across from the window. "The slug must be here someplace."

The deputies came over to join him. A minute later, he found it. "Here," he said.

Drake got his knife out and cut around the drywall to get to the slug. He made a point of not getting too close to the bullet fragment, so as to preserve it. When he had the area of drywall cut, Drake removed the entire chunk and place it in a large evidence bag.

"It's a little mangled, but we may get something off this," Drake said.

"Good eye," Grendel said grudgingly. "Do you have any other evidence?"

"I'm afraid not. I saw the shooter stretched out on the ground beneath a tree. I was about to fire over his head to get his attention when he shot the window. I fired back and he jumped up from the ground and took off running. I chased after him, but he had a vehicle stashed down the road. The rear plate was covered in mud. I only have a make and model—a Chevy truck with a covered bed. Dark in color."

He didn't add that he'd already given the same information to Tucker Powell. It wasn't that he didn't trust the sheriff's deputies to do their job, but they weren't as invested in the Roy Carlton case as he and the other rangers were.

"Tell me about the attempted abduction," Grendel said.

Mari explained the incident. When she mentioned that Sam had arrived before the deputy Grendel gave him a narrow look. It was almost as if Grendel suspected he was responsible.

"I came to let Ms. Lynch know that her ex-husband had escaped," he explained. "I was glad to be here so quickly to help search for him. And that's when I found the dead body of Jeff Abbott."

Grendel stared at him, then muttered something under his breath. "Why did you call us if this is a Rangers case?"

He was starting to wonder the same thing. "Look, I think it's important to have these attempts on record. We believe they're related to Roy Carlton's escape but don't know that for sure. There could be something else going on here that we're not aware of."

His phone buzzed from a text. It was from Tuck, announcing he and the others were ten minutes out.

He texted back a quick okay sign, glad to know they'd be there soon.

"Okay, we'll look into this," Grendel said. "And I would appreciate if you would keep us informed on what you find out, too, Hayward. This ranch is within our jurisdiction."

"Of course." Sam didn't hesitate to agree but knew that passing key information on to the deputies wouldn't be at the top of his list. "Thanks for coming out to take the report."

"You need to show us that tree where you saw the shooter," Grendel said.

"Okay." He shrugged into his sheepskin coat and settled his cowboy hat on his head. "Let's go."

He followed Grendel and Drake outside, closing the front door securely behind him.

"You really think this is all related to her ex-husband escaping from jail?" Drake asked.

"Yeah, I do." Sam led them to the tree. The three of them crouched around the area and played their flashlights over the trampled ground. Sam hadn't taken the time to inspect the ground, deciding to head inside to make sure Mari and Theo weren't okay instead.

Now he saw the shell casing the shooter had left behind. Drake carefully placed it in another evidence bag. "We'll get this checked for prints."

"Thanks." Sam rose to his feet. He doubted the shooter had left his prints, but anything was possible. And it was a good find. They had a shell casing and a mangled slug. Both could help narrow down a potential shooter.

The two deputies spent a few more minutes looking around, then headed to their respective squads. Sam jogged back up to the house.

"Did they leave?" Mari glanced over her shoulder, looking at him in surprise. She was making scrambled eggs for Theo and the domestic scene reminded him of Saturday mornings with his grandmother.

"Yeah. But the good news is they found a shell casing. It doesn't sound like much, but the evidence will help when we find him."

"I hope you're right." Her gaze was troubled. "Are you ready to eat?"

"I—uh, sure." He shrugged out of his coat and hung up his hat. "I should warn you that the other rangers I'm working with on this will be here soon."

She lifted her brow. "I'll make more bacon."

"You're not obligated to feed us," he protested. Even as his stomach rumbled loudly.

"Sounds like I do." She managed a smile. "Truly, it's no bother. I'd rather keep busy."

He could understand that. One of the reasons he liked working in law enforcement was that it was never boring. He picked up his coffee mug. "Do you mind if I have a little more?"

"Please help yourself."

Moving toward the pot, he caught a whiff of her flowery scent. Why was he so attracted to her? It wasn't as if he hadn't seen beautiful women before, because he had.

Having made mistakes in the past, he wasn't too anxious to repeat them. He gave himself a stern, silent lecture to stay focused. He was here to find Roy Carlton, uncover who'd tried to kidnap Theo and why, and who'd murdered Jeff Abbott.

Nothing more.

When Mari finished with the scrambled eggs, she filled two plates, setting one in front of him. She took a seat beside Theo, and then looked at him. "I would like to say grace."

"Ah, okay." The first thing that popped into his mind was that his grandmother would have loved Mari. Then he lowered his head and clasped his hands together.

"Dear Lord, we thank You for this food we are about to eat. We ask that You continue to keep us all safe in Your care. Amen."

"Amen." He lifted his gaze. "I haven't prayed in a long time."

She tipped her head to the side. "God is still there, waiting for you."

He nodded and dug into his meal. He couldn't help but wonder if God had sent him here last night and kept him here throughout the early morning hours.

If anyone deserved to be in God's protection, it was Mari and her son, Theo.

And he added a silent prayer that he and the other rangers would be granted the strength and wisdom they needed to keep them safe.

Chapter Five

She ate her scrambled eggs and bacon even though she wasn't hungry. Only because she would need her strength to get through this.

Having Sam staying in the ranch house made Mari feel safe. A feeling she would never again take for granted. After the abduction attempt of her son, followed by the gunfire shattering the front window, she wondered if they'd ever be safe again without Sam being there.

They ate in silence for a few minutes until Theo began to fuss. "I want to get down."

She hesitated, glancing at Sam. Was it safe for Theo to run around the house the way he usually did? At almost five years old, her son had an abundance of energy.

"He should stay in the living room and kitchen area," Sam advised. "My fellow rangers should be here soon. They'll help do another search of the property to make sure the—uh—" He hesitated, obviously not wanting to say too much in front of her son. "That the area is clear," he amended.

"Okay." She rose and crossed to the sink to get a dishrag. After wiping Theo's hands and face, she pulled his chair back so he could climb down from the booster seat. "You heard Mr. Sam. You need to stay here in the living room where we can see you."

"What about my horses? And my tractors?" Theo pouted.

She glanced at her half-eaten breakfast. She was about to go to his room to grab his favorite toys when Sam spoke.

"Theo, please wait in the living room until your mother is finished eating."

Her son glanced at him warily. The only real father figure in Theo's life had been her father, whom he called Pop Pop.

Then to her surprise, Theo nodded and went into the living room, scooping up his stuffed dog.

"Thanks." She resumed her seat.

"I didn't mean to interfere with your parenting," Sam said in a low voice. "But I was hoping to give you a few more minutes of peace to enjoy your meal."

She simply nodded and dug into her eggs, which were already lukewarm. "It's not always easy being a single parent. Theo is a good boy most of the time, but he sometime pushes the limits." She managed a half smile. "I will be both happy and sad when he starts full-time kindergarten in the fall."

"I can imagine." She noticed Sam's gaze followed her son as he played with Charlie, having his stuffed dog jump from one sofa cushion to the next. "I want you to know I'll do whatever is necessary to protect you and Theo."

The sweet promise made tears prick her eyes. It had been a long time since anyone had cared about her. And Sam's kindness only reinforced how awful Roy had been.

Not that she needed any reminders about what her ex was capable of after what she'd experienced over the past twelve hours.

"I really don't understand why Roy would kidnap Theo." She finished her eggs and bacon, pushing her plate away. "It doesn't make sense. I don't have money to pay any sort of ransom."

Sam's gaze was curious. "What about selling off some of the land? Wouldn't that bring in some extra cash?"

She shrugged. "If there's a willing buyer, sure. But we're far enough from Austin and San Antonio that commuting back and forth to work wouldn't be easy. There's also a new housing development going up just outside of Austin, too. I wouldn't get top dollar for anything I sold off, and that probably wouldn't be enough of a motive to kidnap a small boy."

"Maybe Carlton is desperate," he suggested.

She cradled her coffee mug in her hands, eyeing him over the rim. "You're the one who told me he had help escaping from the hospital. Wouldn't those same helpers give him cash to disappear across the border into Mexico? I just can't fathom why he'd come here to the first place you and the other rangers would search for him."

"I agree his thought process doesn't make any sense." Sam stood and carried his dirty dishes to the sink. She rose to do the same. Then turned to find Theo standing beside her.

"You said I could play with my toys." His whiny tone grated on her nerves. Then she felt bad, knowing it was just her own lack of sleep making her crabby.

"Sure. Stay here, okay? I'll get them." She gave Sam a quick glance, thankful when he smiled and nodded. Then she hurried down the hall to Theo's bedroom and filled her arms with as many of his favorites as she could, then lugged them to the living room.

She put them on the floor near the Christmas tree. Theo dropped on the floor beside her and grabbed the tall horses, his favorites.

"Giddy up!" He was at that age where he loved cowboys, horses and action figures. She hoped he liked the cowboy action figures she'd purchased for his birthday.

Rising to her feet, she abruptly stopped when she saw Sam peering out the door. "What is it?"

"Nothing to worry about," he said with a smile. "The guys are here."

"Oh, sure. Bring them inside. I'll make them breakfast, too."

"Wait until we check the area. That comes first." He opened the door and stepped outside onto the porch. A few minutes later, he returned with the three additional Texas Rangers.

"Mari, I'm sure you remember Tucker, Marshall and Jackson." He gestured to each man in order.

"Yes, of course." She dried her hand on a dish towel, offering a smile. "Thanks for coming."

"We want to find this guy," Tucker said, frowning at the plywood over the window. "We were wondering if you could draw a map of the property."

"Absolutely." That was a good idea. She went to Theo's room to get his large drawing book and water-soluble markers, then returned to the kitchen. She hesitated, imagining the property, and began to draw.

She started with the house, the barn, the paddock where the cattle were kept in the winter.

"How many acres total?" Sam asked.

"Two hundred and fifty." She glanced up. "I know that sounds like a lot, but just remember that property in general is only worth what someone is willing to pay."

"What's that?" Tucker asked, leaning over her other shoulder and tapping to a square she'd drawn on the map not far from Whistling Creek.

"There's a small ranch house back there that was originally built by my grandfather. We use it sometimes as quarters for ranch hands helping in the summer. It's rustic, but I do have propane gas, water and electric out there."

The rangers looked at each other. "Does Roy know about it?"

She frowned. "I can't imagine how he could know about it. We didn't live here when we were married, I was a schoolteacher in Austin. I don't remember mentioning it either."

"We'll check it out, anyway," Marshall said.

"It's about seven miles from here, and it will take you a long time to get there on foot," she warned. "I have several four-wheelers, though, if you'd like."

"Thanks, but the sound of the four-wheeler engines will scare off anyone trying to hide nearby," Sam said. "We'll stick to checking the area closest to the main living quarters on foot, first. We'll check the old ranch house later."

"Of course. That makes sense." Too bad her father had sold the horses. Riding the ranch had been one of her favorite pastimes. Yet living here alone and raising a small son, she doubted she'd have been able to keep the horses anyway.

When she finished with the rough map, each of the rangers including Sam took a picture with their cell phones.

"Thanks. We'll head out now," Tucker said. He glanced at Sam. "You staying here?"

"Yeah." Sam walked them to the door. "Call me if you find anything."

"Will do." The guys headed outside. Sam closed the door behind them.

She busied herself at the sink, washing dishes. Sam refilled his coffee cup, then resumed his seat at the table. It took all her willpower not to glance over her shoulder to see if he was watching her.

Despite her silent promise to never get married again, she was keenly aware of Sam Hayward. His rugged good looks, his warm brown eyes, and his kindness and determination to keep her and Theo safe. She knew that the Texas Ranger would do the same for anyone in a similar position, but she was still touched by his steadfast presence. She knew Roy would have to go through Sam, and the other rangers, too, before he'd get to her.

Oddly, she enjoyed having a man to cook for. It had been just her and Theo for over a year now. She'd always imagined having a large family.

But that dream had been shattered when Roy had become physically abusive. And then was arrested for murder.

No, a large family of her own wasn't in her future. She had decided it would be best to focus on the blessings God had given her. A warm home, livestock to care for, and Theo.

She didn't need anyone or anything else.

* * *

As Mari washed and dried dishes, Sam did his best to keep from staring at her. He had wanted to head out with Tuck, Jackson and Marsh to scour the property, but leaving Mari and Theo alone was out of the question. The plywood-covered windows wouldn't stop a bullet, and they also limited her ability to see anyone approaching from outside.

But he should have asked one of the other guys to stay behind. This closeness to Mari was distracting.

"Will you play with me?" Theo asked.

"Ah, sure." He set his coffee aside and took the horse the young boy offered. "This one is a beauty—he looks like a thoroughbred. Does he have a name?"

"I call him Flash." Theo picked up another horse. "And this one is Speedo, because he's faster than Flash."

"I see." He had to give the kid credit for having a vivid imagination. "Those are great names."

Theo chatted more about his horses and how they were going to race each other again, soon.

"Sam, I need to head outside to gather eggs," Mari said. "I don't want to wait too long. The guys have been outside for a while now. I'm sure if anyone was hiding close to the house, barn or chicken coop, they'd have found him."

It was a good point. Still, he hesitated, then stood. "Maybe I should do that." He glanced pointedly at the shotgun. "You and Theo should be fine for a few minutes, right?"

She frowned. "You know how to gather eggs?"

He had a vague memory of doing that chore during those summers at Cameron's ranch. "Sure. How hard can it be?"

Arching a brow, she crossed to the pantry to pull out a crocheted basket with at least a dozen small egg pockets. The soft yarn was constructed to protect the eggs from slamming into each other. "You'll want to use this. Be careful not to break them even if the hens peck at you. I count on the income I get from selling eggs. It's not much, but it's something."

That gave him pause, but then he nodded. "I will."

The task was more difficult than he'd remembered and probably took him twice as long as it would have taken Mari. The heated chicken coop was warm enough, but the hens didn't like his intrusion. Mari had warned him about getting pecked, but he hadn't anticipated how badly those sharp beaks hurt.

When his basket was filled, he carried it inside and gratefully handed it to Mari. "Here you go."

"Thanks." She filled the sink with water, and carefully washed the eggs. Then she handed him the basket again. "One more pass-through should do it."

One more? He tried not to wince or look at his bloodied and scratched hands. "Got it."

The entire process gave him a better appreciation for Mari's grit and determination to provide for her son. He knew eggs weren't very expensive, so it wasn't like she made a ton of money off this chore. He imagined she sold cattle and chickens, too.

The idea of her scrimping by bothered him. And made him that much angrier with Roy Carlton.

They really needed to find and arrest the escaped convict ASAP.

After handing off the second basket of eggs to Mari, he washed up and texted the guys. See anything suspicious?

It took a moment for them to respond. One by one they checked in.

From Marsh. Clear to the west.

From Tuck. Clear to the north.

And Jackson. Nothing to the east.

The front of Mari's property faced south. He appreciated the guys spreading out in different directions. Should they go all the way to the original ranch house? If Roy Carlton didn't know about it, his accomplices probably didn't either.

And being seven miles away meant the shooter would have had to walk all that way. Or drive across the property. Driving meant leaving tire tracks behind. He made a mental note to check it out later, just to be extra cautious.

He still couldn't figure out why Roy wanted Theo in the first place. Money from selling acreage seemed to be the only answer. But at Mari pointed out, there had to be a buyer willing to pay.

Did Carlton already have a buyer?

The thought brought him up short. That hadn't occurred to him until now.

"Mari? Has anyone offered to buy the ranch from you or your father?"

She glanced up from where she was kneading bread. The yeasty scent made his mouth water. "Not recently, why?"

"When exactly?" he pressed.

She thought about it. "Maybe three years ago? I didn't pay that much attention because I was going through a lot back then, having left Roy and filing for divorce. And my dad didn't think the buyer was serious."

"Did you father mention a dollar amount? Or the guy's name?"

"No name, and the dollar amount was maybe 1.5 million, which is far less than what it's worth on paper. But it sounded like my dad didn't believe the guy had the money or the ability to get financing." She shook her head. "That's the biggest problem with people wanting to buy and finance ranches. You have to make enough of a profit for a bank to agree to a large loan. Without that, the sale likely wouldn't go through."

He was silent for a moment, wondering if she would allow him to go through her dad's personal paperwork to get more information.

"Why are you asking?" She put the lump of bread dough aside.

"What if Roy had tried to grab Theo to force you into selling to someone at a bargain basement price?" He moved closer, keeping his voice low so Theo couldn't hear. "That same person could have helped Roy escape the hospital."

She frowned. "Even buying at a bargain basement price would take a significant amount of money. Like I said, the guy offered 1.5 million. And anyone who would pressure me into selling would likely not go to a bank for a loan, which would mean they'd need to have that kind of money sitting around." She shook her head. "There has to be something else going on here."

"Maybe Roy wanted you to drive him across the border." He shrugged. "But that didn't work, so he thought shooting at you would force your hand."

"You said the shooter took off in a truck last night, but you couldn't get the license plate because it was covered in mud," she protested. "Why not use that to head to the Mexican border?"

It was another good point. He fell silent, filtering through additional theories.

But any way he looked at it, the entire situation didn't jell. Especially when factoring in the murder of Jeff Abbott.

When his phone rang, he quickly answered. "Tuck? What's going on?"

"Hey, I found some tire tracks not far from the spot where we believe Jeff Abbott was murdered. You may want to come out here to see for yourself."

He absolutely wanted to take a look. But did he dare leave Mari and Theo alone in the house? The guys hadn't stumbled across anyone lurking outside. He remembered the scene of the actual murder was roughly fifty yards away from where he'd found the garbage bag.

"Okay, I'll be right there." He stood and crossed to where Mari was cleaning the flour from her cutting board. "I need to check something out. Will you and Theo be okay for a few minutes?"

"Of course." Her smile didn't quite reach her eyes. She

glanced at the shotgun she had near her pantry. "This time, I won't hesitate to shoot."

"Good." He hated the idea of her needing to take such drastic action, but he was proud of her willingness to protect herself and her son. "This shouldn't take long. Fifteen to twenty minutes at the most."

"Okay." She hesitated, then added, "I can make breakfast for the others, too, if they're hungry."

"Only if you let me reimburse you for the cost of bacon," he said. "Those guys eat like hounds."

This time, her smile brightened her eyes. "No need to worry about the bacon. We're not destitute. It's the least I can do for the way y'all are looking out for me. For us," she amended, glancing at Theo.

He wanted to insist but decided to worry about that later. Right now, he needed to get out to check out the tire tracks. Had the crime scene techs missed them? It was dark, so maybe.

"Keep the weapon close," he murmured. Then shrugged into his jacket, grabbed his hat and headed outside. He purposefully went out the front, scanning the area around the driveway. The curve in the driveway prevented him from seeing all the way to the road. No one was by the tree, though, so that was good.

He turned and rounded the corner of the house, heading down along the same path he'd taken the night before. It seemed like days ago, instead of mere hours. A lot had happened since he'd arrived and ultimately stayed at the Whistling Creek Ranch.

The thought had him making a mental note to have one of the guys stand guard over Theo and Mari so he could head back to the hotel long enough to shower and change his clothes.

He kept a keen eye out for anything he or the others may have missed, but there was nothing unusual. The sun was slowly warming the air, and he noticed the cattle were moving around more.

Several of them looked at him curiously as he walked by. They weren't exactly guard dogs, he thought with a grim smile.

He was more than halfway down to Whistling Creek when he heard the crack of gunfire.

Without hesitation, he spun on his heel and broke into a run, hoping and praying the shot had been fired by Mari and not someone else.

Like Roy Carlton.

Chapter Six

Mari had finished the dishes when the kitchen window shattered seconds after her brain registered the sound of gunfire.

Not again!

She ducked, her heart pounding in her chest. That had been too close! Grabbing the shotgun, she ran into the living room to scoop Theo into her arms. Then she headed down the hall to her master bedroom, intending to use the closet for a hiding spot. It was the only place she could think of to buy time. Especially since the gunfire had come from the front of the house.

"The scary man is back," Theo sobbed.

She couldn't argue. "We're okay. Mr. Sam will be here soon." After yanking open the closet door, she stepped inside and set Theo on his feet.

"Mommy," he cried, clutching her legs. She hated how scared he was. No child should suffer this much terror and danger. "I want my Charlie!"

The stuffed dog was likely in the living room, so going back for it was not happening. She held the shotgun with the muzzle pointing to the floor and pulled her phone from her pocket. She needed to call this in because she had no idea how far away Sam had been when the shooter had taken aim and fired at the house.

Was he close enough to have heard it? There was no way to know.

Fingers shaking, she dialed 911 with one hand.

"Hello, what is your emergency?"

"This is Mari Lynch at Whistling Creek Ranch." She did her best to remain calm despite the fact this was the second call like this she'd made in a handful of hours. "The gunman is back, he shot at me through the kitchen window."

"Are you safe?" The dispatcher asked.

"We're hiding in the closet of my room." Theo's sobbing ripped at her heart. "Please hurry. I'm afraid he'll come inside the house."

"Stay on the line with me. I've dispatched two deputies to your location."

It was the same pat answer she'd gotten earlier, and that response had taken far too long. Almost twenty minutes before those deputies arrived. Normally she loved living on the ranch, but not now.

Not when she and her son were in danger.

"I can't. He might come inside the house to find us. Just hurry." She disconnected the call and shoved the phone into her pocket. Then she gripped the shotgun with two hands and prepared herself mentally to fire at the first sign of danger.

She would not hesitate. Not this time.

It wouldn't help to think the worst. If she had Sam's personal cell number she'd call him. But she didn't. All she could do was to wait and pray.

Come on, Sam, where are you?

Theo's sobbing subsided, enabling her to hear better. She tried to tuck him behind her, but he wouldn't budge, gripping her legs so tightly she couldn't so much as take a step.

That was okay. If the intruder did get inside, there was no way she could miss at this close range.

But she desperately hoped it wouldn't come to that. She didn't want Theo to be even more traumatized than he was already.

Please, Lord Jesus, keep us safe in Your care!

One minute passed. Then another.

"Mari? Theo? Are you safe?"

Sam's voice was a welcome relief. Yet she didn't move out from their hiding spot. For all she knew the gunman was hiding inside somewhere, waiting to take one last shot.

"We're okay!" She shouted as loudly as she could. "We're hiding!" She didn't know how much to say in case the gunman was listening. The last thing she wanted was to give their location away.

"Stay where you are!" Sam called.

She didn't respond, hoping the gunman would figure out that he was about to get caught. If he was hiding inside the house. In a way she hoped he was. She would be able to breathe easier once the gunman was found and arrested.

Roy? Or someone else? That was the tough question.

"Mommy? Is that Mr. Sam?" Theo asked with a loud sniffle.

"Yes." She didn't lower the weapon but glanced down at her son. "He's going to make sure we're safe. He won't let the scary man find us."

"I like Mr. Sam," Theo whispered.

His innocent words made her chest tighten. She was happy Theo had someone to look up to, but it was so wrong that her young son was frightened out of his mind.

She heard movement, doors opening and closing, floorboards creaking.

"Clear!" someone said.

"Clear!" Sam chimed in.

She understood Sam had at least one of his rangers with him. It didn't take long for Sam to come into the master suite. "Mari? Are you and Theo okay in there?"

"Yes." A wave of relief hit hard. A few minutes later, Sam

opened the closet door. She slowly lowered the shotgun when she saw him. "Thank you for getting here so quickly."

"I shouldn't have left at all." Sam's grim expression softened when he glanced down at Theo. "Are you all right?"

Theo nodded, but then said, "I need Charlie."

"Oh, yes. Your stuffed dog. I'll get him." Sam lifted his gaze to her. "Pack a few things for you and Theo. We can't stay here."

She wanted to protest, but knew he was right. Yet that didn't mean it would be easy to go. She needed the ranch to be profitable for Theo. "I understand, but what about the livestock? I can't leave them to the elements."

Sam grimaced. "Do you have a neighbor who can help?"

"Tom Fleming lives on the next ranch with his wife, Irene, but he's in his midsixties." She nibbled her lower lip. "I hate to put more pressure on him. He has his own chores to do."

Sam held her gaze. "I can't tell you what to do about the ranch, Mari. But staying here isn't an option."

Letting out her breath in a heavy sigh, she nodded. "I'll call Tom. I helped him out last spring when his wife was ill. I'm sure he can help for a day or two."

"Good. Make it quick and then pack a bag."

"There's one last piece of plywood downstairs," Jackson said. "I'll use it on the kitchen window."

"Thank you." Mari called Tom Fleming, grateful when he readily agreed to gather eggs and check on the cattle. She gave him a little information about the danger, only because he could hardly miss seeing the boarded-up windows.

"You and Theo are welcome to stay with us," Tom was quick to offer. Out here, neighbors helped each other when able.

"I don't want to put you and Irene in danger. The Texas Rangers are here and watching over me." It occurred to her that Tom could be in danger just by coming over to the property to help with her chores, so she added, "Make sure to keep your shotgun handy when you stop over. I doubt my ex-husband will attack you. It's me he wants, but I would feel better if you were armed."

"Will do. Be careful out there."

"Thanks." She ended the call, wondering if she had done the right thing by asking for Tom's help. If something bad happened to Tom or Irene, she'd feel awful.

"Mari?" Sam poked his head into the bedroom. "Ready?"

"Almost." She quickly pulled out a small suitcase and stuffed a change of clothing and toiletries inside for her. Then ducked into Theo's room to do the same. She added some of his toys to help keep him busy, wherever they ended up staying.

Five minutes later, she had the suitcase and the shotgun in the kitchen, ready to go. Jackson and Sam were just finishing with the plywood.

"Charlie!" Theo grabbed the stuffed dog from the table and held it to his chest. "Can I bring him?"

"Of course." She forced a smile, then glanced toward Sam. "What's the plan?"

"Unfortunately, the shooter took out the tires on both SUVs," Sam said. "We'll need to borrow your four-wheelers."

She opened the junk drawer and pulled out the keys. "I have three of them. Is that enough?"

"We'll make it work." Sam took the keys. "I'll take you and Theo on one. Jackson will grab the other, meeting up with Tuck and Marsh. Let's go out the back."

She pulled on her coat, helped Theo with his, instructing him not to let go of Charlie. She held Theo's hand as she followed Sam through the house. Sam had both the suitcase and shotgun with him. Jackson stayed close behind. The late December breeze was chilly as they stepped outside. As if he owned the place, Sam headed straight for the barn where the four-wheelers were parked.

"These won't get us all the way to Fredericksburg which is slightly closer than Austin," she warned as she climbed up on the closest one. Sam lifted Theo up and placed him in her arms.

Then he tucked the suitcase and shotgun on the storage space located in the back, strapping both items securely in place.

"We'll use that map you drew of the property to head to the original ranch house," Sam said. "We need to check it out anyway. And if no one has been there, it will be a good place to stay for a day or two."

She nodded. They could make it work.

The minor discomfort would be worth it to keep Theo safe.

Sam fired up the four-wheeler, relieved to note that Mari apparently kept up with making sure the ranch equipment was in working order. He'd half expected to find the battery was dead, or the engine filled with sludge gas, but it sounded great.

He nodded at Jackson, who shoved the barn door open before jumping on the second four-wheeler. Sam would have to go slow, having both Mari and Theo riding with him, so he'd given Jackson instructions to head to the creek to drop off a key to Tuck and Marsh, then head straight for the original ranch house. Sam wanted to be sure that he wasn't taking Mari and Theo into a trap.

Sam drove out of the barn first, followed by Jackson. But his fellow ranger hit the gas and sped ahead, anxious to join the other rangers.

It had occurred to Sam that the shooter must have been watching the ranch house, waiting for him to leave before striking out again. He kicked himself for leaving the south side of the property open, making the wrong assumption the shooter would hide out back.

A mistake he wouldn't make again.

The more attempts the gunman made against Mari, the more he believed the shooter had to be her ex-husband, Roy Carlton. Maybe this was all about simple revenge. Carlton held a grudge against Mari and wanted to take her out of the picture before escaping to Mexico.

The attempt to grab Theo was the only part that didn't fit

with that scenario. Not that anyone claimed Roy Carlton was rational or logical. The guy should be on his way to Mexico by now, rather than making a grab for his son and shooting at Mari's home.

He drove slowly down the tree line toward Whistling Creek. Imagining Mari's rough sketch in his head, he waited until there was a break in the trees to head northwest.

Theo's tiny hands clutched his jacket, while Mari held on to his shoulder. Under different circumstances, he would have enjoyed riding the property with them.

Up ahead he heard the roar of Jackson's four-wheeler. The guy had made it down to the creek in record time. He could imagine Jackson handing off the key to the third machine, then turning to reach the original ranch house well ahead of Sam.

He glanced over his shoulder at Mari, who appeared to be scanning their surroundings. Over the roar of the engine, he said, "Let me know if I go off course."

She nodded. "You're doing fine."

He hit a particularly hard bump, causing Theo to cry out in fear. He forced himself to slow down, despite the deep sense of urgency pushing at him to get Mari and Theo to safety.

Jackson was at the ranch house by the time they arrived. Sam parked his four-wheeler next to the empty one, grateful to see that there were no footprints or tire tracks in the slight dusting of snow around the building, other than Jackson's.

His fellow ranger came out of the house, waving them inside. "It's all clear."

"Thank the Lord Jesus," Mari whispered behind him.

He waited for her to slide off first. Once she had Theo in her arms, he hopped off and grabbed the suitcase and shotgun from the small cargo area. He led the way up to the house, scanning their surroundings. He could see why her grandfather had chosen the location, although it was much farther from the main highway. Maybe that had been an intentional move on his part.

It was cold inside, but he noticed Jackson had taken the time to build a fire in the wood-burning stove.

Mari stood holding Theo's hand, looking around curiously. "It's rather dusty, but otherwise it looks the same as the last time I was here."

"Good. That means no one has been inside recently." He was reassured by both the layer of dust and the lack of footprints in the snow.

Jackson's phone rang, and his buddy moved away to answer the call. Sam pulled his own phone, surprised to see there were two bars of service.

Not great, but not terrible. The biggest problem was their isolated location. Even if he called for backup, none would be forthcoming in anything close to a timely manner.

"I just got a call from our boss." Jackson turned back to Sam. "Owens has contacted the others, too. Unfortunately, we're not going to be able to stick around. He wants me to head to the hospital to interview more staff members about the night of Carlton's escape. Tucker is being sent to chat with the city manager and Marsh was told to follow up with the medical examiner on Abbott's autopsy."

"Go," Sam said without hesitation although he wished he could take a more active role in the investigation, too. "It's obvious no one has been in the area. We'll be safe here."

Mari's gaze held concern but she didn't argue. She took Theo closer to the warmth radiating from the stove and pulled some toys from the bag for him.

"I hate to leave you here," Jackson said, keeping his voice down so as not to alarm Theo. "But Owens has a point. Finding and arresting Roy Carlton is the quickest way to eliminate the danger to Mari and Theo."

He nodded. "I agree."

Jackson hesitated, then added, "Be careful. She's beautiful and the kid is cute, but you're on the brink of becoming emotionally involved."

Jackson wasn't telling him anything he didn't already know. "I hear you loud and clear."

"Do you?" Jackson arched a brow, flashing a skeptical gaze. "Why do I feel like it's already too late?"

"It's not. I'm fine." His denial was quick, but even he knew he wasn't being entirely honest.

Despite his best intentions, he had let Mari and Theo get too close. In his defense, it was impossible to remain objective when an innocent woman and her young son were constantly under fire from a ruthless gunman.

"Famous last words," Jackson shot back, before stepping outside. Minutes later, he was on the four-wheeler and heading back to Mari's barn.

The interior of the original ranch house was warming up nicely. Almost too cozy, with the three of them staying here. He glanced at Mari, crouched near her son. "I'm heading out to get more wood."

She glanced up. "Okay. There's a woodpile about fifty yards from the back door of the house. We do have a gas furnace but I keep it really low to preserve fuel. It would be nice to use the stove for heat as much as possible. Oh, and I can head down to the utility room to flip the breaker so we have electricity. I generally keep it off during the winter."

"I'll check it out." He frowned, then added, "You should keep the door locked, though. And the shotgun handy."

"I will." Her green eyes held a steely determination. He thought about how she'd looked holding the gun ready while standing in the closet.

He wanted to step forward and gather her close, but with Jackson's warning echoing in his ear, he turned to head back outside.

There was barely a quarter inch of snow on the ground. He wondered why it hadn't melted, but the wind coming from the north likely contributed to it sticking around.

He worked quickly, hauling split logs from the woodpile

and neatly stacking them along the side of the house close to the back door. By the time he finished, he felt certain they'd have enough wood to heat the place for at least the next twenty-four hours.

They should have Roy Carlton in custody by then. Although it would help to identify his accomplices. One if not two people would have been involved in helping him escape.

He stomped the stray bit of snow from his boots as he rapped on the front door. As directed, Mari had locked it behind him.

"Hey." She opened the door to let him in. "Thanks for doing that."

"Of course." He shrugged out of his coat and removed his cowboy hat. Glancing in the living room, he saw Theo was curled up on the sofa with a blanket and his stuffed dog, Charlie. His eyes were drooping as if sleepy.

He followed Mari into the kitchen. "Does he usually take naps in the morning?"

"Never." She crossed her arms over her chest, watching her son for a long moment. "He was up early, though, and has been through a lot."

So had she. "I'm sorry. I wish I hadn't left you alone."

"This isn't your fault, it's Roy's." She turned away and opened a few cupboard doors. "There isn't much to eat as far as lunch and dinner goes. Canned soup and cans of beef stew are the best I can offer."

"That's okay, we'll survive." He frowned as she moved jerkily from one cupboard to the next poking through the supplies.

Then she abruptly stopped and placed her hands on the countertop, her head bowed as if struggling to hold herself together.

"Hey, don't fall apart now." He hoped his voice didn't betray his panic. "We're safe here."

"Are we?" Her voice was thick with anguish. "How long will it take before the gunman finds us here? A couple of hours?"

"Please, don't." Ignoring Jackson's warning, he crossed over to put his arm around her. "I promise I won't leave you. I'll stay close until Roy has been arrested."

To his surprise, she turned and stepped into his arms, burying her face against his chest. He cradled her close, whispering reassurances. It only took her a few minutes to pull herself together.

"Sorry about that." She sniffled and swiped at her eyes. "I didn't mean to cry on your shoulder."

"I'm here for you, Mari. No matter what you need." His own voice sounded husky to his ears.

"I wish—" She abruptly stopped and shook her head. Then she went up on her tiptoes to kiss his cheek.

He hadn't meant to take things any further, but somehow he'd captured her mouth in a warm kiss.

Chapter Seven

Sam's kiss warmed Mari's heart. It had been so long since she'd been held and kissed. Even though she knew Sam probably only intended to offer her comfort, she couldn't deny wishing for more.

Far too soon, Sam broke off the kiss. "I'm sorry," he murmured.

She frowned. "Why? Because you didn't want to kiss me?"

"What? No." He looked shocked, then chagrined. "But I did take advantage of our situation. And I shouldn't have."

His comment proved what she'd thought—that he wasn't interested in her as a woman. And wasn't that for the best?

"You didn't. I'm the one who almost fell apart. But I'll be okay." She straightened her shoulders and lifted her chin. Theo needed her to remain strong. To be able to provide for him. They would get through this.

She'd learned the hard way that being alone was better than being with the wrong man.

"Mari…" His voice trailed off as his gaze searched hers. "I care about you, very much. But I also need to keep you safe."

And those two things were mutually exclusive? Maybe. She didn't ask but forced a smile. "I understand."

She turned to grab the cans of soup, desperate to change the subject. "We'll have this for lunch and beef stew for dinner."

"Sounds great." He sounded as enthusiastic as if she'd offered him a four-course meal. "What can I do to help?"

"Nothing. I can manage." She rummaged in the cupboards for a saucepan. The gas stove worked well, and even though she didn't have money to spare, she'd turned the electricity back on, too.

Thanks to Roy, money was the least of her worries.

For a moment she felt herself sliding back into a sinkhole of despair. She and Theo didn't deserve this. Then again, God never said that His children wouldn't face challenges. But God did provide the strength and courage to overcome them.

She would do better in leaning on her faith to get through this.

When she noticed Sam going through some of the cupboards, she turned to face him. "What are you looking for?"

"Something to wipe the dust off the table," he answered absently.

Why was he sticking so close? She'd feel better if he'd have stayed outside for a while longer.

"I can take care of it." She wasn't used to having help with basic household chores. "Sit down and relax."

He hesitated, then nodded as if sensing she needed space. After settling into the rocking chair next to the stove, he tipped his head back and closed his eyes.

Grateful to have him out of her way, she quickly rinsed the saucepan and then filled it with three cans of soup. She would have loved to have crackers or bread to go along with the meal, but that wasn't possible. She didn't keep perishable groceries here.

When she was finished with that, she began cleaning the kitchen counters, table and other surfaces. Staying busy helped to a certain extent. She wasn't afraid of Roy finding them here, not with Sam on guard.

Yet cleaning did not keep her from ruminating over Sam's heated kiss. And her instant response to his embrace. She'd acted like a starving woman wanting more.

How embarrassing.

Glancing at Theo, she debated waking him from his nap. His sleep schedule was going to be messed up if she allowed him to sleep too long.

Sam rose and fed more wood into the stove. The interior of the ranch house had warmed up nicely. She averted her gaze, thinking that being here with Sam was more intimate than earlier at the ranch house. Maybe because the boarded windows were a constant reminder of the danger.

Or maybe it was just the aftermath of his kiss. She really needed to find a way to get over it.

"Mommy?" Theo lifted his head, his brown hair sticking up on one side. "Where are we?"

"We took a ride on the four-wheeler, remember?" Having finished with the kitchen, she crossed over to sit beside him. "We're at the old house."

"Oh, yeah." He yawned widely and blinked adorably. "I remember now."

Maybe she shouldn't have mentioned how they'd been forced to leave to escape danger. He'd seemed to sleep peacefully without nightmares. But Theo didn't ask anything more as he scooted off the sofa. "I hav'ta go to the bathroom."

"This way." She glanced at Sam. "Will you stir the soup please?"

"Of course." He finished with the wood stove, brushing the bark from his fingers.

By the time Theo had finished and washed his hands, she heard a voice from the kitchen. She followed her son back to the main living space, not surprised to discover Sam was on the phone.

Another reminder that he was here working the case of her escaped ex-husband. Not hanging out for fun and games.

"Thanks for the update," Sam said before ending the call.

"Did they find him?"

"Not yet." He looked as if he might say more but held back when Theo darted toward him.

"Will you play with me, Mr. Sam?"

"Sure. But I think it may be time to eat lunch."

Mari nodded, crossing to the stove. It was early, but that was okay. "Sam, will you grab a pillow for Theo to sit on? I'll dish up the soup."

A minute later, they were seated at the table. She took Theo's hand and bowed her head. "Dear Lord Jesus, we are grateful for this food You have provided. Please continue to keep us safe in Your care and give the Texas Rangers the wisdom and strength to find the truth. Amen."

"Amen," Sam echoed.

"Amen. Can't I have bread with my soup?" Theo asked with a frown.

She had the bread dough rising back at the house, but going back wasn't an option. "I'm afraid not. But chicken noodle is your favorite, right?"

Theo's lower lip stuck out. "But I like bread."

She swallowed a sigh. It wasn't his fault they were making do here at her grandfather's ranch house.

"I love this soup," Sam declared. "It's good without bread."

Theo eyed him for a moment, then mimicked Sam's movements. It made her heart squeeze to realize how much her son looked up to Sam in just the short time he'd spent with them.

Then she worried about how Theo would react once the threat of Roy had been eliminated and Sam wasn't around any longer.

Sam did his best to keep Theo preoccupied as they finished lunch. The kid was impressionable, and that was a good thing.

But it did make him wonder what Mari and Roy's life was like prior to her divorce. He didn't want to pry into her personal life, but it was obvious Theo didn't remember his father very well.

If at all.

"I'll clean up," he offered when they were finished.

"Are you always this helpful?" she asked with a frown. "I mean, most men leave kitchen duty to women."

"My grandmother would give me the stink eye from heaven if I didn't offer to help," he joked. "She always made Granddad pitch in."

"That surprises me," Mari admitted. "Especially from that generation."

"It's common courtesy." He didn't add that there wasn't much of anything else to do. Keeping his voice down, so Theo wouldn't overhear, he added, "What do you think of taking Theo outside to build a small snowman?"

She hesitated. "Is it safe enough?"

"I think so, if we stay in the backyard." They had his sidearm and her shotgun. He didn't anticipate that Roy or his accomplices would find them there so quickly. "Just for a short time. Enough for him to burn off some excess energy."

"Okay." She smiled. "That would be great."

The task of washing their dishes didn't take long, then they headed outdoors. He was surprised at how much fun they had playing in the snow. Theo was all about building a big snowman, but they had to make it a small one as there wasn't that much to work with.

"He's a mini-snowman," Mari declared. "Perfect size, Theo, don't you think?"

"Yep." Theo stuck his tongue out and licked the snowman's head. Sam was taken aback but Mari bit her lip as if holding back a laugh. "He doesn't taste good, though," Theo announced.

"We don't eat or lick them, we just look at them." Mari shook her head ruefully then slapped her gloved hands together to get the excess snow off. "Let's go, Theo. It's time to head back inside."

"Aw, do we hav'ta?"

"Yes. You're shivering," she pointed out.

Sam hadn't noticed, although now that he looked at the boy, it was so obvious he was chilled to the bone. "You heard your mother. We need to get inside."

Theo stared at him for a moment as if gauging if he should argue, but then dashed toward the door. "I win!"

"How is it that I'm more exhausted after building that snowman than he is?" he asked as they went inside.

"Trust me, it's one of life's many mysteries." Mari sighed. "Theo is proof that energy is wasted on the youth."

The rest of the day passed without incident. He played with Theo as Mari warmed up the canned beef stew for dinner. As dusk fell, Mari had turned the kitchen light on. He'd asked her to flip it off, preferring to sit in the darkness with only the faint glow from the wood-burning stove as light.

If Roy or his accomplices had found out about the house, it made sense that they'd wait to strike at night. No doubt having learned from their earlier mistake in taking a shot at Mari through the kitchen window in broad daylight. He didn't want Mari or Theo to be an easy target.

"I'm going to walk the perimeter," he said when they'd finished eating. "Shouldn't take longer than ten to fifteen minutes."

"Okay." She glanced at the shotgun he'd propped in the kitchen corner. "We'll be fine."

He settled his hat on his head, shrugged into his coat and headed outside. The darkness wasn't complete thanks to the reflection of the moon and stars against the snow. He stood for a moment, listening intently. Then he stepped away from the house and began to walk.

There were no footprints in the snow beyond the spot where he and Jackson had parked the four-wheelers. He hesitated, wondering if he should stick closer to the house, but then remembered how the gunman had used the tree for cover prior to shooting Mari's living room window.

He hiked in a circle, scouting any area a gunman could use as a nest. The good news was that there were no lights inside to make it easier for anyone to aim at Mari or Theo.

Not that he wouldn't try. Sam had to assume at this point that the gunman was feeling desperate.

After making a circle around the property, he headed back inside, well within the fifteen-minute time frame.

"Anything?" Mari asked as he stomped snow off his boots.

"All clear." He hiked a brow when he noticed she'd made a pallet on the floor near the wood-burning stove. "Are you and Theo sleeping in here?"

"For now." She grimaced. "I'm not sure how much gas we have in the LP tank. It's better if we use gas heat at a bare minimum."

"Sure thing." He didn't mind sleeping on the floor. Far better for Mari and Theo to use the sofa. "Whatever works."

He took a moment to bring in more wood for the stove, enough to last the night. He was hoping for an update from the guys, but so far they hadn't learned very much. Marsh had called to let him know the medical examiner had declared Jeff Abbott's death a homicide. He had been killed by the shotgun blast at close range. And Jackson had mentioned how one of the hospital employees had noticed a blue minivan leaving the parking garage shortly after the nurse had found Carlton's room empty, and the deputy locked in the bathroom with his own cuffs.

He'd hoped for more, but every small piece of information would help build the big picture.

Even though the convict should never have escaped in the first place.

Mari made hot chocolate out of water, which Theo loved. Then she changed Theo into his superhero footie pajamas. Sam listened as Mari recited a bedtime story from memory, then tucked a quilt around Theo for added warmth. It didn't take long for the little boy to fall asleep.

"Should I lift him onto the sofa?" he asked in a whisper.

Mari nodded. When that was done, she made sure his dog Charlie was within reach, then moved over to the kitchen table so their talking wouldn't disturb him.

"Can you fill me in on what's going on?" she asked.

"We haven't learned as much as we'd hoped," he admitted. "Abbott's cause of death is no surprise. And they're following a few leads from the hospital."

"I just don't understand any of this," Mari whispered.

"I know." He reached out to take her hand. "I wish I could tell you more. I'm sure we'll have more leads by morning."

She stared at their clasped hands for a moment, then gently pulled away. Her hot chocolate was gone, but she held on to the mug as if it were a lifeline. "What concerns me the most is that Roy isn't a nice man," she whispered.

He frowned. "You mean because he murdered Hank George?"

She shook her head but didn't say anything. A chill snaked down his spine.

"He hurt you?" Sam pressed. "Physically hurt you and Theo?"

"Me, not Theo." She stared into her empty mug for a long moment before lifting her head. The anguish in her eyes hit hard.

"How badly?"

She sighed and shook her head, dropping her gaze again. "It started with shouting and swearing, nonstop comments about how useless I was and how he never should have married me."

It was all Sam could do to sit calmly, as she described the abuse she'd endured. When she didn't add anything more, he asked, "When did it turn physical?"

"About a year after Theo was born." She turned to look at her sleeping son. "I started to stand up for myself, and he slapped me." She grimaced. "I should have left right then and there, but I didn't. Not until he hit me a second time."

"I hate that you had to go through that."

"My fault for marrying him." She set her empty mug aside. "I packed up Theo and went home to Whistling Creek. My dad wanted to beat Roy to a pulp, but I told him that wouldn't solve anything." A faint smile creased her features. "But my dad did come with me to get the rest of our things and brought his shotgun along, too. Roy stood back and let me take whatever I wanted without uttering a single objection."

Good for her dad, he thought. And wished he'd been around to help back then. "I'm glad. Good riddance. You're far better off without him."

"Yes, I know." Her brow furrowed. "Roy had some nerve trying to kidnap Theo."

"We'll find him." He tried to sound confident, although it was not reassuring that Carlton had eluded them even this long. "One thing Jackson learned is that a hospital staff member noticed a blue minivan leaving the parking lot shortly after your ex-husband escaped."

She looked up at him. "Really? You think Roy was inside?"

"It's a lead." As if on cue his phone rang and Jackson's name popped up on the screen. Still keeping his voice low, he answered, "What's up, Jackson?"

"Will you ask Mari if the name Cindy Gorlich means anything to her?"

He settled his gaze on her. "Mari? Do you know a Cindy Gorlich?"

"No, why?"

"That's a negative, Jackson. What role does Gorlich have in this?"

"She works as a nurse and reported her blue minivan stolen. I've interviewed her and she claims she told one of the sheriff's deputies about the theft, but I can't find anyone who admitted to talking to her."

"That's interesting. Do you think she's lying?"

"I don't know," Jackson said. "Keep in mind, the sheriff's department already has egg on their face over Carlton's escaping in the first place. Deputy Erickson admitted to getting too close to Carlton, allowing him to grab his sidearm. From there, it was easy enough to force Erickson into the bathroom and use his own cuffs to restrain him."

The story sounded worse every time he heard it. "So, what, you think they're covering up another error by not coming forward with the stolen vehicle report?"

"Why not?"

"Yeah, that's possible." He hoped heads would roll at the sheriff's department after this fiasco but he wouldn't bank on it. "Have you dug into Gorlich's background?"

"We're doing that now. No flags yet. But I thought you should know. And we were wondering if it was possible that Carlton was having an affair with Cindy Gorlich prior to his arrest."

"Hang on." He lowered the phone. "Are you aware of Roy having any girlfriends after your divorce?"

"No." Mari frowned. "If Roy was seeing someone, I didn't know anything about it." She paused, then added, "Honestly, I may have been tempted to warn his girlfriend about his physical abuse, for her sake. I would not have wanted anyone else to suffer either."

He believed her. "Thanks." He lifted the phone. "Mari has no knowledge of her ex having a girlfriend. But maybe canvassing the area would come up with someone who saw them together."

"More than two years ago?" Doubt laced Jackson's tone. "Most people can barely remember what they ate for dinner the night before."

"We have to try." Sam's face flushed, as he added, "Sorry. I would be there helping if I could."

"Yeah, yeah. Coming from the guy who has the gravy assignment," Jackson teased. "We'll ask around and dig a little deeper. How are things by you?"

"Quiet. We're good. Keep me updated, Jackson."

"You know it." His fellow ranger disconnected the call.

As Sam lowered his phone, he thought about Jackson's comment. For a gravy assignment, he was feeling mighty tense.

The responsibility of keeping Mari and Theo safe was heavy on his shoulders. He'd made mistakes in the past, one that had nearly cost his fellow rangers' lives.

He refused to make a similar mistake in judgment this time. He needed to stay hypervigilant in his quest to protect Mari and Theo.

Chapter Eight

Roy likely had a girlfriend. Mari wasn't sure why the news bothered her. She'd been thankful to have him out of her life, and to be granted sole custody of Theo. What her ex did in his free time was his own business.

Some women were attracted to men in prison, or maybe Roy had started seeing someone while they were still married. After everything that had transpired in the past twenty-four hours, she wouldn't put anything past him.

"You should get some sleep," Sam murmured. "Take the sofa with Theo. I'll sleep on the floor."

Startled by the offer, she nodded. Although she shouldn't have been surprised. Sam had been nothing but a gentleman and their steadfast protector during this nightmare. She had no doubt that he'd risk his life for her and Theo, if needed.

She prayed it wouldn't come to that. The Texas Rangers and the local police were searching for her ex. Roy couldn't hide forever.

Especially if he continued to seek revenge by coming after her and Theo. Or kidnapping their son for ransom. Or whatever he was up to.

"Good night." She stood and crossed to the sofa. Theo was

sleeping on one end. She picked up the edge of the quilt and slid underneath so that her legs were stretched out alongside her son's.

The warmth from the wood-burning stove helped her to relax. They were safe here. And tomorrow? She winced, thinking about her ranch chores that Tom Fleming would need to do for her, in addition to his own.

Maybe they could head back to the main ranch house just long enough for her to check the cattle to make sure they had enough water and to gather eggs. With the four-wheeler, it wouldn't take that much time. And that way, she could grab additional food from her fridge and pantry.

Satisfied to have a plan, she closed her eyes and tried to sleep. Yet she was keenly aware of Sam moving around the living room, adding more wood to the fire before stretching out on the pallet she'd made on the floor.

His kiss had been wonderful. The moment that thought crossed her mind, she did her best to ignore it. Remembering their brief embrace would not help her fall asleep.

Just the opposite.

She silently prayed for God to continue watching over her, Sam and Theo. Between the prayer and the cozy atmosphere she drifted off to sleep.

Several times during the night, Sam added wood to the stove for added warmth. She doubted the floor was comfortable, but when she heard him softly snoring, she couldn't help but smile.

By the time the first rays of dawn beckoned on the horizon, Sam was up and moving around in the kitchen. Theo was still asleep, so she carefully disentangled herself from the sofa and quilt, then joined Sam.

"Good morning," she whispered.

"Morning." His smile warmed her heart. "Did you sleep okay?"

"About as well as you did. But thanks for keeping the stove going. That was nice."

"Anytime." He glanced around the kitchen. "No way to make coffee, huh?"

She chuckled at the wistful expression on his face. "There is an old-fashioned percolator here. I'll see if I can find it." She paused, then added, "I'm not sure the coffee that was left here is much good, though. It's probably stale."

"I'm not picky." He leaned against the counter, and she was keenly aware of how he watched as she silently checked various cabinets for the percolator. If things were different...

But they weren't.

The percolator was in the last cabinet she checked. She set it on the counter and began setting it up. Sam watched the process with interest.

"We've been spoiled by technology, haven't we?" he said in a low, wry tone.

"For sure." She found the coffee grounds in the fridge and filled the metal filter of the percolator. "One thing about old technology, it doesn't break down as easily."

"True," Sam agreed.

"Mommy?" Theo sat up on the sofa, rubbing his eyes. "I'm hungry."

"I know." She waved at the percolator. "You'll know when the coffee is ready. I need to take care of Theo."

"Go ahead," he said with a nod. "I'll grab more wood from the back door, too."

She wanted to ask if that was necessary, since she didn't think they'd need to stay much longer, but held her tongue. He was the expert. And she also knew his fellow rangers would call the minute they had Roy in custody.

After getting Theo washed up and changed into regular clothes, taking a few minutes to freshen up herself, she returned to the kitchen with her son.

"I found a container of oatmeal," Sam said. To her surprise he already had a pan of water warming up on the stove. "Figured that would work well for breakfast."

"No oatmeal," Theo pouted. "I want eggs and bacon."

She stifled a sigh. "Not today. But I can make another cup of hot chocolate if you'd like."

Theo's eyes widened and he nodded eagerly. "Yay! Hot chocolate!"

She'd hoped that would distract him from the oatmeal, which she knew wasn't her son's favorite. But if he was hungry enough, he'd eat it.

"You haven't heard anything from the other rangers?" She glanced at Sam questioningly.

"Not yet." He shrugged. "It's still early, though."

It was early in the morning, barely seven thirty, but Roy had been on the run for what seemed like forever. She bit her lip and told herself to be patient.

"I was hoping we could head back to the ranch house, just briefly." She stirred the oatmeal. "I want to be able to gather more eggs, check the cattle and maybe grab more food if we're going to be here for a while."

"I don't know if that's a good idea," Sam hedged. "We're safe here."

They were, but she had her livestock to consider. She dropped the subject for now, concentrating on finishing their makeshift breakfast of oatmeal and hot chocolate.

Theo squirmed on the pillow in his seat as she set their meal on the table. "Wait until we say grace," she warned when he reached for his hot chocolate. "Besides, it's too hot."

With an exaggerated sigh, he sat back. "Hurry up."

"We need to take time to express our gratitude," Sam said.

"What does that mean?" Theo asked.

She took Theo's hand. "It means we give thanks to our Lord Jesus for providing this food we are about to eat. And we also thank the Lord for keeping us safe. Amen."

"Amen," Sam echoed.

"Amen," Theo said. "Now can we eat?"

She couldn't help but laugh. He was still too young to fully grasp the idea of God and faith. But she was touched that Sam had participated in every prayer.

Supporting her in so many small yet important ways.

It occurred to her this partnership was what her parents had experienced. She and her dad had been devastated over losing her mother. But that loss had brought them closer together, too.

Until she'd married Roy, that is. Her dad had never liked him. Less so after she'd come home with Theo sporting a bruised lip and cheek.

They ate in silence for a few minutes.

"Have you considered my request to head back?" she finally asked.

He grimaced. "I don't know if we should. I would offer to go, but I can't leave you and Theo here alone."

"I'm sure the gunman has figured out we're not staying there anymore," she pointed out.

"Yeah, that's kind of what I'm afraid of," Sam admitted. "They may decide to expand their search of the ranch. I'm sure this house is still listed on the title."

She hadn't considered that. "It is, yes."

"I'll call Tucker when we're finished. See if there's been an update in the case," he said.

She nodded, masking her disappointment. She didn't want to take Theo into danger. But the meager supply of canned goods wouldn't last long. And Theo would whine over having soup again for lunch without bread or crackers.

When they finished eating, she filled the sink with soapy water. Sam moved into the living room to make his call. She strained to eavesdrop but couldn't hear much over Theo's chattering.

"I wanna play with my dump trucks," he said, shooting her a reproachful look. "How come you didn't pack them?"

There hadn't been time, and they were too big. She glanced at him, striving for patience. "I'm sorry I couldn't bring them along, but you have your horses, right? Play with those for now."

He thrust his lower lip out stubbornly. "I want my trucks."

She did her best not to snap at him. He wasn't old enough to understand. And she didn't want to remind him of the danger that had caused them to come here in the first place. "Maybe later."

"Show me your horses," Sam said. "Flash and Speedo, right?"

"Right!" Theo ran to the living room.

She met Sam's gaze over her son's head. "Thanks."

He smiled briefly, then said, "We can make a short trip to the ranch house. The sheriff's department had a deputy watching the place all night. No sign of any intruders."

That was good news. "Thanks so much." She almost asked if they couldn't just stay at the main house but decided not to push it. She took a moment to call Tom Fleming to let him know she'd be there to do the morning chores so he wouldn't have to bother, then finished the dishes. She let them dry in the sink, anxious to be on their way.

When she glanced toward her son, her heart squeezed as she saw how Sam was playing along with Theo, pretending to ride the horses across the pallet still covering the floor.

He was so good with her son. But this was also a temporary situation. Easy to help keep a kid occupied when you weren't the child's parent on a full-time basis.

Yet watching them play only made her wish for something she'd never have.

A loving husband and more children.

Sam hoped and prayed he wasn't making a huge mistake by taking Mari and Theo back to the main house. According to Tuck, the deputy hadn't seen anyone lurking around, which was good.

Unfortunately, the rest of the news wasn't nearly as reassuring. There was still no sign of Roy Carlton, the missing blue minivan or a dark truck with mud-covered license plates.

How many accomplices did Carlton have, anyway? One? Two? A handful?

No, it was hard to imagine the guy having more than one or two people helping him. And when they figured out who those individuals were, they'd be tossed in jail right alongside Carlton for aiding and abetting a fugitive.

"What time should we head out?" Mari asked.

"Soon." He set Flash aside and rose to his feet. "But I need to walk the perimeter again, first."

"Play horsey with me," Theo protested.

"I will for a little while," Mari said, dropping down beside her son. "Mr. Sam has work to do."

He shrugged into his coat and placed his hat on his head before heading outside. The early morning light was bright, making him squint. Without hesitation, he made the same loop as he had last night, noticing there were plenty of wildlife tracks in the snow, white tail deer, foxes and coyote.

And thankfully, no human footprints other than his own.

He vacillated between leaving Mari and Theo here while he did the chores and taking them along. When Mari and Theo had been washing up and changing clothes, he'd taken stock of the food situation. The lack of canned goods and other items had convinced them a short trip back to the ranch house was in order.

He'd tried to convince Jackson, Tucker and Marshall to meet him at the ranch, but they were still following up on leads related to the investigation.

Satisfied their current location was secure, he headed back inside the house. Theo was arguing with Mari about wanting his trucks. Without a television or any other electronics to keep him occupied, the little boy was growing more insistent about having the rest of his toys.

"We'll take that trip up to the ranch house now," he said, interrupting Theo. "Make a list of the items you need."

"I have entered them in the notes section of my phone." Mari smiled and stood. "Thanks for doing this, Sam. I appreciate it."

"It's not a problem." He waited patiently for Mari to get Theo in his winter gear. Despite his excitement to get out of the house, he wiggled so much it was no easy task to get him in his coat, hat, mittens and boots.

And she sighed when he insisted on taking Charlie, his stuffed dog, along for the ride.

When the little boy was finally dressed, Sam led the way out back to where he'd left the four-wheeler. He jumped on first, starting the engine, then hopped off and helped Mari and Theo get situated.

"Ready?" he asked, glancing over his shoulder. Mari was holding on to the sides of his jacket, with Theo snuggled between them.

"As ever," she shot back.

Like yesterday, he took it slow, minimizing the bouncing along for their sake. The roar of the engine seemed incredibly loud in the otherwise peaceful setting.

There were several four-wheeler tracks along the ground, but he knew that he and Jackson had left them behind. Besides, he was certain he'd have heard anyone else out there on one of these things.

But all had been quiet last night.

For Mari and Theo's sake, he prayed the peace would last, and the gunman would focus his efforts elsewhere.

It took fifteen minutes for the ranch house to come into view. He drove up the hill along the tree line, sweeping his gaze over the area. The cattle, barn and chicken coop all looked undisturbed. So much so, he worried Mari's neighbor hadn't come out to take care of the afternoon chores after they'd left.

If Mari noticed anything amiss, she didn't mention it. She clung to him as they navigated the rocky terrain, reminding him of their heated kiss.

Don't go there, he silently warned himself. *Stay focused!*

He pulled to a stop beside the cattle. "Do you want to check the water level now?" he asked.

"Yes, please." She scrambled off the four-wheeler and ducked beneath the plank fence. The placid faces of the cows turned to look at her curiously as she spoke to them.

"How are you doing out here? Warm enough, I hope." She talked to them as if they were pets. "Looks like you have plenty of water. Go on, now, shoo!" She waved her arms. At first the cows simply stared at her, then began ambling around the pasture as if knowing this was their daily exercise routine.

"I'll walk up to the chicken coop," she said, waving him off.

He hesitated, then nodded. He knew from his brief experience in gathering eggs that the chickens would put up a squawking fuss if anyone had tried to hide in there.

Holding on to Theo with one hand, he drove up along the fence until he was next to the chicken coop. Then he climbed down and lifted Theo up and onto his feet.

"Stay close. We won't be here for long," he said.

"Okay." Theo ran over and climbed up so that he stood on the lower plank of the fence. The kid had been so quick and agile that Sam figured he'd done it before.

He continued scanning the paddock and outbuildings. Seeing nothing amiss, he joined Theo at the fence.

"My Pop Pop had horses," Theo said in a wistful tone. "But he had to sell them to make money."

"I'm sorry to hear that." He wondered how long ago that had been.

"I miss Pop Pop," Theo said. Then the kid looked up at him. "Are you going to be my daddy?"

Whoa, where had that come from? He scrambled for an acceptable answer. "I'm afraid not. Your mommy has to find a man she loves and get married for you to have a new daddy."

"Why?" Theo's brow furrowed. "Why can't you just be my daddy?"

He didn't have an answer for that one, but thankfully Mari

emerged from the chicken coop. She must have had another of those knitted basket things in there, because she carried one full of eggs. "There's your mom. Now we can go inside and get some of your toys."

"Okay." Thankfully, Theo dropped the subject of Sam becoming his daddy. The kid jumped down from the fence and ran over to his mother. "Mr. Sam said we can go inside to get more toys."

"I heard him." Mari smiled. She looked so happy to be back home, doing mundane chores, that he wondered if he was being overprotective by not allowing them to stay here.

He turned away, calling himself all kinds of a fool to let her mess with his head. This was a brief visit long enough to stock up on food and toys for Theo.

Walking to the back door, he frowned when he realized it wasn't locked. Then again, they had left in a hurry the day before.

"Stay behind me," he cautioned, pulling the door open. He eased his weapon from its holster and stepped across the threshold. A horrible scent washed over him, causing him to take a hasty step back, bumping into Mari.

"What's wrong?"

"You can't go inside." He glanced over his shoulder, half expecting to hear gunfire. "Get Theo onto the four-wheeler. Hurry!"

She looked as if she might argue but took her son's hand. "Come with me, Theo."

For once, the kid didn't argue. Sam pulled the door open again and cautiously stepped inside. He made his way past the bedroom doors, frowning at the complete disarray in both Mari's and Theo's rooms. It seemed as if someone had searched the place. Looking for what, he wasn't sure. Sam came to an abrupt halt when he saw a man lying on the floor in front of the wood-burning stove.

Roy Carlton. Killed by a bullet to the center of his forehead.

Chapter Nine

Cradling Theo on her lap, Mari shivered as she waited for Sam to emerge from the house. Other than the sound of mooing and munching hay from the cattle, she didn't hear anything suspicious.

Yet there had been a reason Sam had refused to let her enter her home. And she knew it couldn't be anything good.

"I wanna get down," Theo whined.

"We're waiting for Mr. Sam." She tried to mask her fear of what was taking him so long. "He'll be here soon."

After what seemed like eons but was only about ten minutes, Sam stepped out of the house, his expression grim. "Marshall is on the way."

"Why?" She held his gaze. "Is there a reason I can't go inside to get food and more toys for Theo?"

"Mari." He came closer, his gaze dropping momentarily to Theo before looking at her. "I have some bad news. Roy is—gone." Despite the mild word, she knew he really meant dead.

Roy was dead? She was ashamed of the sense of relief that washed over her. Even though Roy was Theo's father, she was glad he was no longer a threat.

"And someone left him inside," Sam continued.

Wait, what? She gaped in horror. "Who?"

"I don't know." He rested his hand on her knee. "I'm as frustrated and upset as you are. We had a deputy stationed outside, watching the place. I can't begin to fathom how this happened."

A deputy had been there while someone killed Roy? No, she realized the murder must have happened elsewhere, and Roy's body placed here. Why? To incriminate her? That made no sense. It would be easy to prove she was with Sam the entire time.

"I don't understand what's going on," she whispered.

"I know. I wasn't expecting this either." Sam swept the area with his keen gaze. "I think someone searched your room and Theo's, but there's no one there now. I doubt the killer is hanging around. I'm sure he dumped Roy, searched the place then got out of here as quickly as possible. Yet I need you to stay alert."

She shook her head as a wave of helplessness washed over her. At first she'd thought the danger was over now that Roy was gone. But clearly, Sam didn't feel the same way. And why search her and Theo's rooms?

"You think whoever did this will continue to come after us?"

"That's exactly right. Your ex was left here for a reason. Either to send a message to you or to whoever Roy was working with."

First Jeff Abbott was murdered and left on her property and now Roy. She bit hard on her lower lip to keep from losing control. All she wanted was to run her ranch, caring for the livestock and supporting her son.

But this? Why was she being dragged into this mess?

Unless...her blood ran cold. Had Roy told someone dangerous that she knew something? Key information that could be used against them? Maybe information that was thought to be hidden in their rooms?

It seemed the only logical explanation. Not that any of this came across as remotely logical.

She heard Sam talking on the phone and realized he was speaking with someone within the sheriff's department. He was polite yet pointed in relaying his annoyance at how a dead body had been left inside her home while it was supposedly being watched by a deputy.

"Please do," Sam said in a curt tone. "We'll be waiting for you."

Outside? She glanced down at Theo in concern. She could handle the cold weather, but her son would get chilled if they stayed out here much longer.

"I'm sorry. I'll get you and Theo warmed up as soon as possible," Sam said, reading her thoughts. "I can't leave until I can hand the crime scene over."

"I understand." She drew in a deep breath. "I guess we can head into the barn."

He hesitated, glancing around the area behind her ranch house again. "Please stay here for a little while longer. Marsh should be here soon. I caught him when he was on the road heading to Austin."

She nodded in agreement. Being alone in the barn with Theo wouldn't provide the sense of safety that came from sticking close to Sam. She wished she'd brought her shotgun along, but it hadn't seemed necessary.

Obviously, a wrong assumption.

Danger still lurked behind every corner. Not from Roy himself but from whatever he'd gotten himself involved with. At least she knew now why her ex hadn't made his way down to the Mexican border.

"How long has Roy been…" Her voice trailed off.

"I can't say for sure. We'll need the medical examiner to give us that information." Sam paused, then added, "He still could have been the shooter taking out your living room and kitchen windows. I plan to make sure his hands and clothing are tested for gunshot residue, to help answer that question."

"Okay." The way he spoke so calmly of evidence and clues

helped keep her calm. Maybe they'd learn something from this that would put an end to the danger.

Yet she couldn't deny being angry with Roy for dragging her and Theo into this in the first place. Ironic that she'd been safe the entire time he was in prison, only to be smack in the center of danger when he'd escaped.

"Marsh is out front." Sam glanced up from his phone. "Let's take the four-wheeler around."

She nodded, scooting back to give Sam room to jump onto the seat. He hit the gas and drove around the side of the building closest to the tree line that led to the creek. The trip didn't take long, and she was glad to see Marshall standing outside his SUV.

"What happened with the other SUVs that were damaged by gunfire?" she asked, as Sam agilely hopped down.

"We were able to change the tires of one SUV, the other was towed to Fredericksburg," Sam said, reaching over to pick up Theo, then setting him on his feet. He helped her down, too. She felt a little ridiculous standing there with a crocheted basket of eggs but she wasn't going to waste them.

"Ms. Lynch." Marshall gave her a solemn nod. "I'm sorry to hear about your ex-husband."

She didn't know what to say to that, so she simply shrugged. "I hope you find the person responsible."

"We will." Marsh turned to Sam. "You cleared the house?"

"Yes. The two bedrooms had been searched, and of course you know what else we found." Sam tipped his head toward Theo. "The lack of blood indicates he wasn't killed there. The sheriff's department is sending a couple of deputies out too. They had someone out front watching the place."

Marsh hiked a brow and shook his head. "They're really not batting a thousand, are they?"

"Not at all. The deputy claimed he only left for a couple of bathroom breaks." Sam's expression turned thoughtful. "Do you think one of them is dirty? Maybe being paid to look the other way?"

"It's possible. First a deputy allows Roy to escape from the hospital, then a deputy is supposedly on guard duty while a dead body is dumped inside." Marshall sighed. "It's a stretch that the deputy assigned to watch the place is involved. That seems rather obvious. But I agree, the sheriff's department is not looking good. There may be someone inside setting both of these deputies up for failure."

She shivered and not from the cold. A deputy working for the bad guys? Pulling strings and allowing Roy to escape, and then to be murdered? How could she and Theo possibly be safe if one of them was dirty? She tried to remember the name of the deputy who'd responded that first night. Oh, yes, Deputy Strawn. He'd seemed concerned and had taken her statement along with pictures of the window. Hard to imagine he would be involved.

From now on, she decided she would only trust the rangers. Especially Sam.

She and Theo would be safe with God and Sam Hayward watching over them.

After finding Roy Carlton's dead body, Sam had cleared the rest of the house. The two tossed bedrooms bothered him, but it could be that the shooter was looking for something to use to implicate Mari in Roy's death.

He'd initially intended to take Mari and Theo back to the original ranch house, but now he wasn't so sure if that was the right way to go.

He'd felt certain that Roy had been the one shooting at her. But his murder, so much like Jeff Abbott's, gave Sam pause. Obviously someone was eliminating those involved in the original murder of Austin City Manager Hank George.

What role Abbott had played was unclear, but Roy had been arrested, charged and found guilty in a court of law. After spending two full years behind bars—the trial hadn't happened until more than a year after his arrest—he'd managed to escape.

Only to be murdered and left here on Whistling Creek Ranch. Had the goal been to scare Mari? Possibly.

As if she needed another reason to be afraid.

"You should know Jackson has another lead," Marsh said in a low voice. "A staff member who cleans the emergency department, guy by the name of Zach Tifton, called in sick the day of Roy's escape. Jackson is on his way to Tifton's apartment now. Maybe Tifton had been hiding Roy Carlton there at some point." Marsh shrugged. "Guess we don't have to worry about that issue now."

"We still need to know who helped Roy escape," Sam insisted. "In my opinion, both hospital employees, Zach Tifton and Cindy Gorlich, are still suspects. Either one or both could have been hired by the same person who shot and killed both Abbott and Carlton."

"You think they were taken out of commission by the same perp?" Marsh asked.

"I don't know for sure, but that's the way I'm leaning." He frowned. There were more holes in his theory than pieces of fabric holding it together. Yet his gut told him they were on the right track. "The timing of both murders, one right before Roy's escape and one a day after, is suspicious, don't you think?"

"Yeah, when you say it like that it's glaring. For sure the same person is behind this." Marsh paused, then added, "Or the same group of people are behind it."

The mere thought of a group of thugs being involved was depressing. But Marsh was right. They really had no idea what was behind all of this.

A motive strong enough to kill an innocent mother and her son.

He frowned when he realized Mari and Theo were shivering in the cold. "Let's get them into your SUV so they can warm up."

"Not a problem." Marsh turned and jogged over to start the SUV.

Sam moved closer to Mari. "You and Theo can sit inside the SUV for a few minutes, okay?"

"Thank you." Mari held the basket of eggs in one hand, ushering Theo forward with the other. "How long until we can head back to the ranch house?"

"I'm not sure. We'll see what happens when the others arrive." He wasn't trying to be vague on purpose. Was it safe to return to the original ranch house? He knew Mari and Theo were more comfortable there, but he needed to make this decision based on facts, not to make Mari happy.

Once they were huddled in the back seat with the heat flowing through the vents, he headed back to the front of the ranch house. Examining the front porch, he frowned when he spotted a drop of blood.

"Marsh, over here." He gestured to the drop of blood. "Seems as if Roy was brought in this way."

"And where was the deputy while this was happening?" Marsh asked. "A bathroom break? Really?"

Sam turned to see two sheriff's department SUVs rolling up Mari's driveway. "Guess we'll find out."

"If we can trust them to tell the truth," Marsh muttered under his breath.

Sam silently agreed but kept his expression impassive as the two deputies emerged from their cars.

"You're Hayward, right?" the larger man asked. "We met the other day."

"Yes, I'm Texas Ranger Sam Hayward, and this is Ranger Marshall Branson." He noticed neither deputy stepped forward to shake their hands. So that was how this was going to go. Adversaries rather than partners.

"We're Deputy Adam Grendel and Deputy Trey Drake." The four of them stood there with a good six feet between them. "What's this about a dead body being taken inside last night?"

Swallowing his irritation, he explained how he'd taken Mari and Theo to the original ranch house for safety, only to return this morning to find Carlton's dead body.

"The back door was open?" Grendel snorted. "That's probably how they got inside."

"There's blood on the front porch." Sam held the man's gaze. "Easy enough to have it tested to see if matches Carlton."

There was a long moment of silence as the two deputies digested that.

"I cleared the house, and it looks as if the bedrooms were tossed," Sam went on. "We know Jeff Abbott was killed down at Whistling Creek and left there, too. I'm no medical expert, but there's not nearly enough blood on the floor to indicate Carlton was killed inside. I believe he was dumped here as some sort of warning."

"What kind of warning?" Drake asked. "To you?"

He suppressed a sigh. "More likely a warning for Ms. Lynch. She's been targeted several times now, starting back with an attempted abduction of her son."

"She knows something," Drake said, his expression suspicious. "We need to take her in for questioning."

Over his stone-cold dead body, Sam thought, but didn't say. "I've spoken to her at length. She has no idea why she's being targeted or how Roy Carlton escaped from prison. We need to figure out if Carlton was the shooter before he was killed, so I want his clothing and hands tested for gunshot residue."

"Sam is right. We've been working this case per the request of the governor," Marsh said. "We asked you to come out as a courtesy, since this transpired under your watch."

"This isn't our fault," Grendel snapped.

"You better watch it," Trey Drake added. "This is still our jurisdiction."

"No, it's not. I am putting you on notice that we'd like to interview the deputy who was assigned to watch the place. We're calling the shots from here on out."

Both deputies bristled at that, but thankfully the arrival of Tucker and Jackson prevented the tense situation from disintegrating into a full-blown shouting match.

Sam walked away, to keep himself from saying something he might regret. He waited for Tuck and Jackson to join them.

"Medical examiner is on the way," Tucker said. "He's not happy about driving all this way out to the ranch for the second time in two days."

"Join the unhappy club." Marsh jerked his thumb toward the deputies. "Those guys are jerks."

"Nothing new there," Jackson said. "We got similar attitude when asking about Deputy Erickson, the guy who was supposed to be guarding Carlton prior to his escape."

"Where are Mari and Theo?" Tucker asked.

"In the SUV, keeping warm." He hesitated, then said, "All was quiet last night down at the original ranch house, but I'm having doubts about staying there indefinitely. Especially after this latest incident."

His fellow rangers were quiet for a long moment. "The fact that Carlton's body was dumped here is concerning. But if no one has been around the original ranch house, it should be safe enough," Jackson finally said. "Especially with one of us standing guard."

One of *them*—not Sam—was the not-so-subtle distinction. And Sam understood Jackson's concern. Every cell in his body rejected the idea of leaving Mari and Theo with someone else watching over them, but he managed to nod in agreement. "Whatever you think is best. But I am worried that this killer is escalating. If I were involved in this scheme, whatever it is, I would be concerned that I'd be targeted next."

The rangers exchanged a look. "Maybe we need to get that message out to our two hospital employee suspects," Tucker drawled. "That might encourage them to cooperate with us."

"If they're guilty, yeah," Marsh agreed. "But for all we know, there was someone else involved."

"I know you've questioned Mari," Jackson said. "But there must be something we're missing. Some key reason why this guy is coming after her."

"I'm open to suggestions," Sam said, doing his best not to show his frustration. "And frankly, Mari is, too. She has expressed her concerns about why this is happening several times. If she knew anything, she would tell us to protect her son."

Another long silence hung between them.

This time, the arrival of the medical examiner ended the conversation. Dr. Earl Bond slid out from behind the wheel, approaching them with his field kit.

"You guys need to figure out what's going on," he grumbled. "This is getting ridiculous."

"We're doing our best. This way." Sam turned to take the lead. He paused on the front porch, pointing out the drop of blood. "What do you think, Doc? Could this be from our victim?"

"Get your crime scene techs here to take a sample and I'll let you know." Despite his annoyance at the long drive, Earl Bond looked around with interest as Sam took him inside the house.

"I didn't touch him," Sam said. "Based on the stench and the bullet hole in his head, there was no reason to get close. I believe he's been gone for at least a couple of hours."

Dr. Earl Bond grunted and went to work, donning booties, a white coverall, mask and gloves. He knelt beside the body and went to work.

"One more thing, Doc," Sam said, breathing carefully through his mouth to avoid the worst of the smell. "We would like his hands bagged for gunpowder residue. And his clothing preserved, too."

"That's not a problem." Dr. Bond quickly placed two paper bags over Carlton's hands and taped them around the wrist to keep them in place. "The sooner your crime scene techs get out here, the better. Gunpowder residue can dissipate over time."

"I'll check to see how far out they are." Gratefully, he stepped back outside. Then frowned, when he saw Marshall getting in behind the wheel of his SUV. "Where's Marsh going?"

Tucker arched a brow. "He's taking Mari and Theo back to the original ranch house using the SUV instead of the four-wheeler. Why?"

"No reason. I'm glad they're going back to where it's safe." At least, that was what he said out loud.

But deep down, he was irked that Marsh had made that decision without telling him.

Then he realized the three rangers had likely discussed it among themselves, making the decision while Sam was busy inside.

Leaving him little choice but to go along with the plan.

Chapter Ten

"Where is Sam?" Mari eyed Marshall with confusion. "Isn't he coming with us?"

"He'll meet up with us later." Marshall slid behind the wheel. "I'm hoping you know a way we can get across to your grandfather's ranch house without wrecking the SUV."

"I—uh, sure." Swallowing a protest, she began giving directions. The old driveway was little more than a dirt road, and they had to cross the pasture to the west to get to it. As the SUV bumped and swayed over the uneven ground, she gave Theo's hand a reassuring squeeze. The poor kid had been through a lot and was handling it better than she could have hoped.

She kept the basket of eggs in her lap. Not exactly the food supplies she'd hoped for, but better than nothing.

"I want my trucks," Theo whined. "How come we didn't get my trucks?"

"I'll see if Mr. Sam can bring them later." She caught Marshall's keen gaze on her in the rearview mirror. "If not, we'll play with your horses again. This is Mr. Marshall. Can you say hi?"

"Hi," Theo mumbled, hiding his face against Charlie.

Marshall's eyes darted to Theo for a moment, before looking out at the dirt road. She wondered if he had a child of his own or was baffled at how kids behaved. Being a single parent wasn't easy. Kids needed constant attention and room to run and play. Which normally wasn't a problem living out on Whistling Creek Ranch.

Unfortunately, the only outdoor activity Theo had experienced lately was building their mini-snowman. She told herself not to dwell on what she wasn't able to provide Theo. Best to focus on the positive side of their situation.

Thanks to God's grace and the Texas Rangers, they were alive and unharmed. And Roy was dead. He would never hurt her or Theo again.

The nagging thought about why she and Theo had been targeted wouldn't leave her alone. Roy must have told someone about her, making them believe that she knew details of the crime. Or maybe Roy had bragged about how much her ranch was worth.

She almost wished the killer would simply come up and talk to her so she could reassure him that she knew nothing and had very little cash. Maybe then they would leave her alone.

Talk about wishful thinking. She gave herself a mental shake. There was no point in speculating. She needed to trust in God's plan.

And in Sam and his fellow rangers' ability to get to the bottom of this mess.

"That's the house up ahead," she said, leaning forward in her seat. "Do you see it?"

"Yep." Marshall seemed like a nice enough guy. She didn't doubt that he'd protect her and Theo.

But she missed Sam. Which was ridiculous since she barely knew him.

Marshall pulled up to the front of the house. It looked unchanged since they'd left it—what, not even two hours ago? So much had happened, it seemed longer. She helped Theo out of the SUV, then grabbed her basket of eggs. Holding Theo's hand, she followed Marshall inside.

There was a chill in the air, and Marshall didn't hesitate to cross over to add more wood to the stove. She set the basket of eggs on the counter and quickly washed them.

"I want my trucks," Theo repeated, this time stamping his foot for emphasis. It would have been cute if not for her frayed nerves.

"Can you tell me about your horses?" Marshall asked.

She flashed him a grateful look.

Theo eagerly played with Marshall and his horses, reinforcing the little boy's need for a father figure. Not that Sam, Marshall or any of the others were volunteering for the job.

Well, they were stepping up to help now, but only on a temporary basis. And she was truly grateful for their kind and seemingly endless patience.

Playtime came to an end, though, when Marshall's phone rang. She watched as he rose to his feet and pulled out his phone.

"Branson," he answered curtly.

There was a long pause as Marshall listened to whatever the caller was telling him. She couldn't help watching him curiously, but his impassive gaze didn't reveal any indication of a change in the case.

Not good news, then, she thought with a sigh. Of course it couldn't be that easy.

"Okay, I'll let the guys know. Someone will head in to interview him again."

"Interview who?" she asked after he'd slipped his phone back into his pocket.

Marshall slowly nodded. "A suspect we believe may have been seen riding in the blue van with your ex-husband."

"His possible girlfriend, Cindy Gorlich?" she guessed. "She's the one who reported her van was stolen, right?"

"No. The other hospital employee, Zach Tifton." Marshall

grimaced. "The witness description was vague, but we haven't found Zach yet to interview him. He never answered his door yesterday and we couldn't see anything suspicious through the windows. Without a search warrant or probable cause, we couldn't enter the premises. With this added information of a witness describing him as possibly with Carlton, we'll get what we need to do the search."

She understood the laws were there to protect the innocent, yet still felt irritated at how Marshall and the other rangers had their hands tied while trying to find out who was responsible for the attempted kidnapping of Theo and shooting at her.

"I'm glad." It was something, a step in the right direction. Even if it seemed like things were moving in slow motion.

"Roy never mentioned seeing anyone?" Marshall asked.

She swallowed a sigh. "Sam already asked me this. No, I was not aware of any girlfriend. And wouldn't have cared, even if I had known about it."

"Sorry, we're still trying to put the puzzle pieces together," he said with a chagrined smile. "We know Carlton killed Hank George, but there's obviously something more going on here than a simple murder."

"Yes." A strange thought struck. "What if Roy didn't murder Hank George?"

Marshall frowned. "We know he did. His fingerprints were on the gun, his DNA at the scene of the crime."

She nodded. "Yes, you're right. There was a lot of evidence against him. When you guys were talking about the deputies not doing a good job, I couldn't help but wonder if the fingerprints, gun and DNA were planted there to implicate him." She flushed. "Or maybe I just watch too many crime shows."

Marshall smiled, but then his gaze turned thoughtful. "That is an angle we hadn't considered. Although I would think that Carlton would have cried foul to anyone who would listen about being framed."

"You would think so." She shook her head. "Don't mind me. It's been a long couple of days."

"I understand." Marshall's gaze was sympathetic. He glanced around the room. "I'll bring in more wood," he offered.

"Sam stacked a bunch of wood just outside the back door, so no need. We'll be fine."

"Mr. Marshall do you want to see my snowman?" Theo asked.

"Ah, sure." Marshall glanced at her as if for approval. She nodded, and quickly put Theo's coat, hat, boots and mitten back on before following the pair to the back door.

She stayed inside, watching as Theo ran toward the mini-snowman they'd made. It was already beginning to melt thanks to the bright sunlight.

She was about to turn away to begin lunch, when the sound of gunfire sent her heart to her throat.

Theo! Yanking the door open, she rushed outside in time to see Marshall scoop Theo into his arms, bolting toward her.

"Get inside, hurry!"

She turned and darted back inside, holding the door open for Marshall and Theo.

"Get down, stay away from the windows," Marshall said as he put Theo in her arms, pulled his phone and called Sam for backup. "Sam? Gunfire at the original ranch house. I need you guys here right away!"

Theo sobbed as she held him close. She was thankful her son wasn't hurt but was equally horrified to know the gunman had found them here, at her grandfather's original ranch house.

Almost as if he'd been sitting out there and waiting for the right time to strike.

She fought the urge to cry, sick with the realization they weren't safe, anywhere.

The call from Marsh about gunfire at the ranch house made Sam wish for the tenth time that he was the one out there with Mari and Theo.

"Tuck, you and Jackson take the SUV. I'm going on the four-wheeler." He didn't waste another second in running to jump onto the four-wheeler. The all-terrain vehicle could get him there faster than using an alternate route.

At least, that was what he hoped. Especially since he knew exactly where to go.

He never should have left them alone. And he also shouldn't have assumed the original ranch house was safe.

They couldn't stay at Whistling Creek any longer. Mari wouldn't like it, but there wasn't another alternative.

Not after this.

He drove as quickly as he dared, not wanting to flip the machine, but desperate to make good time. When the ranch house came into view, he didn't slow down as he raked his gaze over the area.

Marsh's SUV was parked out front and appeared undamaged. He hadn't wasted time in getting details from Marsh as to where the shots had come from and knew the shooter had been stationed out back.

And could be making his way up to the house right now.

Gunning the engine, Sam drove around the corner of the house. Scanning the trees, he searched for signs of a shooter with a rifle and scope, much like the guy who'd taken up residence outside Mari's house when he'd shot through her living room window.

He didn't see anything, but that didn't mean much. What he did notice was a bullet hole in the mini-snowman he, Mari and Theo had built yesterday.

He kept moving, doing his best to draw the gunman's fire. But to no avail.

After rounding the next corner of the house, he went back to where Marsh's SUV was parked. Killing the engine of the ATV, he jumped off and ran up to the front door.

"Mari? Marsh? Are you okay?"

The door opened, revealing a grim-faced Marsh. "No one is hurt. But we need to get out of here."

"I know." He stepped inside, his chest tightening when he saw Mari and Theo sitting on the floor, tucked behind the wood-burning stove.

With the cast-iron stove as protection, it was probably the safest spot in the house.

"Are you sure you're both okay?" He couldn't help but cross the room to kneel beside them.

Mari sniffled, her eyes red and puffy from crying. "We're not hurt."

He put a hand on Theo's back, wishing more than anything he could do more for them. Then he stood and turned to face Marsh. "Did you get a line on the shooter?"

"He was directly across from the back door," Marsh said. "I noticed the flash of his scope a second before he fired. Thankfully, I was already grabbing Theo and turning to head inside."

He wanted to thank Marsh for saving their lives but knew that was their job. His fault that he cared more for Theo and Mari than he should.

"Tuck and Jackson are bringing the other SUV," he explained. "Looks like yours isn't damaged, which is good. We should all drive out together, keeping Theo and Mari in the front vehicle and the other covering from behind."

"You're assuming the shooter hasn't already made his way around to the front to lie in wait for us," Marsh said. "I've been checking every window, but just because I haven't seen him doesn't mean he's not out there. There's a lot of land to use as cover."

That was true. Sam knew he couldn't afford to make another mistake. "Okay, then what's the plan?"

There was a long moment of silence before Marsh said, "We don't have another option. We'll drive out while keeping Mari and Theo covered. Even if this guy does try to take another shot, he'll have to go through us to get to them."

Since he couldn't come up with anything different, he nodded. "Okay. Tuck and Jackson should be here soon."

"Where are we going?" Mari asked. "I mean, once we leave here."

He hadn't given their destination much thought. Other than getting them away from the shooter. If he had his way, he'd stick her in a plane and send her and Theo to another state, far away from the ranch.

But that wasn't a feasible option. Rangers only had jurisdiction in the state of Texas, and they needed to be close enough to continue working the case.

"We'll find a motel," he finally said. "At least we'll have easy access to food."

"Are you going to tell the deputies where we're going?" she pressed.

"No." He glanced at Marsh, who nodded his agreement. "Only the four of us rangers will know your location."

She nodded and pressed a kiss to Theo's head. "Okay. But I'll need to make sure Tom Fleming can continue helping with the ranch chores."

"Call him now," Sam suggested. He glanced at his watch. "We have a few minutes before Tucker and Jackson will be here."

She scooted out from behind the wood-burning stove, her face flushed from the heat. Without thinking about it, Sam reached to take Theo into his arms. The little boy wound his arms around Sam's neck and buried his face against his chest.

"I'm scared," Theo whispered.

Sam's heart squeezed in his chest. No child should be in this position. "It's okay, I'm here. We're all safe now." He did his best to sound reassuring.

Marsh raked his hand through his hair. "Maybe I should have scouted the place."

"Even if you had, finding a guy hiding in the woods wouldn't be easy." He cleared his throat as Theo continued to cling to him. It hurt to know how frightened he was. "It's my fault for suggesting we continue using this place. I should have known it was only a matter of time before the perp showed up."

Marsh nodded, and they were both quiet while Mari spoke with Tom Fleming, her closest neighbor.

"I'm sorry to do this to you and Irene," she said. "I feel terrible asking for favors." There was a pause as she listened, before she said, "Yes, I know. And I appreciate that. Thanks again, Tom." She lowered her phone and turned to face him. "I feel awful. Tom has his own ranch chores, too. I really can't impose on him for long."

"I know." He felt bad for her plight. The sound of a car engine had him heading toward the front window. "Tuck and Jackson are here."

"Good." Marsh joined him at the window.

Without being asked, Tuck parked the SUV right next to the other one, leaving just a few feet between them. Tuck and Jackson slid out and glanced around before stepping up to the front door.

Marsh was there to let them in.

Sam quickly outlined his plan. "We don't know the shooter's location. He may have taken off because he missed or he's waiting up ahead somewhere along the dirt road to take another shot."

"I doubt he's gone," Tuck muttered. "Seems like he wouldn't come this far not to finish the job."

Mari's face paled, making Sam wince. They were used to talking about this stuff, but it was different to be the intended victim.

"I want Marsh to drive the first SUV. Tuck, you take the second. I'll stay in the back seat of Marsh's car with Mari and Theo hiding in the back seat. Jackson, you ride with Tuck, but in the back seat as if you're protecting them, too." He shrugged. "The shooter will hopefully assume we have them in the second vehicle, not the first. It's not much of a decoy operation, but it's all I have."

"That works," Jackson agreed. "Especially if you make sure they both stay out of sight."

"That's the plan." He glanced around. "Ready?"

"I hav'ta go to the bathroom," Theo said, lifting his head from Sam's chest.

"I can take him." Mari stepped forward.

"We'll both take him." From this point forward, Sam wasn't going to let Mari and Theo out of his sight.

He couldn't help feeling responsible for this most recent incident. Even though he knew Marsh had done everything right.

The trip to the bathroom didn't take too long. Theo wanted his stuffed dog and his horses, so Mari bundled them into a small blanket in lieu of a bag.

"He deserves to have something familiar with him," she said in a low voice.

"I agree." Sam put his hand in the center of her back. "We're going to move quickly once we're outside, okay? Just get into the back seat and I'll hand you Theo, and crawl in beside you. Make sure to get down on the floor."

She nodded in understanding and shrugged into her coat. As always it took another moment or two to get Theo bundled up, but apparently sensing the seriousness of the situation, the little boy didn't argue.

Marsh stepped out first, with Mari right behind him. Within minutes, Mari and Theo were down on the floor, with Sam hovering nearby.

Marsh pulled away from the ranch house first. Sam glanced through the rearview mirror to see that Tuck was driving the second SUV, with Jackson positioned in the back, pretending to cover two people just like Sam was.

This would work. It had to.

Marsh kept his speed steady, not too fast over the rocky terrain but not too slow either. Sam scanned both sides of the dirt road but didn't see anyone.

They were roughly past the halfway point, taking a curve in the road when the crack of gunfire rang out.

Marsh hit the gas, and so did Tuck. Sam hunched over Mari and Theo, knowing there was little they could do but to keep going.

And pray.

Chapter Eleven

Another gunshot rang out. Mari flinched at the sound, even though she didn't think their vehicle was hit.

At least, not yet.

Hearing Sam's whispered prayers for safety helped keep her calm. She hadn't expected the shooter to be waiting for them, but it was clear Sam had. He'd planned for the worst, and she mentally braced herself for what would happen if their vehicle was struck and disabled by a bullet.

She had faith in Sam, Marshall, Tucker and Jackson's ability to get them out of this mess. But she was upset by the constant danger. Roy was dead. Why were they still coming after her and Theo?

What on earth did they want?

"Tuck's SUV took a round," Marshall said. "They're still moving, but slower now. The gap between us is widening."

"We can't leave them behind," Sam said.

"Tuck is waving at us to keep going," Marshall responded calmly. "He and Jackson can take care of themselves."

Sam's jaw clenched, but then he looked down at her and Theo with a resigned gaze. She felt terrible for making him choose between backing up his team and protecting them.

"I'll call to get the deputies out here," Sam said after a long moment. He swayed from side to side as Marshall picked up the pace, while pulling his phone from his pocket. "They need to offer assistance to Tuck and Jackson."

"Good idea." Marshall was preoccupied with driving while she listened as Sam made the call.

The gunfire had stopped now, making her wonder if the shooter believed she and Theo were hiding in the second car. She sent up a silent prayer for the rangers' safety.

Please, Lord Jesus, keep those brave men safe in Your care!

"Now!" Sam barked into his phone. "They're taking gunfire, understand? They need you now."

She held Theo's hand and lightly stroked his hair. He clutched Charlie close, but wasn't crying. As awful as it was, she suspected her son was becoming accustomed to the sound of gunfire.

No child should be put in this position. What had Roy gotten himself involved with? Who had killed him? And why?

She had no answers, only dozens of unanswered questions.

Marshall must be closer to the road now, because she heard the wail of sirens. Her heart squeezed at knowing they'd left Tucker and Jackson behind.

"I'm sure the shooter will take off," Marshall said.

Sam nodded, but then dug for his phone again. A minute later, he said, "Tuck? Are you both okay? Where's the shooter?"

"We're fine." She was so close to Sam she could hear both sides of the conversation. "He hit our engine block, though, so we had to stop and get out of the car. We returned fire, but didn't get a good look at him."

She swallowed hard, imagining the two rangers exchanging gunfire with someone who'd tried to kill her and Theo.

"Deputies are on the way," Sam was saying. "Hitch a ride with them. We'll catch up with you, later."

"Roger that," Tucker said before ending the call.

"I'm so glad they're both unharmed," she whispered. "That was close."

"Too close, but thankfully our plan worked. He shot at both of us, but only took out one of the vehicles. The wrong one," he added.

But it could have gone the other way. She could tell by Sam's grim expression that he'd feared they'd all perish in the most recent shooting event.

And they could have.

God was watching over them. And knowing that gave her the inner strength she needed to keep going.

The sirens from the sheriff's department vehicles were louder now. She couldn't see, but Sam's gaze tracked the cars, so she could imagine them going around their SUV to reach the dirt road driveway.

"Can we trust them?" she asked.

"The call went out on the radio to dispatch, so yeah. I don't think they'll pull anything now." Sam looked at her. "How are you holding up?"

"My legs are starting to cramp," she admitted. Being down in a crouch like this wasn't normal.

"Marsh? Are we far enough that they can get up on the car seats?"

"Give me a couple minutes. I'm almost at the point where I can get off this road and onto the main highway."

"I can wait." She shifted a bit. Her main concern was Theo's safety. They didn't have a car seat for him.

The minutes passed slowly. Finally, Sam said, "Okay, you can get up now."

He leaned back and she slowly straightened into a normal sitting position. She stretched her legs out as far as possible to relieve the pressure. Then she reached for Theo.

"We need to stop and get a car seat for him," she said as she buckled him into the middle space between her and Sam.

Marshall met her gaze in the rearview. "We'll stop when we get closer to Austin."

Austin? She frowned. "Why there?"

"There are more hotel options," Sam said. "Especially on the outskirts of town. And that is the city where the original murder took place of City Manager Hank George." He frowned. "We need to be close enough to continue following up on leads in the investigation."

"Okay." Easy enough to accept that rationale. The sooner they figured out what was going on, the quicker she and Theo could return home.

To their normal, boring and safe life.

It would seem different after spending so much time with Sam and the other rangers. But she quickly pushed that thought aside. She would take the mundane routine over being in constant danger, any day.

Yet that didn't mean she wouldn't miss Sam.

He's not yours to care about. She gave herself a mental shake. There was no point in wishing for something she couldn't have. Even if Sam was interested, any sort of relationship between them would be impossible. She lived and worked on the ranch. Texas Rangers were sent to work cases all over the state.

And besides, she doubted Sam would want anything to do with a ready-made family.

Unfortunately, memories of his warm kiss wouldn't leave her alone. Logically, she knew she was in a vulnerable position. Her life and Theo's depended on Sam and the others.

Marshall, Tucker and Jackson were all nice, brave and good-looking men. But she wasn't attracted to them.

Not in the way she was so keenly aware of Sam.

"Should we stop at the shopping center?" Sam's question interrupted her tumultuous thoughts.

She glanced over to the discount shopping store. "That would be great. Thank you."

"No problem." Marsh met her gaze briefly in the rearview mirror. She hoped her thoughts about Sam hadn't been obvious to him. "I'll wait for you in the car. That way, I can drop you off near the front door and pick you up, there, too."

"Works for me," Sam agreed.

"That would be wonderful." She was grateful for the opportunity to get Theo a proper car seat, and maybe a couple more toys to keep him occupied. It was bad enough to know her son was in danger; she needed to keep him calm and happy.

"Wait a minute," Sam warned as Marshall pulled up to the front door. She unbelted Theo as Sam ran around to open her door. He was on high alert as they slid out of the SUV and headed inside.

It felt odd to do something as normal as shopping thirty minutes after nearly being struck by gunfire. The good news was that there were plenty of after-Christmas sales on toys. The car seat wasn't cheap, but she was able to find some action figures marked half off.

"Would you like a change of clothes for you and Theo, too?" Sam asked. He didn't appear concerned at how quickly their cart was filling up. "Grab what you need since I'm not sure how long we'll be staying in the hotel."

"Okay."

"Will we be home for my birthday?" Theo asked. "And how will Billy the elf know that I'm being good while we're at the hotel?"

"I—uh, don't know." His questions had caught her off guard.

"When is your birthday, Theo?" Sam asked.

Theo held up two fingers. Sam frowned. "You're not two years old, you're going to be five, aren't you?"

"No, my birthday is two," he insisted. "Day two."

"January second," she clarified. "We call it day two of the new year."

"Oh, I see. Of course. Day two." Sam nodded as if the explanation made perfect sense. "Well, Theo, I'm going to do everything I can to make sure you're home by your birthday."

"Goody," Theo clapped his hands excitedly. "I want to open more presents."

She suppressed a sigh. She didn't like that he was all about the gifts, but knew most kids were. And for Theo, Christmas overshadowed his birthday.

She tried to make it a special day, but based on what they were going through now, it would be more than enough to have the shooter arrested and the danger over, for good.

Walking through the store, easing past other shoppers searching for a discount in the after-holiday sale, he thought about Theo's upcoming birthday.

He didn't like making promises he may not be able to keep. Telling the boy that he'd have him home by his birthday wasn't smart. Yet the kid had been through a lot and deserved something positive to look forward to.

The little boy's birthday was four days away. Surely they'd have the gunman in custody by then.

Although Roy Carlton's murder had brought their investigation to a grinding halt. Or rather, the murder had forced them to take a sharp detour from their original theory to something more complicated.

He still didn't trust the sheriff's department.

"No more," Mari scolded her son. "You have enough toys."

Sam wanted to let the kid have whatever he wanted but knew better than to interfere. He stopped in the electronics section to pick up a cheap laptop, hoping to get more work done while they were hiding out at the hotel.

When they went through the checkout, Mari's eyes widened in horror at the amount.

"We can get rid of some of this," she said, grabbing at some items. "We don't need it all."

"It's fine." He rested his hand on her arm. "Please, Mari. I don't mind. It's the least I can do. Besides, the bulk of the cost is the computer, followed by the car seat. And that's a necessity. The rest isn't that much."

She gazed up at him for a long moment, before acquiescing. "You shouldn't have to pay for this—my situation isn't your fault," she protested weakly.

"Or yours," he pointed out. "As far as the toys go, consider them an early birthday present for Theo."

She nodded, but still looked concerned as he handed over his credit card. He admired her desire to stay independent, but these were extraneous circumstances.

And he knew her inability to work the ranch would put them in a hole, financially.

Before heading outside, he called Marsh. "We're ready."

"Be there in two."

As promised, Marsh pulled up to the main doors. Sam stored the bag of clothing and toys in the back, leaving Mari to secure Theo's car seat. The little boy protested having to climb inside, but Mari was firm.

"Now. Or no toys."

The boy glanced at Sam, then did his mother's bidding. Sam could only imagine how difficult it must be for Mari to be a single mother, dealing with Theo every day.

Not an easy job, especially while running a ranch.

Once they were settled at chain motel, Sam reached out to Tucker. "Where are you?"

"Heading to Austin." Sam could hear talking in the background. "Deputy Grendel has agreed to take us to get a rental SUV."

"No sign of the shooter, then?"

"Knowing he was armed and dangerous, we didn't stick around," Tucker admitted. "But the plan is to head back later to look for shell casings."

"Understood." Shell casings would be nice, especially if they matched those found beneath the tree outside the front of

Mari's ranch house. But that wasn't worth risking their lives either. He gave Tucker the name of their motel. "We have a pair of connecting rooms. Meet us here when you're finished. We need to follow up on our next move."

"Got it. Later." Tucker ended the call.

"Are you leaving us here alone?" Mari asked, her gaze troubled.

"No." He crossed over to where she sat on the edge of the bed. Theo was thankfully distracted by his new toys, especially the action figures and the cartoons on the television. He sank beside her. "One of us will always be with you and Theo."

She nodded, dropping her gaze to her entwined hands. He slipped his arm around her shoulders, giving her a reassuring hug.

"I'm sorry," he murmured. "I wish there was more for me to do to make you and Theo feel safe."

"We are safe with you." She glanced up at him, her green eyes direct. "I can't tell you how happy I am that God brought you to the ranch house when we needed you the most."

He was touched by her comment, and smiled at how she'd met him with the business end of a shotgun. "Me, too."

She leaned against him. He wanted very badly to kiss her again, but couldn't bring himself to do that in front of Theo.

"Sam?" Marsh hovered in the opening between their connecting rooms. His arched eyebrow seemed to indicate he could read Sam's thoughts. "Owens wants to chat with us."

"Yeah." He forced himself to release Mari. "I'm coming."

Was it his imagination or did Mari's fingers linger on his arm before he moved across the room. He glanced over his shoulder to find her watching him. It was all he could do not to turn and go back to her side.

He wasn't sure why he felt so deeply connected to her. He should have learned his lesson after last time.

But here he was, about to make the same mistake all over

again. Okay, he knew Mari wasn't anything like Leanne. She wasn't a criminal or involved in this mess.

Yet getting emotionally involved wasn't smart.

"Skating on thin ice," Marsh murmured as he joined him in the next room. "Better watch out that you don't fall through and drown."

"Yeah, yeah." He wasn't in the mood to discuss his complicated feelings for Mari and Theo.

Or maybe the problem was they weren't all that complicated. He liked her. Respected her. Admired her. And cared about them both.

More than he should.

Marsh sighed, then pulled out his phone. A moment later he had their boss on the line.

"Where have you been?" Captain John Owens didn't sound happy. "The trail is going cold."

"Sorry Cap," Marsh said. "We experienced more gunfire getting the two targets away from Whistling Creek Ranch."

"Gunfire? Anyone hurt?" Owens asked.

"No injuries, but we're down another SUV," Sam said.

"Our budget is spiraling out of control on this case," Owens muttered. "Did you get the shooter?"

"No." Marsh winced at admitting the failure. "The good news is that we have the targets safe just outside of Austin."

"I'm getting a lot of heat from the chief on this," Owens said in a blunt tone. "First a prisoner escapes, then he's found dead. And we have squat to go on."

"Any updates from the crime scene techs?" Sam asked, more to distract their boss from the lack of progress. "And what about getting those search warrants for Cindy Gorlich and Zach Tifton?"

"I have the search warrant for Tifton here. I just need one of you guys to head out to execute it." Owens still sounded testy. "I'm working on getting search warrants for Gorlich, too."

"I'll grab and execute the warrant for Tifton," Marsh offered.

Sam felt a little guilty letting Marsh do the legwork while he stayed here with Mari and Theo. "Tuck and Jackson will be here soon. I'll grab one of them to go with me."

"Good. I'll keep working on the warrant for Gorlich, although the judge is making noises that we don't have enough evidence against her. The witness seeing a man matching Tifton's description was enough for us to get that warrant."

"I picked up a computer today, so I'll dig into Gorlich's social media," he offered. "If we can find some connection between her and Roy Carlton, the judge should grant the warrant."

"Do it," Owens said. "I need something for the upper brass, soon."

"We should know soon about whether or not Roy Carlton has gunshot residue on his hands or chest, too," Sam said. "I asked the medical examiner to protect both areas."

"That would be nice," Owens said. "Get back to me ASAP."

"Understood. We'll be in touch." Marsh quickly ended the call, shaking his head with a grimace. "He's right, we should have more intel by now."

"I know." Sam crossed to the desk where he'd left the laptop. "I'll start on this end right away."

"I'll head out to the office," Marsh said. Their headquarters were in Austin, which was another reason staying in a motel here was better for all of them.

Leaving Mari and Theo alone in the other room wasn't easy, but he forced himself to concentrate on the task at hand. Yet digging into Cindy Gorlich's social media didn't reveal any connection to Roy Carlton.

Was it a coincidence that her van was stolen? Maybe since it was a make and model known to be easier to steal than most.

He decided to search for a connection between Cindy and Zach but was quickly interrupted by a phone call from Tucker.

"We're five minutes away," Tuck said.

"You should head out to back up Marsh. He's executing

a search warrant for Zach Tifton's place," he said. "We're fine here."

"Sounds good. We'll talk more later."

Sam lowered his phone, feeling guilty all over again for sitting here while the others did the legwork on the investigation.

Giving up on social media, he used a simple case search to dig into Cindy's past. Almost immediately, he reached for his phone.

"Tuck? Cindy Gorlich has several open financial cases against her, including a pending eviction from her apartment." He rose to his feet. "She needs money. Get over to headquarters. This may be enough to get a search warrant for her, too."

"Roger that. We're on our way."

Sam ended the call, then contacted Owens, convinced they were on to something. Anyone suffering a financial crisis could be swayed into doing something crazy.

Like helping Roy Carlton break out of the hospital.

Chapter Twelve

Hovering in the doorway between their connecting rooms, Mari overheard Sam's comment about Cindy Gorlich having financial trouble.

"Does this mean Roy wasn't having an affair with Cindy?" She asked.

Sam swung around to face her. "That may have been the wrong assumption," he admitted. "It's looking more like she may have been paid to help your ex-husband escape."

She nodded, wondering why that made her feel better. It wasn't as if she still loved Roy. Not just because of the way he'd verbally and then physically abused her, but he'd killed Hank George in cold blood.

She hadn't known the man she'd married. And he'd only pretended to care about her. Why he'd bothered to marry her in the first place, she had no idea. Unless he'd wanted to look like a legitimate family man.

Whatever. That was in the past. No point in playing the what-if game. Besides, she firmly believed God's plan was to give her the blessing of a son.

"We plan to search both Cindy's apartment and Zach Tifton's place." Sam's voice intruded on her thoughts. A flash of anticipation lightened his dark brown eyes. "Hopefully we'll find key evidence that will help us find out who hired them."

"I hope so, too." She glanced back over her shoulder to make sure Theo was still watching cartoons. The motel offered a channel featuring children's movies, and Theo was thrilled to have extra television time. "I need to call Tom Fleming. Do you have any idea how long we'll be here?"

"No, sorry." Sam gave her an apologetic glance. "I wish I could say we'll have this wrapped up by tomorrow, but it's better if we take it day by day."

She understood where he was coming from. She tried not to sigh as she reached for her phone to make the call. Tom was nice enough about the inconvenience, and she made a silent promise to make it up to Tom and Irene later, bringing them eggs and maybe some steaks from her last butchering along with fresh bread.

"Everything okay?" Sam asked.

"Yes." She knew Tom would only gather eggs twice a day, rather than her usual three times in the winter months, but that couldn't be helped. "Is there something I can do?"

"I'm afraid not." Sam held her gaze for a moment, then seemed to change his mind. "Can you fill me in on what you remember about your ex-husband's activities prior to your divorce? Any unusual behavior? Or maybe places that he went that were outside the norm?"

She checked Theo one more time, smiling at the picture he made curled up on the bed with Charlie, before stepping into the room. "I didn't know anything about Roy's plan to murder Hank George. To be honest, once I left him to go back to the ranch with Theo, I refused to communicate with him directly. My dad helped me get a lawyer to first file for separation and then divorce. From that point on, I referred Roy to Larry Eastman for everything."

Sam nodded. "Okay, but what about prior to that? You said he grew more abusive, first verbally, then physically. Was there anything you noticed prior to the change? I recall Roy worked in construction."

She sat on the edge of the bed, thinking back to those difficult years. "Yes, he did work in construction. He was good at doing drywall, referring to himself as a rocker." She shrugged. "Whatever that means. There were many new homes going up in the Austin suburbs at the time. I do remember something about how Longhorn Construction, the company he worked for, had lost a key contract. I didn't think much about it at the time, but that may have been when he started drinking more." She stared down at her hands for a moment. "I soon learned to stay away from him when he'd been drinking, because he turned mean and nasty."

"I'm sorry you had to go through that," Sam said, coming over to sit beside her. "Did you get the impression he needed money?"

She frowned. "Not that I was aware of. But honestly, he handled all the bills. When I left that night with Theo, I only took our clothes and my car. Nothing else, even though I worked as a substitute teacher and had money in our joint checking account.

A flash of anger darkened his eyes. "That's not right. I hope you got some of that money back after the divorce."

"No, I didn't, because the money was gone." She remembered how awful she felt leaning on her father for financial support. "I didn't care, I was just so happy to be away from him. Then Roy was arrested for murder, and well, you know the rest."

"Yeah. So, other than the lost building contract you don't remember anything else."

"No. I wish I did." She grimaced. "What I regret the most was giving up my full-time teaching job. I should never have allowed Roy to have that much power over me." Looking back, it was glaringly easy to see her mistakes. Too bad she hadn't been smart enough to avoid some of them.

"Will you go back to teaching once Theo is in school?" Sam asked.

"Maybe." She had considered it. "Running the ranch takes a lot of time and energy, but more so during the spring, summer and fall. I've thought about doing substitute teaching work, especially in the winter. It would pay better than my egg money," she added with a smile.

He frowned. "I don't like knowing you're having trouble making ends meet."

"We're doing okay. We're blessed to have a roof over our heads and food to eat. That's more than some people have."

"True." He slipped his arm around her shoulders. The urge to lean against him was strong. "You're an amazing woman, Mari."

His kind words brought tears to her eyes. She blinked them back, reminding herself that he was just being nice because of her situation.

She managed a smile. "Thank you. You're pretty wonderful yourself."

"Ah, Mari," he murmured, hugging her close.

His musky scent filled her head, making her long for more. She gave in to temptation, resting her head in the hollow of his shoulder. On some level she wished she could stay in his arms like this, forever.

He brushed a sweet kiss against her temple. The gesture only increased her awareness of him. She lifted her head to look up at him, at the same moment he lowered his mouth to hers.

Their second kiss was even more powerful than the first. Slipping her arm around his waist, she pulled him closer. Sitting on the side of the bed was awkward, but she didn't move, didn't dare break off their embrace.

Because she wanted this, too much.

"Mommy!" Theo's cry was like a bucket of cold water sluicing over her head. She jerked away from Sam, jumping guiltily to her feet.

"I'm here, Theo." She hurried through the connecting door, to find Theo rubbing his eyes with his fists. Had he fallen asleep? "What's wrong?"

"The scary man," he whispered, clutching Charlie. "I saw him."

A chill snaked down her spine and she glanced at the window overlooking the parking lot. Then she relaxed, realizing Theo must have had a nightmare. "It's okay, sweetie. We're safe here. Mr. Sam will protect us."

As if on cue, Sam came over join them. "Hey, Theo." He rested a hand on her son's head. "Don't worry, I looked outside. No one is out there."

"'Kay," Theo mumbled. Her son rested against her. "I don't want the scary man to come back."

"I know, and Mr. Sam is here to make sure that doesn't happen." She met Sam's gaze, surprised to realize there was a hint of self-reproach in his gaze.

Sam obviously regretted their kiss. Swallowing hard, she looked away, stroking a hand down Theo's back.

Of course Sam wasn't interested in her that way. And she understood that most men weren't jumping at the chance to have a ready-made family.

She needed to remember this situation was temporary. That Sam was only there to keep them safe.

Tearing himself away from Mari and Theo wasn't easy. He wanted nothing more than to wrap mother and son in his arms, but they weren't his family.

The guys were right, he was too emotionally invested in them. He needed to think and act like a lawman, not as a potential husband and father.

The mistakes he'd made in the past lingered in his mind. Leanne Columbus had come across like an innocent woman in a troubled relationship. Not unlike Mari's situation with her ex-husband. They'd needed key intel on Leanne's boyfriend Colin

Farley related to a murder and she agreed to work with them to set up a meeting because she wanted him arrested. But Leanne had played him for a fool, luring him into a trap that had resulted in her so-called abusive boyfriend shooting at them, nearly killing Tuck and Marsh.

He didn't believe Mari had shot and killed Jeff Abbott. But he really didn't know for sure that she was telling him the truth about her memories of Roy Carlton's activities before his arrest.

Logically, he didn't want to believe she'd purposefully hold back information. Especially knowing her son was in danger.

But he wasn't sure he could trust his judgment either.

He crossed the threshold of the connecting door to put badly needed distance between them. Eyeing the computer, he tried to come up with another way to help investigate the case. They should have known about Cindy Gorlich's financial troubles before now, and he worried that he was dropping the ball on other clues, too. There was so much going on that made it difficult to keep track of everything that needed to be followed up.

He called Tucker. "What's the scoop with the search warrants?"

"Marsh and Jackson are going through Tifton's apartment. They haven't found anything obvious yet, other than it appears the guy hasn't been there lately, as evidenced by old garbage and a small stack of mail."

His gut clenched. "Do you think Tifton is dead?"

"That's one theory. The other is that he skipped town for a few days. When they finish the search, they're going to meet me at Cindy's place. I'm here now, keeping an eye on things until they arrive."

"That's good." There was always the possibility that Cindy might try to destroy evidence. Although if that was her intent, she likely would have done that already. "Is she home?"

"Looks like it," Tuck agreed.

Sam glanced at his watch, wishing he could head out to assist with the search. He almost suggested Marsh and Jackson come to the motel but then remembered how the last time he'd left Mari and Theo, the shooter had tried to take them out.

"Will you keep me updated?"

"Sure thing," Tuck drawled. "How are things at the motel?"

"Quiet." Which was a good thing. Even if it made him feel useless. "Later."

"Later," Tuck agreed.

"Sam?" He turned, sliding his phone into his pocket to find Mari standing in the doorway. "Theo is hungry."

"So am I," he said with a smile. "Let's grab lunch. There's a fast-food restaurant across the street."

"That would be wonderful." Her brow furrowed. "Is it safe for us to leave?"

He hesitated, then shook his head. "Better if I place a carry-out order."

"That works." She smiled wryly. "Theo loves chicken bites. I'll have the grilled chicken sandwich."

"That can be arranged." He used an app on his phone to place their order. Then crossed to the window to scan the parking lot. There was no sign of anyone lurking around. He couldn't see how the gunman could know where they were staying. Even the sheriff's deputies didn't know their location.

And he intended to keep it that way.

Fifteen minutes later, he'd picked up their food and had spread out their meals on the small table in his room, having closed and stored the computer in a shoulder bag.

As always, Mari bowed her head to say grace. He longed to take her hand in his but didn't, following her lead and bowing his head, too. "Dear Lord Jesus, we thank You for the blessings You have bestowed upon us. We humbly ask that You continue to keep us safe in Your care. Amen."

"Amen," Theo said.

"Amen," he echoed. "I like how you focus on the positive side of things," he added. "Especially when it would be easy to wallow in the negative."

"I have faith that God has brought us along this path for a reason." She smiled and unwrapped Theo's chicken bites, breaking them in half, then opened several packets of ketchup. "Be careful, they're hot," she cautioned.

They ate in silence for a moment. He was touched by her faith in God. He remembered how he'd prayed when they were leaving the original ranch house and felt a little ashamed that he'd only done so in a time of extreme need, rather than showing his gratitude for everyday blessings.

"I loved your prayer, Mari. I need to do better."

"Sam, you're doing fine. God is always listening, no matter what." She lightly touched his arm, sending a zing of awareness skipping along his skin. "He knows your heart."

"I hope so." It was all he could do not to lean over and kiss her again. He cleared his throat. "Thanks for reminding me of what is important in life."

"Anytime." Her smile brought another wave of awareness washing over him.

The moment was broken when his phone rang. Sam fished it from his pocket, saw the caller was Tucker, then rose to his feet to move away so as to not disturb Theo. "What's up? Tell me you have something."

"Well, we didn't find anything in Cindy's apartment, but when we confronted her about her financial situation and mentioned that the search warrant included her financial records like her bank statements, she broke down sobbing," Tucker said. "She claimed she was about to be evicted from her apartment when a man contacted her about helping Roy Carlton escape. He offered her ten grand, made in two five grand payments. Desperate to dig herself out of debt, she took him up on the offer."

Sam felt a surge of satisfaction. Finally they were getting somewhere. "Who contacted her? What's his name?"

"She claims he never gave her a name, only referred to himself as one of Roy's friends," Tuck explained. "She said he told her not to ask questions, and she half expected the call to be some sort of scam. But then the first five grand was deposited in her bank account within two hours of the call. That was enough for her. She claimed all she had to do was to leave her keys in the van and declare that it was stolen. She didn't think it was that big of a deal."

"She's wrong. Aiding and abetting an escaped convict is a very big deal," Sam pointed out.

"Oh, I arrested her on the spot, so she is finally seeing the error of her ways," Tuck said with a sigh. "We grilled her hard, but she stuck to her story."

"What about the payments themselves?" he asked.

"Yeah, we have our tech guy tracing the source of the deposit. Seems like it came through some crypto currency account in an offshore bank, so it's going to take some time."

That didn't sound reassuring. Sam had a bad feeling tracing the money would take too long. Every minute the gunman was out there, Mari and Theo remained in danger. He wanted this guy caught and arrested ASAP. "What about the phone number the guy used to contact Cindy? Can we track that?"

"Call came from a disposable cell phone purchased at a discount store with broken security cameras," Tucker said. "From what our tech guy is saying, the phone was used for only a few days in several public areas in the city, before it went dark, likely destroyed. Not helpful as far as narrowing a specific location of our perp."

In other words, another dead end. He blew out a breath, staring out the window at the small parking lot. Who was this anonymous guy claiming to be Roy's friend? Jeff Abbott? It would make sense to have Abbott get Roy out of jail, then to kill him so he couldn't talk.

Carlton must have died for the same reason. To keep him from talking. But why? What did they know? Who was the mastermind behind all of this?

And how did Mari and Theo fit into the puzzle?

"Sam? You still there?" Tucker asked.

"Yeah. But why does it feel like we're no closer to uncovering the truth?" He didn't bother to hide his frustration.

"I hear you," Tucker agreed.

"Do we know for sure Cindy wasn't involved in the shooting incidents?" It occurred to him that ten grand was a lot of money to simply allow a car to be stolen.

"She was out at a local pub the night of the first shooting," Tuck said. "And she was working the following day. We didn't find any weapons, not that she couldn't have gotten rid of it. Still, she's a blubbery mess right now. Honestly, I don't think she is capable of shooting anyone."

"And what about our other search warrant?" Sam pressed. So far, they had nothing to show for the day's work. And very few additional avenues to investigate.

"Unfortunately, Zach Tifton is still missing. Owens has instructed us to reach out to his friends and family to find him."

Again, Sam wished he could be out there, doing the legwork to follow up on leads. "Okay, but now that we know Cindy Gorlich was paid to let Roy steal her car, Tifton is likely off the hook."

"Possibly, but based on his calling in sick and being missing, boss wants us to tie up that loose end. Hey, speaking of which, Owens is on the other line now. Talk later." With that, Tucker ended the call.

Sam lowered the phone, still staring outside. This case was confounding on so many levels.

Movement from across the parking lot caught his attention. He narrowed his gaze. Was that a man in a ski mask? No rifle this time, but his instincts were screaming at him that this guy was likely armed.

"Mari, grab Theo and go into your room. Hide in the bath, understand? Keep your head down until I come and get you." He'd barely said the words when the crack of gunfire had him jumping back from the window in the nick of time.

A bullet punctured the glass, whizzed past the two double beds to lodge in the wall between the bedroom and bathroom. He drew his weapon, took aim and fired back.

Theo began to cry, gut-wrenching sobs that were difficult to ignore. Sam stood to the side of the window, eyeing the opposite side of the parking lot warily. Returning fire had caused the gunman to drop out of sight.

He was about to tell Mari to call 911, but her voice calm and strong from the other room indicated she already had.

Help would be there soon. He just needed to survive long enough for the local cops to arrive.

Chapter Thirteen

Stretched out in the bathtub with Theo tucked in front of her, Mari prayed. Theo's crying ripped at her heart, but as much as she tried to reassure him that they were fine, gunfire still echoed around them.

Sam was firing back at the gunman, which gave her hope for their ability to escape yet also made her worry for his safety. She trusted Sam to protect them, and she couldn't bear the thought of losing him.

Please, Lord Jesus! Protect us all!

Hearing the shrill wail of sirens helped her to remain calm. This motel was located just outside of Austin, which meant the police department would respond, rather than the sheriff's deputies.

She still didn't trust the deputies after the incident at the ranch. Roy's dead body had been placed in her living room while the deputy was supposedly outside watching the house.

The sirens were much louder now, and the gunfire had stopped. "The police are here, Theo," she said, pressing a kiss to his head. "We're safe now. The police will keep us safe."

"I want Mr. Sam," Theo sobbed. "And Charlie."

"Charlie is right here." Theo had the dog when she'd picked

him up from the bed. She tucked Charlie in closer, frowning a bit when she felt the beginning of a small opening in the stuffed animal's belly. She made a mental note to repair the dog when they got home.

"Mari? Are you and Theo okay?" Sam asked.

"Yes." Her voice sounded hoarse, as if she'd been screaming. She cleared her throat and lifted her head to look over the edge of the tub. "We're not hurt."

Sam stood in the doorway, his gaze full of regret and maybe a hint of anger. Not at her, she knew, but at the situation.

"I need you to stay there for a moment, until the Austin PD clears the area." He hesitated, then added, "I'll be back as soon as possible."

"I understand." Being in the tub wasn't exactly comfortable, but she wasn't about to complain. She knew there could have been more than one shooter outside. And there was evidence to preserve, too.

"I wanna get out of here," Theo whined.

"I know, but we have to wait for Mr. Sam to come back." She kissed him again. "I know, why don't we sing songs?"

Theo sniffled loudly, then nodded. "Okay. I wanna sing the bus song."

No surprise as it was his favorite. They sang together, for several minutes. When they finished the "Wheels on the Bus" song, she suggested another a church song they'd recently learned, called "Jesus Loves Me."

After three songs, Sam returned. "Sounds like you're ready for the church choir," he said with a smile. He offered her a hand. She took it, grateful for his strength.

Once she'd gotten out of the bathtub, Sam leaned over to lift Theo into his arms. Her son rested his head on Sam's chest. "Was that the scary man?"

"Yes, but he's gone now," Sam said reassuringly. "You don't have to worry about him."

"Why does he keep coming to scare us?" Theo asked, his tear-streaked face tearing her apart.

Sam sent her a panicked gaze, clearly not sure how to answer. Unfortunately, she didn't have a good response to her son's good question either. "We don't know, sweetie, but he'll go to jail for a long time." She didn't add, when they finally caught him.

Thankfully, it was enough to satisfy Theo. He lowered his head back to Sam's chest, content in his arms.

Theo needed a father. She had to tear her gaze away from the image Sam and Theo made, before she broke down sobbing, too.

Charlie was in the bottom of the bathtub, so she bent to scoop him up. Turning the dog over, she poked the bit of stuffing back into the small opening.

Then frowned when she felt something hard and unyielding. What in the world?

Examining the underbelly more closely, she gasped when she felt something move. What was in there? She used his fingers to rip the opening to the point she could pull whatever was in there, out.

A small USB drive plopped into her hand.

"Sam?" She turned to stare at him. "I found this inside Charlie. And I didn't put it there."

Sam's eyebrows levered upward. "Who gave Theo the stuffed animal?"

"Roy." She turned the USB drive over in her hand as if there would be something on the outside that would help explain what it was and why it was in the dog. "He bought the dog when I first discovered I was pregnant. I took it with us when we left, mostly because I wanted Theo to have something from his father."

"May I?" Sam asked holding out his hand.

She dropped the drive in his palm, then pushed the stuffing back inside Charlie. In that moment, she realized this was the reason Roy had tried to kidnap Theo. It wasn't because he'd wanted his son; he was after the USB drive he'd hidden in the dog.

"This is great news, Mari," Sam said, breaking into her thoughts. "Whatever is on this drive is likely the key to blowing this investigation wide-open."

"I hope so." She wished she'd noticed the sutures in Charlie sooner, but who paid attention to a stuffed animal? It had never occurred to her that Roy would do something as crazy as hiding evidence in Theo's toy.

Was this the reason they'd been in nonstop danger?

"We need to get out of here," Sam said in a low voice, interrupting her thoughts. "It's a crime scene, and the techs need to get inside to find the slugs from the weapon."

She wanted to ask about the shooter. "Is he—gone?"

"Yeah. DOA," he admitted. She assumed that meant dead on arrival of the police officers. "We can't interrogate him, but knowing who he is may help us track down who hired him."

"That's good." Not that a man lost his life but having something to go on. For the past few days it has felt as if they were stumbling around in the dark without flashlights.

Maybe now, with the USB drive and the dead gunman, they'd find exactly what they'd need to put an end to this nightmare, once and for all.

One glance at the bullet-ridden wall was sobering. Swallowing hard, she followed Sam and Theo outside to where a slew of police officers were tapping off the crime scene and marking evidence.

Through the throng, she saw Tucker running toward them, concern etched on his features. "Everyone okay?"

"Yeah," Sam said. She noticed he hadn't mentioned the USB drive to the local cops. "We need another place to stay. One that accepts cash with no questions asked."

"I'll have Marsh look into that," Tucker agreed. He raked

his gaze over her and then looked with sympathy at Theo. "Rough day."

"You could say that." She tried to keep her tone light, but tears pricked her eyes. Blinking them back, she drew in a deep breath and added, "But God was watching over us and that's all that matters."

"I couldn't agree more," Sam murmured. "Tuck, can you drive us out of here? Hold on, we'll grab Theo's car seat."

"Yes, this way." Once Sam had removed the brand-new seat they'd purchased only a few hours ago, Tucker drew them through the sea of cops to the spot where he'd left his SUV.

To her surprise no one stopped them. "Don't we need to give statements?"

"I told the local cops that we would do that later," Sam said, an edge to his tone. "They didn't like it, but nothing is more important than your safety."

She nodded, grateful for the reprieve. It wasn't as if she had much to tell them anyway. Sam had seen the shooter, then told her to take Theo into the bathtub. And that was all she knew.

Well, except for finding the USB drive.

Sam didn't bring it up until they were all settled in Tucker's SUV and were heading away from the motel crime scene. "As soon as we get settled in another motel, I need you to get a computer."

"What's the rush?" Tucker asked.

"Mari found this." Sam held up the USB drive. "Roy Carlton hid it inside Theo's stuffed dog."

Tucker let out a low whistle. "That's great news. And explains a lot. It could be that the USB drive is the driving force behind these attacks. And why the bedrooms were searched."

"Yeah." Sam tucked the drive back into his pocket. Then he pulled out his phone. "I'll have Jackson get the computer and meet us at the motel."

"Good plan," Tucker agreed. He tapped a message that had

come up on the SUV's screen. "Looks like Marsh has secured a place for us. Let Jackson know, okay?"

Mari sat beside Theo, grateful to have the rangers gathered around them. She tried to let go of her anger toward Roy for putting her and their son in danger. There was no point in wishing things were different.

All that mattered was uncovering whatever information was on the USB drive and who was ultimately responsible for shooting at them.

And while she would miss Sam terribly once this was over, she would be more than happy for her life to go back to normal.

Hopefully in time to celebrate the new year and Theo's fifth birthday.

Sam couldn't wait to see what was on the USB drive. He turned to glance at Mari and Theo in the back, grateful to note the little boy seemed calmer now. The way Theo had clung to him after the shooting had been touching. Sam had been reluctant to let him go.

There was no denying the child looked up to him as a father figure. The realization should have scared him, but it didn't.

Just the opposite.

He'd prayed like he'd never prayed before the entire time Mari and Theo were hiding in the bathtub. God had been watching over him. It was the only explanation as to how he'd hit the shooter, since he'd never gotten a good look at the guy.

The gunman's face hadn't been the least bit familiar, but the first officers on scene noticed the tattoo of a cobra on his arm, which indicated he may be part of a newer drug cartel known as the Rey Cobras, operating near the border. A fact that only muddied the waters of the investigation.

Why on earth was a drug cartel involved? Had Carlton been working for them? And if so, was that the reason Roy Carlton had shot and killed the city manager, Hank George?

"Mr. Sam?" Theo's voice broke into his thoughts.

He turned in his seat. "What do you need?"

"Did you forget my new toys?" Theo's lower lip trembled as if he were about to cry again.

He hid a wince because he had indeed forgotten Theo's new toys. "I—uh, yes, I'm sorry. We'll get you some new ones, okay?"

"More action figures?" Theo asked.

"Absolutely." He wasn't sure when they'd have time to make another run to the store, but he couldn't bring himself to disappoint the little boy. "The same ones we bought before."

"Soon?" Theo asked hopefully.

"Ah—" He glanced helplessly at Mari.

"The new motel room will have the same children's TV station as before," Mari said. "We'll find something fun to watch until it's time to get more toys."

Theo seemed to consider this, then nodded. "Okay."

Crisis averted, Sam thought. He felt terrible for what Theo and Mari were going through. How had the member of a drug cartel found them in the first place? He didn't like any of this and made another promise not to use plastic anywhere near their new location.

He would have preferred a formal safe house, but that would mean going up the chain of command. And he wasn't ready to do that. Oh, he trusted Captain Owens, but the governor's office had been the one to ask for the rangers' help in the first place. And considering this all started with the city manager being murdered, politicians—even the mayor—could be involved.

Yeah, somehow, there seemed to be far too many fingers in this pie. Too bad he wasn't in the mood to share. Not after this latest attack.

"Do you want me to swing past a store?" Tuck asked in a low voice. He waved to the left. "There's a department store up ahead."

Sam hesitated, then shook his head. "Better to wait until later. We need to know what is on this USB drive." He didn't add his hopes that discovering what was on there might be enough for an arrest and the end to the danger.

He knew Mari would prefer to return to the ranch house as soon as possible.

"Your call," Tuck said with a nod and kept going. Up ahead, Sam could see the name of the motel Marsh had secured for them using cash.

Now if Jackson could just get there with the laptop computer, they'd be all set.

As promised, Marsh was standing outside waiting for them. He held up two room keys and gestured to the door beside him.

Tuck pulled right up to the door and threw the gearshift into Park. Sam pushed out from the passenger seat, then opened the rear doors for Mari and Theo.

"I can do it," Theo said, pushing his hands away. In a spurt of independence, Theo worked on the strap holding him in place.

Mari shrugged, getting out and coming around to stand beside him. Theo released the buckle then scrambled down from the car seat.

"See? I did it all by myself."

"That you did," Mari agreed. "Come inside now, okay?"

Marsh held the first motel room door open for them. The hour was almost three in the afternoon, although it seemed later since they'd been on the move since early that morning. Marsh handed Sam the key. "Connecting rooms," he said. "As requested."

"Thanks. I'll open this side." He followed Mari and Theo into the room, quickly unlocking the connecting door.

"I wanna watch cartoons," Theo said, bouncing on the bed.

"Let's see what they have." Mari pointed the remote at the television. It didn't take long for her to find the children's channel. "Oh, look! This is one of your favorites."

Theo settled down on the bed, clutching Charlie close. Sam hoped the boy would be preoccupied for a while.

"What happened at the motel?" Marsh asked.

Sam quickly filled him in. "I hope Jackson gets here soon with the computer."

"He's five minutes out," Tuck said. "And we should get an ID on the shooter soon, too."

"Too bad we can't question him," Marsh said. "Almost seems as if that entire fiasco was a suicide mission."

"Maybe." Sam frowned. "I hadn't thought of that. You made sure we weren't followed, right?"

"Right." Marsh nodded. "But we need to stay on high alert, regardless. I can't put anything past these guys."

"Yeah. Obviously there is more than one perp involved." The USB drive was burning a hole in his hand. He stepped up to the window, glad to see Jackson pulling into the motel parking lot. "Jackson's here now."

"I'm nervous," Mari said softly. "I can't imagine what is on that drive."

"Hopefully a full confession," Sam said. Although that didn't make sense. Carlton had already been sent to prison for murdering the city manager. Why bother to break out of jail to hide his own confession?

"Sounds like y'all had a busy day," Jackson drawled as Marsh opened the door to let him in. "What's this about a secret drive?"

"Set the computer down and we'll find out." Sam stepped forward. The moment the computer was turned on, he inserted the USB drive and double-clicked to open it.

Mari, Tuck, Marsh and Jackson all crowded around him. To his surprise, there were several documents on the drive. He opened them in chronological order according to the date, starting with the oldest document first.

"Is he really talking about the Rey Cobras cartel?" Jackson asked.

Sam nodded slowly, feeling a little sick to his stomach as he read what was almost like a journal of Roy's descent into the life of crime. "Roy was recruited by the Rey Cobras, also known as King Cobra cartel, to sell drugs. The shooter at the motel scene had a cobra tattoo on his arm, which the local cops identified as part of the same cartel." He glanced back at Mari, who had paled at the news. "You didn't know about that?"

"No." Her voice was barely a whisper. "Roy wasn't the greatest husband in the world, but selling drugs? I never would have expected him to do something like that."

Sam knew people desperate for money were easy targets to be drawn into criminal organizations. If Roy's construction company had lost contracts, it would make sense he'd try to do something else to supplement his income.

"How does the King Cobra cartel fit into the murder of Hank George?" Tucker asked.

Sam clicked on the next document, which held more information about the King Cobra cartel, and specifically Roy's contact known as Jose Edwardo. "Marsh, get the name of Jose Edwardo to Owens."

"On it," Marsh agreed.

Sam clicked on the next document. "Okay, this one mentions a person with 'political clout' as being involved. He mentions Jeff Abbott being involved, too, which may explain why he was murdered. There are also meeting dates and times taking place three years ago." He glanced at Tuck and Jackson. "Hank George? His political clout?"

Jackson shrugged. "Then why kill him? I'd lean toward the mayor himself."

"What about the guy who has taken over the city manager's job?" Tucker asked. "What's his name? Doug Granger?"

"Yeah, maybe." Sam wished Roy had been a little more specific. But there were still two more documents to review, so he moved on, clicking on the next document. He frowned at the blank page.

"Do you think he was arrested before he could finish?" Tucker asked.

"I hope not." He minimized that document and clicked on the last and most recent one. Thankfully, it wasn't blank.

And when he began reading, his pulse kicked into high gear. "Roy Carlton claims he was set up to take the fall for Hank George's murder."

"I'm not sure we should believe that," Jackson drawled.

"Normally, I wouldn't, but it's interesting he's writing this but had not used it as part of his defense," Sam said. He kept reading, then sat back. "Check out that last paragraph. He was told he'd be 'richly rewarded' for cooperating and going to jail if convicted." Sam turned in his chair to face Mari. "What do you think?"

She slowly shook her head, looking confused and upset. "I'm shocked Roy would go along with something like that. Giving up two years of his life for money? Roy was not known to be patient."

"They did help him escape," Tucker mused.

"Yeah, then killed him so he couldn't talk." Sam sighed, rubbing his hands over his face. "We need to know which person with political clout is involved."

"And working with a drug cartel," Jackson agreed. "That's a big problem."

Yeah, it was. And Sam had no idea how they'd get the answers they needed.

Chapter Fourteen

Drugs. Her life and Theo's were in danger because of drugs. Well, that and murder, she silently amended.

The news was shocking, and even now, looking back, she couldn't say that Roy's behavior had ever hinted to the fact he was using drugs.

More likely selling them.

She shivered, hating knowing that Roy had been killed because of sheer greed. Rather than working harder, getting another part-time job, he'd gone down the path of becoming a criminal.

Going as far as doing jail time for the promise of a *rich reward*.

The only encouraging part of reading Roy's notes hidden on his USB drive was that he hadn't murdered anyone. Someday, when Theo was old enough to ask questions about his biological father, she wouldn't have to tell her son his father had killed a man.

Not that selling drugs or getting involved in a drug cartel was much better.

Swallowing hard, she moved away from the small table to check on her son. Engrossed in a children's movie, he didn't seem to notice her hovering in the doorway between their rooms.

Her heart ached for what Theo had been through. Nearly being kidnapped, then shot at multiple times. No wonder he had suffered nightmares.

And likely would for months to come.

"Okay, boss has issued a BOLO for Roy's contact, Edwardo," Marsh said. "He has a criminal record for selling drugs and possession. He was extradited back to Mexico last year, but I assume he snuck back over the border."

She hoped finding Jose Edwardo would help put an end to the danger.

"We need to interview the mayor and this new city manager, Granger," Sam said. "If either of them balks at that, we'll get Owens to pave the way for us."

"Good idea," Tucker agreed. "I'll call the mayor's office now to get the request on record. He's less likely to be available."

Tucker moved past her to make the call. "Hello, Rachel? This is Texas Ranger Tucker Powell. I need a meeting with Mayor Beaumont ASAP." A pause, then he said, "I don't think you understand how important this is. However, I'm sure I can contact my boss Captain Owens to facilitate a meeting, or even the governor's office, if needed." Another pause, then Tucker's expression revealed his satisfaction. "Yes, ma'am, four o'clock this afternoon works just fine. Tell the mayor we will see him, shortly."

Tucker noticed her listening and winked. "Sometimes charm doesn't work and you have to pull out the big guns."

She couldn't help smiling back. "Whatever gets the job done."

"Exactly." His expression sobered. "I'm sorry you and your son are in this position."

"It's okay." Tucker was being sweet, and while she appreciated his kindness, she couldn't help glancing over at Sam.

He was the one she cared about, far more than she should. "I know you will protect us."

Tucker nodded and moved back to the group. "We're set for four o'clock this afternoon. We'll need to come up with something more other than the USB drive to convince Beaumont to cooperate with us."

"I was thinking about that," Sam said. "If we believe Carlton's claim that he didn't kill Hank George, then who did? With the DNA evidence and his fingerprints on the murder weapon, the investigation stopped, right?"

"Yeah," Marshall said. "I see where you're going. We know Hank George was killed in his home but left in an alley behind a restaurant. We need to pick up where the cops left off, searching for video from neighbors' homes and/or businesses in the area where his body was found. They probably didn't bother to keep going after getting Carlton in custody."

"Let's do it," Jackson said. "We don't have a lot of time."

"We'll spread out," Tucker agreed. "I'll take the businesses closest to the dump site. Marshall, you and Jackson go back and canvass the homes in Hank George's neighborhood."

"I'm in," Jackson said without hesitation.

Mari could tell Sam wanted to go with them, but of course he nodded. "I'll stay here, but if you find something send it to me and I'll put it with the other information we have." He gestured to the computer. "I'll also send the documents we found on the USB drive to Owens."

"Good. We're getting closer to uncovering the truth, I can feel it." Jackson reached for the door. "We'll keep in touch."

"Later," Sam said, as the three rangers headed out.

There was a long moment of silence when they were alone again. She told herself not to think about their kiss but to stay focused on the investigation. "What are you going to do now?"

"Dig into social media again." Sam shrugged. "I've been checking Doug Granger's postings, but so far I haven't seen anything remotely suspicious. From what I can tell, the guy is clean. We'll still interview him, but the mayor seems a more likely candidate with his election coming up."

"What about the mayor's social media?" She moved closer and dropped into the second chair. "Maybe we'll learn something there?"

"It's possible." Sam sat beside her. "I doubt he'll be in pictures with cartel members but it's worth a shot."

She leaned forward to see the screen as he began to search. There were dozens of posts for Mayor Beaumont, including several fundraisers for his reelection campaign. She tapped one of the photographs. "Do you think his needing funds for his campaign is a part of this?"

"Maybe." Sam continued poking around. "Looks like Beaumont has at least a few deputies supporting him."

She frowned. "That seems odd. Why the sheriff's department? Austin city is protected by the Austin Police Department. The sheriff's department only has jurisdiction within the courthouse, at the jail and in the counties that are outside of Austin. Including Whistling Creek Ranch."

"True," Sam scowled. "We already know the deputies goofed up protecting Carlton in the hospital. And let Carlton's dead body get placed in your house." He turned to meet her gaze. "Goes back to our original thought that maybe one of them or more are dirty."

She nodded, not wanting to believe it, but couldn't ignore the deputy on the screen shaking hands with Mayor Beaumont as if they were good buddies.

Maybe they just golfed together. Or had friends in common. Yet when she leaned forward, she noticed the deputy looked familiar. She put her hand on Sam's arm to stop him from scrolling. "Wait a minute, I think that's Deputy Strawn. You remember, he was the one who responded to my call that first night when Roy tried to kidnap Theo. He seemed nice and concerned about the event."

"Interesting, but not exactly proof of wrongdoing," Sam said. "Let's keep looking for connections."

"Mommy, my movie is over," Theo called.

She reluctantly stood. "I'll see if I can find something else for him to watch."

Sam nodded without looking up from the computer screen. The sense of camaraderie seemed to have evaporated. She told herself it didn't matter as they were working to find those responsible for shooting at them.

Stepping into the next room, she found Theo standing in front of the television, moving from one foot to the other. "Do you have to go to the bathroom?"

He nodded and quickly ran toward it. She sighed and took the remote. She didn't like Theo to have so much screen time, but without other toys to keep him occupied she didn't have much of a choice.

Better screen time than to risk going back to the store.

It didn't take long to find another children's movie. When Theo returned, she lifted him up onto the bed. "Would you like to watch this show?"

He nodded and leaned against her. She held him close for a moment, silently thanking God for keeping him safe.

Yet the nonstop danger was wearing her down. This was their second motel in one day. All she could do was to hope and pray Tucker was right about how they were getting closer to uncovering the truth.

Before anyone else got hurt.

Ignoring Mari and Theo was impossible. The moment Mari left to tend to her son, he'd wanted to follow. As if she needed his help to find a new TV program for her son.

He could've asked one of the other guys to stay behind but had chosen to keep his mouth shut. *Not a smart move, Hayward*, he inwardly railed. He should have taken the opportunity to put distance between them. Instead, he'd stayed put.

He was flailing in the deep end of the pool when it came to Mari and her son. They'd managed to wiggle their way into his heart despite his efforts to remain professional.

Giving himself a mental shake, he scrolled through the photos on Mayor Beaumont's page. Other than Deputy Strawn being acquainted with the guy, nothing else stood out as suspicious.

He switched his attention from the mayor to the newly appointed city manager, Doug Granger. Maybe Hank George had been killed because he learned about something criminal going on within the city. And they needed someone who would look the other way, like Doug Granger, in that position instead.

Yet why? That was the part that didn't make any sense. What power did the city manager have?

Maybe building permits? Hadn't Roy Carlton been working construction? He began to dig into Longhorn Construction, the company Mari had mentioned, but there was very little information on the internet about them.

He pulled out his phone to make sure he hadn't missed a call. Nope, the guys hadn't found anything, or if they had, they hadn't clued him in. And the meeting with Mayor Beaumont was barely ninety minutes from now.

For a long moment he stared at the computer. What were they missing? A member of the King Cobra drug cartel had pummeled their motel room with bullets. Roy was set up to take the fall on killing Hank George.

Maybe Mari was right about Mayor Beaumont needing a source of funding for his campaign. He brought up information on state and local campaign donations. Of course, Texas didn't have any regulations relative to how much money could be given via an anonymous donation.

Was it as simple as the mayor getting campaign funds from sketchy sources? Like directly from the drug cartel, itself? If so, why? He didn't quite understand the motive. The mayor of Austin had some power when it came to running the city, but he was accountable to the city council. It wasn't like the mayor could turn his back on a sudden influx of illegal drugs. But maybe there were some ways Beaumont could allow members of the drug cartel to operate in the city.

Wait a minute. He straightened in his seat, going back to the website of Longhorn Construction. Was it possible the company was involved? According to Roy, they'd lost a key contract for a new project.

In searching new construction sites, he identified a company by the name of Tribeca Construction. They had a more robust website, with several photos of other projects they'd completed. Tribeca looked legit, whereas Longhorn seemed a bit sketchy.

He went back to the City of Austin website and found the meeting minutes for their council meetings. As he scanned them, he felt Mari come up behind him.

"What are you looking at?" she asked, leaning over his shoulder.

"Council meeting minutes, going back to about the time the city manager was killed." She was close enough that if he turned his head, he could kiss her. "I'm wondering if this isn't related to contracts with construction companies. Like Longhorn, the one Roy worked for, and this one, Tribeca Construction."

Mari didn't say anything but stayed behind him, reading over his shoulder. He worked hard not to let her distract him.

"Here, this meeting was three months before the murder," he said. "And look at that, City Manager Hank George has expressed concerns over Longhorn Construction for what he deemed were worrisome business practices. He insisted they use Tribeca Construction instead."

"And then he was murdered, allegedly by Roy," Mari said. "I remember something about how Roy was accused of acting out of a fit of anger and revenge in killing Hank. Because he and several of his fellow workers had lost their jobs."

"Yeah. Only now we know Roy didn't kill him, and that this

could all be related to the King Cobra drug cartel." There were still some puzzle pieces missing. Then it came to him. "Maybe the cartel owns Longhorn Construction."

Mari finally moved away to sit in the chair beside him. She frowned. "Why would they bother with a legitimate business? Unless it's about laundering drug money."

"That is possible, but I was thinking more about bringing materials in and out of Mexico which would enable them to move drugs at the same time." He reached for his phone. "And people like employees coming in and out might not be searched for drugs either. I need to update Owens. I think there's more than enough here to get the governor's attention."

He quickly gave Captain Owens the bit of information he'd learned about the construction angle. "Good work, Hayward. Keep digging."

"That's the plan," he agreed. "Have you heard from Tuck, Marsh or Jackson?"

"Not yet," Owens admitted. "Could be there isn't any help-ful video footage."

That was possible, although these days many people had ring doorbell cameras. "Okay, I'll be in touch if I find out any-thing more."

"Oh, one more thing," Owens said. "We have an ID on the shooter you took out at the motel. It's the same guy you told me to issue a BOLO for, Jose Edwardo."

He inwardly groaned. "So that name is nothing more than another dead end."

"Afraid so. Although the local cops did confirm his ties to the King Cobra cartel."

"That's no surprise, considering the cobra tattoo. Thanks."

Owens grunted in response and ended the call. As he set the phone down, Mari looked at him. "Jose Edwardo was Roy's contact, right? I guess it's no surprise he was the shooter."

"Yeah, it's one more connection." And he really wished the guy was still alive to interrogate. Then he thought about the medical examiner working on Roy Carlton's body. He made another call and was put straight through.

"Dr. Bond? Ranger Sam Hayward. Do you know if gunpowder residue was found on Carlton's hands or clothes?"

"Not on the hands," Earl Bond confirmed. "The techs took the clothes."

"Thanks." He lowered the phone. "Sounds like Roy might not have been the shooter, although I believe he was the one who tried to kidnap Theo. He knew he'd hidden the USB drive in the dog, no one else did."

"I think so, too." Mari frowned. "What about the meeting with the mayor? Are you going to tell Tucker and the others to ask specifically about Longhorn Construction?"

"They can ask but I'm sure the mayor will deny having anything to do with them." He shrugged. "According to the meeting minutes, it was Hank's decision to stop using them, not his."

"But that's the point, isn't it?" Mari asked with a frown. "If the mayor is using dirty drug money to fund his campaign, he would want Longhorn Construction to get the contracts."

She was right. He reached for his phone and called Tucker. The call went to voice mail. He left a message, then tried Marsh, next. He didn't answer either.

Fighting panic, he reached out to Jackson. Thankfully, he answered. "Something wrong?"

"I tried Tuck and Marsh but they didn't answer. Are you doing okay out there?"

"Are you checking up on us?" Jackson sounded testy. "As far as I know, everything is fine. They're probably busy, hopefully reviewing video. What do you need?"

"I just wanted you to be aware of another angle to this whole mess, prior to your meeting with the mayor." He quickly filled Jackson in on the construction company information. "This is all stuff that should have come out during the initial investigation into Hank Gorge's murder but didn't."

"We can follow up with Beaumont," Jackson agreed. "But don't expect him to suddenly confess."

"I won't. Although you may want to mention how dangerous it would be to get involved with the King Cobra cartel, or any cartel for that matter," Sam said. "He's asking for trouble."

"Will do. Look, I need to go. I have two more houses to check before we meet with the mayor."

"Take care of yourself." Sam disconnected the call and stared at the computer screen for a long moment.

Yeah, the more he considered the implication of the cartel being involved, the more he didn't like it. Cartel members were known to be brutal and vicious. The last thing he wanted was for any of them to continue coming after Mari and Theo.

As much as he hated knowing he'd killed a man, he was glad there was one less shooter to threaten Mari.

Yet there could be others. He abruptly stood and went to the window, scanning the parking lot. Mari's fingers tapped on the keyboard, but he stayed where he was. Maybe he should have asked one of the guys to stay behind, with them.

His phone rang, and he was relieved to see Tucker's name on the screen. "Hey, did you find something?"

"I did. I have a ring doorbell camera from two doors down from Hank George's house. Apparently the owners were gone during the time of the murder, so they were never interviewed by the cops."

"Don't keep me in suspense," Sam said dryly. "What does it show?"

"The video shows a young Hispanic man guy walking down the street toward Hank's house late at night. There's one streetlight that gives a brief glimpse of his profile, but the rest of the angle isn't great. There's no video of him pulling the trigger, but he does walk straight up to the house within thirty minutes of the estimated time of death." Tucker paused, then added, "He looks similar to the shooter from the motel. I'm sending it to the lab to see if they can sharpen the image to say for sure."

"Jose Edwardo," Sam said thoughtfully. "He was Roy's contact within the cartel. And now he's dead."

"Yeah, I know. Mighty convenient if you ask me," Tucker drawled.

"I'm getting the feeling the person with political clout is getting rid of the evidence, including anyone who might be tempted to talk to the authorities." Sam didn't like it one bit. "You better get to that meeting. Maybe you can scare Beaumont into talking if he's the one involved."

"We'll do our best," Tucker promised. "By the way, we're sending Marsh back to your motel. We don't need three of us to do this interview. And we don't like leaving you there alone."

"Okay, we'll watch for Marsh." He wasn't about to complain. "Call me when the interview is finished."

"Will do." Tuck ended the call.

He lowered his phone, then glanced over to where Mari was staring at the computer screen. The intensity of her gaze drew him closer. "Did you find something?"

"I found another picture of Mayor Beaumont with Deputy Strawn," she said. "There's a woman standing between them. She isn't tagged in the photo, so I'm not sure who she is."

"Let me see that." It was his turn to lean over Mari's shoulder. The date and time of the photograph was from November of last year. More than a year ago.

The woman looked familiar, but he couldn't place her. She wasn't Cindy Gorlich, but maybe another hospital employee? Although that didn't make sense, since Deputy Strawn wasn't the one who had been standing guard over Roy during his escape. That had been Deputy Erickson.

He straightened, his mind racing. He had seen this woman before, but when? And where?

Was it possible she was the key to blowing this case wide-open?

Chapter Fifteen

"Mommy, I'm hungry!"

"Coming." She glanced at her watch, realizing it was past Theo's usual dinner time. "Is there a vending machine or someplace we can get pretzels or crackers for him?"

"Yeah, I'll find something." Sam stood and reached for the door. Then glanced at her over his shoulder. "Don't open the door for anyone, not even the maid. Marsh should be here, soon."

"I won't." She crossed the threshold to join Theo. "Mr. Sam is going to find a snack. Is your show over?"

"No, but I'm hungry." He held up the dog. "Charlie is hungry, too."

She smiled. "I'm glad you have Charlie to keep you company."

That was the wrong thing to say, because it reminded Theo of the toys they'd left behind. She swallowed a sigh when he asked for his action figures again, and his horses.

She wanted to tell him to be content with being safe but didn't. "I know, sweetie. We'll get to the store soon."

Theo huffed and threw himself backward on the bed. "Soon is never," he pouted.

He wasn't entirely wrong about that. She had no idea if it would be safe enough to stop by a store to get a few things. She had the impression Sam was waiting to see how the meeting went with the mayor before making those decisions.

"I'm sorry, but we're waiting for Mr. Marsh to return." It was the best she could do.

Hearing the door opening from the other room, she crossed over to check on Sam. He held up a mini bag of pretzels. "Will this work?"

"Perfect, thanks." She opened the bag and carried them to Theo. "Look, Mr. Sam found pretzels."

"Yum." Theo eagerly took one and popped it into his mouth. He'd get crumbs on the bed but that was the least of her worries.

"Be good for a little while longer, okay?" She gestured to the television. "Watch your movie."

Theo nodded, the pretzels doing the trick. She hurried over to the next room.

Sam was back at the computer, scrolling through the sheriff's department website. She sat beside him. "Who are you looking for?"

"The woman in the photo." Sam glanced at her. "She looks familiar, but I can't place her. I found Deputy Strawn here on the list of deputies—his first name is Joe." He clicked off that page and went back to social media. "It's a stretch, but he might have a social media presence. Most cops don't, but some do."

"Safety reasons?" she guessed.

He nodded. "No point in making it easy for someone to find you."

She could understand that. She watched as he found several Joe Strawns, but none that lived in the area.

"Nothing," he said with a sigh.

"She's not the mayor's wife?"

"No." He went back to Mayor Beaumont's publicity page. "This is Arianna."

The slender blonde woman standing beside her husband

didn't look anything like the short and stocky, dark-haired woman standing between Deputy Strawn and the mayor. "She looks much younger than Beaumont," she observed.

"Yeah, second wife." Sam frowned. "I don't remember there being any sort of scandal about his divorce from the first wife."

She sat back in her seat. "Why would he get himself mixed up with the cartel?"

"We don't know for sure he is, but money is the most common motivator."

"I guess." She couldn't imagine crossing that line for what had to be a stressful job in the first place. Give her the quiet ranch life any day.

A knock at the door startled her. Sam jumped up, used the peephole, then opened the door. "Hey, Marsh."

"Mommy! My show is over!" Theo called.

She grimaced. "I'm afraid he's tired of watching movies and cartoons."

"We can head out to pick up a few things," Marshall offered. "We'll need to grab food for dinner, anyway. Should be safe enough while the guys are meeting with the mayor."

"Really?" She turned toward Sam, who nodded. "That would be wonderful. I'm sorry it's been so difficult with Theo. He's used to having his own toys and attending his preschool classes. If we were home, I'd set up a play date for him."

"You don't have to apologize, Mari," Sam murmured. "I wish we could put an end to the danger once and for all."

She did, too. "Thanks. I'll get Theo's coat."

As she dressed Theo in his winter gear, she heard Sam and Marsh discussing the case in a low rumble of voices. She couldn't help but wonder if the mayor was really involved or someone else.

Roy had mentioned someone with political clout. He could have at least written down initials.

She suppressed a sigh as she shrugged into her coat. Maybe

Tucker and Jackson would get something from their meeting with the mayor.

"Enhanced video confirms it," Marsh was saying as she and Theo went into their room. "Jose Edwardo is the one who approached Hank George's home the night of the shooting."

"Too bad the cops didn't investigate further," Sam muttered. "That would have been enough for reasonable doubt."

"Not necessarily, with having DNA and the murder weapon with Roy Carlton's prints." Marshall shook his head. "I can't say that I blame them. And even if they had seen this guy on the doorbell camera, doesn't mean they would have suspected him of being the shooter."

"I guess you're right," Sam agreed. He met her gaze, then smiled at Theo. "Are you ready to get some toys?"

"Yeah! Toys!" Theo jumped up and down with excitement. Then he cocked his head to the side. "Are these my birthday presents?"

"Yes, these are birthday presents from me and Mr. Marsh," Sam said, ignoring her frown. "But you need to be a good boy, okay? And that means listening to your mom."

"I will!" Theo continued hopping from one foot to the next. "Billy the elf knows I'm a good boy."

"Settle down," she said. "Or we won't go."

Marsh went out of the room first, glancing around before moving away from the doorway. She went next, with Theo beside her with Sam covering them. A few minutes later, they were settled in Marsh's SUV and heading to the store they'd passed on the way to the motel.

The trip to the store didn't take long. Of course, Theo wanted several toys and action figures.

"Pick two," she said firmly. "One present from Mr. Marsh and one from Mr. Sam."

Sam looked as if he might argue, but she narrowed her gaze in warning. Theo couldn't have everything he wanted. Besides, he had two presents waiting for him at home.

Although she really did wish they'd be able to return to the ranch sooner than later.

They were on their way to a fast-food restaurant when Sam's phone dinged. He pulled out his phone and grimaced.

"Bad news?" she asked.

"Yeah. According to Tuck, the meeting with the mayor was short and not very sweet. The guy insisted he knows nothing and became annoyed when they pointed out how a member of the drug cartel was shot and killed outside your motel, Mari. And he also said he has nothing to do with which construction companies get building contracts. They were in and out within fifteen minutes. And that was after he'd made them wait almost an hour to meet with him."

"That's a bummer," Marsh said. "I guess it was too much to hope he'd give anything away."

"Yeah. Traffic is a snarled mess, so the guys are stopping at headquarters to update Owens before heading out to meet us at the motel." Sam turned in his seat to look at her. "I'm sorry we don't have better news."

"It's not your fault." She had hoped for more, but it wasn't like they weren't trying. "Nothing else from other cameras in the area?"

"Oh, yeah, there was a text here about a black truck being seen near the restaurant ten minutes before Hank George's body was found." He shrugged. "Could be the same one I saw being used by the shooter, but they didn't get a plate number either, so there's no way to trace it."

Another dead end. She tried not to show the depths of her despair. They'd already found and examined the information on the USB drive Roy had hidden inside Charlie. What else did these men want with her and her son?

"Maybe they should have told the mayor about the USB drive," she said. "There's no reason for them to keep coming after us."

The two men exchanged a look. "I don't know if that's

good enough," Marshall said. "But we'll discuss the idea with our boss."

"Roy knew he hid the USB drive in the dog," Sam said thoughtfully. "But the mayor and whoever else is involved might believe he told you something incriminating."

"I don't know anything!" Her voice came out sharper than she intended. "I wish I could tell them that face-to-face."

Marshall pulled up to the drive-through window. "Let's order and discuss our options when we get back to the motel."

"Sure." She couldn't help feeling dejected. It seemed for all their efforts they were right back where they'd started.

Sam could tell Mari was at the end of her rope. The stress of being in danger, along with the lack of progress on the investigation, was taking a toll.

He wanted nothing more than to wrap her into his arms and reassure her that everything would work out. But it wasn't smart to make promises he might not be able to keep either. All they could do was to keep praying for safety and guidance.

"Grab extra food for Tucker and Jackson, too," he suggested.

"Will do." Soon the enticing scent of burgers and fries filled the interior of the SUV, making his mouth water. Marsh made the short trip back to the motel in record time.

"I'm hungry," Theo said, scrambling from the vehicle.

"Don't forget your action figures," Mari said dryly. "You wanted them, remember?"

"Oh, yeah." Theo came back for them. "My heroes are hungry," he declared.

He and Marsh hung back so Mari and Theo could sit at the table. He bowed his head, waiting for Mari to say grace.

"Dear Lord Jesus, we ask You to please keep us all safe in Your care. Please guide us to the truth. Amen."

"Amen," he echoed, knowing they desperately needed the truth to be revealed. How else could they eliminate the threat to Mari and Theo?

"What do you think about getting the USB drive information out there," Marsh asked in a low voice. They were sitting on the edge of the bed eating their burgers. "She might be right about the danger being over once the bad guys know we found the USB drive hidden by Carlton."

"I would feel better if Roy's USB drive actually named the person with political clout," he said. "I mean, as it stands now, there isn't much to go on."

"No, but the reverse is true, too, isn't it?" Marsh asked. "I mean, what information could Mari have that wouldn't have already been revealed?"

He made a good point. "We might need to talk to Roy's cell mate. Maybe Roy said something to him about who was involved."

"That's possible." Marsh sighed. "But prison snitches aren't exactly good witnesses. The general public is far more likely to believe the mayor's version of the story, rather than someone who'd been convicted of a crime."

"That's true. Unless of course we can find other evidence to support his claim." Sam abruptly straightened. "Maybe we need to head back to the ranch house. Someone searched the place—maybe Roy did hide something in Theo's room."

He hadn't realized Mari was listening in until she turned in her seat to glare at them. "I told you, Roy didn't live with us in the ranch house. I went there to live with my father after leaving him. I filed for separation, got an order of protection before filing for divorce."

She had said that, but he couldn't let the idea go. "Are you saying Roy was never in the ranch house for a family gathering? A holiday? Never?"

"Yes, he was there briefly," she admitted. "But I don't see why he would hide something there."

For the same reason Roy hid the USB drive in Charlie, he thought, but didn't say. "When was the last time he was at the ranch?"

She took a moment to think about that. "Three years ago at Christmas," she admitted. "We were already split up but he showed up unannounced to give Theo a gift. A toy truck," she hastened to add, "So nothing that could have something inside. And he was only in the house for five minutes, and never alone. My dad made it clear he wasn't welcome. There wasn't time for him to have gone into Theo's room to hide anything."

Was he on the wrong track here? Maybe.

"He was arrested just two weeks later," she added. "And from that point forward we had no contact until the divorce was final and I was granted sole custody of Theo." She scowled. "I don't think there's anything at the house."

Before he could respond, his phone rang. "Tuck," he said, glancing at the screen. "What's up?"

"We found Zach Tifton," Tucker announced. "Unfortunately, he's dead. Murdered in almost the exact same way Carlton was, bullet hole in the center of his forehead."

"How?" he demanded. "We never found anything that connected him to Carlton's escape."

"I don't know, but we're heading to the crime scene now," Tucker said. "Just wanted you to know we won't be there anytime soon."

"That's fine. Marsh is here and there's been no sign of anyone lurking around." He couldn't believe Tifton was dead. Murdered. "Keep us informed, will you?"

"Yep. Later." Tuck disconnected the call.

"What happened?" Mari asked.

"Another murder." He glanced at Theo, but thankfully the little boy was eating and playing with his action figure at the same time. "Zach Tifton, another employee at the hospital."

She paled then shook her head. "That doesn't make any sense."

She had that right. He finished his meal, then balled up the garbage. Sitting around in the motel room wasn't going to get them the answers they needed.

He really wanted to head back to Mari's ranch house. Or at least, send Marsh.

As if reading his mind, Marsh nodded. "I can head over there alone but it might be better for us to stick together."

He hesitated, trying to decide what was better for Mari and Theo. "Together," he finally said. "I think that's for the best."

"Okay." Marsh didn't argue. "Let's do it."

Mari's expression was troubled as she cleaned up the mess from their dinner. She went into the bathroom for a wet washcloth and wiped Theo's face and hands.

He caught her hand, offering a reassuring smile. "We'll be fine. No one knows where we are or have reason to believe we're heading back to the ranch."

"I trust you," she said in a low voice. "I just think it's a waste of time."

Maybe it was, but so was sitting around the motel for the rest of the evening. Tuck and Jackson might get something from the crime scene of Tifton's murder, but if not?

They still had nothing to prove Mayor Beaumont was involved with the cartel, and with these recent murders. Jeff Abbott was his stepson—why had he been killed, too? Just because of his friendship with Roy?

Maybe. It was beginning to look as if the answer to keeping the association with the cartel a secret was to kill anyone who might know something incriminating.

Which brought him right back to the attempts on Mari and Theo. Roy could have said something to them, and therefore the mayor and/or his associates wanted her silenced.

Permanently.

"Having second thoughts?" Marsh asked, as Mari took Theo into the bathroom. "We don't have to go."

"I want this to be over for them." He gestured to the connecting room. "Don't you think it's strange they're still in danger?"

"Yeah, but it doesn't sound like Roy had a chance to hide

anything either." Marsh shrugged. "The offer still stands for me to go alone."

"Or we wait until Tuck and Jackson are finished with the Tifton crime scene." Sam sighed. "Be honest. Am I just looking for an excuse to get out of here?"

Marsh held his gaze for a moment. "I think you would do just about anything for those two." He jerked his thumb in the direction of Mari and Theo's room. "And you won't rest until you know for sure there's nothing at the ranch house that might help us get to the bottom of this. I agree we need to double-check to make sure."

He nodded slowly. "We'll do everything possible to keep them safe."

"That we will," Marsh agreed.

"We're ready," Mari said, bringing Theo into their room. They were both dressed in their winter coats and Theo was holding on to one of his action figures.

"Okay, great." He shook off the sliver of apprehension. "Like earlier, Marsh will go out first. Mari, you and Theo will follow him, okay?"

Mari nodded and moved closer to Marsh. He opened the door, glanced around for a moment before moving through. Mari and Theo stayed close behind him.

Sam was the last one out. A tall man stepped out from the shadows and he froze, recognizing Deputy Joe Strawn.

Then Sam quickly moved toward the cop, pulling his weapon in a smooth movement and placing himself in front of Mari and Theo. "Stop where you are, Strawn. Don't make me shoot."

"Why would you shoot a cop?" Strawn asked. The deputy was still half in the shadow, making it difficult to see if he was holding a gun down at his side. "I'm here to talk to you and Ms. Lynch."

"No." He heard the sound of Marsh urging Mari and Theo toward the SUV but didn't dare take his gaze off the deputy. "Throw down your weapon and put your hands in the air."

For a long moment the deputy didn't move. Then he lifted his right arm. There was a gun in his hand, the barrel pointing in his direction.

"Stop!" Sam shouted. But Strawn didn't listen. Strawn moved slightly forward, enough for him to see the guy's resigned gaze. The way he moved with excruciating slowness, it was almost as if he wanted Sam to shoot him,

"Drop the weapon," Sam repeated, his tone desperate. "It doesn't have to end like this."

Strawn simply aimed his weapon at Sam, and sensing his finger tightening on the trigger, Sam had no choice but to fire. The bullet from his weapon slammed into Strawn's chest, sending the deputy stumbling backward against the wall of the building. He slowly slid to the ground.

Only then did Strawn drop his gun.

Chapter Sixteen

"Joe! No, Joe!" a woman shouted. Recognizing Deputy Joe Strawn as the man Sam shot, Mari turned to see a small, dark-haired woman running toward the fallen deputy an expression of sheer anguish on her face.

What in the world? It appeared as if they were a couple, the way she sobbed over his inert body.

"Get inside," Marsh growled near her ear. Theo was thankfully inside the SUV already, and Marsh stood close behind her but she didn't budge. She didn't understand what had just happened. Why the deputy had stood there, as if waiting for Sam to shoot him?

Suddenly another man stepped forward, lifting his weapon toward Sam. Without thinking, she broke past Marshall's arm and rushed the gunman.

"Get back!" Sam yelled, but it was too late. She hit the stranger hard, barely registering that he wasn't the mayor as they'd originally thought.

Her body collided with his. She landed on top of him, hard enough to make teeth rattle. The man with the gun tried to shove her aside, lifting the weapon in his hand again.

"Stop! Police!" Marshall ran forward just as the gunman

fired in Sam's direction. The gunshot was so loud she couldn't hear anything for a long moment. Sam ducked and rolled again to avoid being hit.

Please, Lord Jesus keep Sam safe!

The desperate prayer echoed in her mind seconds before Marshall ran forward, grabbing the weapon from the gunman's grip. "You idiot!" The gunman screamed in fury, his gaze locked on Strawn. "You could have shot them all! You failed the mission!"

Was he talking to Deputy Strawn? Maybe. It was hard to tell with the dark-haired woman weeping over the injured deputy.

"Shut up, Granger. You're under arrest for the attempted murder of a Texas Ranger, and any other charges I can add down the line. You have the right to remain silent and I strongly suggest you use it," Marshall said.

Granger? It took her a moment to place the name. Doug Granger was the newly appointed city manager.

Did that mean Mayor Beaumont wasn't involved? Or were the two of them working together? She grimaced as Marshall yanked Granger to his feet, continuing to read him his rights.

Shaken by the events, Mari pushed herself up and off the asphalt parking lot to limp toward Sam. But then she stopped, realizing Theo was crying her name in the back of the SUV.

"Mommy! Mommy!"

"I'm here. I'm fine, see?" Turning away from Sam, she hurried over to the SUV, pulling him up from the back seat and gathering him close. "I love you, Theo. I love you. Everything will be okay." She kissed the top of his head as his arms gripped her tightly around the neck.

She rocked him back and forth, whispering soothing words as his cries slowly subsided to hiccupping sobs.

"Are you hurt?" Sam called.

She shook her head, unable to speak. That had been close. Far too close. Sam looked as if he'd come to her side, but then abruptly turned to move toward the fallen deputy.

The short, dark-haired woman was still sobbing, her head down on his shoulder.

From where she stood with Theo, she watched Sam check for a pulse, then drop his chin to his chest in a gesture of defeat. In that moment, she understood the deputy was dead.

After a long moment, Sam stood and crossed back toward her and Theo.

"No vest?" Marshall asked, after he'd cuffed Doug Granger's wrists behind his back.

"No. He wanted me to shoot him," Sam said in a low voice. "I just wish I knew why."

"Maybe he thought death was better than facing the cartel," Marshall said.

"I guess." Sam glared at Granger, but the city manager remained silent.

"Joe did it for me." The dark-haired woman lifted her head, tears streaking her face. Mari recognized her from the photograph in which she'd stood between Strawn and the mayor. "He did it for me and our daughter, Ashley. To protect us."

"You're married?" Sam asked. The sound of police sirens filled the air, no doubt called in by other patrons of the motel.

She nodded, sniffling hard. "Yes. And we were forced to help…" Her voice drifted off. Then she added, "I work for Mayor Beaumont."

"Are you Rachel?" Marshall asked. "His administrative assistant?"

She nodded again, avoiding looking at Mari and Theo, likely out of guilt. Rachel had to know that her husband had come here for the sole purpose of killing them.

Instead, he'd sacrificed himself.

"I'm afraid you're under arrest, too," Marshall said, stepping forward. "I assume your boss is in on all of this?"

Rachel grimaced and looked away without responding. Mari tore her gaze from the grief-stricken woman, knowing she needed to work on forgiveness. Maybe later. Right now, she was too numb to feel even a little sympathy for her.

"No more guns, Mommy," Theo whispered. "No more."

"We're safe now," she murmured, wishing she could reassure the little boy that he'd never see or hear another gun. But she wasn't sure if their nightmare was really over. Sam had killed Deputy Strawn and they'd arrested Doug Granger, but if Mayor Beaumont was still involved, wouldn't they need proof to bring him down?

And if so, how long would that take? Hours? Days? Weeks? She couldn't bear to think about it.

"Where's your daughter now?" Marshall asked as he placed plastic straps around Rachel's wrists. "Is she safe?"

"She's with my mother." Rachel Strawn stared at the ground for a moment, then finally added, "I'll tell you everything you need to know if you make sure my daughter is safe."

"We can do that," Marshall agreed. "What's your mother's name and where does she live?"

"Marion Cummings and she lives in San Antonio." Rachel gave Marshall the address.

He nodded, pulled his phone from his pocket. "Tuck? I need you and Jackson to get to San Antonio ASAP, to take a Marion Cummings and a young girl named Ashley into protective custody."

"Thank you." More tears welled in Rachel's eyes. "We were only supposed to help with hiding the true origin of the campaign funds, but then Joe was told to eliminate the threat or risk our daughter being taken to Mexico and now…" Her voice trailed off again.

And now Joe Strawn was dead.

"As a deputy, he should have known better. He should have come to us," Sam said. "We could have helped him."

Rachel winced and looked away. "Joe was addicted to painkillers after being shot on the job two years ago. The mayor found out about it and threatened to leak the information so he'd lose his job and his pension if he didn't cooperate."

"Better fired than dead," Sam shot back. "I didn't want to shoot him."

"I know. I was afraid he would do something like this. That's why I followed him here." She sniffed again, her gaze going back to her husband. "I guess he's not in pain any longer."

Sam and Marshall exchanged a grim look. The local police arrived then, preventing further conversation. To get out of the way, Mari took Theo back into the motel room, leaving Sam and Marshall to speak with the authorities.

It sounded as if Rachel would testify against Mayor Beaumont. Would that be enough to ensure her and Theo's safety?

She prayed it would. Because right now, she wanted nothing more than to go home, putting this horror and grief behind them.

Even if that meant leaving Sam. As much as she liked, no— *loved* and respected him, she couldn't add to Theo's stress level. The little boy would suffer nightmares enough as it was. Especially now that he was afraid of guns.

The best thing for her son would be to return to their normal routine.

One that didn't include Sam Hayward.

Sam couldn't get the image of Joe Strawn's resigned gaze out of his mind. He kept replaying the sequence of events over and over in his head, wondering if he could have done something different.

Each time, he came to the same conclusion. The deputy had chosen his path. It hurt to know that in those last few seconds Sam hadn't been able to change the deputy's mind. After hearing about his daughter being threatened, Sam couldn't help feeling bad for the guy.

Granted, the cop should have gotten the help he needed to get off using the pain meds and then he should have gone to the authorities right away when the mayor forced him into a life of crime. All Sam could do now was to pray that the little girl and her grandmother would be safe from the long reach of the cartel.

"Ranger Hayward?" Rachel's voice had him turning toward her. "I need to talk to you."

Hesitantly, he crossed the parking lot to where she stood, still cuffed, beside a squad. "Ma'am, you have the right to remain silent," he said. "And the right to an attorney."

"I don't care about that." She lifted her chin. "I want you to know the truth."

He hesitated, unwilling to do this here. "You really need to wait for your lawyer," he tried again.

"I waive my rights. I'm afraid Mayor Beaumont and Doug Granger will get away with this." She sniffled again, glancing at her dead husband. "I want you to know exactly what happened. This all started when I noticed a slew of anonymous donations in relatively small amounts, anywhere from five hundred to a thousand dollars coming into Beaumont's campaign."

Just as they'd thought. "From the cartel?"

"Yes. And Hank George had expressed his concerns about the construction company using so many hired hands and goods from Mexico, so he got rid of the contract. Next thing I know, he's dead and Roy Carlton was arrested for his murder."

"We already figured out that much," Sam said. "But what about Jeff Abbott?"

"That was awful," she said. "Jeff visited Roy in jail, then showed up at the office to tell the mayor—you know he's Jeff's stepfather—about the proof Roy had hidden at the ranch of his innocence. That caused a huge fight. A few weeks later, I was told to contact my husband. That was when Mayor Beaumont told Joe to eliminate the threat." She swallowed hard. "He didn't want to, but Beaumont said the cartel would find Ashley and kill her. So he did that and helped Roy Carlton escape, too so that it would be easier to eliminate him. Joe killed Abbott and left him on the ranch, hoping to implicate Ms. Lynch so that he could get in the house to find the evidence Roy claimed was there. Only Roy surprised him by showing up to kidnap his own son, apparently to get access to the evidence too. Joe said he found Roy hiding in the bushes and dragged him out of there, forcing him to talk. That's when he learned about the evidence Roy had hidden in his son's stuffed animal."

It was all starting to make sense now. "So he took shots at Mari and Theo, trying to get them out of the way."

She grimaced. "I think he only wanted to scare them. Joe wasn't heartless. He didn't want to kill anyone, especially not a young woman and her son. Beaumont made him do it!"

"Okay, I hear you." Sam pulled his phone from his pocket to call his boss. "We need to arrest Beaumont, send teams to both City Hall and his private residence. We have a witness that will testify against him."

"Got it," Owens agreed.

"Are my mother and daughter safe?" Rachel's gaze clung to his. "Will you let me know?"

"It's going to take some time for the rangers to reach San Antonio," he said. "But I will make sure someone lets you know when they're in protective custody."

"Thank you." Rachel closed her eyes and hung her head for a moment. "We shouldn't have let things go this far," she whispered.

That was a massive understatement, but he didn't say anything. Rachel Strawn had already learned the hard way about how bad choices could result in even worse consequences.

He turned away, about to head into the motel to check on Mari and Theo, when he saw two officers kneeling beside Joe Strawn.

"I don't understand why he wasn't wearing a vest," the first officer on the scene said with a frown. "It's a standard part of the uniform."

"Suicide by cop," his female partner said with a shrug. "Wouldn't be the first time."

Sam went still as he once again remembered the resignation in Joe's eyes. The way Joe had wanted him to shoot.

So much death and destruction for what? Money? Power?

He shook his head in frustration. After crossing to the motel room door, he rapped on it with his knuckle. "Mari? Theo? Are you okay?"

There was no response for a moment, then the door opened barely an inch. "Sam?"

"Yes." He waited for Mari to open the door wider. He stepped inside, noticing that she carried Theo with her. The little boy looked at him warily. "Everything okay?"

"We'd like to go home." Mari didn't meet his gaze. "As soon as possible."

He didn't like the sound of that. She was already pulling away from him, acting as if they were barely acquaintances. As if they'd never hugged, kissed or supported each other.

She was ending things before they'd had a chance to develop into something more.

"I promise to take you and Theo home as soon as we know Mayor Beaumont has been taken into custody." He gestured to the bed. "Sit down, Mari. Rachel told me everything and has agreed to testify against Beaumont. You and Theo don't have to be afraid anymore."

"She did?" Mari looked surprised. "I thought she was worried about her daughter?"

"Tucker and Jackson are headed to get her mother and daughter now." He glanced at his watch, surprised more than an hour had passed. "They should be in San Antonio any minute."

"So it really is over," she whispered.

hju"Are you sure about that?" She finally met his gaze. "What about revenge?"

"Beaumont is the one who is at risk of being hurt in revenge from the cartel," he said softly. "Not you and Theo. Unfortunately, your ex-husband is the one who pulled you into this. According to Rachel, her husband is the one who fired shots at you, on Beaumont's orders. And Strawn killed Abbott and your ex, too. They probably wanted Roy to lead them to his hidden evidence, which is exactly what he did."

She closed her eyes for a moment, then nodded. She looked stronger now. "I understand. But we'd still like to go home."

"Soon." He sent Owens a text about letting him know when Beaumont was arrested. Then he sat beside Mari and Theo on the edge of the bed. "I'd like to sleep in your living room for a few days, just to be safe."

Her head snapped around to face him. "You just said we were safe," she accused.

"Yes, but I can't just leave." He hesitated, trying to put his thoughts and feelings into words. "I care about you and Theo. I want to spend some time with you. This way, I can make sure your windows are all repaired."

"I—don't think that's a good idea." She turned away, shifting Theo in her lap.

His stomach dropped. "Why not? No pressure, I only want to help."

"Mr. Sam, I want my toys," Theo said interrupting the moment.

"I know, we'll leave soon." He searched her gaze. "Mari? What's going on?"

"Theo is afraid of…" She gestured to the empty holster on his belt. He'd handed his weapon over to the responding officers as they'd be tasked with investigating the shooting. "He was very scared with everything that happened."

"I see." He turned and knelt in front of Theo. "Theo, I'm sorry you were frightened. But remember how I promised to keep you and your mom safe?"

Theo nodded.

"Well, to do that I had to fire my gun. But then I gave it to the police officers, see?" He made a point of showing his empty holster. "You don't have to be afraid anymore. Because I love your mom and I will do everything in my power to keep you and your mom safe."

"Love?" Mari repeated, her eyes widening.

He looked from Theo up into Mari's wide, green eyes. "Love," he repeated. "I fell in love with you and Theo, too. But I know you don't feel the same way. I only ask that you allow me to stay at the ranch long enough to ensure the window repairs are finished. After that, I'll leave. If that's what you want," he amended. Because in truth, he didn't want to go away from her.

He wanted to stay and celebrate the new year with her. And Theo's birthday, too.

But that wasn't up to him. He wouldn't push himself into Mari's life.

"Oh, Sam." Her eyes filled with tears. "That's so sweet. To be honest, I have fallen in love with you, too."

"Thank the Lord Jesus," he said in a heartfelt prayer. "Mari, I love you more than anything. Just give me a chance to show you how much."

His phone dinged with a text from Owens. It was brief.

We got him.

Hallelujah, he thought. Beaumont was in custody.

"I guess we'll both have to figure out how to make things work," she said with a frown. "You travel a lot and I can't leave the ranch."

"We'll make it work." He bent to give Theo a kiss on his head, then rose to his feet, drawing Mari up, too. Bringing both Mari and Theo into his embrace, he dropped a chaste kiss on Mari's cheek. "Love always finds a way."

"I know." To his surprise, she lifted up to kiss him on the lips. "Thank you for everything, Sam. For saving our lives and for being here when we needed you the most."

"Thank you, Mari." He frowned. "Although I was not happy you charged Doug Granger like an angry bull. Marsh would have taken care of him."

"I was so mad when he turned the gun on you," she admitted sheepishly. "I acted without thinking."

He sighed and hugged her and Theo close. "Well, don't do that again."

"I won't." She grimaced. "I'm still sore from the tackle."

He'd loved the way she cared enough to risk her life, but absolutely didn't want her anywhere near danger ever again. "Beaumont is in custody." He held her gaze. "It's over for good, Mari."

"That's wonderful." Her smile lit up her whole face. "Let's go home, Sam."

Home. The word resonated deep within. And he knew if he had his way, he wouldn't leave Mari and Theo ever again.

Chapter Seventeen

New Year's Eve

The past few days had been wonderful. Mari couldn't believe how easily Sam fit into their lives. Oh, she knew this was a temporary reprieve, because Sam would still have to travel with his job, but during the time they had together, Sam was an equal partner. They shared a camaraderie she'd never experienced before.

When she'd suggested grilled steaks, potatoes and salads for dinner, he'd immediately volunteered to cook. And she wasn't sure how, but he'd gotten her windows replaced within twenty-four hours of their return to the ranch, too. The routine ranch chores didn't take nearly as long with Sam's helping hand. She had no doubt that her father would have loved Sam, which was the exact opposite of how he'd felt toward Roy.

Theo still had the occasional nightmare, but with Sam sleeping on the living room sofa, one of them was quickly able to help soothe Theo's fears.

"Can I stay up to see the New Year?" Theo asked when they'd finished eating.

"You can try," Mari agreed. "But it's okay if you fall asleep because we can celebrate the New Year in the morning, too. Don't forget, day two is your birthday. You don't want to be sleepy on your birthday, right?"

"Right." That seemed to satisfy him.

Sam met her gaze across the kitchen, and the promise of a new year kiss in his gaze made her blush.

He'd been so sweet, she sometimes pinched herself to make sure she wasn't dreaming.

"I heard from my boss yesterday while I was out shopping." Sam's tone was casual, but his gaze had turned serious.

"Oh?" She mentally braced herself. "About Beaumont?"

He nodded. "Beaumont gave up the cartel members he knew by name in exchange for a lesser sentence." He paused, then added, "Unfortunately, he was found dead in his cell the following morning. Apparently, the cartel has members inside the prison."

She sucked in a quick breath. "That's horrible."

"Yes. But we have issued several arrest warrants for those members. We'll continue keeping Marion and Ashley in protective custody and the federal marshals are working to get Marion, Ashley and Rachel new identities so they can start over. We know Roy spoke to Abbott shortly before his escape was arranged, so that part of Rachel's story pans out, too. And Longhorn Construction is out of business for good." He smiled. "I suspect the cartel members will head back to Mexico rather than risk being caught."

That was good news, although she still couldn't believe so many people had lost their lives over this. Then again, each of those involved had made a choice.

Bad choices. And she couldn't help but be relieved that Roy wasn't around to pose a threat any longer.

"I guess all we can do is to pray," she murmured.

"Yes," he agreed.

She joined Sam at the sink to finish the dishes. Then they all headed into the living room. She was doubly glad now that she still had her brightly lit tree. Mari was about to sit on the sofa, urging Sam to join her, when he took Theo's hand.

"Are you ready?" Sam asked Theo.

Her son nodded, looking excited. Then he turned to face her. "Mom, Sam asked me and I said yes."

"Yes, to what?" She was confused, but Sam just chuckled.

"He forgot the first part," Sam said with a wry grin. "Remember Theo? We practiced this morning. I asked you if I could marry your mom and you said yes."

"Yes!" Theo jumped up and down with excitement. "I said yes!"

She laughed, tears of joy pricking her eyes. She met Sam's gaze and her heart filled with joy.

"Ah, Mari. I love you so much." Sam pulled out a small ring box featuring a beautiful, shiny diamond ring. "Will you please marry me?"

"Yes, Sam. I would love to marry you." She let him put the ring on her finger then jumped up to hug him. They kissed, then he bent to lift Theo up so he could be a part of their embrace.

"Happy New Year, Mari and Theo," he said in a husky voice. It wasn't even close to midnight, but that didn't matter.

"Happy New Year, Sam." She kissed him again, then nestled her head into his shoulder. With God's love and grace enveloping them, she couldn't imagine a better way to start the new year.

And their new life together.

* * * * *

Alaskan Wilderness Peril

Beth Carpenter

MILLS & BOON

Beth Carpenter is thankful for good books, a good dog, a good man and a dream job creating happily-ever-afters. She and her husband now split their time between Alaska and Arizona, where she occasionally encounters a moose in the yard or a scorpion in the basement. She prefers the moose.

Books by Beth Carpenter

Alaskan Wilderness Peril

A Northern Lights Novel

The Alaskan Catch
A Gift for Santa
Alaskan Hideaway
An Alaskan Proposal
Sweet Home Alaska
Alaskan Dreams
An Alaskan Family Christmas
An Alaskan Homecoming
An Alaskan Family Found

Visit the Author Profile page at
millsandboon.com.au.

But they that wait upon the Lord shall renew their
strength; they shall mount up with wings as eagles;
they shall run, and not be weary;
and they shall walk, and not faint.
—*Isaiah* 40:31

To Teri,

You taught me how to play jacks,
how to put on makeup and how to dance the hustle,
but most importantly, you taught me what
best friends are all about. Thank you for being my friend.

Chapter One

"Less than three months until summer," Hannah Yates reminded herself as she wedged her SUV between Sue Ann's pickup and the pile of snow plowed into the corner of her store's tiny employee parking lot.

Now that March had arrived, the sun was high enough to begin melting the snowbanks on south-facing slopes in Anchorage during the day. By June, the snow would be gone, the mountains would be green again, and tourists would be flocking to the store, snapping selfies beside the enormous fuchsia basket Hannah always hung out front and shopping for gifts and souvenirs. But first came the rest of the winter and breakup, the messy season when snow melted, roads and parking lots turned to ice, and cars wore coats of road grime.

Hannah managed to squeeze out her door without dinging Sue Ann's truck and opened the back gate of her SUV, revealing the precious things she'd picked up at auction earlier. She grabbed a cardboard box and carried it to the rear door of Hannah's Alaskan Treasures, downtown's most popular antique store, and Hannah's pride and joy. Propping the box on one hip, she dug out her keys and let herself in.

Sue Ann, her store manager, appeared through the curtain

separating the workroom from the front of the store and hurried to hold the door for Hannah. "I hope you got the carnival glass you wanted." Sue Ann pronounced the "I" as "ahh." She had lived in Alaska for twenty-five years now, but she'd never lost her Kentucky accent.

"Thanks." Hannah set the box on her workbench. "No, I didn't get it. The bidding got too rich."

Sue Ann raised her eyebrows. "Nicole again?" She opened the box and began removing the bubble wrap on the items inside.

"Uh-huh." Hannah's sister, who had her own antique store in South Anchorage, delighted in competing with Hannah at auctions and sales. Even though their inventories didn't have that much overlap—Nicole specialized in antique jewelry, coins, and small decorative items while Hannah focused on furniture and home accessories—there always seemed to be something they both wanted. "The carnival glass wasn't a big deal," she told Sue Ann, "but there was a jewelry box I really hated losing out on. The inlay was just gorgeous. Let me show you."

Hannah grabbed her phone and pulled up the photo showing intricate patterns of light and dark wood inlaid to form the shape of a blooming trumpet vine meandering around the box. A heart-shaped padlock held the box closed. "The detail was incredible. It's hard to see in the photo, but there were veins in the leaves and stamens in the flowers."

Sue Ann zoomed in to study the pattern. "Nice. Did it come with a key?"

"No, it was sold 'as is' with the lock still on, but it felt empty. The lock looked more decorative than secure, so it shouldn't be hard to get off. There were several bidders. I dropped out at two hundred dollars, but Nicole kept going until she got it for five hundred. I told her I can't see how she can make a profit after paying that much, but—"

"She said to mind your own business," Sue Ann predicted

as she finished unwrapping the top item in the box. "Which it looks like you did. I love this stained-glass lampshade."

"Gorgeous, isn't it? I got a great candelabra and a classic silver bowl, too. And a box of blown glass Christmas ornaments. I also found a chest of drawers," she added as she rolled the furniture dolly from the corner of the workroom. "It's nothing particularly valuable, but it had a great shape and I got it for a song because it's grungy and the bottom drawer is stuck closed. Once I repair and refinish it, it will look fantastic."

"Need a hand bringing it in?" Sue Ann offered, but just then the bells on the front door jingled, signaling a new customer. "Sorry, I've got to get that. Tiff isn't in yet." She returned to the front of the store, leaving Hannah to deal with the chest by herself.

Fortunately, it wasn't a particularly big piece, and she was able to unload it and roll it into the workroom without much trouble. Once she'd closed the back door and shed her coat, she scrubbed off the dirt, thrilled to find intact Birdseye maple veneer on the curved drawers, rather than the pine she'd expected.

The back door rattled and then opened. "I know. I'm late." Tiffany, a college student who worked at the store part-time, said as she rushed in, slipping out of her coat as she did. "Class ran long today." She hung her coat and bag on a peg on the wall and ducked through the curtains before Hannah could do more than nod hello.

Once again, Hannah breathed a little prayer of thanks that she had Sue Ann to manage all the hiring and scheduling, leaving her to concentrate on inventory. She returned to the chest of drawers. The top was solid maple. It had minor water damage, but a deep sanding would take care of that. She'd originally planned to paint the piece, but it would be a shame to cover that beautiful wood grain.

The top three drawers slid open easily to reveal yellowed vintage wallpaper liners, but the bottom drawer wouldn't budge. She turned the chest upside down to see if she could find the problem. Surprisingly, she was able to slide out the bottom divider panel without removing any nails. It wasn't even glued. Once she had moved that out of the way and exposed the drawer runners, it became clear why the drawer wouldn't open. Someone had put a screw through the bottom stile, directly into the center brace of the drawer. Odd.

She pulled a Phillips screwdriver from its holder on the pegboard and removed the screw. After she turned the chest right side up, the bottom drawer opened easily, revealing a Styrofoam rectangle cut to the exact dimensions of the drawer with two one-inch holes in diameter near the center. Hannah put her fingers in the holes and removed the foam. Underneath, another thicker layer of foam filled the drawer, but in the center was a circular cutout, and in that cutout lay a wooden ball about the size of a large grapefruit.

Someone had gone to a lot of trouble here. She picked up the ball and carried it to the workbench where the light was better. It was a wood inlay globe of the world. The continents and islands were made of light-and medium-colored wood, while the oceans looked like walnut. A giddy feeling bubbled up inside her. Almost certainly, this was the work of the same artist who had made the marquetry box Nicole won at the auction.

Hannah pulled a magnifying glass from the drawer for a closer look. Tiny triangles of dark wood edged with even darker strips gave the subtle appearance of waves in the ocean. The continents, too, were composed of minuscule shapes, with rough triangles along major mountain ranges and rounded shapes on the plains. An intricate compass rose floated in the center of the Atlantic Ocean, and a starburst marked the North Pole. Twenty-four longitudinal lines of tarnished silver flowed from pole to pole.

It was an incredible work of art. How could someone cut such tiny, precise shapes, much less inlay them in such an intricate pattern? She considered calling the auction house to report the unexpected find, but the terms of sale were "as is," which meant the globe was hers.

Hannah ducked through the curtain to show it to Sue Ann, but she was busy with a customer going through a stack of quilts. Tiffany was ringing up a set of copper molds for another customer. The front door opened and Charlie Cutlass, one of Hannah's favorite suppliers, stepped inside carrying a plastic bin. Hannah set the globe behind the counter and went to greet him.

"Hi, Charlie. I hope you've got more of those animal puzzles. We've almost sold out." Hannah reserved a section of the store for what she called "future antiques," where she sold works by local craftspeople on consignment. Charlie specialized in wood, turning bowls and candlesticks on his lathe and using his jigsaw to cut Christmas ornaments, whirligigs, and toys. His puzzles in the shapes of moose, bears, puffins, and eagles were always a favorite souvenir gift for children. She cleared some room on his display table.

"I do." He unpacked several puzzles, along with some animal-shaped ornaments with raffia hanging loops. Hannah helped him add them on the display rack. Then he unwrapped two rolling pins, made by gluing various woods together and then turning them on a lathe, forming stripes of distinct colors along the length of the pins.

"Oh, these are gorgeous!" Hannah ran her finger along the polished wood. "People will love them."

"I hope so. Is forty too much?" He pointed to the tag, which he'd already marked with the price and his initials. When they sold a consignment piece, the store kept a quarter and paid the rest to the artist.

"No, not for something as beautiful as this. If anything, you're low."

"Well, let's try it at that price and see if they sell."

"Sounds good." Hannah signed a receipt listing all the items

Charlie had brought. "Oh, I got something at auction today you'd be interested in. Let me show you."

He followed her to the counter. "The Linacott auction?"

"Yes. Today was the first day. Tomorrow and Saturday will be the high-dollar furniture and art, but that's out of my price range."

"I'll bet you had quite a crowd there. Lots of rumors floating around about that lady."

"Oh? Like what?"

"People said that if a collector was looking for something specific, Candace Linacott could find it, but they'd better not ask too many questions about where she got it."

"You think she imported things illegally?" Hannah asked as they came to the counter.

Charlie shrugged. "Who knows? Maybe people were just jealous of her success. You remember, shortly after she died, someone broke into her house on the coastal trail. I don't know if they ever figured out what was stolen. That was, what, three years ago? I wonder why it took them so long to hold this auction."

"The story I heard was that she left everything to a distant relative in Australia who had never even met her, so it took a while to get it all organized. And, apparently, she had stuff in storage lockers all over town. Some of it was incredibly valuable. Just think how easy it would have been for whoever handled the estate to overlook those rental payments and for the storage facility to throw out those antiques and collectibles thinking they were just junk." Hannah shuddered.

"Yeah, or auctioned it off to an upscaler who would have painted over a Chippendale or some other treasure."

"Speaking of treasure…" Hannah took the globe from the shelf and handed it to Charlie. "What do you think of this?"

"Wow!" Charlie pulled the piece close to his eye. "The detail is incredible. It's not brand-new, but it doesn't look that old, either. Do you know who made it?"

Hannah shook her head. "Believe it or not, I found it in the drawer of a dresser I bought. No provenance. I was hoping you might know."

"I don't, but I know someone who might." Charlie pulled out his phone and swiped through a few screens. "Here it is. Peter Morozov from up north. He specializes in wood art." Charlie passed her his phone, and Hannah entered the information into her own phone.

"Thanks, Charlie. I'll let you know what I find out."

They chatted for a few more minutes, and then Charlie took his leave. Once Hannah had emailed the expert, she took the globe with her to the workroom and began to unpack the other items. She'd unwrapped the bowl and was reaching for silver polish when her phone chimed. A text from Nicole.

Got the lock open, and already sold the box for a sixty-per-cent markup!

She didn't add, "Na-na-na-na-na," but Hannah could read between the lines. Hannah should never have mentioned her misgivings about the price Nicole had paid. At that point, the money was spent, so even if Hannah had been right, it wouldn't have been helpful. Hannah sighed. Here she was, thirty-one years old, and she was still letting her little sister draw her into these petty battles. Time to be gracious.

Congratulations, she texted back, before turning her attention to the photos Nicole had attached. That box really was lovely, with the flowering vine pattern weaving over the top and sides. Even the interior of the box, shown in the second photo, was inlaid with a diamond pattern of light and dark woods. Beside the box lay an index card that had presumably been inside. Hannah enlarged the photo to see if she could read the card. Nothing but a few scribbles: N, S CW 30: E CCW 45: CR

Before she could study it further, she noticed a new email. The expert wanted photos of her globe. She set it on her worktable beside a ruler for scale and took three. Almost immediately after she'd sent them, her phone rang.

"This is Peter Morozov. Am I speaking to Hannah Yates?"

"Yes, hello, Mr. Morozov. Did the photos make it all right?"

"They did, and please call me Peter. Hannah, I believe you may have a Dimitri Karas there."

"K-a-r-a-s?" Hannah confirmed as she jotted down the name.

"That's right. Prolific artist, passed away two years ago. I can't quite make out the fine detail from your photograph but look closely. Is there a letter *K* embedded in the pattern anywhere?"

"Let me see what I can find." Hannah picked up her magnifying glass and studied the globe for a few moments. "Yes! I can see four *K*s as part of the pattern in the compass rose."

"Excellent! Most of his work is chests and jewelry boxes, but every year he would put out a few balls, either globes like yours or decorative Christmas ornaments. Lovely, intricate work. Once, I even got the chance to examine one of his puzzle boxes, but they're incredibly rare."

"Puzzle boxes?"

"Yes, he made a few custom ones for select clients, little cubes about eight inches tall with the puzzle embedded in the inlay pattern. Two years ago, one sold for just under twenty thousand."

"What would you estimate a globe like mine would be worth?" Hannah asked.

"Well, if I can verify that your globe is indeed a Karas original, I'm willing to pay you, say, five thousand dollars."

Wow. And Hannah thought Nicole overpaid at five hundred for the jewelry box. Trying to keep the excitement from her voice, she asked, "And how much will you turn around and sell it for?"

He chuckled. "That depends. I happen to know two or three people who collect Karas, so I'd just have to see who wants it most. You could try selling it yourself, of course, but it's a niche market."

He was right about that. Her store customers generally weren't the sort to buy five-thousand-dollar knickknacks. She could try to sell the globe online, but that brought its own set of headaches. She would do a little research, but his price seemed reasonable. "I might be interested in a sale. Will you be in Anchorage anytime soon?"

"I'm afraid not. My first grandchild is due to make an appearance in the next week or so, and I can't miss that."

"Ah, congratulations. I can see why you wouldn't want to travel."

"Thank you. Any chance you could bring it to me? I'd be willing to add another five hundred to cover your expenses if you will bring it to Fairbanks."

Fairbanks. A sudden pang pierced Hannah's heart. She'd grown up in Fairbanks, but she hadn't been back in thirteen years, not since the summer of her best friend's funeral. She'd briefly considered attending her high school class's ten-year reunion, but with Lindsay gone, there didn't seem to be much point. Besides, she might have run into Lindsay's family and the last thing she wanted was to cause them any more pain. But she'd heard that Lindsay's parents had retired and moved to Idaho. Maybe it was time to visit Fairbanks again. "When would you want to meet?"

"The sooner the better."

She considered. "Let me check on a few things. I'll see if I can get a flight tomorrow morning."

"Tomorrow works. I'll text you my address. Let me know your plans."

"I will. Thanks." She hung up the phone. Five thousand dollars! She'd only paid fifty for the chest of drawers. A little research on her laptop verified that a Dimitri Karas jewelry box would sell to a collector for something in the neighborhood of eight thousand dollars, and a Karas Christmas ornament with a star pattern had sold at auction for a little over six thousand three months ago. Five thousand for her globe sounded more than fair. She pulled up the photo of the jewelry box Nicole had sent and zoomed in. Sure enough, she could make out a K in the design of one of the leaves on the vine.

Should she tell her sister the box she had sold for eight hundred dollars might be worth ten times that? Probably not. Besides, if Hannah planned to fly to Fairbanks tomorrow, she had more urgent things to do than torment Nicole. Still, she couldn't resist sending her a photo and text. Look what was in the drawer of that old chest!

Checking online, Hannah found a flight in the morning, but she couldn't get on a return flight the same day, so she reserved one for the next morning, Sunday. It would mean missing her usual church service, but that couldn't be helped. By the time Hannah had booked her flights and hotel, and set up a meeting with Peter Morozov, it was almost closing time.

She ducked through the curtain to the storefront, where Tiff was ringing up a customer. Sue Ann tidied up a nearby display of *ulus*, traditional Inuit crescent-shaped knives, while two or three customers casually browsed in the same area.

"Did you call the expert Charlie recommended?" Sue Ann asked Hannah.

"I did, and it's definitely the same artist that made Nicole's box. You're never going to believe what the expert said." Hannah told her all about the offer and Peter's request that she bring the globe to him.

"Five thousand dollars!" Sue Ann squealed, and the customers all looked in her direction. In a quieter voice she added, "That's incredible."

"I know. I figured I'd better head up to Fairbanks before he changes his mind. I booked an early flight for tomorrow morning and I'm meeting up with him at ten. I plan to stay overnight and fly back the next morning. You're okay running the store without me, right?"

"Absolutely. Where are you staying in Fairbanks?"

"At the Young Hotel near the airport. It's a seven thirty return flight, so I should be back in time to open Sunday afternoon. I know you have that Bible study on Sundays."

"Don't worry about it. I have Tiff and Cheryl scheduled to
open that day, and my class ends at two. Ooh, I'm so excited."

"Me, too." Hannah noticed that one of the customers, a tall
blond man wearing shades and a black down jacket, was hovering nearby with a gold pan, as if he was ready to check out.
Tiff was busy talking to another customer in the crafts area.

Hannah stepped up to the counter and the man set the pan
down and reached for his wallet. Hannah smiled. "This pan
dates back to the 1899 gold rush in Nome. We acquired it from
the great-granddaughter of a miner who went there in early
1900. The provenance is on the attached card."

The man just grunted and looked away while she rang up and
bagged his purchase. He paid cash, took one last look around
the now-empty store, and left. Hannah followed him to the door
and locked it, then turned the sign to Closed.

Tiff immediately headed for the curtain leading to the back
room. "Sorry, I have to go. Study session."

"Okay," Sue Ann called, but the clang of the back door closing was her only answer.

Hannah raised an eyebrow. "A study session on a Friday
night?"

Sue Ann chuckled. "More likely a date."

Together, Hannah and Sue Ann went through the closing
routine. Once they had finished, Hannah encased the globe in
bubble wrap and tucked it into her tote next to the cash bag. "I
think I'll grab some dinner at Kriner's Diner after I make the
night deposit. Then I'd better head home and pack."

Sue Ann grinned. "Breakfast for dinner again, huh?"

"Kriner's has other things on the menu," Hannah protested.

"Yeah, but you're not going to order them." Sue Ann knew
her so well. "Bradley is cooking tonight so it will probably be

moose burgers for us. Have a great trip. I can't wait to hear all about it."

"Thanks, Sue Ann. See you in a couple of days." Hannah set the alarm at the store, and they drove off in different directions.

Hannah deposited the day's cash and headed for the diner, where she declined a menu and put in her usual order. She was tempted to take the globe from her tote to study while she waited for food, but since she'd wrapped it up, she contented herself with studying the photos she'd taken. The longer she looked, the more details she noticed, like flowing shapes along major rivers, and the way the equator was made up of several razor-thin lines of wood, rather than one piece.

The waiter brought her waffles with a side of reindeer sausage. Hannah bowed her head for a silent grace and then continued to study the photos while she ate. An alert popped up on her phone. The store security system had gone off!

Maybe it was a false alarm. She pushed the plate away and pulled up the security camera view. A dark figure in a hooded down jacket climbed through the smashed front window and ran through the store until he disappeared from the camera's view just past the front counter.

Hannah threw enough cash to cover her dinner and tip on the table and called to the waiter, "Sorry, I have an emergency."

"Do you want me to box up the rest?" he asked as Hannah pulled on her coat, but she shook her head.

"No time, but thanks." She ran to the parking lot, jumped into her SUV, and headed for the store.

By the time she arrived, the police were there. Broken glass littered the sidewalk and glinted from the seat of a chair displayed in the window. Hannah identified herself, and one of the police officers took her aside. "Looks like a smash and grab. Can you spot anything missing from your window display from here?"

Hannah looked it over. The items in the bookcase seemed undisturbed, as did the floor lamp and the throw she'd arranged over the arm of the chair. The side table was knocked over, spilling a vase and book onto the floor, but they appeared undamaged.

She showed the officer the camera footage of the burglar heading straight for the back of the store, not even stopping to check the till. Maybe he'd guessed that the cash drawer would be locked up in the safe in the back. He seemed tall, but with the low lighting, she couldn't make out his face or anything distinctive about him. "It doesn't show him coming back, so I assume he left through the back door."

"It was standing open when we got here," the police officer confirmed. "Do you have cameras in the back?"

"No." It hadn't occurred to her that she might need them.

"Okay. Well, once we're done, we'll have you do a walk-through and figure out what's missing."

"Will you be taking fingerprints?" Hannah asked.

He shook his head. "Too many people in and out of a store for fingerprints to mean much. Besides, it looked like in your video that he was wearing gloves."

A green pickup truck pulled up to the curb, and Sue Ann jumped out of the passenger seat and ran to pull Hannah into a hug. "I got the alert. Are you okay?"

"I'm fine," Hannah assured her. "You didn't have to come."

"We brought plywood," Sue Ann's husband, Bradley, said as he joined them. "Once they're done here, we can board up the window until you can get it repaired."

"Thank you. I hadn't even thought that far ahead. I guess I won't be going to Fairbanks tomorrow."

Sue Ann gasped. "Did they steal the globe?"

"No, I had it with me."

"Oh, thank goodness. Then you have to go," Sue Ann insisted. "You've got the flight all booked and that appointment with the expert. I can handle cleaning up the glass and getting the window fixed and whatever else needs doing tomorrow. Sir?" She tapped the police officer on the arm. "I'm Sue

Ann Bolton, Hannah's store manager. Hannah has an important meeting in Fairbanks tomorrow. I can sign police reports or whatever you need done, right?"

"When will you be back?" he asked Hannah.

"Sunday morning," she answered.

"No problem, then. You'll just need to sign the report in the next week or so. Technically, you have a year to file a report, but your insurance will want it before they process your claim."

"I'll call the insurance agent, too," Sue Ann told her. "See, no reason to put off the trip."

Bradley nodded. "We've got you covered."

"All right then, I'll go. Thank you." Hannah wrapped her arms around both of them. "You're the best."

Chapter Two

On the flight the next morning, Hannah wasn't so sure that Sue Ann and Bradley had done her any favors urging her to take the trip. It had been close to ten last night before the police had finished and allowed them to board up the window. Oddly, the only things that seemed to be missing from the store were the candelabra and a box of Christmas ornaments she'd gotten at the auction and left in the back room. The police surmised that the burglar had heard the sirens and fled before he'd had a chance to grab more. It was close to midnight when Hannah finished packing. Then she'd been up at four thirty to catch the seven o'clock flight.

But by the time the flight attendant asked for seats up and tray tables folded, Hannah had gotten her second wind. She nudged the small backpack with the globe inside farther under the seat in front of her and looked out the window. The braided Tanana River looped along the southern edge of Fairbanks, while its smaller tributary, the Chena, meandered through the center of town, reminding Hannah of hot summer days when she and Lindsay would float along it on inner tubes. Snow covered the soccer fields where they had played together. And over there was the neighborhood where Lindsay had lived in a rambling house with her parents, her brother Jace, and a menagerie of dogs, cats, and the occasional rabbit or guinea pig. Hannah had spent almost as much time at Lindsay's house as she had her own.

She still thought of Lindsay often. Whenever she saw kids dressed in their soccer uniforms, or came across the cross-country ski teams practicing, or when certain songs came on the car radio, Hannah would be transported back to when the two of them were almost inseparable. If only they'd been together that last night, it might have changed everything.

The plane landed, and Hannah collected her luggage and her rental car, a small SUV in a distinctive shade of orange, shivering as she did. Years of living in Anchorage's relatively mild climate had made her forget just how cold Fairbanks could be in March. She set her daypack holding the globe in the passenger seat, cranked up the heat, and checked the time. She still had forty-five minutes before her appointment, plenty of time for a quick drive through town.

Not much had changed in thirteen years. Oh, there were new buildings, new roads, but the town still seemed familiar. Out of curiosity, she drove by the house where she'd grown up. The birch sapling her dad had planted the year before they left had grown tall, its white-barked trunk thick and sturdy. The current owners had painted the house a pleasant grayish blue. Two sleds were leaning against the porch railing. It looked like a happy family home, just like it had been for Hannah and Nicole.

Nicole hadn't been in Fairbanks that last summer. Dad had taken a new job in Anchorage, and Nicole had opted to transfer to school there for the last semester of her sophomore year. Since Hannah was a senior, she and her mother had stayed in Fairbanks until Hannah graduated and Mom could sell the house, which had ended up taking longer than she'd hoped. Hannah didn't mind. She and Lindsay stayed busy making plans for fall, when they would be roommates in the dorm at Arizona State. Lindsay's mom, Judy, used to laugh and say it was only because levelheaded Hannah would be with her that she'd even considered letting Lindsay go to college so far away. But they never made it to Arizona.

Instead, it all ended that Friday evening in July. Lindsay had called, all excited. She'd heard about a party at someone's house out in the country and she wanted Hannah to go with her and some of their classmates. Hannah knew the guy whose parents were away, and she had a fairly good idea what would be going on at the party. She'd tried to talk Lindsay out of it, but Lindsay was determined to get out from under her strict parents' control. "Come on. We're eighteen. In a month, we're going to be college students. We need to cut loose, at least once, while we're still in town."

Hannah had refused to go, but at Lindsay's urging, she'd agreed to cover for her. Hannah's mom, a nurse, was working an overnight shift at the hospital that night, so Hannah was the one who answered the landline when Judy called to check on her daughter. Hannah told her that Lindsay was in the bathroom, but that they were fine and that her mom would be home soon, when the truth was her mom's nursing shift at the hospital didn't end until seven the next morning and Lindsay was, even then, on her way to the party.

Three hours later, Hannah's mom called from the hospital to say Lindsay had been brought in by ambulance and was going in for emergency surgery.

Hannah had rushed to the hospital and found Lindsay's parents already there, in the waiting room. They both looked as though they had aged decades that night. Hannah hurried to them, "I'm so sorry—" she started to say, but Judy held up a hand.

"Stop." Her voice shook with suppressed anger. "I can't deal with you right now. Not with Lindsay in there fighting for her life. Go home, Hannah."

Russell's expression, when he met Hannah's eyes, held sympathy, but he nodded, reinforcing his wife's directive. So Hannah went. It wasn't until the next day that she learned the rest of the story. The car Lindsay had been riding in had gone off the road, rolled down an embankment, and hit a tree. The driver's blood alcohol level tested at twice the legal limit. He and the other two passengers were severely injured, although they eventually recovered. But Lindsay, who had been in the passenger seat on the side of the car that slammed into the tree, died in surgery.

Not wanting to make things worse, Hannah stayed away from Lindsay's parents at the funeral, blending into the crowd. Lindsay's mom seemed almost disoriented, and Hannah got the feeling if Judy hadn't had her husband to lean on, she would have melted into a heap of misery and never moved again. At the end of the service, the family left the church first. Neither of Lindsay's parents looked up as they made their way down the aisle, but Lindsay's brother, Jace, glanced toward Hannah. And in that moment, Hannah could read in his eyes all the pain and suffering Lindsay's death had caused. Pain and suffering that might not have happened if Hannah hadn't lied.

According to a classmate who stopped by Hannah's store a few months ago, Lindsay's parents had retired and moved south. Jace was now running the family's outdoor outfitters. Angeles Adventure Store had flourished in the past few years, and was about to open a branch in Anchorage, but Fairbanks was still their headquarters. Maybe after her appointment, Hannah should drop by the store and see if Jace was there. Or maybe not.

Hannah couldn't remember a time when she didn't have a bit of a crush on Lindsay's older brother, although she went to great lengths to make sure nobody ever knew about it. Jace, with his dark hair and laughing eyes. In her memory, he always seemed to be on his way to some great adventure, but when he passed Lindsay and Hannah, he would slow down long enough to flash a smile and talk for a moment. In high school, Hannah used to have this fantasy that one day Jace would notice that she was more than just his pesky little sister's sidekick and would fall madly in love with her. Now, she'd be thrilled if he didn't hate her.

No, it would be better to steer clear of Jace while she was here. Better to concentrate on her own business. She turned her car toward Peter Morozov's address and ten minutes later, she pulled up in front of a tall taupe-colored house with modern angles. It sat next to a forested greenbelt, and she noticed a couple with a border collie strolling down the pathway nearby. The numbers on the front porch verified that Hannah was in the right place. She climbed out of the car and was walking around to collect her pack from the other side when a man stepped out of the trees in the greenbelt and approached her.

"Hi. I'm Peter's neighbor, Jim White. Peter said you're bringing him something special today. Unfortunately, he was called away this morning, but he said he wouldn't be long and asked if I would have you wait at my house until he could return."

Hannah hesitated. Peter had her number. If he had to cancel, wouldn't he have contacted her? Then she realized her phone was still on airplane mode. She turned that off and a text popped up. So sorry. Have to run out. Family emergency. Will contact you later today to reschedule.

There was no mention of a neighbor. Something here didn't seem right. Jim White stood, waiting. Hannah eased a couple of steps backward. "Thanks, anyway, but I'll just contact Peter later."

The man moved closer. "Peter would kill me if I let you go. He's excited about whatever it is you're bringing him. I have coffee and donuts. We can chat until he arrives, and maybe you can give me a sneak peek."

"I appreciate the offer." Hannah was at the driver's-side door of her car now. "But no."

His smile slipped. He stepped forward and wrapped his hand around her arm. "We can't disappoint Peter—"

Hannah took a quick look around. The couple with the border collie was gone, but another woman with a German shepherd came into view. Hannah spoke loudly. "Let go of me!"

The woman stopped. "Are you okay?" she called, pulling her phone from her pocket. The dog bared his teeth.

Jim White dropped Hannah's arm and stepped back, holding up his hands. "Everything's fine. Just a little misunderstanding."

Hannah didn't wait to see if he apologized. She jumped into her car, locked the doors, and started the engine. When the man didn't immediately move from in front of her car, she backed up and then pulled into the street, waving her thanks to the dog walker as she passed by.

Her heart was still racing when she pulled out of the neighborhood and onto the main road a few minutes later. Maybe Jim White was just an overzealous friend of Peter's, but better safe than sorry. She stopped at a red light and pulled out her phone to text Peter, but before she could get more than two words typed, the white truck behind her honked and she realized the light had turned green. She pulled forward.

She clicked on the radio, hoping for some calming music, but a news bulletin came on instead. She was about to change the station when she heard, "A pregnant woman was injured downtown this morning by a hit-and-run driver while crossing the street. She has been taken to Fairbanks Memorial Hospital. Her condition is unknown at this time. If anyone has information about this incident, please contact police through the anonymous tip line." It gave the number and email address for the hotline.

Could it be Peter's daughter who was hit? That would explain the family emergency. Whoever it was must be frightened and in pain. Hannah said a prayer for the woman and her unborn child. Could the hit and run have any connection to Hannah's altercation with Jim White? She glanced at her daypack, holding the Dimitri Karas globe. That was ridiculous. Nobody would go to such elaborate lengths for a wooden globe worth five thousand dollars. But she still didn't feel safe.

Where should she go now? It was too early to check into her hotel. Besides, she didn't want to be alone. She supposed she could go to a coffee shop or mall somewhere, but before she headed downtown, she passed a direction sign for Ice Alaska. Perfect. When she lived in Fairbanks, she'd gone to see the International Ice Sculpture Championships every year. There were always crowds of people there. She made a quick right turn and followed the direction signs to the park.

Sure enough, there were plenty of cars in the parking lot, and a tour bus pulled in just behind her. She put on a hat, gloves, and scarf, grabbed her daypack, and followed a group of tourists to the admission gate. A love seat with a heart-shaped back carved from a block of ice stood outside the gate. The tourists stopped to take photos of each other posing there, allowing Hannah to step to the front of the line for admission. She paid and made her way inside the park.

A wonderland of ice surrounded her. This area was an ice playground for children and a few fun-loving adults. Directly in front was a ship carved from ice. Children and parents climbed steps to various levels and then took the ice slides down. There were several photo stations, with animals, fairies, and other creatures carved from ice with an opening for visitors to insert their own faces. Child-sized saucers of ice rested here and there, and children were sitting in them, spinning on the ice. A direction sign pointed toward an ice maze.

Hannah stepped aside and texted Peter that she had gotten his message. She started to ask about his neighbor, but she hesitated. Maybe it was all a setup. Peter had seemed trustworthy on the phone, but what did she really know about him? A minute later, her phone rang.

"Hannah, it's Peter. I apologize, but I'm not going to be able to meet with you today. My daughter was hit by a car this morning, and she's going in for an emergency C-section right now."

"I'm so sorry," Hannah told him, feeling bad about her suspicions. "I understand completely. I'll keep your family in my prayers."

"Thank you. We can use all the prayers we can get. I'll give you a call in the next week or so and see about reimbursing you for your travel expenses since we weren't able to meet."

"Please don't worry about that. You just concentrate on your family."

"I will. Thanks."

Hannah tucked the phone into her pocket and whispered another prayer for Peter and his family. She wanted to catch a plane and head home right away, but the reason she'd booked a hotel in the first place was that she couldn't find a seat on a flight to Anchorage this evening. She was stuck in Fairbanks until tomorrow morning. Might as well make the best of it.

She left the playground area and headed toward the single block competition. These were sculptures carved from a block of ice around eight feet high, five feet wide, and two-and-a-half feet thick, and as she recalled, they weighed over seven thousand pounds. The extreme cold here meant the ice on the nearby pond froze thick and clear, perfect for carving.

Looking at the sculptures, Hannah found it hard to believe they were all created from identical blocks of ice. Some were solid and strong, like the grizzly rearing on his hind legs, and the medieval castle that seemed to grow from a rocky mountainside. Others were ethereal, a ballerina with her arm and leg extended gracefully, and a giant dragonfly. Many of the sculptures captured minute details like the individual scales and flowing tresses of a mermaid. A stylized teardrop was composed of smooth flowing lines, emphasizing the clarity of the ice. After it got dark, colored spotlights would make the sculptures even more beautiful. She should come back and see them again tonight.

She moved on to the multi-block sculptures, where blocks had been stacked and carved by teams into enormous works of art. She walked along the path, joining groups of visitors who oohed and aahed over the ships, castles, herds of animals, friezes, and even a life-size elephant.

Hannah thought about the year she'd visited the ice sculptures with Lindsay's family. It had been a rare sunny, twenty-five-degree day. She and Lindsay had been about fourteen, so Jace would have been sixteen, but they'd played on the ice as joyfully as any little kids. Lindsay's dad Russell had insisted on taking photos of everything in the park. Hannah was pretty sure she still had a print somewhere of her and Jace in the iconic Titanic pose on the bow of an ice ship. So many good memories.

If only she could go back in time to be with Lindsay again, whispering about the cute new guy in history class and complaining about the extra math homework Mr. Tolliver had assigned. Holding up bunny ears in group photos and making jokes about how the sculptor should have carved goose bumps on the hula dancer.

Even better, if Lindsay could be with Hannah here today. They'd had such plans. They were both going to study nursing at Arizona State, and then explore the country together as traveling nurses, taking assignments here and there as opportunity and interest dictated. After a few years they would return to Alaska, where Lindsay was confident they would both find handsome husbands, buy houses down the street from each other, and let their kids grow up together. Lindsay had always wanted a big family.

Hannah sighed and looked at her watch. She could grab a late lunch somewhere and then it would be time to check into her hotel. She got her hand stamped for re-entry, in case she decided to come back tonight, and made her way to the parking lot, just in time to see a big man in a green parka smash out the back window of her rental. His cohort reached through and grabbed her suitcase.

"Stop!" Hannah yelled. She ran toward the two vandals. The bigger guy looked up and then sprinted toward her. Belatedly, she realized no one else had left the park at the same time as she did. She turned and dashed toward the entrance, but the man was faster. He got a hand on her daypack, pulling her off-balance, and she tumbled forward onto the frozen ground, sending a pain shooting from her knee. He tried to jerk the backpack away, but the chest strap across the front refused to break, and he only succeeded in flopping Hannah around like a beached fish.

A dog barked. "Hey! Let her go!" a male voice called from somewhere nearby.

Her attacker ran away, calling, "Rocky! Let's go!"

She lifted her head in time to see him jump into a white truck. The other vandal slung her suitcase into the bed of the truck and swung into the passenger seat. The truck roared out of the parking lot.

Something wet brushed against Hannah's cheek and she let out a little scream before she realized it was a dog, licking her face. A big, furry yellow dog wearing a service vest.

"Scout, get back." A man ran up beside her and crouched. "Are you hurt? Don't try to sit up yet."

But Hannah rolled to her side and looked up at the face of her rescuer. She blinked, sure she was imagining it, but a second look confirmed it. She knew those hazel eyes, the heavy eyebrows with a funny little bend in the middle, the little clef in his chin. "Jace."

His mouth dropped open. "Hannah?"

Chapter Three

An hour later, Jace stood out of the way, watching Hannah as she spoke with yet another police officer. She'd changed surprisingly little since he'd last seen her, the summer after she graduated from high school. Her face had more character now, the lines around her nose and mouth were a little deeper, and her long hair was honey-blonde now rather than sun-streaked like it used to be. Somehow it all combined to make her even more attractive than she'd been as a teenager. She still greeted everyone with a friendly smile, even in today's situation, while those soft eyes of hers, more gray than blue, still seemed to look past the surface and see the person inside.

Even the rip in the knee of her pants, exposing torn and blood-stained thermal underwear, looked familiar. How many times had Hannah and Lindsay scraped their knees on rocks and trees? And just like she always had, Hannah ignored the injury and carried on.

Scout, sitting at Jace's side, gave a little whine. "I know." Jace reached down to scratch behind the dog's ears. "You've been patient for a long time. It shouldn't be much longer." The police had dismissed him, but Jace wasn't going to abandon his little sister's best friend until he was sure she was safe. Thinking of Lindsay, he felt that familiar pang of loss.

Lindsay, with her sudden enthusiasms and her oversize laugh. She was always spouting ideas. "We should go ice-fishing this weekend." "Let's try making Korean dumplings at home." "Let's get a potbellied pig."

And Hannah had been right there with her, gathering the ice gear, looking for dumpling recipes, finding out what pigs ate. They hadn't been able to sell Mom on the idea of a pet pig, but they had ended up with a guinea pig named Sheba. When Lindsay died, it seemed like the laughter that had once filled their house died, too. Not that there weren't happy times and celebrations in the years since, but they all missed the unabashed joy that Lindsay had brought to their family.

Lindsay's sudden death hit them all hard, but it was hardest on his mother. She and Lindsay had always been close, but in the months before the accident Lindsay had started to chafe at her parents' rules, resulting in some epic arguments. And then, before Mom could find a way to repair their relationship, Lindsay was gone. Mom blamed the driver. She'd blamed Hannah. Most of all she blamed herself. And she blamed God. Time and prayer had healed her relationship with God, and she'd eventually found a way to forgive the others and herself, but she still harbored some residual resentment for Hannah, less for her role in the accident than for her disappearing act afterward.

In a lot of ways, his mom had lost not one but two daughters that evening. Hannah used to spend so much time at the Angeles house, she had her own assigned coat hook in the mudroom. But after the funeral, Hannah left Fairbanks and had never spoken to anyone in his family again. It was as if she wanted to put any memory or connection with Lindsay behind her. At least that's what Mom believed. Jace wasn't sure. Hannah had always been a loyal friend, and Jace knew Lindsay's death had hurt her deeply. If she chose to stay away from the Angeles family, Jace figured she had her reasons.

Hannah was still speaking to the policeman, who nodded and finished writing something before closing the book. Hannah moved a few steps away and pulled out her phone. She still moved with the athletic grace that had earned medals when she and Lindsay were on the high school cross-country ski team. Jace approached her, reaching into his pocket to push the autostart button for his Jeep as he did. "All done?"

"Oh." She turned. "I didn't realize you were still here."

He shrugged. "I thought you might need a ride if the police take your SUV in for evidence."

"That's kind of you." She looked toward the shattered window. "The police say they're done with it, but I've called the rental car company and they're arranging to have it towed. They offered a replacement, but I figured it wasn't worth the hassle since I'm leaving in the morning and the hotel has an airport shuttle." Scout stepped closer to her, and she smiled at him. "May I pet your dog?"

"Sure. Scout, sit."

The dog sat, and Hannah buried her gloved hands in the fur on both sides of his face and massaged his neck. He closed his eyes in pleasure. Hannah laughed. "Sweet boy. What is he, golden retriever?"

"Mostly. Also some Saint Bernard, and a little border collie, according to his DNA test."

"He's a beauty. What kind of service dog is he?"

"He's in general training right now, but the plan is to make him an avalanche rescue dog. He just had his first birthday last month. In another two months, he'll move into formal training."

"Oh, so you're a volunteer puppy raiser?"

"Exactly. I try to take him out often so that he gets used to crowds and distractions."

Hannah gave a rueful smile. "Certainly plenty of distractions today. I don't think I've formally thanked you for rescuing me. If not for you and Scout, that guy would have stolen my backpack, and he might have really hurt me." Hannah shuddered, and Jace rested a hand on her shoulder.

"I'm glad I was here. Are you sure you don't need medical attention?" He looked down at her ripped pants.

She shook her head. "It's just a scraped knee. I've lived through a few of those in my life."

"That's true." He jingled the keys in his pocket. "So, how about that ride?"

"If you're sure it's not too much trouble, I'd appreciate it."

"No trouble at all." He guided her toward his Jeep. While he got Scout settled in the back, Hannah shrugged out of her backpack and climbed into the passenger seat, setting the pack in her lap. He climbed in and turned up the heat. Hannah held her hands in front of the vent. "This feels good."

"Yeah. Twenty below gets cold after a while, no matter how many layers you're wearing."

She chuckled. "I guess I've gotten soft, living in Anchorage. It's usually ten or twenty degrees warmer there in the winter. Not so hot in the summer, either."

"I know. We're getting ready to open another store there, and I've been going back and forth a lot."

"I'd been seeing them raising the building," Hannah told him, "but I didn't realize it was your store until I saw the sign two weeks ago. Congratulations."

"Thanks. So, where to?"

"My hotel, I guess. I have a reservation at the Young." Hannah waited for Jace to pull out of the parking lot. "I heard that your parents retired, and you're the big boss of Angeles Adventure Store now."

Jace chuckled. "That's right. The buck stops here."

As far as Hannah knew, it had always been a given that someday Jace would take over the store. Now she wondered if Jace had ever resented that. "How's that working out for you?" she asked.

"I like it." Jace tossed a smile her way. "The store is doing well. We've got great employees, so that helps. Even the construction of the new store has been on time and under budget, which people tell me is a minor miracle."

"Did you ever consider a different career?" Maybe she shouldn't have asked that. The question was too personal, especially from someone he hadn't seen in thirteen years.

But Jace answered without hesitation. "Oh, sure."

"Really? What?"

The corners of his mouth twitched. "When I was twelve, I was all set to be a professional skateboarder. But after I broke my arm trying a new trick and couldn't fish the whole summer, I decided storekeeper was a safer profession."

"Oh, I remember," Hannah said. "You hated that cast."

He grinned. "Yeah, especially after you drew little hearts all over it. My friends really gave me a hard time about that."

Hannah could feel the heat rising in her cheeks. "Sorry about that."

"Nah. It was funny. And I needed something to laugh about that summer." He pointed to a big box store up ahead. "They took your suitcase. Do you need to stop and replace anything before I take you to your hotel?"

"I suppose I do, if you have time."

"It's no problem. I'm officially on vacation. Tomorrow, I'm taking the train to the cabin for a few days before I travel to Anchorage for the grand opening next Saturday."

"The cabin, huh?" Hannah smiled. She'd been to the family cabin with them many times. "How fun. Who's going with you?"

"Just me and Scout this time. I want to concentrate on his search-and-find skills." He pulled into the store's parking lot and found a spot in a corner near the back. "Can you find everything here or do you want to go to the mall?"

"This is fine. It shouldn't take me too long."

"No hurry. It's good for Scout to be in busy places like this."

They got out of the car, and Hannah shrugged into her daypack and fastened the chest strap.

"I don't think they're going to let you take that inside," he cautioned.

Hannah looked torn. "I really don't want to leave it in the car, after all that's happened."

"You mean, those guys who took your suitcase?"

"Yeah." She fingered the strap. "Not to mention the incident early this morning."

Jace took a step closer. "What incident?"

"I was supposed to deliver an item to a man here in Fairbanks, but he was called away on an emergency. Someone who claimed to be his neighbor was there and tried to get me to come inside his house and wait. He may well have been just an overly friendly neighbor, but there was kind of a weird vibe coming off him, so I left."

"Good for you, trusting your instincts. Did you report him to the police?"

"Not immediately, but I told them about it after the car window was smashed."

Jace wanted to know more about this item she was delivering, but a busy parking lot wasn't the best place for that conversation. "Okay. Scout and I will stay here and guard your backpack while you shop."

"Thanks. I'll be quick." She removed the pack, set it in the seat and hurried off. Jace glanced at the pack, wondering about this mysterious item inside. Two scary incidents in one day. No wonder Hannah didn't want to leave her backpack unguarded.

While he waited, Jace checked the weather report for the cabin. It looked like a front might blow in while he was there, but they weren't forecasting more than a few inches of snow, so it shouldn't affect his plans. True to her word, Hannah was back in a remarkably short time, carrying a couple of shopping bags, which she stashed on the floor before setting the backpack on her lap again. "All set."

"Great." Jace pulled out of the parking lot. "Are you sure you'll be okay at a hotel by yourself after all that's happened?"

"I'll be fine. I've been thinking about it, and I figure they must have followed my car from the meeting place this morning and that's how they found me at Ice Alaska. Now that I'm not driving that car anymore, I don't see how they could find me at a hotel. I'll take the hotel shuttle to the airport tomorrow morning."

He made a right turn, heading toward the hotel. "If you don't mind my asking, what is this item you're carrying in your backpack that's so valuable?"

"That's what's so strange. It's not all that valuable, relatively." Hannah unzipped her pack and pulled out something covered in bubble wrap. "It's a wooden globe made by a well-known artist who died not too long ago. The dealer was going to pay me five thousand and probably sell it to a collector for around seven. But you'd have to know about the artist and his work to appreciate the value." She took off her gloves and used a fingernail to pull off the tape and remove the wrapping.

Jace stopped at a traffic light and turned to look at the globe in her lap. It was a pretty thing, inlaid in different colors of wood, but he never would have guessed it was worth thousands. "It's nice."

"It is, but you'd be lucky to get a hundred for it at a pawn shop unless the owner was particularly knowledgeable or spent time on research. I can certainly see someone smashing a window to grab the globe if they saw it, but it wasn't in the car, so they had to have known about it ahead of time. All this activity seems excessive for the money involved."

"Seven thousand is a lot of money to some people."

"True, but see that woman with the bag?" Hannah pointed to a woman crossing the street in front of them carrying a canvas purse. "That's a vintage Louis Vuitton monogram, easily worth three thousand, and it's probably got cash and credit cards inside. Wouldn't that be an easier and more obvious target than this globe?"

"I see what you mean. Are you sure the globe isn't some incredibly rare antique or something?"

"From what I saw, Dimitri Karas globes like this have consistently sold at auction for six or seven thousand. Depending on the size and complexity, his jewelry boxes go for eight to twelve, and the dealer I was supposed to meet said a puzzle box sold for just under twenty thousand a few years ago."

"A puzzle box? Interesting. Could your globe be one?"

"Not likely." Hannah turned the globe over in her hands. Jace had never noticed how pretty Hannah's hands were before, with those long, graceful fingers and nails painted the color of the inside of a seashell. "From what I read, the artist only made a few and they were all boxes. But it is an intriguing idea."

"Yeah." The light changed and Jace pulled forward. "But not worth putting you in danger. Maybe we should put it in the safe at the store."

Hannah shook her head as she rewrapped the globe and returned it to her daypack. "Good idea, but the logistics don't work. It's Saturday afternoon, and I have an early flight tomorrow morning. First thing Monday morning, though, I'll go to my bank in Anchorage and put it into a safe deposit box."

The only problem with that, of course, was that whoever was after Hannah's globe wouldn't know it was safely locked away. Jace hated the thought of someone going after Hannah over some piece of wood. Or for any other reason. It was funny, even though they hadn't seen each other in over a decade, the minute he'd recognized her in that parking lot, he'd immediately felt the same protective instincts he'd always felt for Lindsay and Hannah.

Well, maybe not quite the same. Hannah was all grown up now, and there were some new feelings mixed in there that weren't brotherly, exactly. "Just be careful, okay? It doesn't sound like these people have a lot of scruples." He turned into the parking lot of the Young Hotel and stopped in the portico by the front door.

"I will." Hannah gathered her shopping bags and the pack, then turned to look at him. "Thank you, Jace, for everything you've done for me today." She leaned across the seat and brushed a kiss against his cheek. "It meant a lot."

"Anytime." He smiled at her. Such a strange coincidence, running into her again after all these years. He would have liked to spend a little more time with her, catch up on her life. Maybe he should say something about exchanging phone numbers. But before he could say anything, she was out of the car.

"Goodbye."

He watched her through the glass doors as she made her way to the front desk and tapped on the bell there. He'd wait until he was sure they'd kept her reservation, although judging by the small number of cars in the parking lot, there should be plenty of empty rooms. Someone stepped out from between two cars at the back of the lot and walked toward the building—a large man wearing a green parka. Just like the parka Hannah's assailant wore. Jace leaped out of the car and ran inside.

"Hannah, let's go."

The clerk had just appeared through the door behind the desk. Both she and Hannah looked at him in alarm. "Why? What's going on?"

"Come on, I'll explain in the car." He grabbed her shopping bags and put his other hand against the small of her back to urge her toward the door.

"Ma'am, is this man bothering you?" the clerk asked.

"No, everything's fine," Hannah told her, although she looked uncertain. But she did allow Jace to usher her to his Jeep.

The man had disappeared, but that didn't mean he wasn't still nearby. Jace jumped into the driver's seat and drove out of the parking lot, making a few unnecessary turns through a neighborhood until he was convinced no one was following.

"What is going on?" Hannah demanded.

Jace explained about the man in the green parka.

Hannah frowned. "Are you sure it was the same guy? It's not like green parkas are that unusual."

"Maybe not, but two-hundred-and-fifty-pound guys in green parkas are."

"How could he have found my hotel?"

"I can't be sure, but I'm not going to risk it." He turned toward home. "You're staying with me tonight."

Chapter Four

"Excuse me?" Hannah stared at Jace. Did he just announce that she would be staying with him without asking her? She wasn't ten years old anymore, and he wasn't her babysitter.

Jace flashed a rueful smile. "Sorry, that came out a little more dictatorial than I'd intended. What I meant to say was I would feel a lot better if you weren't alone in a hotel tonight. I bought my parents' house when they moved to Idaho, so there's plenty of room." In the back, the dog whined, and Jace grinned. "See, Scout wants you to stay."

She chuckled. "So you're blaming your bossiness on Scout?"

"Well, maybe not entirely."

"Uh-huh. Just because you're in charge of Angeles Adventure Store now doesn't mean you're the boss of me. However…" Hannah glanced over her shoulder. She didn't see a white truck behind them, but that didn't mean it wasn't out there. "I admit, I wasn't looking forward to spending the evening alone in my hotel room, imagining scary scenarios. So, if that's an invitation—"

"It is."

"Then I accept. Thank you. Let me just call the hotel." She

dialed the hotel, cancelled the reservation, and assured the desk clerk once again that she was fine and hadn't been kidnapped.

Next, since she'd given them her itinerary, she texted Sue Ann and her parents in Arizona to say she'd decided to stay with a friend, rather than at the hotel. On the off chance either of them tried to reach her through the hotel, she didn't want them worrying. She decided to wait until she returned to Anchorage to tell Sue Ann about all the scary things that had been happening. Otherwise, Sue Ann would likely order Bradley to drive all night to Fairbanks to collect Hannah and act as her personal bodyguard. Hannah should probably let her sister know as well, but she hadn't told Nicole that she was going to Fairbanks, and mentioning it now would involve questions and explanations that she didn't want to get into. Besides, Mom would no doubt fill her in when she called Nicole in the next day or two.

Hannah had barely had time to return the phone to her pocket when it rang. She answered. "Hi, Sue Ann."

"Hi. It's so nice that you ran into an old friend there in Fairbanks. I'm sure you have a million things to talk about, so I won't keep you, but I wanted to let you know we got everything cleaned up and the window fixed this morning. We were able to open the store this afternoon."

"That's great news."

"Yeah, Lupine Glass really came through, in spite of everything."

"What do you mean, in spite of everything?" Hannah asked.

"Oh, we weren't the only ones hit last night. Same thing happened to Timeless Finds on Fifth, and Karen's Kollectibles in midtown."

"What?" Hannah had seen Karen from Karen's Kollectibles at the auction yesterday. "I wonder what that's all about."

"Who knows? By the way, a man came in looking for you this afternoon," Sue Ann continued. "He said his name was John Smith. Tiff told him you were in Fairbanks but would be flying home tomorrow, and he said he'd come back to the store tomorrow afternoon."

"I don't remember meeting anyone named John Smith. What did he look like?"

"Tall. Blond. As I said, he talked to Tiff, so I didn't get a good look at his face."

"Huh, doesn't ring a bell, but I suppose I'll find out what he wants tomorrow. Thanks for handling the repairs on the window."

"All in a day's work. I'll see you tomorrow. Safe travels."

If she only knew. "Thanks. Bye, Sue Ann." Hannah hung up the phone and mused, "Is it just me, or does the name John Smith sound fake?"

Jace shrugged. "I suppose there are quite a few legitimate John Smiths in the world. Why?"

"Oh, that was my manager. She said a tall blond guy named John Smith was looking for me at the store today."

"What store?"

"That's right—you wouldn't know. I own a store in downtown Anchorage. It's mostly antique and vintage furniture and housewares, with a consignment corner for local craftspeople."

"That's great. You always did like old things. You and Mom used to love looking at antique quilts. What's the name of the store?"

"Hannah's Alaskan Treasures."

"I think I've seen it. On Third? It never occurred to me that you might be the Hannah on the sign. Are you still working as a nurse, too?"

"I never studied nursing," Hannah told him. Without Lindsay, she hadn't had the heart to follow that plan. "I got a business degree from UAA instead. I worked for a utility company for a few years, but then my grandmother left my sister and me a little money, and I used my share, along with a business loan, to start my store."

"I'll definitely check it out next time I'm in Anchorage." A furrow formed between Jace's eyebrows. "But what about this John Smith looking for you? Do you think he's connected to the guys who stole your suitcase?"

Hannah thought about it. "It doesn't seem likely, does it? I mean, they know I'm in Fairbanks, so why would they have a guy looking for me in Anchorage? But after the break-in yesterday—"

"You mean today."

"No, my store was broken into yesterday evening after we closed. Oops, I should have told the Fairbanks police about that."

"Okay, let me get this straight." Jace frowned. "Your store was broken into yesterday evening. Then this morning, someone tried to lure you into his house, and this afternoon two men broke into your car and stole your suitcase. And all because of that?" He nodded toward her pack.

"I can't think of another reason."

"I think we need to find out more about that globe." Jace turned into his neighborhood, followed a curving road for several blocks, and turned right onto the last street.

Hannah spotted the familiar yellow house—only it wasn't yellow anymore but a muted sage green with crisp white trim. Stone pedestals now anchored the base of the wood timbers that supported the gabled roof on the front porch. Snow mounded over a new row of low shrubs beside the porch, but the giant lilac bush next to the garage was still there. It all looked completely different, and yet somehow the same. Hannah leaned closer to the window. "I love the updates."

"Thanks. I needed to paint anyway, so I figured while I was at it, the porch could use a facelift." He pressed a button and the garage door opened.

"You picked out all the colors and trim?"

"Yes, and did all the painting and stonework, too. It took me all of last summer." He pulled in and shut the garage door behind them.

"I'm impressed. Can't wait to see what you did on the inside."

"Well, that's something of a work in progress."

Hannah saw what he meant when they stepped into the kitchen. She surveyed the changes while she removed her snow boots and placed them on the mat beside the door. The lower cabinets were the same golden oak they had been when she and Lindsay used to bake chocolate chip cookies here. An old-fashioned timer shaped like an apple still rested on the tile countertop, necessary because she and Lindsay tended to start talking and forget about the cookies in the oven. However, light gray cabinets with frosted glass inserts had replaced the oak cabinets on the walls, coordinating nicely with gleaming stainless-steel appliances.

Jace filled a dog bowl on a rubber mat with fresh water, and Scout immediately began to lap it up. "I'm waiting for the rest of my order to arrive," he told Hannah. "I'll be tearing out the cabinets between the kitchen and the eating area and putting in an island with a quartz countertop." He opened a drawer and removed a countertop sample showing a white background with gray veining. "Here's what I ordered."

"That will look great," Hannah replied. "Are you planning to make one side an eating bar?"

"Yes, with room enough for three stools."

"Nice."

Jace pulled out a chair from the round oak table. "Have a seat. I'll get the first aid kit and we can take care of that knee."

"It's nothing. I can clean it up later."

"I know you can, but it's easier if someone else does." He disappeared through the laundry room door and returned with the kit and a wet cleaning cloth. After kneeling in front of her, he pulled back the torn cloth of her pants and enlarged the hole in her thermal underwear to reveal her injury. "This doesn't look too bad." Gently, he began to wipe her knee. She flinched as he hit a tender spot, and he stopped. "Sorry, I know this hurts."

Scout came to sit beside her, as though to offer comfort. Hannah rested a hand on the dog's head. "I'm okay. Go ahead."

Jace finished cleaning the wound, patted the area dry, and applied ointment and a bandage. "All done." He closed the first aid kit and stood up.

"Thanks. You're good at this."

"I've had some training with search and rescue, which is how I got into puppy raising in the first place."

Hannah ruffled the dog's ears. "Is Scout your first?"

"No, I've raised two other puppies, Dakota and Ted."

"I don't know how you give them up after having them in your life for a year."

"It's not easy, but I just keep reminding myself that they're moving on to something better." Jace stopped on his way to the laundry room to open the refrigerator door. "Since I'm leaving tomorrow, I don't have a lot of choices for dinner, but I do have eggs and bacon." He looked toward her. "Are you still a fan of breakfast for dinner?"

Hannah laughed. "Yes, I am. Imagine you remembering that."

"Oh, I remember a lot." His smile slowly faded. No doubt he was thinking of Lindsay. And about Hannah's part in her death.

At least, that's what Hannah was thinking about. Being here, in the kitchen where she and Lindsay had spent so much time together, how could she think of anything else? But if Jace wasn't going to mention Lindsay, she wouldn't either.

Jace dropped off the kit and returned to the kitchen to pick up Hannah's shopping bags. "I'll take these to your room." To Hannah's relief, he led her toward what used to be his mother's quilting room at the back of the house rather than upstairs to the room she'd so often shared with Lindsay, with its quirky dormer window overlooking the street out front.

The old sewing room now contained a Craftsman-style daybed, covered with a log cabin quilt in shades of blue, green, and coral. A small table with a sewing machine remained on the far wall, but the quilting frame and large cabinet that used to hold fabrics of every imaginable color were gone. "Mom and Dad usually come up for a month or so in the summer," Jace explained, "and Mom can't go without sewing for that long, so she keeps a machine here."

"It's nice that they have a place to come back to." Hannah set her pack on the chair next to the sewing table and ran her finger over the tiny hand stitches in the quilt on the bed. "Your mom is so talented."

"I know. Her latest project is making lap quilts for people in nursing homes." He placed the shopping bags next to the pack. "Okay, well, I need to get a couple more things packed for the cabin. You know where the bathrooms are and everything. Let's plan to eat in about an hour. Okay?"

"Sounds good. Thank you again, Jace."

He waved away her thanks and she was left alone with her thoughts for the first time since surprising the thieves in the parking lot. She changed from her torn pants to the bulky gray sweatpants she'd picked up at the store. They looked ridiculous with her dressy black sweater, but they would do until she could get home. It only took a minute to arrange the basic toiletries she'd purchased on the counter of the bathroom across the hall. She returned to her room, unwrapped the globe, and sat down on the daybed while she examined it.

Could Jace be right that it was a puzzle box? The ones Peter had mentioned were cubes, but he'd also said they were custom-made for select clients, so it was certainly possible that someone, possibly Candace Linacott herself, had commissioned a puzzle globe. If this was a one-of-a-kind Karas puzzle box, it might well be worth far more than either she or Peter had realized, assuming anyone knew of its existence. But as she turned the globe over in her hands, she couldn't see any visible openings or other clues that would lead her to believe it wasn't a solid piece.

After a soft knock on the open door, Jace appeared, holding

a yellow sticky note. "Hi. It just occurred to me that you might want the Wi-Fi passcode for your phone."

"Thanks." She reached out and accepted the note.

He noticed her torn pants, folded on the bed. "Want me to throw those in the wash for you?"

"No, they have to be dry-cleaned, and besides, they're ruined. Throw them away, unless you think your mom might use the wool flannel in a quilt."

"I'm sure she could. You know how she hates to throw away good fabric." He nodded at the globe in her hands. "May I see it?"

"Of course." She handed him the globe. "See the letter K worked into the design on the compass rose? That's a signature for this artist."

"Neat." He sat at the desk chair and ran a finger over the smooth surface of the Pacific Ocean. "Where did you get it, anyway?"

"At an auction. Candace Linacott, who was a well-known antiques dealer and collector in Anchorage, passed away three years ago, but they just held the estate auction on Friday."

"Candace Linacott." Jace tapped his finger against his chin. "That name sounds familiar. Wasn't she involved in some scandal years ago? Something to do with gold coins stolen at the Anchorage airport. Or was it walrus ivory?"

"Walrus ivory," Hannah confirmed. "I'd forgotten about that. Her employee was caught at the airport trying to pick up a bunch of illegal carvings. Only Alaska natives are allowed to carve walrus ivory, but there was some scheme to export the ivory, have the carving done overseas, and then claim it was genuine Alaskan native art. The police didn't charge her, though. As I recall, she convinced the investigators that she was a victim of the scheme, rather than a collaborator. The gold coins were a year or two before that."

"That's right. That was the one where they found a courier

in one of the bathroom stalls, drugged and unconscious, and the gold coins he'd been carrying were gone."

Hannah nodded. "My eighth-grade history teacher was fascinated with that whole story and kept us up to date with all the details. There were five coins in the collection, I believe, all very rare. The courier was just changing planes in Anchorage, on his way to deliver them to a museum on the East Coast. He said he couldn't remember anything about the assault. The kids in my history class were divided on whether he was in on the heist or not, but my teacher pointed out that he was drugged, so it wasn't surprising his memory was foggy. Later, an airline employee who police identified as a 'person of interest' was found dead. But Ms. Linacott didn't have any connection with that one, as far as I know."

Jace raised his eyebrows. "I didn't realize the antiques and collectibles business was so dangerous."

Hannah laughed. "Ordinarily, the biggest danger I face is throwing out my back trying to move some heavy piece of furniture, but I suppose anytime someone has something valuable, there are people who want to take it away."

Jace turned the globe over to look at the Antarctic end. "So you bought this on Friday at the auction, and your store was broken into that night?"

"Yes. Actually, I didn't exactly buy the globe. I bought a chest of drawers, and it was inside."

"Like someone had forgotten it was there?"

"No, much more deliberate. The drawer had a foam insert and it had been screwed shut. Whoever put it there was hiding the globe."

Jace frowned. "Do you think it was Candace Linacott?"

"Who else would it be? The chest itself wasn't particularly valuable, at least compared to most of the antique furniture in her house. In fact, considering how grimy and neglected it looked, I'm sure it wasn't in her house. It must have been found in a storage unit. She had units rented all over town."

"Why would she rent storage units all over town?" Jace asked.

"Presumably because she didn't have room for all her stuff."

"But why all over?" Jace continued. "Why not rent multiple units at the same place?"

Hannah sat up straighter. "To make it harder for someone to find something she'd hidden there?"

"That was my first thought." He handed her the globe. "Better wrap this up again and keep it safe until we can figure out why these guys want it so badly."

Chapter Five

The next morning, Hannah woke up early. She showered and used the blow-dryer she found in the bathroom drawer to dry her hair. Since her straightening iron and makeup had been in the stolen suitcase, her morning routine was reduced to tying her hair back in a ponytail and getting dressed. At least she had clean underwear, thanks to the three-pack she'd picked up at the box store yesterday. She tucked the comb and toiletries she'd bought into her daypack along with the globe.

The scent of coffee lured her to the kitchen, where she found Jace pouring batter onto a griddle. "Pancakes!" Hannah exclaimed. "I haven't had those in ages."

"Blueberry pancakes." Jace sprinkled frozen wild berries evenly over the cooking pancakes. "There's coffee in the pot. Could you get the orange juice from the fridge and syrup from the pantry, please?"

"Sure." Hannah retrieved those items and set forks, napkins, and juice glasses on the table before filling a mug and taking her first sip of coffee.

Jace flipped the pancakes. "You said your flight is at seven thirty, right? I'll plan to drop you at the airport on my way to the train station, if that works for you."

"That's perfect. Thanks."

"It's no problem. Could you hand me some plates?"

Hannah retrieved two plates from the cabinet where they'd always been, and Jace served up the pancakes. He poured himself a second cup of coffee, stirring in a spoonful of sugar before sitting down at the table. He bowed his head. "Lord, we thank You for Your blessings and for this food. Keep us safe as we travel, and especially watch over Hannah. In Your name. Amen." He smiled at Hannah and picked up his fork.

Hannah tried to remember the last time she'd shared a home-cooked breakfast with someone. Even when she visited her parents in Arizona, they usually just helped themselves to coffee and pastries at their own convenience rather than sit down together. There was something very intimate about sharing the first meal of the day. But at the same time, she couldn't help noticing all the empty chairs around the oak table and thinking of the people who used to fill them.

Once they'd finished breakfast, Hannah offered to wash up while Jace transferred the last few items from the refrigerator into his ice chest and then loaded it into his Jeep. Scout, already in his service vest, followed on his heels, obviously worried that he might be inadvertently left behind. Hannah was just wiping the last plate and returning it to the cupboard when Jace stepped inside. "Looks like we're all set. Are you ready to go?"

It felt wrong, leaving Lindsay's house without even mentioning her name, but Hannah was taking her lead from Jace. If he didn't want to talk about Lindsay, she wouldn't push it. So she just smiled and hoisted her daypack over one shoulder. "Ready." But as she walked to the garage, she said a silent prayer of thanks for the wonderful memories made in this house, for sending Jace to her yesterday just when she'd needed him, and for the blessing of growing up with Lindsay as a best friend.

This early on a Sunday morning, there was little traffic on the road. They made their way through town and were almost to the airport, driving along next to a relatively deserted portion of the road when their headlights picked up something ahead. "What is that?"

As they drew closer, it became obvious. A car was parked across the road, blocking both lanes. Jace slowed the Jeep to a crawl. "That's strange. Do you see anybody? You'd think if they broke down, they'd leave their flashers—" Scout suddenly began barking. Jace glanced into his rearview mirror and jerked the steering wheel to the right. "Hang on!" He pulled the Jeep across the ditch and into the field. Scout let out a startled yelp.

"What are you doing?" Hannah yelled.

"That white truck is behind us."

Hannah looked back to see the truck racing up the road toward them. Jace maneuvered around the abandoned car and back onto the road on the other side. The white truck did the same, but it had to slow down to make its way across the ditches, which gave Jace time to speed away, turn off the main road, and wind through a couple of neighborhoods. He finally pulled into the parking lot of an empty store and parked behind a Dumpster. When he turned to look at Hannah, he was breathing hard. "Did you get a license plate number?"

"No." She hadn't even thought of it. She put her hand over her still-racing heart.

"I didn't either. These people are serious, Hannah. You'd better call the police. Or maybe we should just go to the station."

"No. You saw yesterday—these things take hours. I'd miss my flight. Worse, you'd miss your train, and it only runs once a week."

"Yeah, but—"

"It's fine. I'll call from Anchorage and report it. It's not like we have the plate number or anything that could really help them, and they already know about the white pickup truck. Just drop me at the airport."

"I'm not going to do that." His face was set in stone.

"What? Why?"

"It's not safe. Think about it, Hannah. They knew you would

be coming to the airport, and when. They couldn't have left that car in the middle of the road for very long, or the police would have been there. They must have been watching for you to drive by and called ahead to have someone set the trap."

"But airports are public places with lots of security. I'll be safe there."

"What about when you get home to Anchorage? Are you parked at the airport there? What if they jump you on the way to your car? Or follow you home?"

"Mine is the first flight of the day. They can't beat me back to Anchorage."

"They can't, but what if they're working with John Smith, or someone else you don't know about?" Jace paused briefly. "You need to ride the train with me."

"The train? How would that help?"

"It's going to Anchorage, too. You'd still get there today, but they wouldn't know you were coming."

"But I'm scheduled to work at the store this afternoon," Hannah protested.

"Surely you have some system for when people call in sick or have an emergency and can't show up."

"Of course we do. I just—" She studied his determined face for a moment. "You're not going to budge on this, are you?"

He shook his head. "Nope."

"Okay, fine. I'll ride the train with you and Scout." At least that way, he would still get his vacation at the cabin, and she would still get home.

"Good." He glanced at his watch. "We have just enough time for a quick stop before we go to the train station."

A few minutes later, they were circling behind Jace's family's store. He pulled into a narrow drive labeled Private and swiped a card through a box there. The barrier rose, and he continued down the ramp to the basement parking garage. It was one of the many perks enjoyed by employees of the Angeles Adventure Store, as Hannah knew since she'd worked there part-time for two summers. "Come on in," he told her. "I just need to pick up a few things for my trip to the cabin."

"Okay." Hannah grabbed the daypack, not daring to leave it alone even in a secure parking garage, and followed Jace and Scout to the elevator. Jace's was the only car there, but of course it was too early to be open, and besides, it was Sunday. "Are you still closed on Sundays?" she asked as the elevator doors closed.

"Yes. Mom and Dad started the tradition, I've decided to keep it that way. The employees appreciate having the day off." The doors opened and they stepped into the employee break room. Jace led them through a swinging door into the main store. Fishing gear filled the section to their right, tents and camping equipment to the left. Jace headed toward a desk at the back marked Rentals, next to the outdoor clothing section. Another employee perk, Hannah remembered—free rental of the latest outdoor equipment. "Why don't you wait here?" Jace suggested. "I just need to sign out a couple of things for the trip."

"Okay. While you do that, I can cancel my flight." She took care of that and also texted Sue Ann that she was taking the train and wouldn't be in this afternoon after all since she wouldn't arrive until after closing time. Ordinarily she would call, but it was early, and Sue Ann might still be sleeping. Jace and Scout weren't back yet, so she wandered around the store. The old speckled beige tiles on the floor had been replaced with faux wood vinyl planks, and the signage had been updated, but all the departments were still in the same places, and a photo of the store from about fifty years ago still hung on the wall behind the customer service desk, alongside the framed first dollar Jace's parents had earned there.

Jace returned carrying a bulging backpack and a ski bag. Hannah was surprised, since she'd already seen him putting another ski bag into the storage box mounted on the top rack of his Jeep, but she figured maybe he wanted different skis. "Are you ready?"

"All set." They returned to the garage and drove to the train station without incident. Hannah noticed that Jace rejected a couple of parking spaces toward the front of the lot and instead parked between a van and a big truck in the back. Good thinking. Whoever had blocked the road this morning had presumably noted what kind of car they were driving. No use making it easy to find. Jace took a plastic sled from the back of the car and stacked it with an ice chest, a duffel, and the backpack he'd picked up at the store. That left Hannah to carry the ski bags while he dragged the heavy sled along the snow at the edge of the parking lot. A brisk breeze cut through Hannah's sweatpants, and she hurried forward, eager to reach the warm station.

It took a while to buy Hannah a ticket and get Jace's luggage checked in, but before too long, they were boarding the train. Scout, as a service dog in training, was allowed to ride with them in their car, rather than in a crate in the baggage car where pets were normally transported. The dog stretched out in the area in front of their seats and prepared to nap.

Soon they were swaying gently along the tracks. Pristine snow blanketed the ground outside. They passed frozen creeks, twisting and winding through groves of white-barked birch trees and clusters of spruce, their branches drooping gracefully under heavy loads of snow. As they drew closer to Denali National Park, flashes of the snow-covered mountains appeared whenever they passed gaps in the trees.

They broke out into an open area, and there was Denali, the highest mountain in North America. Clouds clung to the sides like fluffy bits of cotton caught on the jagged rocks, but the snow-covered peak rose above them, almost appearing to float in the sky. "Wow," Hannah whispered, never taking her eyes off the mountain until the train curved into the woods and it disappeared. "What a view."

Jace grinned. "Aren't you glad you decided to take the train with me instead of flying?"

"I am," she admitted. When they hit another clear area,

more clouds had gathered, obscuring the mountain, but Hannah would never forget that magical glimpse of Denali. God's creation was every bit as inspiring as a church service. In fact, Hannah was having such a wonderful time, she'd almost forgotten why she was on the train in the first place.

A train employee came through to tell them the dining car was open for lunch. They found a table with a view on the west side of the train, and Scout settled under the table. Hannah set her pack beside her on the seat. After looking over the menu, they both ordered seafood chowder, which arrived promptly. They had just finished saying grace and started to eat when Hannah's phone chimed twice, and then twice more.

'I'm surprised we have a signal," Jace commented, as he passed the breadbasket to Hannah.

"Just one bar." Hannah took a slice of sourdough bread and set it on the plate beside her bowl of salmon chowder. "Sue Ann said that blond man was back. Tiff told him my train wasn't coming in until late and he said he'd be back tomorrow." She flicked to the next message. "That's odd. The other three are from my sister, asking me to call her."

"Why is that odd? Don't you usually call your sister?"

"Not really. We're on more of an occasional text basis." Which was sad when Hannah thought about it. She and Nicole had somehow reached the point where their relationship was nothing but competition over the occasional antique. That just wasn't right. "Three texts, about fifteen minutes apart. I hope nothing bad has happened." She dialed, but even as she pressed the button, the one bar on her phone disappeared. "No good. I've lost my signal."

"We should pick it up again around Cantwell in about an hour. What is Nicole up to these days, anyway?" It was an obvious ploy to get her mind off possible disaster scenarios, but Hannah took the bait.

"Nicole has an antique shop, too."

"Really? I remember you were always fascinated by history and old things, but I never realized your sister was, as well."

Hannah gave a rueful smile. "I don't think she was, back then. It wasn't until I opened my store that she suddenly developed an interest."

"Hmm, sort of like the way she decided to try out for the biathlon team after you and Lindsay did? As I recall, that didn't go well for her."

"No, it didn't." As a freshman, Nicole was a decent cross-country skier, but she hadn't been putting in the hours Lindsay and Hannah had, as members of the varsity team. She had been so winded during biathlon tryouts, trying to keep up with the group, that she'd been unable to hold her rifle steady and had missed every single target. Somehow, in Nicole's mind, her humiliation had been Hannah's fault. "Now that you mention it, maybe that's why she was so eager to open a store like mine, only better."

"Better?"

"Different, anyway. More upscale. Her store is in South Anchorage, in a custom-designed building that looks like a Swiss chalet. She specializes in jewelry, coins, and decorative items, rather than housewares like mine."

"How did she afford a custom-designed store?"

"She was married to a very successful contractor at the time, and he built it for her and set her up in business."

"*Was* married?"

"She's divorced now. Turns out part of the reason her husband encouraged her to start her own store was to keep her occupied so she wouldn't notice how much time he was spending elsewhere. But about a year after she opened the store, his office manager turned up pregnant and he asked Nicole for a divorce."

"What a louse."

"No argument here. But to give Nicole credit, she's landed on her feet. She still lives in the house he built for them on the hillside, complete with a movie theater, ten-person hot tub, and an adventure course on the premises he built for his two teen-agers from a prior marriage. Nicole stayed on good terms with them and let them continue to use the course even after the di-vorce, but they've both moved out of state now. She put in lots of effort to learn all about antiques, and her store seems to be thriving." Hannah smiled. "But then, so is mine."

"So who is winning the antiques competition?"

"I guess that depends on the day. As I said, we mostly carry different inventories, but there's sometimes overlap. At the Linacott auction, for example, I bid on some carnival glass, but Nicole bid it up to the point where I had to drop out, even though that's not something she would usually carry. Sisters!" she exclaimed in exasperation, but then it hit her. Here she was, complaining about Nicole when Jace had lost his only sister, and it was at least partially Hannah's fault.

She glanced at Jace, looking for signs of hurt, but he didn't seem to be thinking about Lindsay right then. "Did you buy anything besides the chest of drawers that had the globe in-side?" he asked.

"A few nice things. A stained-glass lampshade, Christmas ornaments, a candelabra, a silver bowl. Oh, and there was an-other marquetry jewelry box that I now realize was a Dimitri Karas like the globe. Nicole outbid me on that one as well. Let me show you." She found the texts with the photos and handed the phone to him.

"Beautiful. Hey, she says she sold the box the same day she bought it. Isn't that unusual?"

Hannah shrugged. "It happens to me occasionally." But then she realized what Jace was getting at. "Do you think her quick sale might be related to these attempts to snatch the globe?"

"I wonder. Would she have a record of who she sold it to?"

"I don't know. It's possible."

"Why don't you ask her about it when you return her call?" Jace suggested.

"I'll do that. At the very least, maybe she can describe the customer."

They finished their lunch and returned to their seats. Before long, an announcement came over the loudspeaker, "We're crossing Ciamruq Bridge, the second-highest crossing on our trip today. If you look out to the right, you'll get a beautiful view of the Ciamruq River."

Jace leaned forward to peer out the window. "Oh, look. Three, no, four moose are walking along beside the river way down there."

Hannah gave a quick glance, but as always, the distance to the ground made her stomach clench. She closed her eyes and drew in a deep breath, silently counting to four, then exhaling to the count of four. Three breaths later, Jace touched her arm. "It's okay. We're past the bridge."

She smiled at him. "Thanks."

"Still not a fan of heights, huh?"

"Nope." She'd missed out on quite a few popular hikes because she couldn't make herself walk along ledges, no matter how broad they were. "I've tried. I know in my mind I'm perfectly safe, but the rest of me is convinced I'll fall to my death."

"I get it. There's nothing rational about phobias. For me, it's snakes. I was going to share an apartment with this guy in college until I found out he had a pet boa constrictor." He shuddered. "No way was I going to room with a legless reptile."

Hannah had a feeling Jace was exaggerating to make her feel better, but she appreciated it. "Good thing you live in Alaska, then, where we don't have any reptiles."

"Absolutely. I'll take earthquakes, volcanoes, and grizzlies over rattlesnakes any day."

Hannah checked her phone again, but there was still no signal. She kept checking every fifteen minutes or so, until she finally spotted two bars. She was about to dial Nicole's number when her phone rang. Her sister had beat her to it.

"Hannah, I've been trying to reach you all day." The hollow sound of her voice indicated that Nicole was on speaker phone.

"I'm sorry. I've been out of cell phone range. What's wrong?"

"Nothing's wrong," Nicole declared, but her voice said otherwise. "I just need you to come to my house."

"Why? Is it about Mom or Dad?" She and Nicole seldom came to each other's homes except when their parents came to visit. Sad but true.

"No, it's not about them," Nicole answered. "I just need you to come here, right away.

"I can't. I'm on a train."

"What in the world are you doing on a train?" Nicole almost shrieked, as though Hannah had chosen the train for the sole purpose of ruining her plans.

Hannah doubted whatever Nicole was upset about held a candle to what she had been through in the last twenty-four hours, but she didn't want to get into that with her sister right now. "I had to go to Fairbanks yesterday, and I happened to run into Jace Angeles. You remember him?"

"Lindsay's brother? Of course I do."

"Well, he was riding the train to his family's back-country cabin today, and I decided to ride along to Anchorage instead of taking the plane. It's a beautiful trip."

Nicole huffed. "I can't believe you're on a scenic train ride when I'm—" Nicole paused, and Hannah heard what sounded like a paper rustling. In a calmer voice, Nicole asked, "When will you be back in Anchorage?"

"The train is supposed to arrive about seven this evening."

"Come to my house as soon as you get in, okay? Hannah, this is important. Bring all the things you got at that Linacott auction. Everything. I, uh, have something to show you."

"Is it about the marquetry box you got at the auction?"

"N-not really."

"Because I was wondering who you sold it to. Do you know the customer's name?"

"I don't." Nicole's response was immediate.

"Well, how about his description?" Hannah continued. "I don't suppose it was a tall blond man?"

"I—I have to go. Just bring those things immediately once you get back to town."

"Fine."

"And bring that antique you got from Grandpa, too. I'll see you this evening." The call ended.

Hannah slowly returned the phone to her pocket. "That was strange. Nicole wants me to bring the stuff I got at the auction directly to her house when I arrive in Anchorage. I wonder if she thinks the stained-glass lampshade I got might be a real Tiffany. I haven't had a chance to look closely." She turned to Jace, preparing to tell him about the rest of the conversation, but he was staring at her. "What?"

"You just told Nicole you were on the train."

"Yeah. So?"

"Who else did you tell?"

"My manager, Sue Ann. Why?"

"Don't you see? Those guys in the white truck knew what time you would be heading for the airport this morning. Someone is feeding them information."

"It wasn't Nicole. I didn't even tell her I was going to Fairbanks." She paused. "Unless my mom told her. Which, yeah, she probably did."

"Did you give your mom your itinerary?"

"Yes. But Nicole is my sister. We might compete over antiques, but she's not going to help someone rob me."

Jace tapped his chin. "Maybe her phone line is bugged, or her email got hacked, or something."

"That sounds a little paranoid," Hannah said. "Although—"

"What?"

"She kept saying to bring all the stuff I won at the Linacott auction to her house as soon as I arrive in Anchorage, but just before she hung up, she mentioned I should bring the antique I got from Grandpa."

"What's odd about that?"

"I don't have anything of Grandpa's. My grandmother loved antiques, but Grandpa didn't. He was always shaking his head over all her 'clutter.' He used to say that he'd had enough hand-me-downs growing up, and that the only sentimental thing he owned was the memorial flag from his dad's funeral."

"Your great-grandfather was a veteran?"

"Yes, and he was in the Alaska Territorial Police here before statehood. He died before I was born, and my grandpa died when I was about eight. My mother has my great-grandpa's flag down in Arizona, so I can't imagine why Nicole would ask me to bring it. She hung up before I could ask what she meant."

"That is odd." Jace thought for a minute. "What about your manager? Could she be feeding someone information?"

"I trust Sue Ann completely. She's not just my employee, she's my friend. She would never purposely do anything to put me in danger." Hannah's eyes widened. "Except—"

"What?"

"That text. Sue Ann said Tiff told the blond man who asked for me that I was on the train and wouldn't be back until this evening. What if—"

"You can't get off the train in Anchorage," Jace declared. "It's too dangerous."

Hannah drew back. "What do you mean I can't get off in Anchorage? What other choice do I have? There are no other stops between here and there."

"There are whistle stops. The train will stop to let me off near the cabin." He gazed directly into her eyes. "Come with me."

"To the cabin? That's ridiculous. I'll call the Anchorage police before I get off the train and ask them to meet me at the station."

"Okay, and then what? Someone grabs you in the parking

lot, or breaks into your house? They know you have the globe, and they need to get it before you have a chance to lock it up. You should come with me."

Hannah shook her head. "I can't just disappear for a week until the next train. People would be frantic."

Jace thought for a moment. "Okay, get off the train with me, we wait a couple of days for everything to settle down, and we can ride the snow machine to Pika, the nearest town on the road system. That's what I was planning to do next Friday. A driver is scheduled to pick me up there and take me to Anchorage for the grand opening. I can call and they'll send a driver for you."

"But I promised Nicole I would come to her house this evening."

"Text her and say you can't make it. Make some excuse, like you're not feeling well. Don't tell her where you're going. Seriously, Hannah, your life could be at stake."

She thought about it. "You'll take me to Pika day after tomorrow?"

"I promise."

Still, she hesitated. "If I don't show up for work tomorrow, Sue Ann will have the state troopers looking for me."

"Text her too. Just don't give out any information as to where you are. Quickly, before you lose the signal."

Hannah closed her eyes and breathed a prayer, "Lord, guide me." On the one hand, Nicole had sounded upset, and Hannah should be there for her sister. But on the other, what if the blond man was waiting to rob her at the train station? When she opened her eyes, there was Jace, his face filled with concern. Jace, who had been keeping her safe since the moment they reunited.

"All right," she told him. "I'll text them now."

Chapter Six

The train pulled to a stop where Jace had requested. There were several cabins in this roadless area, accessible only by train or snow machine in the winter, float plane or ATV in the summer. The train employees were quite accustomed to flag stops. Jace had half-expected a last-minute argument from Hannah about leaving the train, but here she was, standing beside Scout while Jace took a quick inventory of all his gear. Once everything had been unloaded, the train whistled and pulled away.

Fortunately, the temperature here was a good twenty-five degrees warmer than it had been in Fairbanks. Hannah wandered a few steps away. Next to the track, where the plow had pushed the snow, it was hard-packed and she could walk easily, but once she had gotten a few feet away, her boots sank into the snow up to her knees. "The snow is so soft, I'm postholing." She looked back at Jace. "How far to the cabin? I can't remember."

"Almost three miles, but don't worry. I thought ahead." He opened one of the backpacks and pulled out a pair of oyster-colored weatherproof ski pants. He handed them to her, along with one of the ski bags. "Hope everything fits."

"You brought me skis?"

"And boots. Size seven, right?"

Hannah studied him with narrowed eyes. "So this is why you had to drop by the store. You've been planning to take me with you to the cabin all along."

"Yes," he admitted. "Ever since that ambush this morning, I've been worried that they know more than they should about your schedule, and I didn't want you going to the train station alone."

She put her hands on her hips. "I don't know whether to be angry or flattered. What were you going to do if I refused to get off the train with you?"

"I was going to go with you to Anchorage," he admitted.

"But the train only runs once a week. You would have had to give up your whole vacation to do that."

"Correct." He grinned. "So it's good that you agreed to come to the cabin. Right?"

After a long, tense moment, a slow smile crept onto her face. "I guess. But you have to stop doing this, making decisions without consulting me. I'm a grown woman. I don't need a babysitter anymore."

"Agreed." She was all grown up all right, and she'd matured into a lovely, capable woman. He still felt the need to protect her, but not the same way as when she and Lindsay were kids, acting on all of Lindsay's wild schemes.

While Jace loaded the ice chest, duffel, and backpacks onto the sled, Hannah pulled off one snow boot and pulled the leg of the ski pants up over her sweats. Then she stuck her foot back into the boot and repeated the procedure with the other leg. Jace was impressed with her ability to stand on one foot while pulling on clothes. She unzipped the ski bag and tried on the backcountry ski boots he'd brought for her. "Perfect fit. I can't believe you remember what shoe size I wear."

"Whenever we went on a family ski or to the cabin, I was always the one in charge of gathering ski equipment for the whole group," he explained as he laced up his own ski boots. Then he confessed, "And I happened to see the size inside your boot when you left it by the door last night."

"Tricky." She grasped her ski poles in one hand, dropped the skis on the snow, and stabbed the toes of the boots into the bindings. "I'd challenge you to a race, but I can't remember the way to the cabin."

"It wouldn't be fair anyway." Jace stepped onto his skis and attached a belt around his waist to which he fastened the tow-rope of the sled. "Because I'll be pulling the luggage."

Hannah smirked. "I know."

Jace laughed as he skied forward, dragging the sled behind him. Hannah followed, and Scout brought up the rear, smart enough to let them break trail instead of bounding through the snow on his own. Jace set a good pace up the first hill, but Hannah had no trouble keeping up. Less than thirty minutes later, the cabin's chimney pipe appeared. As they climbed the last hill, the rest of the cabin came into view, and Jace experienced a familiar mix of anticipation and nostalgia. So many great family moments had happened here.

Beside the door hung a welcome sign Lindsay had painted dark blue with white lettering and pale blue forget-me-not flowers scattered across the bottom. It had been a Mother's Day gift, probably Mom's favorite gift ever. She had painted the rocking chair beside the door to match, the blue creating a pop of color against the white snow and brown wood of the cabin.

Jace paused for a moment to savor the sight. It looked like more than a foot of snow had fallen since he was last here, with some clinging to the moose antlers on the gable over the porch. The moose had shed them right in front of the cabin one January, shaking off his huge antlers like a couple of annoying insects while Jace's whole family watched from the front window. Hannah had been there, too. She and Lindsay had been the ones to insist that the moose's "gift" needed to go on the cabin.

Hannah pulled up beside him at the top of the hill and caught her breath. "It still looks great. You must take good care of it."

"I try. I put a new coat of sealer on the logs last summer." He pushed forward. "Come on. Let's get a fire going." They glided down the hill and stepped out of their skis. Hannah hung both pairs on sets of pegs on the porch wall while Jace transferred all the baggage from the sled to the porch and unlocked the front door. Inside, they shed their ski boots and set them to dry on the mat beside the door.

Jace glanced around the room, noticing the battered pine kitchen table, the faded cushions on the chairs, and the worn rug on the floor, and realized while he'd been taking care of the outside of the cabin, he'd allowed the interior to get a bit shabby. But when he looked over at Hannah, she was looking up at the heavy timbers that supported the roof. Her gaze traveled down the walls and all around the front room. "I love this place. It feels so solid, like it will still be here in a hundred years, safe and snug."

Jace felt it, too, every time he came to the cabin. "Sanctuary." He crossed to the stove and, using the firewood and kindling he'd left at the ready last time he was here, made short work of building the fire. Meanwhile, without being asked, Hannah began wiping down the kitchen surfaces. Once they were clean, she unpacked the freeze-dried and other nonperishable foods and arranged them on the shelves, leaving Jace free to shovel a path to the woodshed.

He finished just before the sun reached the horizon. When he stepped inside carrying a load of logs, the scent of chilis, cumin, and stewing meat greeted him at the door. Scout followed him inside, holding his head high and sniffing the air. Hannah stood at the kitchen counter, chopping an onion. Two large cans of hominy sat nearby. "I assumed the pork cubes and hominy were for posole. Hope I didn't overstep."

"No, of course not." He'd planned on making do with canned stew tonight because he'd figured with all the chores, he wouldn't have time to cook the posole until tomorrow, but this was even better. "Smells great."

"I hope it tastes good. Your mom never measured the seasonings, just cooked by feel, so I'm not sure I have them right. The pork needs to cook another fifteen minutes or so before I add the hominy and other ingredients."

"Good. That gives you time to come outside and see the show."

"What show?" Hannah was already grabbing her coat and stepping into her snow boots.

"You'll see." Jace rested a hand on her back and urged her through the door ahead of him and Scout.

As soon as she stepped outside, Hannah's mouth dropped open. "Wow."

Jace grinned. This was exactly the reaction he'd hoped for. The wind this morning must have stirred ice particles into the air, because the sun was a brilliant orange, reflecting off the low clouds and painting the surface of the snow. The light touched Hannah's face, warming her skin until it almost seemed to glow, too, as she stared in wonder at the sunset. Jace had the strongest urge to touch that lovely face, to see if her skin was as soft and warm as it looked. Instead, he reached down to ruffle Scout's ears.

"The earth is full of the goodness of the Lord," Hannah whispered, and Jace recognized it as part of a Psalm his dad liked to quote. She continued to watch until the sun had dropped below the horizon and the orange clouds faded to peach. Then she turned to Jace. "Thank you."

"For what?"

"For getting me to stop for the sunset." She spread her arms, taking in the whole view. "It's been too long since I took the time to appreciate the everyday miracles."

Everyday miracles. He liked that. "You mean like sunsets, and snowflakes, and the smell of good food cooking?"

"Yes, exactly."

"I know what you mean. When you run your own business, it seems like there are never enough hours in the day. But Scout here is good about reminding me to take a break, and spending time at the cabin is even better." He brushed snow off the sturdy porch railing and rested his hand there. "Spending time here always reminds me to give thanks for all I have, and for the privilege of living here in the midst of all this beauty."

"Yes." Hannah shook her head slowly. "Here it is March, and I just realized that today was the first time since New Year's Day that I've skied outside. Seems like it's easier to work out on my ski machine in the basement in the morning before I head to work. And that's just wrong." She drew in a lungful of crisp air and let it out again. "Of course, in two days, I'll have to get to Anchorage and figure out what to do about this globe and the people after it, not to mention dealing with Nicole and whatever had her so agitated. Here in the cabin, trouble seems so far away."

"Maybe we should keep it there." Jace touched her arm. "What if, for tonight and tomorrow, we just enjoy the cabin and forget about all that other stuff?" Not that he wouldn't be constantly turning it over in his mind, but Hannah needed a break. Needed to believe in the sanctuary of the cabin. In the sanctuary of God's love.

Hannah ran a hand over Scout's head and smiled. "I love that idea. Let's do it."

After breakfast the next morning, Hannah cleared the table while Jace poured a kettle of hot water into the dishpan. He went outside to refill the bucket with snow and returned to put it on the stove to melt. While he was working on that, Hannah washed their plates and silverware and stacked them in the dish drainer beside the sink. Without a word, Jace grabbed a dish towel and began drying.

It was almost eerie how well they worked together. Hannah supposed it was just because Jace's mom had taught them the chores that came with a backcountry cabin with no plumbing or electricity, but Hannah didn't remember it all running so smoothly when they were kids. There was the usual grumping and arguing about whose job it was to fetch the wood or sweep the floor. Lindsay would usually come up with some creative reason why it was always Jace's turn, but her parents never let her get away with it. Hannah had never complained about chores—she was just grateful to be included in the Angeles family outings.

She scrubbed the skillet, rinsed it, and handed it to Jace, who wiped it out and set it on the stove to finish drying. He poured kibble into Scout's bowl and set it on the floor. Scout gulped it down as though he hadn't eaten in a month, his wagging tail creating a draft that sent a paper towel drifting from the countertop to the floor. Dodging the tail, Hannah picked up the towel and set it in the kindling bucket. Nothing was wasted at the cabin.

Jace hung the now-dry skillet on its assigned peg and the dish towel on a bar to dry. He picked up a box from the kitchen shelf. "What are these doing here?"

"What are they?" Hannah asked.

"Darts." He opened the box to show her. "I guess I cleaned them last time I was here and forgot to put them away." He carried the box to the cabinet on the living room door that housed the dartboard. He opened the doors, exposing the board, stepped back a few feet, and threw his first dart. Bullseye. Two more darts followed, sticking to the board right beside the first dart.

He pulled his darts from the board and looked at Hannah. "Your turn."

She shook her head. "I haven't thrown a dart in years."

"It's like riding a bicycle," Jace assured her. "Come try it."

Hannah came to stand next to him. She'd never been good at this. She picked up one of the darts Jace offered and threw it. It missed the board entirely, sticking into the door instead.

Jace grinned. "That one didn't count." He handed her another dart. "Here, hold it like this." He put his fingers over hers, adjusting her grip, but the feel of his touch was so distracting, she couldn't seem to concentrate on what he was trying to tell her. Her face grew warm.

"Okay, go," he said.

Hannah let the dart fly. This time it hit the outermost ring.

"Better. One more try." He handed her the last dart and Hannah threw it before he could start fiddling with her grip again.

This time the dart hit three circles out from the middle. Jace nodded approvingly. "There you go. You're getting the hang of it now." He pulled out the darts and looked at her. "Your cheeks are pink. I can damp down the fire if you want," he offered.

"It's fine," Hannah replied quickly. Knowing Jace had seen her blushing only made her blush more, but if Jace noticed, he was kind enough not to comment.

"What do you want to do today?" he asked, as he returned the darts to the box and stashed the box in the cabinet.

"You do whatever you had planned," Hannah told him. "I've disrupted your life enough."

"I was going to give Scout some practice in avalanche search work."

Hannah waved a hand at the shelves under the dartboard stocked with books, games, and puzzles. "Go ahead. I can entertain myself."

"Well, actually," Jace said, "the training would go better with two people. I'd planned on hiding his toy, but if he can search out a hidden person, all the better. If you're up for it."

"Sounds great." Maybe she could repay Jace, at least in a small way, for all he'd done for her. "I would love to play the role of avalanche victim for Scout."

He grinned. "All right then. Let's get ready." He pulled an Angeles Adventure shopping bag from the backpack and handed it to her. "I threw in a few more warm layers for you."

"Thank you!" Hannah retreated to her assigned bedroom

and opened the bag. Inside she found a new set of pale laven-
der thermal underwear, the really soft kind made from bam-
boo, plus wool socks, a fleece zip-neck pullover, and a pair of
insulated ski bibs, heavier than the snow pants he'd given her
yesterday. She quickly pulled on all the layers. So thoughtful.
She knew if she offered to pay, Jace would refuse. Nevertheless, she made a mental note to send him a check for all the
clothes and food once she got back to Anchorage.

When she returned to the living room, Jace and Scout were
already there. Scout was dancing at the door, eager to go. Jace
handed Hannah a red bandanna. "Here, put this against your
skin. Scout will use it later to track you."

Hannah tucked it inside her top and packed one of the water
bottles Jace had already filled into her daypack, along with the
globe. She stepped into her snow boots. "All set."

They went outside. The sun glittered on the snow, and Hannah realized she'd left her sunglasses in the rental car. As if
reading her mind, Jace pulled two pairs of shades from his
backpack and handed one to her. He pulled a squeaky toy from
his pocket and threw it. "Scout, fetch!"

The dog galloped after the toy. Hannah chuckled. "Training
looks a whole lot like playing."

"Yeah, it's basically a game. We'll start with fetch and work
our way to hide-and-seek."

Scout came running back with the toy and deposited it into
Jace's hand, tail lashing so hard it was going in a circle. Jace
threw it two or three more times, working their way into the
woods as he went. The snow wasn't as deep here under the
trees, and they were able to walk without sinking up to their
knees. The next time Scout returned the toy, Jace commanded
him to sit and stay, and then handed the toy to Lindsay. "Do
you still have that bandana?"

"Right here." She pulled it from under her top and handed
it to Jace.

"Great. Take the squeaky toy with you and find a place to

hide behind a bush or tree somewhere. Once you're hidden, I'll send Scout to find you."

"How far should I go?" she asked.

"Not too far the first time, but far enough that Scout can't see where you went from here." He looked at his watch. "I'll give a two-minute head start. Go."

Lindsay trotted away down a game trail through the trees, checking out possible hiding places as she went and mentally counting off the seconds. When she figured her two minutes were just about up, she backtracked for a bit and crouched behind a snow-covered boulder about six feet off the trail, still clutching the squeaky toy. She'd left tracks, of course, but that was unavoidable. A raven in the tree above her gave her a scolding for disturbing his solitude. She held her finger to her lips and whispered. "Shh, don't give me away." The raven gave another squawk and flew to a different tree, still making grumbling noises.

Soon, she heard Jace in the distance giving the command to "Find." A short time later, bushes rustled as Scout made his way along the trail. Jace's footsteps followed. As they drew closer, she caught a snuffling sound and the occasional sneeze. Scout trotted right past the boulder without pausing, but suddenly he stopped, sniffed the air and turned, spotting her. His ears pricked and his tail wagged. Two bounds later, he had knocked her down and was lying on her legs, holding the squeaky toy in his mouth.

"Oof." Hannah laughed at the dog. "If you're going to act like a lap dog, you might want to cut back on those between-meal treats."

Jace ran up. "Good boy. Release." He threw a different toy, and Scout dropped the first one to chase after it. Jace offered Hannah a hand. "Sorry about that. I forgot to warn you. Scout has been trained that when he finds someone in the snow, he's supposed to crawl up next to them or lay on top of them to keep them warm until help arrives. Unfortunately, he's concluded that if they're not prone, he's supposed to knock them down. Are you okay?"

"I'm fine. Next time I hide, I'll know what to expect." She took his hand and let him pull her to her feet. For a moment, their faces were only inches apart. Within kissing distance. Now where did that thought come from?

Jace's gaze went to her eyes and dropped to her mouth. Was he thinking of kisses too? Or was that just a scrap of fantasy left over from her schoolgirl crush? He paused for an instant, and then he took a step back. Hannah had probably imagined the whole thing.

Scout returned, and Jace threw the toy once again. "I need to break him from knocking people down, but I don't know how, without discouraging him from seeking. I've decided to let the professional trainer handle it when she takes over. Are you up for another round, or have you had enough?"

"Oh, I'm just getting started," Hannah replied. Scout was already back with the toy, and Hannah reached down to ruffle his ears. "Right, Scout?"

The dog dropped his toy and stared at Jace, head cocked and ears pricked, waiting for his next assignment.

"All right then," Jace said. "Let's keep practicing."

Chapter Seven

That evening, Jace carried in the Dutch oven with the leftover posole from the porch where they'd stored it overnight, and set it on the woodstove to heat. "This may take a while," he told Hannah. "It's partly frozen."

That comment sparked a memory for Hannah. "Ooh, you know what would be good with it?"

Jace groaned. "You're not going to try to bake, are you?"

Hannah laughed. She couldn't count the times she and Lindsay had attempted brownies, or coffee cake, or bread in the Dutch oven on the woodstove. They'd had the occasional success, meaning the result was more-or-less edible, but most of their experiments had been either charred to a crisp or raw in the middle. Sometimes both. Still, it had never discouraged them from trying, and she was pretty sure she remembered the recipe for corn bread. "Do you have cornmeal, flour, and baking powder?"

Despite his skepticism, Jace checked the metal-lined box where his mom kept her staples safe from mice and other would-be invaders. "We have masa harina for tortillas. Powdered milk. Sugar. I don't see flour, but we have pancake mix."

"That will work, and it already has baking powder in it. How about eggs?"

"We ate all the eggs for breakfast." He dug around a little more. "Well, there is a pouch here of freeze-dried eggs with cheese and jalapenos."

"Perfect. I saw butter in the ice chest." Hannah lifted one of the iron skillets from its peg on the wall, added a chuck of butter, and set it on the stove to melt. She set the next larger skillet on the stove beside it.

Jace watched, a bemused expression on his face while Hannah found a mixing bowl and combined the pancake mix, corn flour, powdered milk, and dried eggs. She picked up the skillet with an oven mitt, tilted it to coat the bottom with melted butter, and poured the rest of the butter into the bowl of dry ingredients. Next, she added water and a squirt of honey, stirring just until the dry ingredients were moistened. The batter sizzled when she poured it into the hot skillet. She returned it to the stovetop and set the larger empty skillet that had been preheating on top as a lid. "There. It should be ready in about twenty minutes."

"If you say so." Jace set bowls and spoons on the table and hung a lantern on the hook above.

"Oh, ye of little faith." Hannah added bread plates and butter knives.

Jace chuckled.

Seventeen minutes later, a hint of smoke had Hannah rushing to remove the corn bread from the heat. She lifted the upper skillet to check her results. The baking powder in the pancake mix must have worked okay, because the corn bread rose just like it was supposed to, but when she ran a spatula underneath to check the bottom, a solid black layer greeted her. She sighed. "It's ruined."

Jace looked over her shoulder. "Maybe not. We could cut off the burned part." Using an oven mitt, he transferred the stew to a trivet on the table.

"You don't have to eat it to spare my feelings."

"Let's try it." Jace cut the corn bread into wedges, severed the burned layer, and gave them each a serving. They sat down at the table, and Jace bowed his head. "Lord, we thank You for this day, for all the progress Scout made in his training today. Bless this food, especially the corn bread Hannah prepared, and if You so please, transform it into something edible, just as You did the water into wine."

Hannah chuckled. "Amen."

Jace spread some butter on his corn bread and took a bite. "It's not bad."

"Yeah, right," Hannah said skeptically. She tried a little taste. "Hey, it really isn't."

"The hint of cheese and jalapeño from the egg mix really jazzes it up," Jace said. "If the stove weren't quite so hot, I think it would have been perfect. Lindsay would be proud."

Hannah stopped eating to look at him. It was one of the few times either of them had mentioned Lindsay.

Jace gave Hannah a gentle smile. "It's okay to talk about her, you know. I'm sure you've been thinking about her. I know I have."

Hannah nodded. "I have. It's just—after everything that happened, I didn't want to do anything to hurt you more."

"It doesn't hurt me to talk about Lindsay." He paused. "Well, it hurts a little bit, but it hurts just as much not to talk about her, you know?"

"I do know," Hannah assured him. "I think about her, a lot. Just last week, these two kids came into the store, and one of them was wearing a horned helmet—"

"Oh, wow." Jace laughed. "I'd forgotten all about Lindsay's Viking phase. When she braided her hair and wore that silly helmet everywhere she went. Mom couldn't even get her to take it off for church. She was, what, seven years old?"

"Eight. We were in Ms. Engels's Sunday school class." Hannah blinked back tears. "Oh, Jace, I miss her. I'm so sorry. If I hadn't lied to your mother about where Lindsay was—"

Jace cut her off. "We all wish we'd handled things differently. Myself included."

Hannah frowned. "You weren't even living at home. You were in the dorm, going to summer school at UAF. None of it was your fault."

"I wouldn't say that." Jace sucked in a breath and blew it out. "You know she was out past curfew drinking with some kids in the woods the weekend before that, right?"

"What? No." Come to think of it, the weekend before Lindsay's accident, Hannah and her mom had driven to Anchorage to spend time with Dad and Nicole. "But that doesn't make any sense. If Lindsay was out past curfew, especially if she'd been drinking, your parents would have grounded her for a decade." The Angeleses were loving but strict parents. Like most teens, Lindsay had rebelled on occasion, especially after she turned eighteen, but her parents told her that if she expected them to pay for her college, she needed to follow their rules. Hannah always sympathized when Lindsay got in trouble, although she'd privately thought the rules weren't that unreasonable. She shook her head. "No way would they have allowed her to spend the night with me that night."

"They didn't know about it. The friend she'd ridden with ditched her, and she needed a ride home, so she called me. I picked her up and dropped her a block away from home. She'd left the window in her room open, and she sneaked inside without our parents finding out. But the next day after she sobered up, I really came down hard on her. I told her I wasn't covering for her again, that next time I'd wake up the folks and let her face the consequences." He huffed out a breath. "If I hadn't been so judgmental, maybe she would have called me again instead of riding with someone who'd been drinking."

"Or if I'd gone with her to the party, I could have watched over her." Hannah stood up and walked over to the window. She stared outside at the expanse of snow gleaming in the moonlight. "I felt terrible that night. And at the hospital, your parents were so upset, and I—" A sob stole her voice.

Jace came up behind her and put his arms around her. "I felt bad, too. But when it came down to it, the guy chose to drink and drive, and Lindsay chose to ride with him."

"She didn't deserve to die," Hannah protested.

"No, she didn't. But I don't believe she would want us to keep beating ourselves up over what we did and what we didn't do. God forgives, and I think Lindsay would as well."

Hannah turned within the circle of his arms. "Oh, Jace. I miss her so much." Tears poured from her eyes. He pulled her close against his chest and stroked her hair. Hannah put her arms around his waist and held on, as though he was the only thing keeping her from being swept out to a sea of loss and misery. Maybe he was. Hannah felt, rather than heard, the single sob that rattled Jace's chest. She looked up to see answering tears in his eyes.

"I miss her, too," Jace whispered. "But I know she's with the Lord now. And someday, we'll all be together again."

"Yes." Lindsay might have made mistakes, but her faith had never wavered. "I know that's true."

Suddenly Jace grinned. "I'll bet in heaven, no one ever burns the corn bread."

Hannah's tears turned to laughter, especially when Jace added, "But if anyone could do it, it's Lindsay."

The next morning, Hannah dressed and packed her few belongings into her daypack and the Angeles Adventure Store shopping bag. She and Jace had agreed to spend the morning working with Scout again, and then Jace would take her on the snow machine to the closest village. Pika was a tiny town, but it was on the road system. From there, they figured Hannah would be able to arrange a ride to Anchorage.

Jace's suggestion to forget her troubles for a day had been

a good one, but now she needed to be making plans, figuring out how to keep herself and the globe safe, as well as how to appease her sister since she'd backed out of their meeting with nothing more than a text reading:

Can't make it this evening. Not feeling well. Talk later.

But her thoughts kept returning to the conversation with Jace the evening before. To Lindsay.

She washed her face and started to comb her hair, but several teeth snapped off the cheap comb she'd picked up at the box store. That was annoying. She opened the drawer below the washbasin to see if she could find a replacement. Lindsay's purple hairbrush lay right on top, next to a couple of rhinestone-encrusted hair clips. Tucked beside them, for some reason, were some painted rocks. She, Lindsay, and Lindsay's mom, Judy, had painted them on a trip to the cabin the week after high school graduation. They'd even roped Jace and Lindsay's dad, Russell, into the project.

They'd had so much fun that day, gathering the rocks at the bend of the creek while they watched the antics of a family of river otters who had taken up residence on the far bank. They'd even seen a moose swim across the stream not too far down-river and a fox trotting by. Lindsay had declared that the creek was her favorite spot in the whole world. Later, they'd brought the stones back to the cabin to paint.

Hannah took the rocks from the drawer and spread them out on the countertop. Hers were painted with flowers, mostly daisies and fireweed. Judy's rocks were heavy on mountains and rainbows. Jace's rock was simple, just a brown line with green down-swept branches, forming a spruce tree. Russell's was a moose, although he'd smudged the antlers and Lindsay had teased him that it looked more like a stegosaurus.

Lindsay, who had the most artistic talent of the group, had done several animal paintings based on the shape of the rocks.

A sleeping red fox like the one they'd seen that day curled around one rock, and a mallard swam across another, the natural rings in the rock looking like water. Hannah turned over the last rock to see a bald eagle, painted in amazing detail, soaring against a blue sky.

She could hear Jace adding logs to the woodstove. "Jace, can you come in here for a minute?" she called.

He stepped inside the doorway. "What's up?"

She pointed to the rocks. "Remember these?"

Jace stepped closer. "Oh, yeah. You gathered them down at the creek that one day."

"Look at this one." She handed him the eagle rock. "Remember how Lindsay said it reminded her of a Bible verse?"

"'But they that wait upon the Lord shall renew their strength; they shall mount up with wings of eagles,'" he quoted without hesitation.

"That's the one. Hannah loved that spot where we gathered the rocks, at the river bend. I was thinking we could take this rock and leave it there, as sort of a memorial."

"That's a great idea."

Hannah hesitated. The rocks had been in a drawer, after all. "You don't think your parents would mind?"

"They would love that idea, and so would Lindsay. Let's do it."

Once they'd eaten breakfast, fed the dog, and banked the stove, they strapped on their skis and headed out. A cold breeze nipped at their noses, but the sunshine on their backs made up for it. The wind calmed as they arrived at the creek, now completely frozen across except for a space about a foot wide in the center where the water rushed too fast to be caught by the cold. An ancient spruce grew tall and thick on the bank. Birch branches, heavy with snow, bowed over the murmuring water. It looked completely different now than it did in the summer when they'd gathered the stones, but every bit as beautiful. Hannah knew Lindsay had loved this spot in all seasons.

The spruce branches had deflected the season's snow away from its trunk, forming a well about three feet deep. Hannah stepped out of her skis and took the eagle rock from her daypack. She carried it to the spruce tree and set it between two roots at the bottom of the tree well.

She returned to Jace and they stood without talking for several minutes, just listening to the birdsong. To the water whooshing past the ice in the middle of the frozen creek. To the wind rustling the tree branches. It was the voice of God's creation, and Lindsay had loved it more than anything. Hannah reached for Jace's hand. "Would you like to pray?"

"I would." He gave her hand a squeeze. "Our Father, we come to You today with heavy hearts. We miss Lindsay. But we also come with thankfulness for those years she was in our lives. Her joyful spirit was a gift to us, and to everyone around her, and we're grateful. Hannah and I are grateful, too, for this opportunity to share this moment of remembrance. In Jesus's name we pray. Amen."

"Amen," Hannah whispered and opened her eyes. "Oh, Jace, look!" On the far bank, a fox, looking dapper with his white shirtfront and furry red coat, watched them curiously. "There was a fox there that day when we gathered the rocks. It couldn't be the same one, could it?"

"No, but it could certainly be his great-something grandson. The cycle of life continues."

"Beautiful." She turned to Jace. "Thank you for coming with me today. Somehow, I feel…" She groped for the word.

"Peaceful?" Jace suggested.

"Yes. And lighter. As though a burden I've been carrying has been lifted." She looked into his eyes, a window to the gentle spirit inside him.

"I feel that way, too." He pulled her into a hug.

It felt so good, standing there on the riverbank with their arms around each other, warm and safe, as if they'd shut out all the dangers and complications and worries of the outside world.

Here it was just the two of them, drinking in the beauty of their surroundings and remembering someone they had both loved. Hannah felt like she could stay there in Jace's arms forever, but Scout chose that instant to notice the fox across the river and let out a barrage of barking. The fox fled, Jace turned to calm the dog, and the special moment was over. But the warmth of the hug stayed with Hannah.

A sudden gust of wind shook the branches and a splat of snow fell to the ground, barely missing them. Jace looked at the sky. "We'd better get back to the cabin. The forecast called for high winds tonight and a couple inches of snow tomorrow morning, but it looks like the front is arriving early." Another gust confirmed his theory.

The wind continued to pick up strength as they skied toward the cabin. When they reached the point where the trail converged with their tracks leading in from the train, Jace stopped, frowning.

"What's wrong?" Hannah asked, but then she spotted it too. The crosshatched tracks of a snow machine covered their own tracks leading to the cabin, although wind-driven snow was already beginning to erase them. "Do you think…" Hannah trailed off, unwilling to put her fears into words.

"It could be the neighbors." Jace's words were optimistic, but he still looked worried. "Eli Jones and his family have a cabin about five miles from here and they sometimes stop by to say hello. Although, when I talked to Eli a month ago, he said something about a Hawaiian cruise."

He examined the tracks more closely. "Whoever it was, they've come and gone. The tracks go both ways." But he stared toward the cabin, that worry line between his eyebrows. Scout, sensing his mood, pressed against his leg, and Jace absentmindedly reached down to stroke his head.

They continued on until they crested the hill, and the cabin came into sight. "Oh, no," Hannah whispered. The blue chair on the porch had been knocked over, and the door stood open.

The welcome sign lay in broken pieces on the snow in front of the porch. The chaos from Fairbanks had somehow followed them. The cabin was no longer a sanctuary.

Hannah's first impulse was to hurry forward, to see what damage they had done to the inside of the cabin, but Jace put out a hand to stop her from moving out of the protection of the woods. She looked at him. "You think they might have left someone behind," she guessed.

He nodded. "It's possible. Let's circle around and approach the cabin from the back, just in case."

They did just that, crouching behind the woodshed, but after watching the cabin for almost thirty minutes, they saw no sign of movement other than loose snow and broken twigs blowing across the clearing. "I'm going closer." Jace had to raise his voice to be heard over the wind, even though he was only a few inches away. "You keep Scout here."

Hannah nodded and grasped the dog's collar. Jace skied up to the cabin and then stepped out of his skis to creep closer to one of the bedroom windows. He looked inside, then moved to the next window and did the same. He circled the cabin, moving out of Hannah's field of vision. After what seemed like forever, the high window from the loft opened and Jace leaned out. "They're gone. Come on in."

Hannah released Scout and the two of them circled to the front porch and stepped inside. She gasped. It looked as though the cabin had been through a major earthquake. All the books and games on the shelves were dumped on the floor. The ice chest stood open, and all the kitchen gear was strewn about. Even Scout's dog food had been emptied from the bag. Jace climbed down the ladder from the loft. "Same story up there. They had to be looking for the globe."

"I had it with me." Hannah pulled off her backpack and took out the object of their search. "They might be back, and they won't be happy if the globe isn't here. Maybe instead of dropping me off at Pika, you'd better come with me to Anchorage."

Jace's mouth was set in a grim line. "I think that's a good idea."

Hannah picked up some of the plates on the floor. "Not broken, fortunately."

Jace laid a hand on her arm. "Don't worry about that. I'll clean up when I get back, once this is all behind us. You get your stuff together, and I'll do the same. We need to head out."

"Okay." He was right, although she hated leaving him with this mess. "Jace?"

He turned back, "Yes?"

"I'm sorry I dragged you into this."

He gave a little smile. "I'm not. Come on, get your things and dress warm. We'll be in Anchorage by nightfall, and we can turn this all over to the police."

Chapter Eight

Jace closed the ice chest and moved it to the front porch. Better to let the contents freeze in case he didn't make it back to the cabin in the next few days. It all depended on what happened once he got Hannah safely to Anchorage and they talked to the police. Hopefully, Hannah could get that globe tucked away in a safe deposit box, or in police evidence, or somewhere secure. But even then, how would she get the word out to would-be robbers that she wasn't carrying it around anymore? And what was so special about that globe, anyway?

He went back inside and scaled the ladder to the loft. After shoving one of the beds there to the side, he located the ring embedded in one of the floorboards. Fortunately, whoever had searched the house hadn't discovered it. He pulled up on the ring and the section of the floor lifted out, revealing a compartment about fourteen inches square and ten inches deep. Inside was a metal box. He pulled out the box, turned the four numbers to the proper combination, and opened the lid. Inside, a portable GPS lay beside Dad's .45 Winchester Magnum pistol.

Too bad there wasn't a satellite phone there as well to call the state troopers. When their store first began carrying the phones, Jace had suggested they get one for the cabin, but Dad had nixed the idea. He said the whole point of the cabin was to get away from work and everyday stresses, and if he carried a satellite phone, work would just follow him. He made a good point, but Jace could have really used that phone right now. He tucked the pistol into his backpack, along with a box of ammunition and the GPS. Dad kept the gun at the cabin as protection from bears, but whoever was after Hannah might be even more dangerous than an angry grizzly.

He shrugged on the backpack and climbed down the ladder. Scout waited at the bottom. Hannah was at the door, about to step into her snow boots. "Wait." Jace ducked into his parents' bedroom and returned carrying a pile of puffy outerwear. He tossed one of the jumpsuits to Hannah. "You can borrow my mom's snowmobile suit and gloves."

"Thanks." Hannah pulled the suit up over her clothes. The temperatures outside weren't that cold, but the wind chill on a snow machine could bring on frostbite in a hurry if the passengers weren't bundled up.

They gathered up their things and stepped outside, into the gale. After Jace locked the cabin door, they had to bend forward to make their way through the blowing snow to the shed. Ordinarily, Jace would never go out in conditions like this, but with the portable GPS unit, he was confident he could find the way to Pika. His first inkling of trouble came when he noticed extra footprints in the snow near the shed. The wind must have blown them clear between the cabin and the shed, but on the leeward side, a few tracks remained, and they hadn't been made by him or Hannah. When they reached the door, he wasn't surprised to find that someone had used bolt cutters to remove the padlock.

Hannah leaned around him to peer at the mangled lock lying in the snow. "This doesn't look good."

"No." When he unlatched the door, a gust of wind jerked it from his hand and slammed it against the wall. He and Hannah stepped inside to find the hoods open on both snow machines.

As his eyes adjusted to the relative gloom inside the shed, he was able to see parts and pieces scattered everywhere.

"Oh, no!" Hannah surveyed the wreckage. "Now what?"

Jace picked up the nearest part, which happened to be a carburetor. "I guess I try to put it back together. Looks like that auto shop class I took in high school might come in handy."

"What if you can't fix it?" she asked. "Whoever did this must intend to come back, or they wouldn't have bothered to disable the snow machines."

"You're right. And the train doesn't run again until Saturday." He considered the options, which were few. "If I can't fix this, we'll have to ski out. We should be able to make it to Pika in under two days."

Hannah picked up a stray bolt that had rolled under the edge of a shelving unit against the wall. "This looks hopeless. Maybe we should start skiing now."

Another gust shook the shed. "We're almost in whiteout conditions," Jace said, "but the wind is supposed to die down tonight. Chances are, since they think we're stranded, they'll wait for the storm to pass before they come back. If we leave first thing tomorrow morning, we should be able to make it to Pika the day after tomorrow. If we left now, that would mean two overnights, and I'm not thrilled with the idea of tent camping in this weather."

"Good point. I don't think we could even set up a tent in this gale. Okay, I don't know much about mechanics, but how can I help?"

Jace considered the best way to attack the problem. "Let's collect all the parts and lay them out on the floor in some kind of order."

Hannah nodded. "I'll go inside and get some lanterns, so we can shut the door and get out of the wind while we work."

"Thanks."

Forty-five minutes later, after they had collected all the parts, it was clear the snow machines weren't going anywhere. The intruders had torn the wires from the distributor caps and broken the spark plugs. For all Jace knew, they could have contaminated the fuel in the tank as well. He couldn't detect any odor other than gas, but then if they'd just added water, he wouldn't. He huffed out a breath. "I suppose we should be grateful that they didn't set the shed on fire."

Hannah shook her head as she gazed down at the assorted parts. "I'm just sorry that your reward for helping me is to have your snow machines destroyed."

"I don't think they're destroyed," Jace said. "I just can't fix them without getting more parts. Once this is behind us, I'll get someone to come over from Pika and haul these to a shop for a complete overhaul. They're due for a tune-up anyway." He put a finger under her chin and tipped up her face so that their eyes met. "And none of this is your fault, so don't start feeling guilty."

She gave a rueful smile. "It's a long-standing habit."

"Well, it's time to change that. And speaking of change, looks like we're going to Plan B. So let's take these lanterns back to the cabin and dig out our equipment for snow camping." Saying the words reminded him of the one and only time his parents had taken them all camping in the winter. Dad had planned on doing all the cooking on a camp stove, but Lindsay and Hannah insisted it wasn't a real camping trip if they didn't roast marshmallows over a fire.

When the wet wood they gathered refused to burn, they had sacrificed most of the marshmallows to use as a fire-starter, leaving only one apiece to roast. When Lindsay's last marshmallow fell into the fire, Hannah offered hers. The two girls had ended up sharing a s'more, the same way they'd shared almost everything. Jace grinned. "We'd better carry plenty of fuel for the camp stove, because I don't have marshmallows this time."

Hannah laughed. "I remember that trip. Best s'more ever. You know, I haven't eaten a s'more in years."

"Me neither. Next time, we'll have to bring a bag of marshmallows." The words slipped out before Jace remembered that Hannah didn't live in Fairbanks anymore. He wouldn't be sharing marshmallows or anything else with her once he'd seen her safely home. And that thought saddened him more than he wanted to admit.

Busy gathering the lanterns, Hannah didn't seem to notice his slip. They stepped outside, where Jace pushed a screwdriver into the hasp to hold the shed door closed until he could return with a new padlock. Bracing themselves against the wind, they made their way to the cabin.

It felt so familiar, being here with Hannah, as if the thirteen years of absence had just fallen away and their relationship had simply picked up where it left off. But no, that wasn't quite true, he realized. Back then, she'd been almost another sister, but now there was something more humming between them. When he'd held her in his arms at the river, looking into her face, he'd wanted nothing more than to kiss away those tears, to bring back that wonderful smile.

Once they'd gotten out of their jackets and boots, Scout went to lean against Hannah's leg. She stroked his head. Jace wasn't the only one Hannah had charmed. She crossed to the stove. "How about if I build a fire and heat up that leftover posole while you get the equipment together?"

"Sounds like a plan." With the two of them working together, it didn't take long to clean up the mess the intruders had left and gather up the camping equipment. Soon, they were sitting at the table, enjoying bowls of hot soup and cold corn bread. Outside the wind still howled, but inside the cabin they were warm and cozy. Tomorrow night might be a different story.

Once they'd finished supper and washed dishes, Hannah took the globe from her backpack and held it close to the light of the lantern in the center of the table. "There has to be more to this than a simple ornament. Maybe there's something special about the design that makes it worth a whole lot more than Karas's other globes."

Jace leaned closer. "You mentioned puzzle boxes."

Hannah nodded. "Peter Morozov, the expert in Fairbanks, said Dimitri Karas made a few, but the ones he described were cubes about eight inches square. But since each art piece he made was custom, there's no reason he couldn't have designed a ball puzzle." She ran a finger over the smooth wood in the Indian Ocean. "But if he did, I can't imagine how it would work. Everything fits together so tightly."

"May I see?"

Hannah passed the globe to Jace. She was right—there didn't seem to be any gaps. Except…was that a crack in the center of the equator, or simply a slight groove? He looked closely at the minuscule strips of dark wood circling the globe. "There's a tiny space here. It's hard to see, because there's dark wood underneath, but I think the two hemispheres might be separate pieces. Can you feel it?"

Hannah ran a fingernail over the line. "Yes! It's shallow, but I can feel a little depression."

"Without more light, it's hard to tell, but if it is a puzzle box, that raises another question. Is it the puzzle box itself the guys in the white truck are after, or is there something inside?"

Hannah ran her fingers over the surface. "I suppose we could smash it," she said slowly. "Although I hate to destroy that beautiful work."

Jace shook his head. "Only as a last resort. If it is a puzzle box, there has to be someone who can tell you how it works. And you could always have it x-rayed to find out if there's something inside. But first, we need to get it and you to a safe place."

"Agreed. And since we're planning to head out before dawn tomorrow, I suppose we'd better get some sleep." Hannah rewrapped the globe and returned it to her backpack. "Thank you, Jace, for everything you've done."

"I can't say I've done much. I thought you'd be safe here, but they found you."

"But you've been with me, protecting me." She leaned toward him, close enough for him to catch a whiff of her scent, clean and natural, like rain. "And you can't imagine how much it means to me that you've forgiven me for my part in Lindsay's accident."

"And you've forgiven me for mine. We both loved Lindsay, and we miss her, but she would want us to be happy."

"Yes, she would." She pressed a kiss to Jace's cheek. "Good night, Jace."

"Good night, Hannah." He waited until she'd disappeared into her room before running his finger over the cheek she'd kissed. It still felt warm. What would a real kiss with Hannah be like? He suspected it just might be life changing. Was that good or bad? If anyone had asked him last week, he would have said he liked his life just the way it was. Now, he wasn't so sure.

But he couldn't let himself be distracted by what-ifs and future possibilities. He needed to concentrate on the here and now, on standing between Hannah and the danger that kept following her. Whatever came, Jace would keep her safe. Somehow.

The wind died down about midnight, as Hannah could attest, since she'd spent most of the night tossing and turning. She should have been sleeping, gathering strength for the grueling trek to come, but her swirling thoughts kept her awake. It wasn't memories of the strange men in the white truck, of Jim White grabbing her arm at Peter Morozov's place, or of the ransacked cabin that disturbed her sleep. Rather, it was thoughts of Jace, of the concern on his face when he'd insisted she come to the cabin with him. Of his warm, woodsy scent when he'd held her in his arms. Of the feel of rough stubble on his cheek when she'd kissed him good-night. Maybe she shouldn't have done that, but she couldn't bring herself to regret it.

When she faced herself in the mirror the next morning, she noticed dark circles under her eyes, but since her makeup bag had been inside her suitcase and she hadn't picked up more at the store, there wasn't a lot she could do about it other than splash some cold water on her face. She dressed in the weatherproof ski pants Jace had provided, knowing the insulated bibs would be too warm once they started skiing.

Jace was already up, working at the woodstove. He looked up and smiled. "Good morning. Coffee in five. Bacon and pancakes in ten." If he'd had any trouble sleeping, it didn't show. In fact, he seemed energized, as though they were about to head out on a grand adventure rather than fleeing danger. But when he turned to pick up a skillet, she spotted the tension in his shoulders. He was putting on a brave face for her. The least she could do was return the favor.

"Coffee sounds great." Scout rushed to greet her, and she ran a hand over his soft fur. "Good boy. Are you ready to go snow camping, Scout? Are you?" She couldn't help but smile as the dog wagged so hard he wiggled all over. She set her backpack next to the other gear and went to the window, cupping her hands around her face to better see into the dark. "It's snowing."

"I know." Jace stirred the batter in a red ceramic bowl. "But that's good. It will cover our tracks."

"True." There was still a little breeze stirring the snowflakes, but nothing like yesterday's wind. "You have the route mapped out?"

"Yes." He nodded toward the portable GPS on the table. "It's kind of a roundabout path, but I'm taking us through the woods as much as I can. We'll be harder to spot, and the trails are too narrow for snow machines." He poured coffee into a cup and handed it to her.

"Thanks." She helped herself to some sugar from the bowl on the table, enjoying the little conveniences while she could. Tomorrow's breakfast would be camp coffee and freeze-dried eggs, at best.

It was still dark when they headed out, their headlamps spotlighting the dancing snowflakes falling from the sky. Jace led the way, dragging a sledload of gear behind him. Hannah and

Scout followed. They all wore packs, including Scout, who carried his own kibble, rolled mat, and collapsible bowls for food and water. Once they were in the woods, the snowfall slowed, and all Hannah had to do was follow Jace's tracks, through the forest, beside the streams, and up and down the hills. She considered herself fit—after all, she worked out almost every day at the gym or on her ski machine at home—but she was puffing like a steam locomotive as they crested a particularly steep hill.

Jace stopped there, pulled out a water bottle, and handed it to her. "You're doing great." Frost clung to his eyebrows and two-day beard, but he was barely breathing hard.

"Thanks." Hannah gulped some water. "It's been a while since I did any backcountry skiing."

"It's different than groomed trails, for sure." He accepted the bottle back and took a drink. "Hear that?"

Hannah raised her head and listened, but the falling snow dampened even the usual forest sounds. "I don't hear anything."

He smiled. "Exactly. You never get that on city trails."

Hannah looked eastward. Trees blocked their view of the horizon, but the overcast sky was beginning to grow lighter. In a nearby tree, a chickadee called, "Dee-dee-dee." Another called back, and a few seconds later a mixed flock of chickadees, nuthatches, and sparrows darted overhead only to alight in a tree on the other side of the clearing. The last of the breezes had died away, and the big feathery snowflakes seemed to dance in the air before settling on Scout's fur.

It had been too long since Hannah had taken a moment to really appreciate the beauty of a snowy day. She smiled at Jace. "You're right."

Scout came up beside him and opened his mouth. Jace squirted in some water and adjusted the dog's pack. "Guess we'd better keep moving. Are you ready?"

"Ready," Hannah assured him, and she kept assuring him on every break throughout the day, even as her leg muscles threatened a mutiny.

Finally, he stopped in a level clearing next to a boulder the size of a school bus, no doubt deposited by some glacier long ago. "How does this look for a camp spot?"

"Perfect." Although in all honesty, she would have said the same if he'd suggested they camp in the middle of a five-diamond ski run in avalanche country if it meant she could stop moving for a while.

But she hadn't earned her rest yet. First, they had to stomp down the snow in the clearing, then put up the tent, and finally, ferry all their gear inside. It was another hour before Hannah leaned back against one of the gear bags with a deep sigh.

"Sore?" Jace asked, as he hung a lantern from a hook on the domed ceiling of the tent and arranged his foam mat and sleeping bag.

"I will be. Right now I'm too tired to feel anything."

"Here." He reached into a duffel and handed her a small bottle of ibuprofen and a water bottle. "Take two of these." Once she'd swallowed the pills, he pulled off her boot.

"What are—?" she started to ask, but when he began kneading the ball of her foot, she smiled and closed her eyes. "That feels amazing."

He chuckled and kept massaging the sore muscles of her foot and calf, then switched to her other leg. By the time he'd finished, Hannah was all but asleep. Jace pulled the insulated ski bibs from a pack and handed them to her. "Better put these on and keep those muscles warm. I'll get started on supper," he added as he dug out a camp stove and a couple of instant meals.

"I'll help," Hannah offered, but Jace waved her offer away.

"I can do it. You rest. Remember to hydrate." He slipped out of the tent and Hannah took another swig of water and changed into the heavy pants. Fifteen minutes later, Jace was back, carrying the foil pouches and two sporks. "Chicken and rice or lasagna?"

"They both sound great. You choose."

He chuckled. "We're talking freeze-dried food here. It won't be great, but we need the fuel. Here, you take the lasagna. You used to love Italian food."

"I still do. Thanks." After a heartfelt prayer of gratitude for safe travel and food, she opened the pouch and took a bite. Maybe it wouldn't be gourmet food under other circumstances, but tonight the dried cheeses and saucy noodles tasted better than any restaurant meal in recent memory. Scout, who was eating his kibble, stopped and shot a hopeful glance her way. She paused, a sporkful of noodles halfway to her mouth.

"Don't," Jace said. "He knows he's not supposed to beg."

"Sorry, Scout. I've been overruled." She put the bite into her mouth and Scout went back to his kibble. In no time, she'd finished the whole meal. Jace collected the empty pouches, rolled them up, and stuffed them in the duffel. She could almost hear his dad's voice reminding them, "Pack it in, pack it out. Leave no trace." Russell always carried an extra bag to pick up after any other campers who hadn't been as considerate. Hannah had learned so much tagging along with Jace and Lindsay's family.

Jace ducked out of the tent again, and when he returned, he was juggling two cups and two water bottles.

"What's this?" Hannah asked as she took the cups from him.

"Hot chocolate. And a hot water bottle to warm up the foot of your sleeping bag."

"Nice." Once he'd slipped the bottles inside the sleeping bags, she returned his cup and took a sip from her own. "Yum! Room service, massage, a hot water bottle… Do you have a mint for my pillow, too?"

He snapped his fingers. "I knew I forgot something."

She laughed. "I don't know why you're being so good to me. All I've done is drag you into a hot mess and gotten your cabin ransacked. You probably wish you'd taken Scout to the dog park instead of to the Ice Sculpture Championships that day."

"Not at all." He met her gaze, and she could read the sincerity in his eyes. "I'm glad I was there, and I'm glad I'm here, with you."

Their eyes held, and Hannah found herself wondering, not for the first time, what it would be like to kiss Jace. Not just a kiss on the cheek, like last night, but a real kiss. She gave herself a mental shake. This wasn't the time for her old teenage crush to come rushing back. There was too much history there. Even if they'd forgiven each other for their own part in Lindsay's accident, it was still there, between them, and she wasn't sure his parents would be so generous with their forgiveness.

Besides, there were practical reasons she shouldn't kiss Jace. They had no future. He was CEO of Angeles Adventure Stores, based in Fairbanks, and she had invested so much of herself in the store in Anchorage. He was just helping her until she could get the globe to the authorities and be safe. Then he would be going home, and they might never see each other again.

Reluctantly, she pulled herself away from his gaze and reached inside her backpack for the globe, which she unwrapped. The workmanship she'd been so appreciative of now seemed to mock her. Was it just an ornament, or was it more? "What secrets are you hiding?" she whispered.

"May I?" Jace asked. She handed it to him, and he examined it for several minutes. "You know, each of the continents has a tiny line around it. Oh, look! If I put my finger in the very center of Antarctica and push, it sinks a little. So does Australia."

"What! Let me see."

Hannah scooted closer and he demonstrated that he could push each continent like a button. When he removed his finger, each one popped back into place. "It has to be a puzzle box. There's no other reason for moving parts and springs."

"You're right. But how does it open?"

"I don't know." He tried a few more spots. "All the continents seem to be buttons, and so do the North Pole and the compass rose, but they don't do anything, at least by themselves. If this is a puzzle box, I assume we would need to press them in a certain order, like a combination lock."

"A combination!" Hannah exclaimed. "That might be what was on the card."

"What card?"

"Remember the photo I showed you of the box Nicole won at auction? There was an index card inside, with letters and numbers. Let me find it." Hannah pulled up the photo on her phone, enlarged the part with the card, and read, "N, S CW 30: E CCW 45: CR."

Jace looked at the photo. "Okay, N, S, and E could be north, south, and east, but what is CW? Something west?"

Hannah tilted her head. "And what is east on a globe, anyway?"

"I suppose it would be the farthest point from the prime meridian, one hundred eighty degrees longitude. The international date line." He pointed to one of the silver longitudinal lines in the center of the Pacific Ocean. "Here."

"But there are no continents on that line until you get to Antarctica. No land at all, except—" she leaned closer "—the Alaskan Aleutian Islands. Look, does it seem like that island right beside the line is a little darker than the others?"

"Maybe. It's hard to see in this light, and it's too small to push."

"Just a sec." Hannah checked inside her jacket where she usually kept a couple of small safety pins. She unpinned one, opened it, and handed it to Jace. "Try pushing on it."

He tried it. "It moves!"

"So, maybe N is the North Pole. S is Antarctica. E is that island. We just need to figure out CR, CW, and CCW. And the numbers."

"The numbers would probably be longitude. Thirty degrees is either here…" He pointed to a spot in Africa. "Or here." He moved his finger to the Pacific Ocean. "Depending on whether it's east or west."

"Maybe that's what the W means," Hannah suggested.

"Okay, but why the C with it? CW is written together."

"Center West? Is there a button at thirty degrees on the equator?"

Jace tried pushing the pin into that area. It slipped into the depression in the center of the equator line but didn't seem to activate any sort of button. Instead, it just slid along the line. "No button. I think the equator might be where the box opens up once we get the combination right."

"Hmm. Like it unscrews?" Hannah gasped. "What if CW means clockwise, and CCW means counterclockwise?"

Jace gently tried to turn the two hemispheres in opposite directions. "It doesn't move."

"You'd need to do the combination first. Try pushing the North Pole, then Antarctica, then turn it clockwise."

"Clockwise from top or bottom?"

"I don't know. Try both."

He did. "No, still can't move it."

"Hmm." She stared at the photo. "Wait. What if you hold the N and S buttons down while you turn clockwise?"

"Let's see." It took him a few moments to figure out how to position his hands so that he could hold it all at once, but when he tried it, the hemispheres shifted. "Eureka!"

"Hurray! Okay, stop once you've turned thirty degrees. Now hold the Aleutian button with the pin and turn counterclockwise forty-five degrees."

Jace did it. "Okay. Now what?"

Hannah frowned. "It just says CR."

"CR," Jace repeated and stopped to think. "Compass rose?"

"Try it!"

He pushed on the center of the compass rose, and with a click, the globe fell into two halves, exposing a white foam ball with a seam in the center. "Yes!"

Hannah blinked. "I can't believe it worked."

"Now let's see what someone was hiding in here." Jace removed the ball and handed it to Hannah.

Holding her breath, she pulled the two pieces of foam apart.

Inside was a transparent plastic box, about two inches square, holding a coin.

"What is it?" Jace asked.

"It looks like a gold coin."

"Nice. What's gold worth now? About two thousand dollars an ounce?"

"Yes, but I'm sure this is worth a lot more. I'm no coin expert, but it looks old. Too bad Nicole isn't here. She knows way more about coins than I do." Hannah picked up the box and examined the coin inside. It featured a woman's profile in classic Greek style, wearing what looked like a tiara with the word "Liberty" written on it. Stars lined the border of the coin, with the date at the bottom. "It was minted in 1854."

"So, really old."

"Yes, and probably rare. Between 1933 and 1974, it was unlawful to hold gold in the United States. When the law passed, everyone was supposed to deliver their gold coins to the government, who melted them down, so most of the gold coins minted before that are gone." Hannah turned the coin over to reveal an eagle with a shield on its chest. One foot held a clutch of arrows, and the other a branch. Around the rim were the words "United States of America" and "Five D." She pointed to the letter S underneath the eagle. "This means it's from the San Francisco mint."

"Is that important?"

"It can be. If a certain mint only produced a limited number of a certain coin, that drives up the value." She handed Jace the coin in its box. "And that pretty much exhausts my expertise on the subject of collectible coins."

"It's more than I knew." Jace opened the lid and examined the coin. "Five dollars, huh?"

"Well, five dollars was worth a lot more in 1854."

"Feels about as heavy as two quarters. It's hard to believe it's really worth all that much, even if it is made of gold."

"Hard to say. At the Linacott auction where I got the chest

that was holding the globe, they were auctioning off some coins. I didn't pay that much attention since I'm not a coin collector, but I remember that a four-dollar gold piece, which apparently is rare, went for more than twenty thousand dollars."

He snapped the box closed and handed it back to her. "In that case, you'd better hang on to it. It's too much responsibility for me. I might accidentally put it into a vending machine."

She laughed. "Not a big concern at the moment." She returned the coin to the foam ball and tucked it inside one hemisphere of the wooden globe. She set the other hemisphere on top. It only took a slight twist to put it back together again. She started to tuck the globe inside her backpack but paused. "You don't suppose..." She trailed off, staring at the globe.

"What?" Jace asked.

Hannah looked up. "You remember when we were talking about that gold coin robbery at the airport? I was in eighth grade, so it would have been seventeen years ago."

"The one where the five coins were missing, the courier was drugged, and later an airport employee found dead? Yeah, I remember."

"Well, what if this is one of those coins?"

Jace raised his eyebrows. "Wait, I thought we decided Candace Linacott was mixed up in the walrus ivory scandal, not the gold coins. Besides, you said she was cleared."

"I said she wasn't charged. What if she was the mastermind behind both? If she managed to get away with robbing a courier, she wouldn't balk at smuggling ivory."

"That's a big leap."

Hannah sighed. "You're right. I have absolutely no evidence that she had anything to do with the gold coin robbery. But if she did, that would explain some things."

"Like what?"

"Like why these men are so determined to get their hands on this globe. According to my history teacher, the coins stolen in that robbery were incredibly rare. Do you remember the value of the stolen coins?"

"No idea. Fifty thousand dollars?" he guessed.

Hannah shook her head. "I don't remember the exact figure," she said, "but it was more than a million."

Chapter Nine

Jace's eyes flew open. Still dark. He wasn't sure if whatever had woken him was part of a dream or real, so he lay still, listening. After a few seconds, Scout gave a low growl. Jace could just make out the shape of the dog with his nose pressed against the door of the tent. Had whomever ransacked the cabin managed to follow their trail despite the wind and snow? Jace pulled on his boots and reached into his backpack to collect his head lamp, his dad's pistol, and the box of ammunition. He loaded the gun. At the click of the bolt engaging, something outside the tent made a scuffling noise.

Scout reacted by pressing against the tent fabric with a whine, but Jace pushed him into the down position and whispered "stay." Scout reluctantly obeyed. Slowly and silently, Jace unzipped the door of the tent. A visual sweep of the area revealed nothing except that in the hours they had been sleeping, the skies had cleared. The new-fallen snow glistened in the light of a full moon. He crept out of the tent and spotted a set of tracks, the kind made by some four-footed creature, crossing close to the tent and then heading into the woods. He blew out a breath and allowed his body to relax.

"What's going on?" Hannah whispered from the door of the tent.

"Nothing important. An animal passed by." He turned on his headlamp to get a better look at the tracks and identify them, but something green flashed in the woods. He trained his light in that direction, and a pair of emerald animal eyes reflected the light back at him. The animal took a step out of the woods, and Jace recognized the tufted ears and flat face. "A lynx."

"I see it," Hannah answered, softly. Scout tried to squeeze past her, but she grabbed the dog's collar. "Oh, no you don't." In a flash, the big cat disappeared into the woods.

Jace turned to Hannah. "You okay?"

"Of course." Hannah put her hand to her chest. "I just thought for a second—"

"Me, too. But it's okay. We're safe."

Hannah pushed the dog back before crawling out the door and zipping it closed. "The snow stopped." She stood and looked around. "It's so pretty."

"Yeah, it is." The temperature had dropped with the clearing skies, but all around them moonlight reflected off the new fallen snow, bathing everything in a silvery light.

Hannah looked toward a particularly tall spruce, its limbs drooping gracefully under their load of snow. Her eyes followed the trunk upward. "Oh, Jace. Look!"

An owl perched at the top of the tree, staring down at them. Scout whimpered. Jace unzipped the tent and let the dog out, convinced the lynx was long gone. He grabbed his sleeping bag, unzipped it, and draped it over Hannah's shoulders.

"Thank you." She flashed him a smile and held out one side of the bag, inviting him in. "Join me?"

"Love to." He pulled the end of the bag over his left shoulder and because it seemed only natural, slipped his right arm around Hannah's waist. She leaned into him, her head on his shoulder. Scout came to sit at their feet.

A million stars twinkled in the blue velvet sky overhead.

A few high clouds drifted, painting ever-changing pictures among the stars. A sweep of green appeared for a few seconds and then it was gone. "Northern lights," Hannah whispered.

"Maybe they'll come back," Jace whispered back to her. With Hannah's warm body pressed against his side, Jace felt as though he could stand there forever, watching the sky. They waited, but the northern lights seemed to be over for the time being. Jace was about to suggest they return to the tent when a sudden streak shot through the sky.

Hannah gasped. "A shooting star! Oh, make a wish, Jace."

But, other than Hannah's safety, Jace couldn't think of anything he wanted in that moment that wasn't already there with him.

Hannah turned toward Jace, moonlight spilling over her lovely face, eyes sparkling like the brightest stars. "With all the streetlights, we can't see the stars like that in Anchorage. I'd forgotten how amazing they are."

He took a moment to study her face. "I'd forgotten how amazing you are."

Her lips parted, and he leaned closer, but just before their lips touched, he hesitated, suddenly unsure. But Hannah slid a hand behind his neck and closed the gap, pressing her lips to his. He tightened his arm around her waist and pulled her even closer. The heat of the kiss seemed to flow through him, warm and wonderful, like nothing he'd ever experienced before. It was like he'd been born to kiss this woman.

After a long moment, he pulled back and paused to look again at Hannah's face, familiar and yet somehow brand-new to him. Was her nose always so perfect, her eyelashes so long, her eyebrows so gracefully arched? He kissed that adorable nose, brushed his lips against her velvety cheek, and couldn't resist a kiss on each eyelid before returning to her mouth.

Her hand went up to cup his jaw. "Jace," she whispered against his lips, and he lost track of the cold, of his surroundings, of everything except for Hannah and the thrill of kissing her. When he finally broke the kiss, she smiled at him. "The lynx, the stars, the kisses—is this really happening or am I dreaming?"

"Let's find out." He leaned in for another kiss.

Wham! A furry missile crashed into them, knocking them to the snow. Scout was lying on Jace's chest, wearing a pleased expression and breathing dog breath into Jace's face. Hannah, sitting on the snow beside him, was laughing so hard tears were running down her face. "You—" she began, but had to gasp for breath before continuing. "You did say find."

"I did." Jace pushed the dog off his chest and sat up. "Buddy, we're going to have a word about your sense of timing."

Hannah grinned and then glanced at her watch. "Speaking of timing, there's not much use going back to bed. The sun will be up in an hour." She stood and offered Jace a hand.

"You're right." Mentally, he shifted gears. This wasn't a date. He was here to protect Hannah, and he shouldn't let himself get distracted. "We have a lot of miles to cover today. We might as well get started." He took her hand and let her haul him to his feet, but he couldn't resist stealing another little kiss before he let go. *Last one*, he promised himself. "I'll get some water boiling for coffee."

Five hours later, the sun had just about reached its zenith for the day. Jace slowed his pace going up a big hill, just enough to give Hannah a rest without it being obvious that's what he was doing. She'd been pushing herself hard, not that he could blame her for being eager to get back to safety, a community... home. He'd thought he was keeping her safe by taking her to the cabin. Instead, here they were, fleeing cross-country for their lives, with no way to contact the authorities. Jace could tell by her ragged breathing that the hours of backcountry skiing were wearing Hannah down.

He was feeling it, too, especially since he was dragging the sled filled with camping equipment. Jace had hoped to be in Pika by noon, but he'd underestimated how much the gear and new snow would slow them down. Now it was looking more like early afternoon. And after they got there, he would still need to call a driver service and wait for a driver to come from Anchorage. Once they got close to the village, they might be able to pick up a cell phone signal and call ahead, but he doubted it. As he recalled, cell service was pretty iffy, even in the town. He reached the top of the hill and paused to rest.

"Why are…" Hannah sucked in a breath "…we stopping?" She pulled up beside him. Scout, always hoping for a treat, ran up and sat in front of them.

"Snack break. We need calories." He handed Hannah an energy bar and tossed Scout one of the dog treats he always carried in his pocket before helping himself to another bar.

"Oh." Hannah leaned forward with her hands on her knees and closed her eyes while she caught her breath. With her long lashes brushing her rosy cheeks, her face reminded Jace of the angel atop his family's Christmas tree. Once Hannah's breathing had returned to normal, she unwrapped the bar and took a bite. "Chocolate almond. Yum." She swallowed another bite. "How much farther to Pika?"

Jace checked his GPS. "About ten miles, but there are a couple of stiff climbs on the way. And we have to take it slow crossing that area up ahead. It's pretty rugged." As long as they stuck to the trail he'd mapped out, they should be fine, but there were several ravines in the area, and new snow tended to camouflage them.

Hannah finished her bar and stuffed the wrapper into her backpack. "Ready?"

"Not yet." This was their first big descent of the day. He snapped a second cord onto the back of the sled and handed it to Hannah. "Can you hold the sled back so it doesn't run over me on the way down?"

"Of course." Hannah tied the cord around her waist.

Jace pushed off. If he'd been skiing unencumbered, he would

have picked a line almost straight down the hill, but with the sled and Hannah in tow, he chose a gentler, more winding route. Hannah followed in his tracks, holding back the sled. They made a good team. Although, after those incredible kisses early this morning, he had a hard time thinking of Hannah as simply a teammate.

What was this between them? A simple attraction fueled by adrenaline and the romance of moonlight, or was it more? Once Hannah had turned over the globe and coin to the police, then what? Did he and Hannah go their separate ways, or—

"Watch for that branch," Hannah called, and he navigated around a stray limb from a nearby currant bush sticking out of the snow just enough to trip an unwary skier. The last thing they needed right now was an injury.

Jace turned his attention to the trail. One thing at a time. He needed to keep his mind on keeping Hannah safe today. Tomorrow would take care of tomorrow.

They made it to the bottom of the hill, and Jace unclipped Hannah from the sled. Scout, who had trotted on ahead, started barking.

"What is it, boy?" Jace called. The dog only barked harder and then took off at a run, away from the main trail. "Scout, no. Come! Come back, now!" he yelled, but he might as well have been whispering for all the good it did. So much for all those hours of obedience training. Scout was still young, and like human teenagers, young dogs sometimes made poor choices. Jace was going to have to go after him.

"Stay here with the stuff," Jace told Hannah as he unclipped the towline from his belt. "I'll be right back." He skied after the dog, who had disappeared down a game trail that veered off from the main trail. Jace had been following for fifteen minutes or so without any glimpse of Scout when he heard another bark, followed by a surprised yip. Jace raced toward the sound and followed the trail around a bushy spruce, only to slide to a stop when he found his way blocked by the back end of a moose.

The moose swung around toward him and Jace ducked behind a nearby birch. Scout stood on the other side of a clearing with his head lowered, occasionally throwing out a nervous bark and probably wishing he'd never started this confrontation. Jace was afraid that yip earlier meant the moose's hoof had landed a blow, most likely a glancing one since Scout was still standing. In between them, a much smaller moose snorted at the dog. Just the situation they didn't need—an agitated mama moose convinced her calf was in danger. "Scout, quiet," Jace commanded, and this time the dog obeyed.

The moose swung her head toward Jace and then toward Scout, trying to decide which was the bigger threat. "It's okay." Jace tried for a soothing voice as he eased farther into the woods, putting distance between himself and the moose. "Nobody wants to hurt your baby."

Scout chose that moment to abandon the standoff and make a run toward Jace and the safety he represented. Unfortunately, the moose interpreted his sudden movement as an attack and lashed out at him. Scout dodged her hoof and ran directly toward Jace, with the mama moose right on his tail. Jace tried to jump out of the way, but his ski caught, and he stumbled backward. A flash of yellow fur streaked past followed by the moose, her bulk catching Jace and knocking him completely out of his skis. He went flying and landed in the snow, but the snow gave way, and he was falling again. He hit something hard, a pain shot from his knee, and then he was rolling in the snow, fruitlessly trying to catch himself. His gloves found nothing but loose snow to grab on to, but finally he came to rest on his back, facing upward. He seemed to be in one of those ravines he'd hoped to avoid.

He sucked in a lungful of air. Okay, he was breathing. So far, so good. Even better, none of his ribs seemed to be broken. No dizziness when he sat up. His knee hurt, but he didn't think it was anything serious. Until he tried to move it and discovered one of his legs was wedged between two rocks.

He tried pulling it toward himself, but the stiff sole of his ski boot was caught on something, and he couldn't seem to wiggle it loose. Lifting the leg from the crack was impossible, because of the angle at which his leg had come to rest.

About ten feet above him, a gap in the snow revealed a patch of sky, quickly blocked by a furry yellow face looking down at him. Scout whined.

"Oh, so now you're concerned about my safety," Jace chided. "I hope the moose have moved on. Stay there, boy. I'll be up in a minute." He tried bracing his free leg against the rock and pushing, but the stuck boot still refused to budge. This was getting ridiculous. Jace was strong and fit, and not seriously injured. There had to be a way to get himself free so that he could climb out of the ravine. He just needed to…or maybe…

Fifteen minutes later, he was forced to accept the truth. He was stuck.

Chapter Ten

Hannah took another drink from her water bottle and checked her watch. How long could it possibly take to catch a runaway dog, especially one that was supposedly obedience trained? Was Scout hurt? Maybe he'd come across a porcupine. Or wolves. Or he could have fallen through some thin ice on a creek. Jace could be trying to figure out how to pull him out of the freezing water without falling through the ice himself right now. And he didn't have any gear with him. She'd better take Jace's pack and go look for them.

But before she could even hoist Jace's pack from the sled onto her back, Scout burst out of the woods and galloped in her direction. She was relieved, even when the dog jumped on her and almost knocked her down. "Hi, Scout." She pushed him down until all four feet were on the ground and gave his neck a good rub. "Where's Jace? Did you outrun him?" She looked up the trail, but she didn't see any sign of him approaching. "Jace?" she called.

There was no answer and her fear returned. Was Jace in trouble? Scout sat at her feet, staring up as though he was expecting a command. Come to think of it, the only time the dog ever knocked her down was after he'd been ordered to "find." Maybe Jace sent him back for her.

She opened Jace's backpack, found a sock, and held it under Scout's nose. "Scout, find." The dog immediately raced back down the trail. She pulled Jace's pack onto her back and followed. Fortunately, it was easy to follow Scout's trail in the new snow. Before long, she found where he'd branched off from the main trail into the woods. In the distance, she could hear Scout barking. Maybe he'd found Jace already.

The trail ended in a patch of trampled snow in a clearing. Scout continued to let out a bark every few seconds, but there was still no sign of Jace. Skiing toward the dog, she spotted something bright yellow. As she got closer, she recognized Jace's skis, one of which had been snapped in half. What could have happened to him?

She picked up the skis. "Jace?" she called, and this time, she got an answer.

"Hannah! I'm down here. Be careful, there's a ravine."

Hannah dropped Jace's skis, stepped out of her bindings and laid down her poles, shrugged out of Jace's heavy pack, and made her way to where Scout was standing. She grabbed onto a sturdy branch and leaned over the edge. Jace lay at the bottom of the ravine, several feet below. Her stomach did a flip, as it always did when she stood on ledges. "Um, hi there."

He chuckled. "Hello. I can't tell you how glad I am to see you. Scout and I had a little run-in with a mama moose, and I wound up here."

"Are you hurt?" She didn't see any blood, but only the upper half of his body was visible from where she was standing.

"Not much," he told her. "Just wrenched my knee a little."

"Can you still climb? I'll get the rope from your pack and throw it down."

Jace shook his head. "Unfortunately, that won't work. I seem to be stuck here."

"Stuck? What do you mean stuck?"

"I mean I can't pull my leg out of this crack between rocks with my ski boot on, and I can't reach to get it off. I'm going to need you to come down here and remove it. The boot, not the leg," he clarified with a grin.

"Down there?" Hannah squeaked.

"Yeah. I know you don't like heights—"

"No, I don't like pistachios. I'm terrified of heights. Are you absolutely sure you can't get loose?"

"Believe me, I've tried. I'm sorry, Hannah. You know I wouldn't ask you if—"

"No, I know. It's okay." She sucked in a breath. "I can do this." She stood at the edge of the ravine, trying to plot a path down, but her vision blurred, and everything began to swim. She stumbled back away from the edge and reached for a tree trunk to steady herself. There was no way she could do this.

"Tie yourself off to a tree," Jace called. "You can hold onto the rope to help you down."

"Hold on to the rope. Right. I'll do that." She closed her eyes and leaned against the tree, feeling the rough bark against her cheek. "Lord, I can't," she whispered. "I can't make myself go over the edge of that ravine. But Jace is down there, and he needs my help. And I need Yours. So please, Lord, give me courage. Amen." She opened her eyes. Scout stared up at her, waiting for her to act. He'd done his part, and now it was time for her to do hers.

She got the rope from Jace's pack, wrapped it around the big cottonwood she'd been leaning on, and tied it in a square knot. Then she tied another knot, because one couldn't be too careful. "In God, all things are possible," she told herself, as she tied the other end of the rope around her waist.

"In God, all things are possible." She walked to the edge and looked down. Her heart pounded, but this time her vision stayed clear. God was helping.

"There's a ledge about four feet down and six feet to your left," Jace told her. "Try that first. But it's covered with snow so be careful putting your weight down until you're sure it will hold you."

"Okay." Hannah moved to her left. *In God, all things are possible.* She turned her back on the ravine, grabbed the rope in her gloved hands, and sort of slow-motion rappelled down the edge of the ravine, until she reached the ledge. She put down one foot and pushed, but the snow held. The second foot held as well. She looked at the ledge, but she didn't have the nerve to look at the bottom of the ravine.

"You're doing great," Jace told her. "I can't see you from here, but is there a boulder or something behind you where you can climb?"

She took a deep breath and checked. "Yes," she called. It was only about three feet down. *In God, all things are possible.* She sat on the edge of the ledge and eased her right foot down until it rested against something solid. She pushed off the ledge to bring her left foot down, but her right foot slipped and skidded. She yelped and grabbed the rope, swinging herself forward and banging her shoulder against the edge of the ravine.

"Hannah!" Jace yelled. "Are you okay?"

To her surprise, she was. Her shoulder had bumped against the rock but didn't hit hard enough to damage anything. "I'm fine," she assured Jace. She was now directly over another ledge, and a foot below that, she could see Jace's black ski boot. Because of the way the wall jutted out, she could no longer see his upper body. Bracing herself against the wall, she let herself gingerly down to the ledge, which proved solid. The boot was now hidden under the ledge. She removed her gloves and felt around underneath until her fingertips brushed heavy fabric. "I can feel your boot."

"That's great. Can you get it off?"

"I think so." She ran her fingers up the boot until they hit the Velcro strap at the top. It made a ripping noise as she pulled it apart to expose the laces. It took a minute to sort out the laces by feel, but eventually she was able to locate a lace tip and pull until the bow untied. She tied the end of one of the laces around her wrist before working the boot loose.

"I can feel that," Jace called. "It's getting looser."

"Good. I'm pulling on the heel. Can you flex your foot?"

It took some wrestling, but with a final tug, the boot slid off his foot. Hannah lost her balance for a second and almost fell from the ledge, but she managed to grab the rope and catch herself. Good thing she'd tied the boot to her wrist, because otherwise it would have dropped another six feet, and she really, really didn't want to climb down there after it.

Some gravel crunched as Jace flexed his foot and wriggled his leg through the opening. "I got it. I'm free!"

"Thank You, God!"

"Amen." A minute later, Jace's hand appeared past the jutting part of the wall. Slowly, he worked himself around, hugging the wall, until his left socked foot was on the ledge with Hannah. When he put his weight on it to swing his right foot around, a little grimace passed over his face, but a second later, he was standing beside her. As soon as he was secure on the ledge, he pulled her into his arms. "Thank you for saving me," he whispered against her hair.

She wrapped her arms around his waist, accidentally banging the back of his leg with the dangling boot, but he didn't seem to mind. "Anytime."

He leaned back so that she could see his face and smiled. "I'll try not to let it happen too often. Now, why don't you give me that boot, so that we can get out of here."

"Brilliant idea."

Climbing up was less scary than getting down, especially with Jace to give her a boost from below. Once Hannah was on solid ground, Jace pulled himself up using the rope, although it was clear each time he used his left leg that he was feeling pain in that knee. Scout whined, and Hannah had to hold him back to keep him from rushing Jace while he was teetering on the edge of the ravine. As soon as Jace was clear of the edge, Hannah let go of the dog's collar. Scout rushed to Jace, sniffing him up and down as though to reassure himself that Jace was all in one piece.

Jace ruffled his ears and then ran his hands over the dog's body. Scout winced when Jace's hand reached his ribs. "Yeah, you've got a bruise there, probably where her hoof caught you. It could have been a lot worse. I hope you learned your lesson about chasing moose." He untied the rope and coiled it into a neat bundle. "Well, we didn't expect that delay, but we should still be able to make it to Pika from here in ninety minutes or so." He limped toward the clearing and picked up the ski poles he'd dropped in the fall. "Have you seen my skis?"

"Unfortunately, yes." Hannah held up the broken ski. "How did this happen?"

"Oh, shoot. The moose must have stepped on it when she knocked me into the ravine." He made a face. "It might take a little longer than ninety minutes, after all."

"Guess we'd better get started, then." Hannah pulled on Jace's pack and slung her own skis and poles over her shoulder.

"I can carry that," Jace protested.

Hannah shook her head. "You're doing well to carry yourself. That knee looks painful."

"I just wrenched it a little. It's nothing serious," he claimed, but there was a definite limp with each step as they made their way through the woods. Once they reached the main trail where the snow was deeper, Hannah stepped into her skis, but Jace was forced to walk, post-holing through the snow with each step while they made their way back to the spot where Hannah had left the sled. There was no way he was going to be able to walk ten miles like that.

Jace must have come to the same conclusion. "I should have packed snowshoes, as a backup," he said in a low voice.

Hannah took off the heavy backpack and set it in the sled. "We have plenty of food and fuel. We'll take it slow."

"Or..." Jace opened the backpack and pulled out the GPS. "I'll set a pin for this location. You just need to follow the route

I've set, and once you reach Pika, you can give my location to Search and Rescue."

Hannah stared at him. "You want me to leave you here? Injured? With moose and lynx running around, not to mention whoever ransacked your cabin? No way."

"It's the only way. I'd slow you down too much if—"

"Get on the sled," Hannah demanded.

"What?"

"The sled. It won't be comfortable. You're going to have to hold most of the gear in your lap, but we can make it work. Give me your tow belt."

He hesitated and then slowly unbuckled the wide belt. "Are you sure?"

"I'm sure," Hannah said as she adjusted the size of the belt. Jace wouldn't be here, wouldn't have gotten injured if he weren't trying to help her. Once this was all over, he would probably want to get as far away from her as possible, but she wasn't about to leave him here alone. "It's better if we stick together. You know this trail better than I do. You can help me avoid the ravines."

"Like I've done so well today," he muttered, but he began unloading the gear from the sled. "Oh, wait. I have an idea." He removed the rope from his backpack. "I can make a harness for Scout, and he can help you pull."

Hannah glanced over at the dog, who was rolling in the snow. Maybe he'd gotten too warm after all that running and adventure. "Are you sure that's a good idea?" If Scout objected to pulling, he might be more hindrance than help.

"I've taken him skijoring. He knows how to behave in a harness."

Hannah considered Jace's idea. If the dog could pull a skier, he should be able to pull a sled. "Okay. Let's try it."

Hannah watched while Jace tied the rope in a series of loops to create a sort of web that went around Scout's neck and across his chest, between his legs, and then back up to come to a vee just above his tail, avoiding the bruised spot on Scout's lower rib cage. He padded the parts around the neck and chest by wrapping a fleece pullover around the rope there and securing it with duct tape, a roll of which any self-respecting Alaskan would never be without. Finally, he tied a loop at the back of the harness, where Hannah would be able to clip the sled's towrope.

"Impressive," Hannah said. She fashioned a second, longer towrope out of rope and extra carabiners from Jace's pack. "Let's get this show on the road."

Jace sat in the sled with the tent bag, the duffel containing their sleeping bags and camping equipment, and Hannah's daypack piled up in his lap. It looked like a miserable ride, but Hannah couldn't think of any way to make him more comfortable.

After adjusting the straps on Jace's pack to fit her, Hannah pulled on the pack and clipped herself and Scout to the sled. "Okay, let's go. She leaned into her skis and pulled forward.

"Mush," Jace called, and Scout leaned into his harness, too. *Less than ten miles to Pika*, Hannah reminded herself. *Easy peasy.*

Chapter Eleven

Jace shifted the duffel in his lap. Nothing like being carried along on a sled like a piece of luggage to keep a man humble. A verse from Proverbs popped into his head. *A man's pride will bring him low, But the humble in spirit will retain honor.* Well, his honor should remain intact. His position on the sled was hurting his back as well as causing his knee to throb, but he wasn't going to complain. Not when Hannah was towing him and all their gear up a challenging slope.

He'd been afraid she was reaching the end of her endurance before, when he was still dragging all the gear, and yet here she was, chugging along, mile after mile. And that was after facing her fear of heights and climbing down into a ravine to save his life. Hannah Yates was one impressive human being. Scout was helping, making up for his earlier faux pas by leaning into the harness and pulling some of the weight, but Hannah was doing most of the work. When they reached the top of the hill, Jace called for a stop. "You need a rest."

Hannah checked the GPS. "But we've still got four miles to go."

"Ten minutes won't make that much difference, and besides, you can't pull the sled down that hill without someone behind to moderate the speed. I'd run right over you."

She frowned. "Then how can we get you down?"

He'd been thinking about this. "It's a sled, right? We'll let gravity do the work. I'll slide down and meet you at the bottom."

Hannah looked down the steep hill and laughed. "You're just bored and looking for a thrill."

"You got me." He smiled and took out a water bottle. "Better drink and eat while you can. There's one more big climb before we get to town."

While Hannah snacked on some trail mix and Scout ate a dog biscuit, Jace unhooked the sled from its towline and pushed forward with his hands until he was balanced on the edge of the slope. The simple plastic sled had no steering or braking capabilities, but fortunately, the slope appeared clear, with no rocks or trees between him and the flat area at the bottom. It brought back memories of fun times at the university sledding hill back home. Lindsay and Hannah used to love sledding. Lindsay would shriek in mock terror, and Hannah would laugh. Jace had always loved her laugh.

"See you at the bottom," Jace said, but before he could push off, Hannah ran up and gave him a big shove, sending him and the sled flying down the hill. Scout barked, Hannah giggled, and Jace couldn't keep the grin off his face.

The zooming sled hit a bump, which sent Jace and all the gear airborne for a split second, and then hit the snow and picked up speed once again. Momentum carried Jace to the bottom of the hill and on past until another bump, this one on the right side of the sled, raised one edge far enough to send Jace and all the luggage tumbling into the snow. Nothing to do but laugh.

By the time Hannah and Scout made it down the hill, he had everything gathered up and was back on the sled. Hannah reached down to brush some snow off his face. "Having fun?"

"You bet." He grinned. "Want to drag me up for another run? You can ride down with me this time."

Hannah chuckled. "I'll take a rain check on that." After re-fastening the towlines to herself and Scout, she started off. The trail was mostly a gentle downhill here, which would lead to a small lake, frozen solid this time of year, and then a final climb up to the town itself.

When they reached the lake, Jace turned on his cell phone, but as he'd expected, there was no signal. Hannah didn't even slow, skiing across the pond in a few strokes, and then climbing up the hill. She'd almost reached the summit when she ran out of momentum. She turned sideways and began sidestepping up the hill, still dragging him. Jace couldn't stand it anymore. He rolled out of the sled and stood up.

"What are you doing?" Hannah demanded.

"Helping, I hope." There wasn't much snow deposited on this windy knoll, and Jace managed to limp his way to the hilltop. Hannah still had to pull the gear, but at least not his weight, too. At the trailhead at the top of the hill, a well-beaten path led into town. Pika consisted of a handful of houses, a modest RV campground that was closed in the winter, and a general store/post office with gas pumps out front.

Hannah pulled out her phone and turned it on. "I'm not getting a signal."

Jace checked his. "Me, neither. But we can call the state troopers from the phone in the general store. I know Lucas and Marti, the couple who own this place."

Hannah frowned. "If we call the troopers, that would mean waiting here until they show up, and that could be hours or even tomorrow. Let's go back to Anchorage first and turn over the coin to the police there."

She had a point. "That makes sense, especially since you've already reported the break-in at your store, and they have an open case."

"I'll call my sister to see if she'll pick us up. Assuming, of course, that she's still taking my calls after I said I'd come by her house and then stood her up."

"You texted that you couldn't come."

"Yeah, but then I lost the signal, so I don't know for sure if the text made it. If she did that to me, I'd be furious."

"I'm sure she'll forgive you once she understands the situation. And if she's not available, I can call the car service in Anchorage and hire a driver to come get us." They'd reached the general store. A battered Jeep Wagoneer was parked in front with the tailgate open. Hannah wriggled out of Jace's huge pack and set it on the sled with the other gear, replacing it with her small daypack. Jace commanded Scout to stay with the gear and then limped up the steps to the porch. He went to hold the door for Hannah, but before he could reach for the knob, the door opened and a man with a gray beard, glasses, and a ball cap stepped out carrying a suitcase, which he tossed into the back of the Jeep.

Lucas followed with another suitcase but dropped it when he spotted them. "Jace, hi!" He gave Jace a one-armed hug and slapped him on the back. "Haven't seen you since Christmas when you and your folks stopped by. Who's this pretty lady?"

"This is Hannah Yates. Hannah, Lucas Sutton. An old family friend."

"Hello, Hannah." Lucas shook her hand and then looked over at the dog and gear they'd left near the porch. "Did you ski in all the way from your cabin?"

"Yeah, we did," Jace said, "and now we need to call for a ride. We can't seem to get a cell signal—"

"I know. It's down again. They need to put in another tower or something." Lucas picked up the suitcase he'd dropped. "You're welcome to use the store phone. Or wait—where are you headed?"

"Anchorage."

"Bill!" Lucas called and carried the suitcase to the Jeep. "This is Jace Angeles and Hannah Yates. They need a ride to Anchorage. You got room for them and the dog?"

"Sure, if they're ready now." Bill, who had closed the tailgate, reopened it. "If you don't mind catching a ride from the Anchorage airport, that is, 'cause I don't have time to drop you anywhere else. I can't miss my flight to Honolulu. I'm meeting my kids and grandkids there."

"The airport is just what we need," Hannah answered. "Thanks."

"All good then." Lucas grabbed Jace's duffel and carried it to the Jeep. "Bill will take good care of you."

Jace loaded the camping gear, ski equipment, and backpack into the Jeep. Lucas frowned when he noticed the limp. "What happened to you?"

"Nothing serious. Wrenched my knee."

"Ouch. You should ice that." Lucas started toward the store. "Let me get you a cold pack."

"If you're coming, come," Bill called out the driver's side window. "I'm already running late."

"I'll ice it when I get there," Jace told Lucas as he urged Scout to jump into the back of the Jeep and got him settled next to the luggage. "Tell Marti I said hello. I'll stop by to visit next time." Jace slammed the tailgate shut.

"Are you sure?" Lucas asked. "Won't take a minute."

"No, I'll be fine. But thanks." Hannah was already in the back seat behind the driver, so Jace climbed into the front passenger seat. Lucas waved as they drove away.

Bill pulled onto the highway. "Sorry to rush you out of there, but you know Lucas and Marti. He would have gone in and asked Marti for ice, and she would insist you need your knee wrapped before you go and spend ten minutes with Lucas discussing which bandage he should use. And then while Lucas wrapped your knee, she would have wanted the whole story of how you got hurt, asked about your family, and caught you up on every mutual acquaintance you have with them. Then she would inspect Lucas's job and decide it wasn't right, and that she'd better take the wrap off and do it again, and that would have reminded Lucas of some long, convoluted story, and next thing you know, I've missed my plane."

Jace laughed. "That's exactly what would have happened."

Bill shook his head. "Salt of the earth, those two, but once they start talking, they just don't stop. How did you hurt your knee, anyway?"

"An unexpected run-in with a moose," Jace told him, deciding to skip the details about falling into the ravine, since Bill seemed to appreciate brevity.

"Oh, yeah? I've had a few of those myself." It turned out Bill didn't mind long, convoluted stories after all, as long as he was the one telling them. He spent most of the two-hour trip into Anchorage entertaining Jace and Hannah with his own adventure-filled encounters with moose and bears. Once he'd run out of tales of his own, he threw in a few secondhand wildlife stories from various friends and relatives.

Meanwhile, every time they passed through someplace with cell service, Hannah's phone would ding and she would tense up. Either her sister was really upset or there was something major going wrong at the store. Jace looked at Hannah with raised eyebrows, silently asking her what was going on, but she shook her head. Either she didn't want to tell Jace about it or didn't want to talk in front of Bill. Not that she could have gotten a word in anyway.

It must have been a warm day in Anchorage because there were puddles in the streets where the snow had melted. As the temperature dropped later, the roads were likely to get slick. It was fully dark by the time they turned onto the road leading into the airport. "Want me to drop you at the terminal before I park?" Bill asked. "Should be able to get a cab there."

"I left my car in long-term parking before I flew to Fairbanks," Hannah told him. "So we'll be fine. We appreciate you letting us tag along."

"My pleasure." Bill turned into the long-term parking lot

and found a spot not far from the shuttle stop. "It was nice talking to you."

"Thanks, Bill," Jace said as he unloaded their stuff. "Have a great time in Hawaii."

"Oh, I will." Bill grabbed his two suitcases and locked the car. "I'll get me some of that guava juice and find a nice chair under a palm tree and feel sorry for you poor suckers back here in the snow and ice." He was still chuckling as he turned a corner and disappeared between two parked cars.

Hannah picked up Jace's backpack and pushed her arms through the straps. "I'll carry that," Jace offered, but she shook her head.

"I've got it. My car is right over there." She pulled a key fob from her own small backpack and pushed a button. The horn beeped and lights flashed on a gray SUV at the end of the row. "How's your knee?"

"A little stiff," he admitted as he picked up the duffel bag. "But it will be fine. What's with all the texts?"

"My sister." She opened the tailgate of her car and set the backpack inside. Scout came to sit beside her, waiting for the command to hop in. Hannah absently ran a hand over his head and then pulled the phone from her pocket and frowned at it. "Something weird is going on."

"How so?" Jace set the duffel beside the pack and turned toward Hannah.

"You remember the day we were on the train? Right after I texted her to say I wasn't feeling well and couldn't come to her house after all, we lost the signal."

"Right."

"Well, it looks like she sent six, no, seven texts right after that demanding that I had to come immediately, even if I was sick. Then she called and left a message. All the messages were telling me to come, but not why. Then nothing for the two days we were at the cabin, but today I'm getting messages again. I didn't want to call her in the car with Bill there, but I'd better do it now. I'll explain about the globe and everything and tell Nicole I'll come to her house as soon as we're done at the police station."

"I'll grab the rest of the stuff while you call." Jace went back for the camping and ski gear and stowed it in the back of Hannah's car. Hannah stood beside the open driver's side door, phone pressed to her ear, not saying anything. Her sister was probably giving her an earful. Jace closed the tailgate and stepped to the side, intending to catch Hannah's eye and see if she needed privacy or support.

But Hannah's face had gone pale, her eyes huge. Something was very wrong. Scout sensed it, too, and went to nudge her hand and whimper. Hannah laid a hand on his head.

"Let me talk to her again," she demanded in a shaky voice. "No, I— All right, I understand. Yes, I have what you want. I'll be right there." She ended the call, and whatever color still remained in her face drained away. She looked like she might faint.

"Hannah." Jace hurried to her and grasped her shoulders.

"Jace," she said, as though she'd forgotten he was there, but then she gave her head a little shake and her features settled into an expression of determination. "Oh, Jace, they're holding Nicole hostage at her house. They want the coin."

Chapter Twelve

Hannah got into the driver's seat and started the engine while Jace loaded Scout into the back seat and then hurried around the car to climb into the passenger side. She drove to the pay station at the edge of the parking lot. Jace pulled a credit card from his wallet and handed it to Hannah, but her hands were shaking so much, she couldn't fit the card into the slot. He leaned across and did it for her. A few seconds later, the bar lifted, and Hannah shot forward.

Jace buckled his seat belt as Hannah streaked through a yellow light, and he gripped the handle on the car door when she swerved off International Airport Road and onto the entry ramp to Minnesota Avenue. Once they'd merged into traffic, he reached into his pocket. "I'll call the police."

"No!" Hannah shot him a wild-eyed look before returning her gaze to the road. "They said no police or they'll kill Nicole."

"O-kay," he replied, slowly. No use pointing out the obvious, that if they were willing to kill Nicole, there was nothing keeping them from killing him and Hannah, too, once they had what they wanted.

Hannah bit her lip as she stared straight ahead. "Look, this isn't your problem. I'll let you out at the traffic light at Old Seward."

"What?" Did she really think he would leave her to deal with these people alone? "No way. I'm coming with you."

"You've already hurt your knee helping me." She flashed him a tortured look. "If you got seriously hurt—"

"Hannah, stop it. You're not to blame for Scout chasing a moose, or for me falling. On the contrary, if you weren't there, I'd still be at the bottom of that ravine. You saved my life—simple as that. Now I want to help you help your sister. So no more talk about dropping me off, okay?"

"Okay," she whispered.

He needed to get her past her panic. "Tell me what we're up against. How many people are there?"

"Only one that I know of. Nicole answered the phone and said she'd been kidnapped, but then a guy took the phone away and said to bring the 'item' to her house immediately. I could hear Nicole in the background, trying to get him to let her talk with me, but he wouldn't put her back on."

She tilted her head, the way she always did when she was thinking. "He must have been holding her since the day we rode the train. That's why she was so insistent I come to her house, and why she mentioned Grandpa's antique—the funeral flag belonging to his father, a territorial policeman. She was trying to tell me to call the police." She slapped her forehead. "Why didn't I get that?"

"Why would you? You had no idea she was in danger," Jace pointed out. He tapped his chin. "If the kidnapping was happening on the same day as those guys in the white truck in Fairbanks were breaking into your rental car, that would mean there are at least three people involved."

Hannah merged onto the Seward Highway and passed a slow-moving minivan. "Then there's the blond guy who keeps coming into the store and asking for me, and Peter Morozov's 'neighbor.' They may be involved, too. And all over a stupid coin." She huffed. "I wish I'd never found that globe."

Jace couldn't disagree, but after all, finding interesting and valuable objects was Hannah's business and she seemed good at it. How could she have known it would put her and her family in such danger?

Hannah took the exit to Rabbit Creek Road. There were no streetlights in this part of town, leaving only Hannah's headlights to cut through the darkness and illuminate the winding road. After following the main road for several miles, she turned off onto a narrow side road with thick forest lining both sides.

Jace wasn't familiar with this part of Anchorage. "Where is Nicole's house, anyway?"

"Way upper hillside. It's on five acres, and like I told you, it has an adventure course out back." Hannah took a curve too fast, and the SUV fishtailed on the slick road before Hannah straightened it out.

"Slow down," Jace said gently. "They won't care if we're a minute late, just that we get there."

"Right." Hannah took her foot off the accelerator. But seconds later, just after they'd passed a mailbox, a loud crack sounded. A ragged hole appeared in the windshield. Simultaneously, the driver's side window exploded into a thousand tiny pebbles of glass. Scout gave a frantic bark.

"They're shooting at us!" Hannah hit the gas.

Jace twisted in his seat to look behind them. Scout had wisely scrambled from the back seat to the floor. A familiar white truck pulled out of the driveway they'd just passed and flashed its lights, signaling them to stop, but Hannah kept driving. Jace could just make out two figures in the truck.

"Looks like your friends from Fairbanks are back," Jace announced.

"Friends don't shoot at friends." Hannah took another curve at a less-than-prudent speed. "Why are they doing this? We're bringing them the coin." She paused. "Unless we've got two separate groups who are trying— Oh, shoot, there's the turn." She hit the brake and skidded onto an even narrower snowy road, but lost control and slid off the shoulder, the passenger side of the car coming to rest against a tree. The engine died.

Jace was still watching behind them. "Flip off your lights!" Hannah did it. A second later, the white truck came around the curve and went on by the turnoff.

"Okay, we've lost them for the moment." He reached across and touched her chin to turn her face toward him, but he saw no sign of blood or bruises. "Are you okay?"

"I'm fine. That bump didn't even set off the airbags." Hannah shook off his hand and restarted the engine, but when she tried to pull forward, the side of the car crunched against the tree and the front right dipped.

Jace rolled down his window and leaned out to see what the trouble was. "Blew out a tire. Come on. We have to get out of here. It won't take those guys long to figure out where we are." He grabbed his backpack from the seat behind him and pulled out the gun, holster, and ammunition before shimmying out the window onto the snow-covered ground. Meanwhile Scout jumped into the front and followed Hannah out the driver's-side door.

Hannah shrugged into her daypack, where she'd stored the globe. "Nicole's house is on the other side of this hill."

Jace put a hand on her arm. "Are you sure you don't want to call the police?"

"I'm afraid if the kidnapper hears sirens, he'll do something to Nicole. I just want to get there and give him what he wants."

Jace figured they didn't have time to argue about it.

"Let's go." He strapped on the holster and picked a path through the trees, which proved to be more of a challenge than he'd anticipated when a sharp pain zinged from his knee, but he couldn't let that slow him down. Rather than follow the drive, he herded Hannah and Scout upward, into the woods. Hopefully the three of them could disappear into the shadows of the trees and bushes before the pair in the white truck found them. Fortunately, the snow wasn't nearly as deep here in Anchorage as it had been at the cabin. Hannah led the way upward through the forest, guided only by the moonlight reflecting off the snow and bouncing through the woods. Scout stayed at her heels, and Jace hobbled along at the rear.

Between the time Jace spent looking back and the pace his tricky knee allowed him, he was falling behind, but maybe that was for the best. If the pair in the white truck came after them, he might be able to slow them down enough to let Hannah escape and make it to her sister's house, where she could turn over the coin and pray that the kidnapper kept his word.

Scout looked back and whimpered. Hannah turned to look. "Jace? Oh no, you're really hurting, aren't you?" She turned and came back.

"I twisted my bad knee when I jumped down, but I'm okay. Go on ahead."

"Not without you." She slid an arm around his waist and pulled his arm over her shoulder. "Come on, let's climb."

Together they made it to the top of the hill. Hannah pointed to a few tiny points of light flickering through the trees far down the hill. "Those are the nightlights from the steps on Nicole's deck. It's not far now."

Still with his arm on her shoulders, they made their way down the steep hill, slipping and sliding on a few spots, which didn't do his knee any good, but they made it without falling. Jace noticed what looked like a metal ladder next to one of the trees. "What's this?"

"Part of the adventure course," Hannah told him. "We must be on Nicole's property now." They pressed forward. The woods were denser here, and for a moment they lost sight of the lights. Then they came around a bush, Hannah stopped abruptly. "Oh no! I forgot about this part."

They were standing on the edge of a bank. Above them, to the right, moonlight glinted off a frozen waterfall that seemed to feed into a narrow gorge. The bottom of the gorge was lost in shadow but, judging by the faint sound of water trickling through the frozen edges of the creek, it was deep. "Is there a way across?" he asked.

Hannah nodded and silently led him downstream until they turned a corner, and there it was—a bridge, if one could call it that. Three ropes, two about waist high and the other at bank level, stretched across the gorge. "This is the only way across?"

"No. There's a hand-tram." Hannah pointed to a cable about twenty yards downstream that connected two wooden plat-forms. "Unfortunately, it's controlled from the other side, and this is the only way to get to it."

Jace took stock. A guy with a bad knee, a woman with a fear of heights, and a dog. Behind them: two guys with guns. Ahead: a rope bridge between them and their goal. He blew out a long breath. "If ever there was a time for prayer, it's now."

Hannah could hardly hear Jace's prayer because her heart was pounding in her ears so loudly. She'd been on that hand-tram. Once. And once was more than enough. Hanging above a rushing creek in what was basically an oversize wire milk crate, she'd felt like her heart might give out at any moment. But right now, looking at the rope bridge, she would give any-thing for the safety of that tram.

"...and lend us strength, Lord. Amen." Jace squeezed her shoulders before releasing her. Hannah opened her eyes. Jace took a limping step toward the bridge.

"What are you doing?" Hannah demanded.

"I'm going to cross the bridge." He hobbled closer. "I'll get the tram on the other side and bring it back for you and Scout."

"That rope bridge? With your knee?" Crossing that rope would require steady steps. If his knee gave out unexpectedly, he could fall to his death. "No way."

"But—"

"I'm doing it." Hannah stepped in front of him and sur-veyed the ropes.

He reached for her shoulders and turned her around so that

she had to look at his face. "Hannah, no. You don't have to do this."

"Yes, I do." She flashed a grin. It wouldn't fool Jace, but it made her feel better. "Look, no offense, but you have a rotten track record for staying out of ravines, and I don't have time to bail you out of another one. I'm going."

He chuckled. "Hey, I blame the moose for that one." Then his expression grew serious, and he searched her face for a long moment as though he was building another argument in his head. Finally, though, he sighed and wrapped his arms around her. "Okay," he whispered, just before his lips touched hers. The kiss was short but full of promise. "You win."

"Lucky me." She turned back to study the bridge. Really? Three ropes? Nicole's ex-husband couldn't have sprung for a few wooden planks across the bottom? And how sound were those ropes anyway? Nicole used to have the course inspected regularly when her stepchildren used it, but they had all moved out of state a couple of years ago. But what choice did Hannah have? If they went back to the road, the guys in the white truck were sure to be there and take the coin. Even if they let her and Jace go, if she showed up at Nicole's house without the coin, Nicole's kidnapper might carry out his threat. The only solution was to get to the other side of that creek, and the rope bridge was their last chance to do it.

Hannah sucked in a deep breath. With God's help, she had climbed into the ravine to rescue Jace. Climbing on solid rocks was child's play compared to stepping out onto a rope, but she reminded herself, "In God, all things are possible." She put her hands on the upper ropes and tested them. So far, so good. She put her right foot onto the bottom rope. It felt solid. But then came the moment of truth. She took her left foot off the solid ground and stepped onto the rope. The bridge swayed, and for a moment so did her courage. She glanced down, and everything went blurry.

Then she heard Jace's whispered prayer, "Lord, please hold Hannah in the palm of Your hand." Her vision cleared.

She eased forward, not lifting her feet but sliding them along the bottom rope. She kept her gaze determinedly on the far bank, never letting it drift down to the depths below. An eon later, she reached the far bank. She stepped onto solid ground and looked back. On the other side of the creek, Jace gave a fist pump. "Amen," she whispered before hurrying to the hanging hand-tram.

Snow had piled up on the platform around the tram. Fortunately, someone had left a snow shovel in the corner, leaning against the railing. It took Hannah several minutes to clear the snow from the decking so that the tram would be able to slide out. Meanwhile, without the benefit of a shovel, Jace was using his boots and a tree branch to clear the twin platform on the other side of the creek. It took Hannah another minute or two to figure out how the locking mechanism worked, but finally, the tram was operational. She climbed into the hanging tram, grabbed the rope that circulated on a pulley, and pulled. With a loud creak, the tram moved along a foot closer to the edge of the platform. Another two tugs, and it was swinging free above the creek.

Hannah's heart missed a beat. She let go of the rope and grabbed the sides of the tram, willing it to stop swinging. In the silence, she heard voices from the other side of the hill. The white truck guys were back! Jace pulled his gun from its holster and loaded it. She grabbed the rope and started tugging, wincing at the loud creaks that might be leading those guys right to their position.

Four minutes later, the tram was over the other platform. Hannah unlatched the gate, and Jace and Scout piled in. With Jace pulling on the lines, they were back across in half the time. They unloaded from the tram, and Hannah locked it in place. She turned to find Jace staring up at the hill across the creek. Something, or someone, was moving through the trees near the top.

Jace limped to the rope bridge as fast as his injured knee could carry him, pulled a knife from his pocket, and began sawing at the bottom rope on the bridge. Hannah unzipped the outer pocket of her own pack, but then she remembered that she'd removed her pocketknife before flying. She watched Jace work, willing the rope to break. A few seconds later, it snapped, falling away into the creek, and he started on the second rope.

Crack! A shot rang out and something ricocheted off a boulder just behind Jace. Scout barked. Hannah grabbed Jace's hand and tugged. "Leave the ropes. We have to get out of here."

With his arm around her shoulders, they stumbled into the woods and kept moving until the creek was well behind them and they could see the lights from Nicole's deck through the trees. Between them and the deck, a snow-covered bench, bird-bath, and trellis marked Nicole's perennial flower garden. An unfamiliar black sedan was parked on the drive that wound around the house from the other side.

"Hold up," Jace said. Hannah stopped and they stood still, listening. "I don't think they're trying to cross the creek behind us."

"No," Hannah agreed. "It would make more sense for them to go back to the truck and take the road around." She turned to him and touched his precious face. "That bullet—it could have killed you." The thought of losing Jace was even more terrifying than the rope bridge.

"But it didn't. I'm right here. We're safe." Jace smiled and pulled her into a tight hug. "We're both okay, thanks to you getting us across the creek."

She allowed herself one long moment in his strong arms before stepping back. "We're okay, but Nicole isn't. We've got to help her."

Jace straightened. "What's the plan?"

Hannah shrugged out of her pack and pulled out the globe

that had caused all the trouble while she surveyed the area, then the holstered gun on Jace's hip. "We need to trade the coin for Nicole."

"I'll take it to him," Jace offered, but Hannah shook her head.

"He's expecting me, and you have the gun. You stay here and cover me. The security cameras should pick me up as soon as I get close enough to activate the motion light over the back deck." She pulled off her hat and laid it beside the pack. "I want to make sure he recognizes me."

"Good idea." Jace pulled the gun from his holster, checked that it was loaded, and ordered Scout to get down and stay. "I'm ready."

"If anything goes wrong, call the police." Hannah took a deep breath and stepped out of the woods. She was still twenty feet from the deck when the floodlight came on. She stopped and held up her hands, making sure the globe would be visible to anyone looking at the security camera.

She waited, but no one appeared. She glanced in Jace's direction, but she couldn't see him in the shadows of the forest. Still, she knew he was there. She went forward, up the steps to the deck, knocked on the door, and then turned and hurried down the steps and away from the deck, where she would still be visible from the door but not so close someone could drag her inside. A few seconds later, more outside lights flashed on and the door opened a crack. Hannah got a glimpse of her sister's face, pale and terrified. Nicole stepped out onto the deck, but a tall man with blond hair was behind her, holding an arm around her throat. Hannah wasn't sure, but he looked like the man who had bought a gold pan last week. "I said not to call the cops," he shouted.

"I didn't," Hannah insisted.

"Then who's that in the woods?"

Hannah must have given it away when she looked back for Jace. She straightened her shoulders and tried to control the quaver in her voice. "A friend. He won't stop you, as long as you do what you've promised." She searched her sister's face and body for signs of injury. "Are you okay, Nicole? Did he hurt you?"

"I'm okay," Nicole called back, but her voice sounded weak. "Just give him what he wants."

"I have it, right here." Hannah held up the globe. "Let my sister go, and it's yours."

He eased Nicole another step forward, and Hannah could see that he was carrying a gun in his other hand. "How do I know you didn't open the globe?"

"I did open it," Hannah admitted, "and I found the coin. It's still inside."

"Show me," he ordered.

Hannah nodded. "All right. I'm going to take out my phone now, because I need to look at the combination. Also, I'll need a pin. Okay?"

"Slowly."

With exaggerated care, Hannah opened her jacket and removed a safety pin. Then she took her phone from her pocket and found the photo Nicole had sent of the card that had been inside her jewelry box. Her hands shook, but she managed to press the right buttons and count the degrees of rotation, until finally the globe separated into two parts. She laid them on the snow-covered bench, and then held up the plastic box containing the coin. "Here it is."

"What's the date and mint?"

She squinted in the low light. "San Francisco, 1854."

"All right." The man shifted his grip on Nicole's neck. "Put the coin in the globe and walk away."

"Not until you let Nicole go."

"I'll let her go once I have the coin."

Hannah shook her head. "How do I know you won't take the coin and a hostage?"

"How do I know your friend won't shoot me the second I let her go?"

They stared at each other for a long moment. Then Hannah spoke. "Take me instead."

"Hannah, no!" Jace called out from the woods.

"It's okay," she called back. "Nobody has to get hurt." She took a step toward the kidnapper. "I'll walk with you to your car, and you can drive away with the coin."

"Stay there." The man shoved Nicole forward and down the steps from the deck, keeping her between himself and Jace. "Turn around," he told Hannah.

Slowly she turned her back on him. A second later, he shoved Nicole forward and wrapped his arm around Hannah's neck. "Show me the coin."

Hannah held up the coin, still in its box. The man looked over her shoulder to read the inscription. "That's the one." He snatched it from her hand and put it in his pocket. "Okay, we're going to my car now, one step at a time." Something poked her ribs, and she realized it must be the gun barrel. "Move."

Chapter Thirteen

Nicole ran toward the woods, momentarily blocking Jace's view of Hannah and the kidnapper. By the time Nicole was past Jace's line of fire, the kidnapper was already dragging Hannah toward the black car.

"Jace Angeles," Nicole whispered. "Is that you?"

"It's me." Without taking his eyes off Hannah and the kidnapper, he got out his phone and handed it to Nicole. "Take this. Hide somewhere in the woods and call 911. Tell them there's a kidnapper in a black sedan taking Hannah. I can only read the last two numbers on the plate: 74."

Nicole stared at Jace. "But he said he'll let Hannah go."

"He'll say whatever it takes to get what he wants. If he thinks he's safer with Hannah, he'll take her along. Also tell the police to be on the lookout for a white pickup in the vicinity. The two men inside shot at us earlier."

Nicole still didn't move, other than a violent trembling. She was dressed in jeans and a sweater, no coat, but Jace guessed it wasn't the cold that was giving her the shakes. Nevertheless, he didn't have the time to help her with her shock right now. He spoke in a gentle but firm voice. "Listen, Nicole, I know you've been through a lot, but you need to be strong for a little longer. I need you to find somewhere safe and make that call. For your sake and for Hannah's. Can you do that?"

Nicole stared at him for a second and then said, "Yes." She moved farther into the woods out of his sight. Jace continued to watch the kidnapper and Hannah. They were almost at the car now, with the man still hiding behind her, only his pale hair and the side of his face visible. They reached the car and as he opened the door, he said something to Hannah. He seemed to be relaxing his hold on her. Good, he was going to leave her behind.

But before the man made it into the car, the sudden roar of an engine and slamming doors announced a new arrival at the front of the house, and the kidnapper grabbed Hannah once again.

The two men who had broken into Hannah's rental car in Fairbanks burst around the corner of the house waving guns. The big guy still wore his green parka. The other guy spotted the two halves of the globe lying on the bench. He knocked them to the ground and shouted to the kidnapper, "Where's the coin?"

The kidnapper had his own gun up and pointed in their direction. He'd released his hold on Hannah, but now she was right in the line of fire. "You're too late, Rocky. Back off."

"I don't think so." Rocky stepped nearer.

The big man in the green parka caught up and took a few menacing steps toward the kidnapper. "Hand it over, old man."

"Let's talk about this later, shall we? I'll just hold on to it for now—"

"That's not going to happen," Rocky said. "If you haven't noticed, you're outgunned."

All three of the men looked as though they could start shooting at any moment. Jace watched helplessly, willing Hannah to move away, but the three men surrounded her. Her eyes darted from face to face, but none of the criminals seemed inclined to back down.

Sirens sounded in the distance. Rocky swore. "We gotta get out of here." He nudged his cohort forward. "You grab Ivan, and I'll take her. Throw them in the truck. One of them has the coin." He moved toward Hannah.

Jace's heart jumped into his throat. Scout whined. Jace reinforced the stay signal. The last thing he needed was for Scout to jump into the middle of this. Or was it? In sudden inspiration, Jace grabbed the hat Hannah had left beside her pack and showed it to Scout. "Find!"

Scout bounded forward from the woods. The men stopped and all eyes turned to the dog as he rushed into the middle of the crowd, cutting off Rocky's path to Hannah. As soon as the dog reached Hannah, he jumped up, knocking her to the snow and out of Jace's line of fire. Jace stepped forward into the light, pointing his pistol at the three men. "Everybody freeze!"

Surprisingly, they all did. Three pairs of eyes glared hard at him. "Drop your guns," Jace ordered. The blond kidnapper and the big guy from the white truck obeyed. Rocky dropped his gun, but then made a dash toward the front of the house. Jace let him go. He ordered the other two men to turn around and put their hands behind their heads.

In the front, the truck engine roared to life. The big guy from the white pickup spit out a curse. But before the white pickup could leave the house, police cars came dashing up the long drive with flashing lights and sirens.

Meanwhile, Hannah managed to get out from under Scout and crawl toward Jace. Scout followed, wagging his tail over this new game. Once Hannah was away from the two criminals and out of Jace's line of fire, she got to her feet.

"Are you okay?" Jace whispered, not daring to take his eyes off the two men long enough to examine her.

"I'm fine," she told him. "Thanks to you and Scout." She ruffled the big dog's ears and looked around. "What happened to Nicole?"

"I'm here." Nicole came out of the woods. "Oh, Hannah. I thank God you're okay."

Hannah opened her arms and the two sisters hugged.

"Police!" came a call from the side of the house.

"We're in the back!" Jace shouted. "Hurry!"

Police appeared from inside and around the edge of the house; guns drawn. "Sir, drop the pistol."

"Gladly." Jace dropped the gun and held up his hands.

It didn't take the police long to sort out who was who and handcuff the two criminals. Judging by the sirens, more emergency vehicles were on their way. Jace removed his coat and handed it to Hannah. "For your sister."

"Thanks." Hannah draped the down jacket over Nicole's shoulders. "Can we go inside?" she asked the nearest police officer.

"Let me check on that." He disappeared around the corner of the house.

While they waited, Hannah set the globe aside, brushed the snow from the garden bench and urged Nicole to sit. Two emergency technicians came from the front of the house. They returned Jace's coat, wrapped Nicole in a warm blanket, and took her vitals.

"I'm fine," she insisted, but her voice sounded as though she was trying to convince herself.

"Your blood pressure is high," the first EMT said. "I think we should get you checked out at the ER."

"That's not necessary," Nicole started to stand, but then sat back down with a thump. "Whoa, did everything just spin around for a second?"

Hannah rested a hand on Nicole's shoulder. "You'd better go in and get checked. You've been through a lot." Hannah's eyes were bright with tears. "I'm so sorry I didn't come that night when you called."

"I'm just glad you're all right." Nicole sniffed and turned to the EMTs. "Okay, let's go." With the EMTs supporting her on both sides, Nicole walked toward the ambulance. Jace and Hannah followed.

One of the technicians noticed his limp. "Are you injured, sir?"

"I just wrenched my knee. I'm okay."

The man nodded. "RICE. Rest, ice, compression, and elevation."

"Good advice. Thanks." As they neared the driveway, they could hear Rocky claiming in a loud voice that the police had no grounds to arrest him. "I was looking for my buddy's house, and I turned into the wrong driveway. Get these cuffs off me!"

An officer was listening to something on his radio. He nodded to the one who was standing with the handcuffed prisoner. "Outstanding warrant in Fairbanks. Hit-and-run."

"There you go." The second officer nudged the prisoner toward a waiting police car. "You have the right to remain silent…"

The EMTs took Nicole to the ambulance, loaded her up, and told Hannah where they were taking her. "I'll be there as soon as I can," Hannah promised. As she watched the ambulance make its way down the drive, Jace slipped an arm around her shoulders.

"Oh, Jace," she whispered. "I—" A sob interrupted whatever she had been about to say, and suddenly all the tears she must have been holding back over the past few days broke loose.

"Shh." Jace pulled her into his arms. "It's all over. You're safe now."

She wrapped her arms around his waist and held on as though he was the only thing keeping her from falling into an abyss, but through her tears he heard her whisper, "Because you kept me safe."

Late the next morning, Hannah balanced the tray she was carrying and tapped on the unlatched door of her guestroom, causing it to swing open. "Nicole?"

"Come in." Nicole pushed back the quilt and mumbled. "What time is it?"

"Time for elevenses." Hannah set the tray on a small table near the window and poured tea from the pot into two mugs.

Nicole yawned. "I can't believe I slept so late." She sat up and propped an extra pillow behind her.

"You needed it." Hannah gave her a mug. "You couldn't have gotten much sleep over the past few days."

"No," Nicole admitted as she accepted a blue-and-yellow flowered mug with a handle shaped like a carrot. She took a sip and then raised the mug and squinted at the bottom. "Is this Spode?"

"Good eye. It's Imperial Garden." Hannah gestured toward the matching teapot. "Isn't it cute, the way the pot looks like it's made of cabbage leaves?"

"And the handle on the lid is a butterfly. That's adorable." Nicole took another sip. "Where did you find it all?"

"Garage sale, believe it or not, marked three dollars for the full set. Something they'd found in an aunt's attic." Hannah offered a plate of tiny shortbread cookies. "I paid them thirty-five."

"You're too soft." Nicole laughed and took a cookie. "Where's Jace?" Once Jace and Hannah had finished with the police, they'd borrowed Nicole's car and gone to meet her at the emergency room. By the time they'd arrived, the doctor had already examined Nicole. With her blood pressure lower if not completely back to normal, he'd released her, and they'd all spent the night at Hannah's house.

"I drove him to the airport early this morning," Hannah answered. And she had been missing him ever since. Considering all she and Jace had been through together, saying goodbye was never going to be easy, but at least it had been relatively drama-free. On the drive to the airport, they'd chatted about the weather, Scout's upcoming training, and the locally made handicrafts Hannah carried in her store. In the chaos of finding a place at the curb to drop him off and the other drivers hovering behind, waiting for the space, there wasn't time for more than a quick hug goodbye. No promises of "see you soon" or "keep in touch." They'd never even exchanged cell phone numbers, Hannah realized with a pang. But she kept her voice casual as she added, "He had to get back to Fairbanks. Some sort of supply chain emergency he had to sort out."

"Oh." Nicole gave Hannah an appraising glance. "How long have you and Jace been…?" Nicole waved the cookie around vaguely before popping it into her mouth.

Hannah shook her head. "We're not together. Jace just happened to be walking his dog at the ice park in Fairbanks when those two guys in the white truck broke into my rental car and tried to take my backpack. He ran them off."

"You were lucky. And then what happened?" Nicole asked.

"And then he drove me to my hotel, but he spotted the same guys lurking around the parking lot, so I stayed at his house instead. The next day those guys had the road blocked off to the airport, so Jace convinced me to take the train with him, and then to stay at his cabin…" Hannah drew in a breath. "Oh, Nicole. I'm so sorry I didn't ride the train to Anchorage and come to your house that day like I'd promised. If I'd had any idea somebody was holding you hostage—"

"I'm glad you didn't. I felt horrible, trying to lure you into a trap like that. I almost blurted out he'd kidnapped me, but he had a gun, and the way he looked at me…" Nicole shuddered. "It was like he didn't see me as human at all. Just a pawn in a game."

Hannah winced. "And I just left you there, in danger. You even tried to tell me to call the police, talking about Grandpa's flag, but I was too dense to get the hint."

"It was a long shot. Besides, I suspect that if you had come and brought the coin that first night, he would have decided it would be safer for him if neither of us lived to tell the tale."

"That's a sobering thought."

"Yeah, well, I had a lot of time to think about it after I went and blabbed about the Angeles cabin, and he sent those two goons after you to find the coin. I could hear him on the phone, yelling at them that he didn't care about the weather, they should have waited for you at the cabin, forced you to give them the globe, and 'dealt with the problem.' It didn't take a lot of imagination to guess what that meant. He ordered them to go back the next morning, but they reported that you'd already left the cabin by the time they arrived, and they couldn't find you or the globe. He called them a few choice names and said they could just forget about getting a cut, that he'd handle everything himself from then on."

"I guess when we're thanking God for keeping us safe, we can add in thanks for sending in that windstorm early so they decided not to wait it out at the cabin. Was it the same two guys who showed up in the truck last night?"

"Had to be. He called one of them Rocky on the phone." Nicole ate another cookie.

"Rocky posed as a neighbor and tried to waylay me on the way to the expert's house in Fairbanks. He and the other guy did a hit-and-run on the expert's pregnant daughter so that he would be tied up when I arrived."

Nicole's eyes widened. "Is she all right?"

"I hope so. Last I heard she was going in for an emergency C-section."

"I hope they both made it okay." Nicole took another sip of tea and set the mug on the bedside table. "So where is the coin now?"

"The police took it for evidence."

"Oh, duh, of course they did. What coin is it and why were those guys so desperate to get their hands on it?"

Hannah shrugged. "I don't know. You're the coin specialist in the family. It was gold, American, but I don't know much more than that."

"Did you take a picture?" Nicole asked eagerly.

"You know, I didn't. We didn't figure out how to open the globe until the night before last when we camped, and we were using lanterns. We were in such a hurry to start skiing the next morning, it didn't even occur to me to take a picture in daylight." Not to mention those kisses in the moonlight that had driven every other thought from her mind. Nicole didn't need to know about that.

"You were camping? In a blizzard?" Nicole looked horrified. But then she'd never been one for spending time outdoors in less-than-optimal weather.

"No, the wind had died down by the time we left the cabin," Hannah assured her. "We had to ski out because they'd sabotaged the snow machines, and so we camped one night on the way to Pika."

Nicole shook her head. "I'm sorry I told them about the cabin and forced you to ski all that way and risk hypothermia sleeping outside in the winter."

"It wasn't too bad. Jace had a good tent and warm sleeping bags. I'm the one who should be sorry. I'm sure I was a lot more comfortable in that tent than you were with a kidnapper in your house."

"Stop." Nicole held up her hand, palm toward Hannah. "It's established that we're both sorry, and we both forgive each other. Can we stop apologizing and move on already?"

Hannah smiled. If Jace were there, he would be telling her the same thing, but in a more tactful way. "Absolutely."

"Okay, then. What did the coin look like?"

"Um, it had an eagle on one side."

Nicole laughed. "So do half the quarters in your cash register. You'll have to do better than that."

"Okay, let me think." Hannah closed her eyes and pictured the coin. "The eagle was holding arrows. Lady Liberty was on the other side, with stars."

Nicole sat up straighter. "Did it say Liberty on a coronet across her head?"

"I think so. Yes, I'm sure it did."

"What was the date and mint?" Nicole demanded.

"San Francisco mint." Hannah was sure of that. "The date was old, eighteen fifty-something."

"Eighteen fifty-four?"

"That sounds right. Why?"

"Because if it is, you actually held in your hand an eighteen fifty-four San Francisco Mint Coronet Half Eagle gold coin, one of the rarest coins out there!"

"Coronet Half Eagle. Why does that sound familiar?" Hannah mused.

Nicole was almost bouncing on the bed. "Because there were thought to be only three in existence, but in 2018, some collector in New England discovered a fourth one and sold it for over two million dollars. It was in all the news."

"Oh, wow. I do remember that story. They thought it was a forgery, but it turned out to be real."

"Yes, exactly. Which means a two-million-dollar coin might be sitting on a shelf in police evidence between a stolen bicycle and a baggy of drugs." Nicole shook her head. "I wonder, is this a fifth coin, or is it one of the original three?" Nicole patted the bedside table beside her tea mug. "Shoot, I don't have my phone. Can I borrow yours?"

"Sure." Hannah took the phone from her pocket, touched the fingerprint reader, and passed it to Nicole, who typed something into the search bar.

"Hmm." A line formed on Nicole's forehead as she read. "It says in the article that three of the four San Francisco eighteen fifty-four Coronet Half Eagles are in museums, and the other is in the hands of an unnamed private collector. You don't suppose Candace Linacott was the private collector? I mean, she obviously had a lot of money, but was she that rich?"

"I don't know, but she didn't seem to have multiple houses or private jets, that sort of thing."

"Never mind." Nicole scrolled down. "The private collector still has his, so this one must be number five. Still incredibly rare."

"You know, Jace and I wondered if the coin might be tied to a robbery at the Anchorage airport a couple of decades ago. Let's see, I was in eighth grade, so you would have been in fifth. Do you remember hearing about it?"

"Something about a courier getting drugged? Let me look it up." It took a minute for Nicole to locate the original news story. "Yes, it says the courier was on his way to deliver five assorted valuable coins to a museum in Boston. He was found drugged in an airport bathroom with no coins and no memory of what happened. Let's see if there's a follow-up story that lists exactly what coins were taken." Nicole swiped through a few things on the phone. "I don't see anything about the coins, but if one of them was as yet an unknown Half Eagle, the museum probably didn't want it publicized that they'd lost something so valuable. Oh, no—a week later, the body of an airport employee who was a person of interest in this case was found in Centennial Park." She looked up. "You think Candace Linacott was involved in this robbery and murder? Why?"

"It's just a hunch. For one thing, she hid an extremely rare coin in a wooden puzzle box, which was hidden inside an ordinary chest of drawers with the drawer screwed shut. And that chest wasn't even stored at her house. I mean, there's no law that says you have to keep your valuables in a safe or vault—"

"But that would make a whole lot more sense, unless you were afraid someone might come with a search warrant and go through your safe looking for stolen property. If this is one of the coins from the robbery, I wonder what happened to the other four mentioned in the article? They could hardly be as rare as the one in the globe, although, they must have been quite valuable, too."

Hannah shrugged. "Sold to private collectors maybe? I suppose we should mention this theory to the police when we give our statements this afternoon."

Nicole made a tsking noise. "I'd say so, and we should ask what measures they're taking to keep that coin safe. What time are we supposed to be there?"

"I told them one o'clock."

Nicole threw back the covers. "In that case, I suppose I should get up and shower. I'm going to need to borrow some clothes until I can get back into my own house."

"Of course. Help yourself to anything in my closet." Hannah started to gather up the tea things, but she stopped and turned. "Nicole, I know we said we were done apologizing, but I really am sorry, and not just because of the kidnapper. It feels like I haven't been a very good sister for the past few years. I should have supported you more through your divorce, but my nose was out of joint because you opened your antiques store after I did. And since then, it seems like we've been more competitors than sisters. But when that kidnapper came on the phone and said he was holding you hostage—" Hannah pressed her hand to her chest. "I was so scared. I know we don't usually say things like this out loud, but I love you, Nicole. I don't know what I would do if anything happened to you."

"The truth is, well, I love you, too." Nicole's voice was shaky, and her eyes glittered with unshed tears. But then she grinned. "And talk about competitiveness, don't be hogging all the blame. I got so sick of hearing Mom go on and on about how well your shop was doing, I decided to show you up. That really is the only reason I opened my store—to spite you."

"But you're so good at it," Hannah protested.

"Running the store, or spiting you?"

Hannah snorted. "Well, both, actually."

"You're right." Nicole laughed. "Ironic, isn't it? It turns out that I really like running the store and looking for beautiful things like that Karas jewelry box. And there's an example of my competitiveness coming back to bite me. I was so eager to sell it for a profit to show you I didn't pay too much, I didn't bother to research the box and see who made it until after it was sold. I could have kicked myself when I went online and saw that it was worth eight thousand or more. Not that I was going to admit that to you. But I am sorry I outbid you on that box. And on the carnival glass, which I didn't plan to buy until you started bidding. I shouldn't have behaved that way toward you."

Hannah shook her head. "Why do we do this?"

"Habit, I guess." Nicole thought for a moment. "I think it goes back to Lindsay."

"Lindsay?" Nicole had never seemed particularly interested in Lindsay. If anything, she'd snubbed Hannah's best friend. "What does she have to do with anything?"

"I was always jealous because the two of you were so close. I felt like I was invisible. I guess I thought that if I could do things as well or better than you and Lindsay that you would accept me and let me into the club. But you never did."

Hannah thought about it. When she and Lindsay were seven, it made sense that four-year-old Nicole couldn't play board games or climb trees, but as they all got older, there was no reason they couldn't have included Nicole. But they never did. "You're right. We did exclude you. I'm sorry."

Nicole shrugged. "I got over it. But I have to admit, it felt like payback watching you crushing over Lindsay's big brother, where you were the invisible one, instead of me."

"What are you talking about?" Hannah tried to keep her voice casual, but she felt her face getting warm.

"Are you really going to pretend you weren't head-over-heels in love with Jace all through high school? Like you didn't have his initials in little hearts all over the inside of your notebook? Everybody knew—everybody but Jace, that is. He was totally oblivious. My friends and I used to laugh about it." She gave a wry smile. "You can add that to the list of things I'm sorry for. Maybe we should be writing this stuff down."

"No need. I'll forgive you for snickering behind my back if you'll forgive me for ditching you."

"It's a deal. And by the way, I don't think I ever told you at the time, but I'm sorry about what happened to Lindsay. And I know you blamed yourself, but what happened to her wasn't your fault."

"Thanks." Hannah sighed. "Jace said the same thing at the cabin."

"Did he now?" Nicole swung her legs to the floor and shoved her feet into the slippers Hannah had loaned her, but she remained seated on the bed. "Just out of curiosity, is the spark still there?"

"What spark?" Hannah asked in her most innocent voice. She gave up the pretense. "How was he looking at me?"

"Like I would look at a Victorian ruby ring marked five dollars at a garage sale. No, scratch that. I'd buy that ring and sell it again, but Jace was looking at you as though you were the most precious thing in his world, and he would do anything to keep you safe."

"Well, that's just Jace. He would have helped anyone in trouble." If Nicole were right about Jace's feelings, he would have said something before he left town. Wouldn't he?

"You think so?" Nicole's expression was thoughtful. "I agree he would have come to the defense of anyone being mugged in a parking lot, but would he have whisked just anyone away to his cabin to keep them safe? Or risked his life confronting a gang of criminals to rescue just anyone's sister? The man is a store manager, not an action hero. It's not as though he was trained in any of this stuff. But when you needed him, he was there. Even though you hadn't seen each other for, what, thirteen years now? He cares about you."

Before Hannah could formulate an answer, Nicole stood and shuffled off toward the bathroom. But before she shut the door, she called over her shoulder, "I hope this time around, you plan to do more about it than doodle his initials inside your notebook."

Chapter Fourteen

Jace watched Scout scoop up a yellow tennis ball and execute a skidding about-face in the snow to bring it back for another turn. The dog would do this all day, given the opportunity, but Jace was on his lunch hour. It had taken him most of yesterday to straighten out the ordering mix-up with one of their suppliers. It might not have taken so long if he could keep his thoughts on business, but instead, his mind kept returning to Hannah.

When the store manager, Bette, had called early yesterday morning to tell him about the mess, he'd taken the excuse to return to Fairbanks. Bette had been working for Angeles Adventure Store for twenty years. She could have taken care of the problem, and she would have if Jace had been out of cell phone range at the cabin like he'd planned, but he'd flown home to handle it himself. Truth was, he was running away.

Seeing Hannah in danger, surrounded by angry men with guns, he would have traded everything he owned and everything he was if it kept her safe, including his own life. And afterward, when he held her in his arms, the intensity of his feelings—well, they scared him. He wasn't an impulsive person. He might have known Hannah since she was six years old, but this adult version of Hannah was a virtual stranger.

And yet, in a matter of days, she'd become the center of his thoughts, the center of his life. It was all happening too fast. It couldn't be real. He needed to put some distance between them.

Hannah didn't protest when he'd told her he needed to catch a plane to Fairbanks yesterday morning. She'd simply driven him to the airport and given him a goodbye hug. Which was good, right? Now that the criminals were locked up and the coin was safe, it made sense that he and Hannah should go back to their own separate lives. Only he was starting to think that there was no going back for him.

Scout nudged Jace's hand with the ball. "Okay. Just a few more." He threw the ball again and checked the time on his phone. Twenty minutes left in his lunch break. Not that anyone would question the boss if he happened to take a long lunch, but Jace liked to set a good example. Then he noticed today's date—his parents' anniversary. Shoot, he'd meant to mail a card Friday, but in all the excitement, he'd forgotten. He took out his phone and dialed. "Hi, Mom. Happy anniversary."

"Thank you! Just a second, and I'll get your dad and put him on Speaker." There were the usual beeping, bumping, and static noises that happened whenever his mom tried to make adjustments to her phone. "Russell. It's Jace."

Dad's voice came through. "Hi, son."

"Hi. Happy anniversary."

"Thanks." Jace could hear the smile in his dad's voice. "Hard to believe it's been thirty-nine years. Seems like yesterday when I spotted your mother across that crowded room—"

"It wasn't that crowded," Mom cut in. "And it wasn't a room. It was a backyard cookout and there were only eight people there."

"Were there eight?" Dad asked. "I only had eyes for one."

"Oh, you," Mom replied and Jace heard the smack of a kiss.

He grinned. His parents seemed to be treating their retirement as sort of a second honeymoon, and Jace wholeheartedly approved. "So, what are your plans to celebrate?"

"Nothing too fancy," Dad said. "We're going out to dinner with friends."

"And I got your dad tickets to a Boise State basketball game this Saturday," Mom added.

"Fun," Jace said. Mom had never been a particular sports fan until he made the team in middle school, and his parents had developed a sudden fascination with basketball. Lindsay and Hannah would come to every game, too, cheering so loudly Jace's teammates used to tease him. There he went again. It seemed as though every subject in his mind eventually led to Hannah.

Without giving any thought to the consequences, Jace asked, "Tell me, Dad. How long from the time you met Mom until you knew she was the one you wanted to spend your life with?"

"Honestly?" Dad said. "Ten minutes. Twenty, tops."

"Oh, phooey," Mom exclaimed. "He didn't even ask me out for three weeks after that cookout."

Dad chuckled. "Jace asked when I knew, not how long it took me to work up the courage to do something about it. Why do you ask, son?"

"Yes, why? Did you meet someone special?" Just from the tone of Mom's voice, Jace could almost picture her raising her head like a bird dog finding a scent. For years, she'd been hinting that it was time he settled down and started a family.

"Not exactly," Jace hedged. Hannah was definitely special, but he hadn't just met her.

Of course Mom wasn't going to let that go. "You did! I can hear it in your voice."

Dad snorted. "Are you sure that voice you're hearing isn't your own inner wannabe grandmother?"

"Like you're not just as eager to be a grandfather," Mom countered. "Tell us about her, Jace."

Jace hesitated, but then he decided to go for it. Maybe his parents could give him some insight. And besides, he needed to fill them in on what had happened before they heard it elsewhere.

"I was walking Scout at Ice Alaska on Friday, when I heard

this woman yelling in the parking lot. Some guy was chasing after her and knocked her down. Scout and I ran over, and the guy jumped into a white truck with his partner and took off. They'd broken into the woman's car and stolen her suitcase."

Dad said, "Thank goodness you were there."

"Yes." Jace took a breath. "The woman was Hannah Yates."

"Hannah?" Mom gasped. "Our Hannah?"

"What other Hannah Yates would he be talking about?" Dad asked. "What was Hannah doing at the Ice Sculpture place? As far as I knew, she hadn't been back to Fairbanks since high school."

"It's kind of a long story," Jace said, "so get comfortable." He told them all about the events of the last few days. Except, of course, for those moonlight kisses. That was between him and Hannah.

"Hannah crossed a rope bridge?" Dad marveled. "When she was in high school, she wouldn't even hike to the water-fall with us because of the ledge along the trail, and that ledge is a good six feet wide."

"I know. She's still scared of heights, but with a whole lot of praying, she did it. Just like when she climbed down into the ravine after me."

"That was very brave of her," Mom said thoughtfully. "Is your knee better now?"

Jace smiled to himself. He could always count on his mother to worry about his health. "My knee is fine. I just wrenched it a little when I fell."

Mom sighed. "I hate that you put yourself in danger, but I'm glad you were there for Hannah. Poor girl. That must have been terrifying to have those men chasing her. And then to find out her sister was being held hostage—it doesn't bear think-ing about."

"It was scary," Jace admitted. "But Hannah was amaz-ing. You should have seen the way she handled herself with the kidnappers."

"But I'm confused," Mom said. "Why does Hannah run a store? She was going to study nursing at Arizona State."

"She never went to Arizona. You know the plan was that once she and Lindsay graduated, they were going to explore the country together as traveling nurses, but Hannah said it just didn't feel right without Lindsay. Hannah ended up getting a business degree from UAA, instead. She opened her antique store in downtown Anchorage a few years ago. It's called Hannah's Alaskan Treasures."

"But I thought…" Mom stopped talking, but Jace knew exactly what she'd thought—that Hannah had gone on with her plans without a backward glance for her friend. Mom sighed. "You know, I was just thinking about Hannah the other day. I was not kind to her that night at the hospital, sending her home like that."

"You were upset," Dad said soothingly. "I'm sure Hannah understands."

Jace wasn't so sure. "Hannah and I talked about Lindsay, there at the cabin. Hannah has been blaming herself all these years. That's why she never got in contact with you after the funeral. She thought you didn't ever want to see her again."

"Oh, dear. I wish I'd called to apologize, but by the time I was together enough to do that, Hannah and her family had moved away to Anchorage, and I never bothered to try to find them. I should have. Hannah may have covered for Lindsay, but the accident was not her fault."

"I know, and I told her that. When we were at the cabin, we took one of those rocks Lindsay had painted—you remember the one with the eagle—and we carried it to the creek where Lindsay and Hannah used to like to go to watch the otters. We had a little memorial service for Lindsay there."

"That's so sweet. So Hannah never forgot Lindsay."

"Never," Jace assured her.

"Would you text me Hannah's phone number?" Mom asked.

"I'd like to call and clear the air, let her know I never really blamed her. I was just lashing out."

"Sorry, I don't have it," Jace said, "but I'm sure you can reach her at her store."

"What do you mean you don't have her phone number?" Mom demanded. "Why not?"

Jace had been wondering the same thing. "I don't know. It just never came up."

Mom continued to press. "How are you going to move forward in this relationship if you don't have her phone number?"

Were they going to move forward? Jace was in Fairbanks; Hannah was in Anchorage. They had just spent an intense weekend together, but were these feelings real and lasting? "I'm just not sure—"

"Yes, you are," Mom interrupted. "You just haven't worked up the courage to do something about it yet. Like father, like son." Mom laughed. "Hannah may have made a mistake, but she was one of the sweetest girls I ever knew, and pretty, too. I'm sure she's grown into a lovely woman, inside and out."

"She has." Jace couldn't deny that.

"Then you'd better stop dilly-dallying and make your move," Mom said. "Women like her don't come along every day."

"Jace is old enough to make his own decision about whether he wants to pursue a relationship," Dad pointed out.

"Well yes, but—"

"Judy." Dad's voice held a warning note.

"Fine. I know you'll make the right choice, Jace. I'll be praying for you. And thanks for the call. It makes our anniversary even more special to know you've found your someone."

"Judy—" Dad repeated.

Mom laughed. "Love you, Jace."

"Love you, too. Bye, Mom. Bye, Dad." Jace hung up the phone.

He called Scout and returned to work, where he sat at his desk and got nothing done. He was supposed to be reviewing the latest and greatest new adventure gear to decide what to order for next season's inventory. Ordinarily this was one of his favorite tasks, but he just couldn't seem to concentrate today.

He'd been at it for an hour when Bette walked into his office. "I wanted to apologize for yesterday. When I called about that order problem, I was thinking you were at the Anchorage store and could handle it from there. I forgot you'd taken the week off. And I sure didn't mean for you to have to fly home and ruin your vacation. I should have taken care of it myself."

"That's all right. It was my decision to come back early." He'd chosen to run to Fairbanks, to put some distance between himself and what he was feeling. But the feelings hadn't gone away. No, the more he turned it over in his mind, the clearer it became. He'd fallen in love with Hannah Yates. It was as simple as that. Question was, did she feel the same?

"Are you planning to fly down for the grand opening Saturday, or are you going to drive tomorrow?" Bette asked.

"Oh, wow. That's the day after tomorrow, isn't it?" It seemed like a year ago when Jace had scheduled a driver to meet him in Pika early Saturday morning and take him to Anchorage for the event. "I'm going to drive." He closed his laptop. "In fact, I'm going home now to pack, so I can drive down this evening. I have some important personal business in Anchorage tomorrow before the grand opening on Saturday. You can handle things here, right?"

"Of course," Bette told him. "Just out of curiosity, does this important personal business in Anchorage have anything to do with a certain antiques store owner there?"

He looked up. "You've been talking to my mother, haven't you?"

"Now why would you think that?" Bette winked. "I always did like that girl. Such a sweetheart. Can't wait to see what kind of a woman she grew up to be. Godspeed, Jace."

Jace grinned. "Thanks, Bette."

Chapter Fifteen

Friday morning, Hannah stacked a new selection of pillow-cases on a table in one corner of the store, while Sue Ann unlocked the front door and turned the sign to Open. A minute later Tracy Schmidt, a regular customer and a friend of Sue Ann's, wandered in and immediately gravitated toward a carved cedar chest Hannah had just set out. Yesterday, Hannah had responded to an online listing for that chest, only to find when she arrived to purchase it that the chest was stuffed with hand-embroidered pillowcases, tea towels, and aprons that the seller had forgotten were there. Knowing how much her customers loved handmade items, she'd negotiated a price for the whole collection.

Sue Ann went to help Tracy, so Hannah just called a greeting. Once she'd finished laying out the pillowcases, she slipped through the curtain into the workroom where she set up an ironing board, started the iron preheating, and switched on her radio. Once the iron was hot, she reached into a basket for one of the aprons she'd washed last night, this one pinafore-style with daisies embroidered across the top.

She spritzed some water onto the apron and ran her iron over the cotton fabric, enjoying the homey smell of freshly ironed cloth. Music played in the background, a modern instrumental interpretation of a favorite old hymn. It was good to be home, good to be back into her normal routine, and yet, Hannah felt unsettled. Sue Ann would say that was to be expected after such a frightening experience, but Hannah didn't feel particularly skittish or nervous, just…off. As if she'd forgotten an appointment or left something behind.

Like maybe her heart.

Hannah sighed. Nicole might or might not be right about Jace's feelings, but she was correct about one thing: Hannah was no longer a teenager, doodling Jace's initials in her notebook. What she felt toward Jace wasn't some girlish crush. In the brief time they had spent together, that spark of attraction had caught and grown into a full-fledged bonfire.

But what was she going to do about it? Jace was in Fairbanks. She was here. Eventually, when the police were done, they would return the globe to her and she could see if Peter Morozov was still interested in having her bring it to Fairbanks, but that could be months, and she didn't want to wait months to see Jace again.

Of course, there was always the chance that Jace didn't share her feelings. Yes, he'd kissed her out there in the wilderness, but that might have had more to do with their situation than with any deep feelings. A few kisses didn't necessarily mean he wanted an ongoing relationship. And even if he did, there was the matter of Lindsay. Jace said his parents had forgiven Hannah, but forgiveness was one thing. Having the person you held responsible for your daughter's death dating your son was a whole other matter. The last thing Hannah wanted was to come between Jace and his family.

She closed her eyes in a silent prayer. Was it God's will that she and Jace should be together? Could they work out things with his family? When she opened her eyes, she still wasn't sure. But she knew she had to try.

Maybe she should give him a call, just to check on him, feel him out a little. She didn't have his cell phone number, but she could surely reach him through the store. But that didn't feel right. When she talked with him, she wanted to see his face, and not in a tiny picture on her cell phone. She wanted to touch his hand. If all went well, she wanted to put her arms around him and feel his kiss.

The song on the radio ended, and a commercial came on. Hannah ignored it, until the words "grand opening" caught her attention. The announcer was talking about special promotions and door prizes for people attending the Angeles Adventure Store grand opening tomorrow. Jace would be there. In fact, he might even be there now, helping prepare for the big event.

Maybe she could drop by this afternoon, ask for him, and casually offer to take him out for a meal after closing. It would be a friendly, supportive thing to do. And if he agreed, it would give her a few hours to gather up her courage before she laid her heart on the line. The very heart that was beating faster at the thought of seeing Jace again.

She hung up the freshly ironed apron and pulled another from the basket, but paused before she picked up the iron. Why wait? She could drive over right now. If Jace wasn't there, she could try again tomorrow. She paused just long enough to un-plug the iron, run a brush through her hair, and apply a fresh coat of lipstick before grabbing her coat, but before she could let Sue Ann know she was going, the bells on the door rang, signaling a new customer. Hannah glanced at the employee schedule on the wall. Cheryl wouldn't be in for another hour. Hannah shouldn't leave Sue Ann alone in the store, not after all the scary things that had been happening.

With a sigh, Hannah set her coat aside and stepped through the curtain into the store. A man wearing a down jacket had his back to her while he examined one of Charlie's wooden rolling pins. The man's dark hair, waving a little where it met his collar, almost looked like...

A dog stepped out from behind the display and woofed a

greeting in her direction—a big fluffy yellow dog. Jace turned and flashed that gorgeous smile of his. "Hannah!"

"Jace!" She hurried toward him. "What are you doing here?"

He caught her in his arms and Hannah's heart swelled. She wrapped her arms around him and breathed in his warm, woodsy scent.

"I got into town late last night, but somehow I never got your phone number," Jace told her as he released her from the hug. His hands ran down her arms and lingered, his thumbs moving over the backs of her hands in little circles. "So, I thought I'd drop by and see if you might have some free time to spend with me today."

"I, uh…" Hannah couldn't seem to form a coherent sentence when he was touching her hands like that.

"She's free now." Sue Ann sidled up to them, a knowing smile on her face. "Hi, I'm Sue Ann Bolton, Hannah's store manager, and I'm guessing you're Jace Angeles." She offered her hand.

"Yes." Jace dropped Hannah's hands so that he could shake Sue Ann's, and Hannah immediately felt the loss.

"I thought so. There aren't too many people who can leave Hannah speechless and blushing." She chuckled. "And this must be the famous Scout, who ran into the middle of a crowd of gun-toting kidnappers and knocked Hannah down and out of danger. I know I'm not supposed to interact with service dogs when they're in their vests, but I really want to give that dog a big hug."

"It's all right," Jace told her, "as long as the handler gives permission. Scout, go say hi."

The dog went to Sue Ann, who heaped him with extravagant compliments and petting. Tracy joined her, and soon Scout's mouth was open in a doggy grin and his fluffy tail kept bumping against a nearby table leg hard enough to rattle the dishes on top.

Hannah stood next to Jace and watched, grinning. After a

few minutes, Jace laughed. "Okay, enough, or you'll be spoiled rotten. Come, Scout." The dog returned, and Jace snapped on the leash.

Sue Ann smiled. "Next time, I'll have a treat for him. Now, Jace, why don't you and Hannah go get some coffee or something? I can handle the store."

"Cheryl doesn't come in until eleven. Are you sure you don't mind working alone?" Hannah asked.

Sue Ann waved away her concerns. "I've got this. Y'all have fun."

"It will take me a while to look through all the new goodies, anyhow," Tracy said, "so Sue Ann won't be alone."

"All right. Thanks. I'll get my coat." Hannah ducked into the back and grabbed her jacket and bag. When she returned, Jace reached for the jacket and held it while she slipped her arms inside. Once she'd buttoned it, they stepped out the front door and he reached for her hand. Neither of them had bothered with gloves, and his hand warmed hers. Scout walked along on his other side. "Where did you want to go?" Hannah asked.

"I'm not sure." He glanced down at the dog. "As a service dog in training, Scout is allowed in restaurants, but I don't usually take him because there's not always a lot of room for a big dog like him."

"Why don't we just grab coffee and walk around Town Square?"

"Sounds good to me." As they strolled along the sidewalk, Jace mentioned, "I talked to Peter Morozov yesterday. You'll be glad to know his daughter has recovered from the hit-and-run, and that she and his grandson are at home and doing well."

"That is good news." They reached the coffee shop a block from Hannah's store. Their walk-up window was closed in the winter, so Hannah popped inside to get them two cups of coffee. She came out and handed one to Jace. "Sugar, no cream, right?"

"Thanks." He looped Scout's leash over his left wrist and transferred the cup to his left hand, leaving his right free to reach for hers, lacing their fingers together and tucking their joined hands inside his coat pocket to keep warm. This was nice, Hannah decided. She could get used to it.

"Have you found out any more about whether the gold coin is tied to that airport robbery like we thought?" Jace asked before he took a sip of coffee.

"It is indeed. The police have it for now as evidence, but once they're done, it will go to the museum where it was originally headed. The coin is—let me get this right..." Hannah closed her eyes briefly to concentrate. "...an 1854-S Coronet Half Eagle, worth more than two million dollars."

"That's amazing. And to think you were carrying it around in a backpack."

"I know. And you remember when we were talking about that walrus ivory scandal? Turns out Ivan Penca, the guy who kidnapped Nicole, spent six months in prison for that crime. He must have gotten a nice reward for accepting the blame and keeping Candace Linacott out of it. As for the two guys in the white truck, Rocky Pearson and Alfred 'Tiny' Lima, they're falling all over themselves to talk to the police, trying to get the best plea deal by implicating the others. It seems they were all involved in the airport robbery. Ivan bribed an airline employee to find out which flight the courier would be on coming into Anchorage. At the airport bar, Ivan distracted the courier while Rocky put some drug in his drink. Once the courier began to feel the effects, Tiny escorted him to a bathroom off the main level, robbed him, and left him there. Later, to make sure the airline employee didn't talk, at least one of the three—depending on who is telling the truth—murdered him and dumped his body in Centennial Park. And it was all under the direction of Candace Linacott."

"Wow."

"I know. Since it all happened at the airport, the Feds have taken over. They suspect once they dig a little deeper, especially into Ivan's travel history, they may be able to clear up several smuggling cases as well."

"What happened to the rest of the coins that the courier was transporting?" Jace asked as they crossed Fourth Street.

"Nobody seems to know, but it's assumed Candace Linacott sold them to private collectors and that's where she got the money to pay Ivan, Rocky, and Tiny. Together the other coins were worth about a hundred and fifty thousand according to the police report. It seems odd that she held on to this one for so long instead of selling it, but maybe she was waiting for just the right collector who would pay top dollar."

Jace thought about it. "Or maybe she got a thrill from possessing something so rare."

"If so, it might have cost her. Her death was listed as cardiac arrest, but I understand the investigators are considering exhuming the body. But if it turns out Ivan and company had anything to do with her death, between the original crimes and the new robbery, breaking and entering, and kidnapping charges, it's going to mean very long prison sentences for the three men involved," Hannah said.

"Just as long as it keeps them far away from you." Jace squeezed her hand. "What about the globe puzzle box?"

"Good news. It seems that, since it was in the chest of drawers I bought, it's legally mine once the police are done with it." They reached the corner and Hannah pushed the crossing button at the light.

"Are you going to sell it to Peter Morozov?"

"I haven't decided yet." She was tempted to keep it. True, the globe was a reminder of the danger they'd been through, but it had brought her back to Fairbanks and thrown Jace into her path, and she could only be grateful for that.

The light changed and they crossed the street and followed one of the pathways that meandered through Town Square. The snow glistened in the sunlight. A couple skated together on the small rink in the center of the square. Mounds of snow covered the beds that city workers would fill with a riot of bright bedding plants in the summer, making this one of Hannah's favorite places in Anchorage.

"That sun feels good," Jace commented, pausing to let Scout sniff at a lamppost.

"A little warmer than Fairbanks?"

"Much warmer. It's supposed to be nice for our Anchorage store's grand opening tomorrow."

Hannah nodded. "I heard your commercial on the radio. Sounds like the grand opening is going to be a lot of fun."

"I hope so. I'm looking forward to it, but that's only partly why I'm here. Once the grand opening is behind us, I want to explore the possibility of moving our headquarters to Anchorage."

Hannah's breath caught. She stopped to face him. "Would that mean you're thinking of moving here?"

"That's the plan."

She grinned. "Are you getting so soft you can't take the weather in Fairbanks anymore?"

He chuckled. "Better weather is just a bonus." He dropped Scout's leash, told him to stay, and took Hannah's cup and set it on the snow next to his. Then he took both of her hands in his and looked into her eyes. "The reason I want to move to Anchorage is because I want to be close to you. I believe that you and I could have a real future together. That is, if you're interested."

She couldn't imagine anything she wanted more. But had he really thought this through? "What about Lindsay? And your parents? Will they be able to forget what I did? Won't Lindsay's accident always be there, between us?"

"Lindsay would be thrilled with the idea of us together. You know she would. She'd probably be picking out her maid of honor dress even as we speak."

Hannah laughed. "She already did, in eighth grade. Purple,

with a chiffon skirt and sequined bodice. You know how she loved sparkles."

"She really did." He stroked Hannah's cheek with his finger. "I've talked with my parents, and they're completely on board with the idea of you and me together. My mom feels horrible about those things she said to you at the hospital. She wants your number so that she can call and tell you herself. So, how do you feel about what I said? Are you interested in having me around?"

She closed her eyes for a moment to savor the feel of his caress before opening them again. "I'm interested. But tell me more about your plans for us."

"You mean long-term or today?"

"Either. Both." She laughed, just for the joy of it. "Let's start with today."

"Okay. Depending on your schedule, I was hoping that we could spend some time together. Maybe catch a movie, then hit the diner and have breakfast for dinner. Or we could do some skiing or skating or…" He leaned closer. "Maybe some kissing."

"Kissing, you say?"

"You know. Like this." He brushed a soft kiss across her lips. Then he slipped his arm around her waist and pulled her closer.

She reached up to take his face in her hands and look into his eyes. "It's all so amazing." She smoothed a lock of hair from his forehead.

"What is?" Jace asked.

"That you and I should find each other again, after all these years." She raised her face for another kiss, but Scout's keen ears must have picked up the word *find*. He jumped onto the two of them, knocking them onto the relatively soft snow on the flower bed next to the path. Jace rolled as they fell so that Hannah landed on top of him.

Scout tried to crawl onto the pile, but Jace pushed him away. "Are you okay?" he asked Hannah.

"I'm fine." She laughed as she got up. "You're still protecting me, I see." She offered a hand.

"I'll always protect you." He took her hand and allowed her to pull him to his feet. "I love you, Hannah. I didn't think it was possible to fall in love this fast, but I was wrong. I really do love you."

"Oh, Jace." Her hand flew to her chest. "I love you, too!"

"That's the best news ever." He gave Scout a stern order to sit and stay. "Now, where were we?" He opened his arms.

Hannah stepped into them and threw her arms around his neck. "I believe we were right about here."

And this time when they kissed, no one interrupted for a good long time.

Chapter Sixteen

Five months later

Hannah flashed her exhibitor pass and wheeled in a dolly with two boxes stacked on top of a mid-century nightstand past the gates of the Alaska State Fair in Palmer. She paused for a moment to breathe in that distinctive fair scent: fried food, farm animals, engine grease, cotton candy, wet grass, and a hundred other aromas she couldn't name. Whenever she caught a whiff of that smell, she was instantly ten years old with a clutch of ride tickets in her pocket and Lindsay at her side, eager to see, taste and experience everything.

She smiled, remembering. She did that now, whenever she thought of Lindsay. Instead of the sadness and guilt she used to feel, she remembered the fun, the laughter, the sheer joy that Lindsay brought to life, and she was thankful to have had such a friend.

She moved slowly along with the crowds, admiring the flower gardens, 4-H exhibits, and Irish dancers performing on an outdoor stage. Soon she reached the vendor area and rolled her dolly past tents selling fireweed jelly and birch syrup, chainsaw sculptures, and specialty soaps, until she came to the bustling Angeles Adventure Store tent. She stopped and parked the dolly out of the way. Several store employees were interacting with customers. Jace was at the back of the large tent, talking with a young couple about the two sea kayaks he had on display.

She'd only been watching him for a few seconds when Jace looked her way, almost as though he could sense her presence. He shot her a smile and held up a finger to indicate he'd be just a minute. Hannah nodded and crossed the tent to a portable dog run where Rosy, Jace's currently assigned service dog in training, was holding court.

Rosy, a six-month-old labradoodle puppy, had already mastered all her basic obedience commands and leash manners. If Rosy had possessed a pinky finger, it would certainly have been raised while she sipped tea with the queen. Since she was a puppy, however, she contented herself with greeting her adoring public with wiggles and tail wags.

Hannah reached into the pen and tousled the red curls on the puppy's head. With her sharp brain and unflappable disposition, Rosy would be a blessing in the life of some special person someday, just as Scout would help save lost hikers and avalanche victims. It had been hard on both Hannah and Jace to send Scout off to "dog college" as Jace called it, but Scout's new trainer kept them up to date. According to her, Scout was progressing well, and she had finally managed to convince him that he didn't need to knock people down in order to rescue them.

Jace walked over to Hannah. "Hi, there." He leaned in for a kiss.

"Hi. I didn't mean to interrupt your sales pitch. I was just on my way to take a shift at our booth and thought I'd stop by and let you know."

"I'm glad you did. I'll be done here and ready for dinner at about six. Can you take a break then?"

"I should be able to if Nicole can cover for me." Hannah

and Nicole had decided to combine their resources and share a booth at the state fair this year, something neither of them had tried before. So far it was working out well, with a higher sales volume than either of them had anticipated.

"All right then," Jace said. "I'll meet you at your tent, and we can grab a couple of corn dogs and some chili fries."

Hannah wrinkled her nose. "You mean halibut tacos and funnel cakes."

"Do I?" He grinned. "We'll negotiate later. Mom and Dad are planning to drive out this evening, by the way. They'll probably stop in at your booth." After one more quick kiss, he went back to the couple and the kayaks.

Hannah pushed the dolly past a dozen more tents that sold everything from hot tubs to jeweled dog collars before arriving at the tent with Nicole's "Hillside Heirlooms" banner hanging above her "Hannah's Alaskan Treasures" one. Nicole had won the coin toss on whose banner went on top, but it really didn't matter because they'd mixed their inventories together. Nicole's beaded shawls were draped over a ladder beside Hannah's antique dressing mirror, and Hannah's curio cabinet displayed a set of Nicole's handblown glass goblets.

When Hannah checked, it looked like both the goblet set and the curio cabinet had sold, along with quite a few other items. Good thing she'd brought in some replacements. Sue Ann was busy counting out change to a woman with a whole stack of baby quilts. Nicole was a few feet away, lifting a tray of vintage brooches from a locking jewelry case to allow a man a closer look. Several people browsed, looking over Nicole's porcelain figurines and Hannah's quirky salt-and-pepper shakers.

After waving a greeting to Sue Ann and Nicole, Hannah made her way toward the back of the tent, unloaded the nightstand, and opened the boxes. Even before she'd finished unpacking, a woman with dark curls had snatched up one of the antique garden gnomes. A slightly older-looking woman, who wore a "Made in Alaska" ball cap, complained, "Hey, I wanted that one."

"Too bad. I got here first." The curly-haired woman smirked.

"Brat," the first woman retorted.

Hannah got the impression the two knew each other well. In fact, based on the similar shape of their eyes and noses, they were most likely sisters. Nicole caught Hannah's eye and smiled. Hannah knew just what she was thinking. That could have been the two of them, not long ago. Their relationship had come a long way in the last few months. Hannah unwrapped another gnome. "I've got more."

"Ooh, let me see." The ball cap woman picked it up. "I like the colors in this one better anyway."

"The hat matches the trim on my house. Let's trade," her sister suggested.

"Not a chance." With a smug smile, the older sister paid Sue Ann for the gnome. The curly-haired sister waited for Hannah to finish unpacking the other three she had brought, but after dithering between them for a good ten minutes, she decided if she couldn't have the one her sister had bought, she didn't want one at all.

Once she was out of earshot, Nicole whispered to Hannah, "She'll be back for that first gnome if she can figure out how to ditch her sister. If she buys it in front of her, her sister will gloat about getting the best one."

Hannah laughed. "Sisters."

"I know, right?" Nicole accepted the box of glass paperweights that Hannah had picked up at her store and turned to arrange them on top of a mahogany ladies desk. "Is Jace here?"

"He's working the Angeles Adventure tent. Okay if I slip off for a little while around six? He said he'd be ready for dinner then."

"No problem. Sue Ann says she's bringing her sister to help later, so we can cover."

For the next two hours, Hannah was too busy helping customers and couldn't talk with Nicole or Sue Ann, but around five thirty, traffic slowed as people switched their attention from shopping to food.

Sue Ann took her dinner break. "I'll be back by six, and my sister, Leigh, will be here then, too, so you can take a break," she told Hannah before she left.

Nicole sold her current customer a garnet ring, but once she'd gone, they had no shoppers for a few minutes. Hannah noticed faint dark circles under Nicole's eyes. "You've put in a long day," Hannah told her. "Why don't you head out? I can cover the booth."

"I'll wait until Sue Ann is back from dinner break at least," Nicole answered.

"That's not necessary. It's slow, and Sue Ann is bringing her sister-in-law to help."

But Nicole wouldn't budge, so Hannah stopped asking. Maybe Nicole wanted to be here, around people. Hannah knew Nicole had met with the prosecutors managing the kidnapping case against Ivan Penca earlier that morning, but she hadn't had time with Nicole since then to ask how it went, and she didn't really want to do it now, when they were sure to be interrupted. It had to be hard for Nicole, anticipating coming face-to-face with her kidnapper in court and having to field questions from his defense attorney. Maybe she hadn't been sleeping well.

Hannah had an appointment with the prosecutors the next week, so she should get a better idea of what to expect then. In the meantime, she should schedule some downtime with Nicole, just the two of them, to talk about it. Or not. If Nicole didn't want to talk, they could just get coffee or something, whatever would help Nicole feel better. At least Rocky and Tiny had already accepted plea deals, so Nicole and Hannah wouldn't need to testify at those trials.

Hannah was refolding and stacking quilts when someone tapped her on the shoulder. She turned to find Judy and Russell Angeles smiling at her. "Hi, there!" Hannah leaned in for a hug, careful not to jostle Judy's giant tote bag. She hugged Russell, too, who was carrying three more shopping bags. "Looks like you two have found lots of goodies. Want me to stash your stuff so you don't have to carry it around?"

"That would be great." Judy passed over the heavy tote with a relieved sigh.

"Now that I have a hand to carry it," Russell said, as he gripped the shopping bags, "I'm going to get some lemonade. Anyone else want some?"

"Not right now, thanks," Hannah answered, and the others declined as well. He went off toward the food vendors while Judy admired a needlepoint stool.

Hannah tucked their bags into a locking trunk she had hidden under a table with a tablecloth that reached the ground. Jace's parents had spent most of the summer in Alaska, much of it at Jace's new home in Anchorage. Hannah had been a little apprehensive the first time she faced them again, but Judy had given a sincere apology for what she'd said at the hospital, and they had been nothing but welcoming and friendly to Hannah ever since.

Nicole was showing a woman her collection of Victorian hatpins when her phone rang. After glancing at the screen, she told the customer, "Excuse me, I need to take his call. Hannah, can you take over?"

"Sure." Hannah stepped behind the jewelry counter and smiled at the woman while Nicole walked away from the tent. "Any particular ones you'd like to see?"

"How about that one?" She pointed to one with an egg-shaped jade top.

Hannah removed the heavy eight-inch pin from the velvet pincushion and handed it to the woman.

The woman eyed it warily. "Kind of dangerous looking, isn't it?"

Judy drifted over to see the pins. "I read that Victorian women sometimes used their hatpins as defensive weapons."

"Interesting," Hannah said. "No wonder they were popular if they could look this pretty and function as a weapon." It was too bad Nicole wasn't carrying a hatpin when Ivan had kidnapped her. Hannah noticed a shorter silver one and plucked it out of the pincushion. "Look at this lily of the valley design."

"That is pretty. May I see?" The customer handed back the jade pin and took the silver one, discreetly checking the price tag. "I'll take this one. My aunt collects old hats, so I think she'd like the hatpin to go with them."

"Who wouldn't? It's lovely," Judy commented, while Hannah wrapped the pin in tissue paper and put it into a gold organza bag along with Nicole's business card.

Hannah ran the woman's credit card and handed over the bag. "Hope your aunt loves it."

Nicole returned, but instead of asking about the sale, she gazed into the distance. Hannah studied her sister's face. "Everything okay?"

Nicole looked at Hannah and blinked. Then she smiled. "Everything is great, actually. Ivan Penca accepted a plea deal, after all. I won't have to testify."

Judy gave Nicole a hug. "That must be such a relief."

"It is, for sure," Nicole replied.

Hannah took a turn hugging her. "I'm so glad."

A voice behind them asked, "So, are those hugs for just anyone or only for your sister?" Jace had arrived, with Rosy on a leash beside him and a paper sack from the fish taco stand in his hand.

"You brought me halibut tacos. You get double hugs." Hannah wrapped her arms around him and gave him a kiss before releasing him. "I thought you wanted corn dogs and chili fries."

"I did, but once I smelled the halibut frying, I decided you were right. But then, you usually are."

Hannah laughed. "I'm going to remind you that you said that. We were just celebrating because Ivan Penca has accepted a plea bargain and Nicole won't have to testify at the trial."

"That is good news." Jace sent a sympathetic glance Nicole's way. "So it's all over."

"It's all over," Nicole repeated. She flashed Jace a little smile. "On to the future."

"Absolutely." He gave a quick nod.

Hannah wasn't quite sure what that was all about, but she didn't have time to think about it because Jace took her hand. "Let's find a picnic table before these tacos get cold."

"Can you wait just a minute? Sue Ann isn't back yet."

"I'm here," Sue Ann called as she walked up from the other direction. "And I brought reinforcements." Sue Ann's friend, Tracy, and her sister, Leigh, both regulars in the store, trailed after her. "Y'all go ahead and have dinner. We've got this."

"Thanks," Hannah said after greeting the trio. "Nicole, Judy, are you coming with us?"

Nicole shook her head. "I want to jot down a couple of notes for inventory and then I'm heading home. I'll see you tomorrow."

"You go on ahead," Judy told Hannah and Jace. "I'll catch up with you after Russell gets back."

"Okay. Have a good night, Nicole. I'll see the rest of you later. I'll be back in half an hour," Hannah promised.

Jace waved goodbye and tugged Hannah along to the seating area where he found a picnic table and set down their food bag. "You hold the table and I'll get us some drinks." He studied the menu printed on a nearby booth. "Pineapple express soda or black bear lemonade?"

"That's a mixed berry lemonade, right? I'll have that."

Jace handed Rosy's leash to her and went for the drinks. Rosy, who wouldn't dream of begging at the table, settled herself under Hannah's bench. Jace returned with their drinks and Hannah handed him a taco from the bag before unwrapping her own. Creamy lime chipotle sauce dribbled from the edge, and she licked that up before biting into tender beer-batter halibut chunks and crunchy cabbage shreds. Delicious as always.

They talked about the successes of their booths and what they might want to change next year while they ate. Once Hannah had finished the last bite of her taco, Jace asked, "Ready for that funnel cake?"

She shook her head and put her hand on her stomach. "I couldn't eat another bite. Maybe later." She stood and stuffed napkins into the bag. "I should get back to the tent."

Jace checked the time on his phone. "You've got a while before they're expecting you. Let's walk a little."

"All right." Hannah couldn't turn down any chance to spend time with Jace. They wandered through the midway, watching happy kids on the carnival rides while Rosy in her vest trotted along beside them. Soon, they were walking past the carnival games.

Jace stopped in front of a booth with rows of balloons attached to the back wall. Stuffed animals and other prizes dangled from the rafters. No one else was at that booth just then. "Think I can pop a balloon with a dart and win you a prize?" Jace asked Hannah.

"I've no doubt you could, but you don't need to. I have everything I need right here." Hannah squeezed his hand. "Besides, they probably don't use real darts anymore. Too dangerous for kids."

The proprietor, who must have been getting something off a lower shelf, straightened up and spoke. "We use beanbags now," he told them. "There's a tack in back of the balloon that will pop it if the beanbag hits in the middle of the balloon. But hey, you can use a dart if you want to. Five bucks a throw." He reached under the counter and pulled out a single dart. It looked to be the same brand as the darts at the Angeles cabin.

"Sounds good to me." Jace handed over a fiver.

There was something off here. Why would the proprietor have just one dart available? Didn't this game usually give multiple chances? "What do you win if you pop a balloon?" she asked.

The man shrugged. "You have to pop the balloon to see. It depends on what the paper inside says."

"Here goes," Jace said before Hannah could ask any more questions. The dart sailed through the air, straight at a red balloon in the corner. Pop. A square of paper floated to the floor.

The proprietor bent down to pick it up and read it. Hannah expected him to reach for one of the toy harmonicas or stuffed animals hanging from the rafters, but instead he leaned over to pull something out from under the counter. He handed a small blue box to Jace.

Jace, in turn, opened the box and pulled out a ring. "Do you suppose it's a real diamond?" he asked Hannah.

Hannah grinned, and looked at the trinket he was holding. Then she took a second look. Three clear stones in the center of the ring sparkled like fire, set on an old-fashioned filigree band the color of rose gold. It was rose gold!

Suddenly, Jace dropped to one knee. "Hannah, ever since I saw you that day at the ice park, my life hasn't been the same. It's been a thousand times better. I love you, Hannah, and I want you in my life forever. I promise to stop at all garage sales and to move heavy furniture for you whenever you ask. Will you marry me?"

He signaled to Rosy, and she sat up on her back legs, her front paws dangling and the expression on her face absolutely adorable.

Hannah gasped and pressed her hand to her heart. "Oh, Jace. Every day I thank God for bringing you into my life. You kept me safe when I was in danger, and you've brought me more happiness than I could have imagined. Yes! I would be honored to marry you."

Jace stood and she let him slip the ring onto her finger before she threw her arms around his neck. Someone cheered, and she looked over to see Nicole, Sue Ann, and Judy clapping and jumping up and down while Russell recorded everything on his phone.

Strangers joined them, stopping to cheer and clap for the proposal. Hannah grinned and waved. Then she held up her hand to inspect the ring. "It's beautiful!"

"Your sister helped me find it. We both thought it was just your style, classic, graceful, and strong." He kissed her forehead. "Just like you."

"I love it! And I love you."

Nicole, Sue Ann, and Russell all came to hug and congratulate them. Judy waited until the others had moved on to Jace before she approached Hannah and took her hand to admire the ring. "Oh, sweetie, I'm so happy to have you in our family." She chuckled. "I'm going to tell you a secret. When Lindsay was, oh, eight or nine, she came to me and said, 'Mama, I want Jace to marry Hannah when we grow up, and then she'll be my sister forever and always.' And I laughed, but in my heart, I prayed that Lindsay's wish would come true. And now God has answered my prayers."

"Judy, that's so sweet." Hannah tried to blink back tears as she pulled Judy into a hug.

"What's this?" Jace came over. "Mom, are you making my fiancée cry?"

"Happy tears," Hannah assured him as Judy stepped back. He put an arm around Hannah's shoulders, and she wrapped hers around his waist. "Jace, I can hardly wait to be your wife. To be part of your family and to make you part of mine. Together, forever and always."

"Forever and always," he agreed. And he kissed her once again.

* * * * *

Romantic Suspense

Danger. Passion. Drama.

Available Next Month

Colton's Deadly Trap Patricia Sargeant
The Twin's Bodyguard Veronica Forand

Hostage Security Lisa Childs
Breaking The Code Maria Lokken

LOVE INSPIRED

K-9 Alaskan Defence Sarah Varland
Uncovering The Truth Carol J. Post

Larger Print

LOVE INSPIRED

Defending The Child Sharon Dunn
Lethal Wilderness Trap Susan Furlong

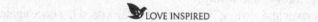
LOVE INSPIRED

Cold Case Mountain Murder Rhonda Starnes
Christmas In The Crosshairs Deena Alexander